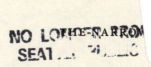
'**I loved this book**. Christine Dwyer Hickey writes such beautifully poised prose. Flawed lives played out in a postcard perfect setting.' Graham Norton

'**Tender, disquieting**… A meticulous dissection of the strains and nuances of the Hoppers' marriage.' *Times Literary Supplement*

'**With a beguiling grace and a deceptive simplicity**, Christine Dwyer Hickey reminds us that the past is never far away – rather, it constantly surrounds us, suspends us, haunts us. This is **a brilliant portrait** of America as we journey with Edward Hopper and his marvellously eccentric wife, Josephine Nivison, through the years shortly after the Second World War. Two young boys, one German, one American, negotiate the ongoing perils of loss, while Hopper's wife poses searing questions, and Hopper himself attempts answers on canvas. The world, as so powerfully evoked by Christine Dwyer Hickey, is bridged by small acts of mercy and hope.' Colum McCann

'Everything about the writing is so carefully balanced – thought and action, feeling and movement, drama and suspense. She leaves space on the page, giving her characters the freedom to behave unexpectedly and to occupy the mind of the reader even when they are offstage. **It is a long time since I have read such a fine novel or one that I have enjoyed quite so much.**' *Irish Times*

'The novel is set up like an artwork itself, with broad brushstrokes and fine lines, layer upon layer, scene upon scene… This is no plot-driven page-turner, rather a slow, ethereal thing, where you stop after each paragraph and let the **achingly beautiful** words resonate. You feel the weight of history but with a lightness of touch.' *Sunday Independent*

'Hickey's writing is **gorgeously lyrical**, whether describing the beauty of the Massachusetts landscape or the often painful life of the creative soul… like an American version of Kazuo Ishiguro's *The Remains of the Day*. It's **beguiling and compelling**.' *Sunday Business Post*

'Christine Dwyer-Hickey is **nuanced and exceptional** at character and voice.' Sinéad Gleeson

Also by Christine Dwyer Hickey

The Lives of Women

Snow Angels

The House on Parkgate Street and Other Dublin Stories

Cold Eye of Heaven

Last Train from Liguria

Tatty

The Gatemaker (*The Dublin Trilogy* 3)

The Gambler (*The Dublin Trilogy* 2)

The Dancer (*The Dublin Trilogy* 1)

THE NARROW LAND

CHRISTINE DWYER HICKEY

atlantic·*fiction*

First published in hardback in Great Britain in 2019
by Atlantic Books, an imprint of Atlantic Books Ltd.

This paperback edition published in 2020.

2 4 6 8 10 9 7 5 3 1

A CIP catalogue record for this book is available
from the British Library.

Paperback ISBN: 978 1 78649 674 4
E-book ISBN: 978 1 78649 673 7

Printed and bound by CPI Group (UK) Ltd, Croydon CR0 4YY

Atlantic Books
An imprint of Atlantic Books Ltd
Ormond House
26–27 Boswell Street
London
WC1N 3JZ

www.atlantic-books.co.uk

To A.C. and J.M.,
who left us in the dead of winter

Contents

'Every man has within himself the entire human condition.'

MICHEL DE MONTAIGNE

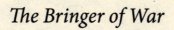

The Bringer of War

1

AT THE TOP OF the terminal steps the boy stops short and the woman pulling him along pulls harder. The boy resists, this time bending at the knee and pressing his weight down into his heels. The woman waits a second and then spins around.

'What? What is it now? What *now*?'

As she turns, her basket swipes the side of the boy's bare leg. A long red scratch springs out on his skin. The leg flinches, but the boy doesn't make a sound. He looks at the leg, he looks at the basket then he looks at her. He leans to the side and allows his suitcase to slip out of his hand.

'I'm not going…' he begins.

'You're not *going*? What do you mean you're not going?'

'I don't like—'

'You don't *like*? What, now, don't you like?'

This is not the first time they've stood in this place having this argument. The last time was two summers ago, the summer of 1948, when she'd turned her back on him to go buy the tickets and he bolted, leaving the shiny brown suitcase Harry had bought him sitting there in the middle of Grand Central. He didn't get very far then. He hadn't got the sense to try for an exit and was still too scared of elevators and escalators and anything, in fact, that moved him towards something he didn't already know or couldn't already see. And so he just plunged into the crowd and began scooting from side to side. It took no time at all between her reporting the matter and the cop dragging him back to where she'd been waiting, under the clock with four faces.

'You the mother?' the cop had asked.

And she'd nodded yes, because she just couldn't bring herself to go into the whole sorry story, and to have to do it too against a blubber of tears.

She had shown her temper back then, smacking the boy on the side of his head – the first and only time she had ever done that. And then shredding the tickets in her hands and flinging the lot in his face, she had yelled, 'Happy now? *Happy?*' with the cop still standing there listening to her. 'Is that what you want? I take a whole day off work just to go with you on a train to Boston. A whole day, just to come all the way back on my own, and this is how you treat me. Well, you can go boil for the rest of the summer in the apartment, go boil like a piece of meat in a pot – you hear me now? You can just go…'

The boy didn't budge. He never even raised his hand to comfort his slapped ear. A slight sulk on his face was all: no shame, no regret, nothing to show any real upset. Just stood there, peering straight through her, like he was trying to figure out what colour wallpaper was inside her head.

And here they are again, two years gone by and the boy now ten years old, so far as anybody knows. The case Harry bought him is back on duty, a little more faded and a lot more scuffed after two years of getting dragged in and out from under his bed, where it had been acting as a secret container for his comic books and bits of paper and God knows what other peculiarities he kept hidden in there.

This time, she is taking no chances. The ticket was bought during yesterday's lunchbreak and a porter Harry knows on the New Haven line has promised to keep lookout in case the boy gets any ideas about jumping off at the next station. It has all been arranged. She will put him on the train, take note of the car number and, when she sees the train pull out of the station, go call Harry in work who, in turn, will call Mrs Kaplan to let her know there have been no complications. When the train pulls into Boston, Mrs Kaplan will board it and they will continue together on to the Cape. After the train, there will be one of those chubby buses, after that an automobile. And then the sea, the sand and Mrs Kaplan's grandson named Richie.

She is tired of telling all this to the boy: the bus, the automobile, the sea, the sand, the grandson named Richie. A dog even! Tired building it all up while the boy, in his silence, pulls it right back down again.

But he promised Harry; he swore it – this time there would be no monkey business. He had seemed sincere in his promise too. Harry even made a few jokes about him running off last time and having to be brought back by a cop. He said it had been on the radio news – the whole of New York had heard about it. The boy sort of grinned when Harry said that, a nice-looking boy, too, when he bothers to smile. The past two years have made such a difference to him: better at school, better at eye contact and, when you can get him to talk, he speaks like any other American boy, practically. He takes more of an interest, too, and she'd been so long telling him, 'Sweetheart, you got to take more of an interest in life.'

She has every confidence that this time he will act like a big boy. She said so a few days ago to Harry who, through the mirror, had cocked one eye at her over his foamed-up face. Every confidence.

She lays the basket down next to the suitcase. 'I asked you a question,' she says.

The boy ignores her.

'What's the matter with you – answer me, please?'

But the boy still refuses to say a word. And so she starts on him. She starts off slow and steady but soon she is letting him have it in shovelfuls. She lets him have it for all the trouble he's been these past two summers when she's had to pay, yes, *pay*, a sitter so she can go out to work while he mopes around the apartment cutting dumb little paper figures out of magazines and playing those dumb little games that he plays with them. She lets him have it over Mrs Kaplan – Mrs Kaplan who has been so kind as to allow him another chance after all the inconvenience two years before. Mrs Kaplan of all people. The woman without whom he would be God knows where, dead at the side of a road in the middle of Europe somewhere. Mrs Kaplan, the woman who had probably put the whole idea in President Truman's head in the first place about saving all those orphans. Anything that comes to mind, she throws at him: his stealing food from the kitchen as if she never feeds him or would refuse him a bite to eat! His wandering around the building in the middle of the night,

5

spooking the neighbours! And as for all those lies that come pouring out of his mouth. Senseless lies! To his teachers; his classmates; the man in the grocery store – to any ear with a hole in it that is willing to listen.

She wants to stop. To pause, anyhow, and think about this barrage of words. But just like it happens sometimes in the typing pool, the words seem to shoot out of their own accord except now they're landing on the boy instead of on the page. And NO, she continues, she won't be tearing up the ticket like before, if that's what he's hoping. He will get on that train and she will go back to work. He will get on that train and do as she says and she will be standing on the platform until she sees the train disappear down, *right* down, the track.

'I don't like…' he says and then, 'I don't want…'

'And I don't care! You hear me? I don't care what you like or don't like, what you want or don't want. You understand? I've had enough of all your likes and your dislikes… of your— wants and your don't-wants. And you know what else? I'm tired. Tired because you kept me awake all night, in and out of the bathroom, light on, light off in the hallway. I'm tired and—'

The boy lowers his head, then swallows. 'Please, Frau Aunt,' he finally says.

She turns away from him. On the concourse below, she watches the crowd dissolve into one big moving mass with umbrellas, hats, purses, suitcases tacked onto it. For the first time, she notices how many soldiers and marines are moving around down there. It's as if the war in Europe is still on. Yet the servicemen seem different somehow, younger and more perked up than before. She remembers then: they've moved on to a new war now, and what she's looking at here is a whole batch of brand new men. She puts her hand in the pocket of her raincoat and pulls out a handkerchief, blows her nose and puts the handkerchief back in. She lifts her face and looks up to the vaulted ceiling and the arched windows beneath it that have taken the rainy, grey daylight and turned it to silver. It makes her think of a church from her childhood. A church she can no longer name where a once familiar service was going on over her head, and at eye level, the elbow of a father on one side and on the other the elbow of a mother. She feels ashamed of herself then for yelling at the boy, for sending him away when he doesn't want to go. For bringing all that up about his private little world, the games that he plays when he goes there. He is, after all, still a child, and as Harry often says, 'God knows what that kid's seen in his time.'

She comes back to the boy, softened. 'Look,' she begins, 'you're a good boy. I know that. But it's been tough, you know? And not just for you but for me too. I try. I do try. But now you need to have time away. Time for you. Time for me – you understand? We'll get along better that way when you get back. A new start we'll have then. New home, new school, new… well, a whole new life, you could say.'

'But I won't know where the apartment is. What it looks like or nothin'.'

'As soon as Harry finds it, I'll write and tell you all about it.'

'And school – how am I supposed to find that? I'll be starting back late, everyone lookin' at me when I walk in the door.'

'Nobody cares about any of that. Other boys start late – those harvest boys, they don't come back till maybe the end of October. You'll be back by the end of September. And you may not even have to change schools, not if Harry finds some place close by.'

The boy keeps shaking his head in that way he has – like it's loose on his neck. She wishes he would stop doing that.

'Look, if you want,' she says, 'I can do what I was supposed to do last time – you know, go with you as far as Boston, and when Mrs Kaplan gets on I'll get off and come straight back. It'll cost more money and I'll get in trouble in work. But I'll do it. If that's what you want.'

'It's okay,' he says, so quiet she only knows he's said it at all because she reads the shapes of the words on his lips.

'It's just a few weeks, sweetheart. A few weeks goes by so quick you won't hardly notice. And you'll have a friend to play with. And the dog, don't forget – I don't know what sort but I bet it's a beauty. You're a very lucky boy. You should know that. A nice big house and garden. A beach of sand. A sea to swim in. And air… think of it – all that fresh air!'

'I don't like fresh air,' the boy says. 'I don't like the boy, I don't like the beach.'

'You don't know the boy! And you've probably never even been to a beach.'

'Harry said he'd take me to Coney Island, but he never did,' he snaps.

'He will. He said he will and he will. But let me tell you, it's not so great, that Coney Island, noisy and dirty and the crowds… But where *you're* going? This is paradise I'm talking about here.'

She brings her face a little closer to his and cuffs her hands around the tops of his arms.

'Are you afraid – is that it? What are you afraid of then? Won't you tell me? Is it all these soldiers? They're going off to the other side of the world, to a place called Korea. It's not like before, you know.'

The boy begins shaking his head again.

'Is it the tunnel then?' she asks. 'Is that it? Does it make you think of the air raids? I promise you there's nothing in those tunnels but railroad tracks and trains. That's all over now. That's all in the past. This is America. You're safe here, sweetheart. Safe.'

She waits for the boy to give her something but he won't even look at her now.

'How can I know how you feel if you never tell me anything. *How?*'

He pulls back for a second then turns on her suddenly and screams in her face. 'I said okay – didn't I? I said I was going – didn't I? How many times you want me to say it? I'm going. I'm going!'

The way he just blasts it out. Right in her face.

'Don't you go yelling at me,' she begins, 'don't think you can just—'

But the boy isn't listening; he is too busy counting the buttons on her coat. Down and then up again.

'Stop doing that,' she says. 'Will you please *stop*? Counting things, it drives me crazy the way you— the way you…'

She takes her hands away from his arms, picks up the basket, settles it on her arm. Then she picks up his case and clamps it to his chest. Her throat feels tight and sore now; she has to push her voice to make it go through.

'And another thing, don't call me Frau Aunt again,' she says. 'I'm tired telling you. We don't speak German in this country – you got that?'

She pulls him by the sleeve of his jacket, down the steps and towards the track. When they reach the barrier, they get in line and she begins rummaging in her purse and at the same time pulling herself together.

'Look, I don't think we should leave it on a sour note,' she says. 'I don't think either of us wants that.'

She edges his ticket out of her pocketbook. 'Did you write a letter back to that boy Richie? Did you write back like I told you?'

The boy turns his head to the side, as if she's not there.

'I'm asking you a question now, if you could answer me, please?'

'I wrote a letter,' he mumbles.

She combs her fingers through his hair and he shakes her hand away.

'Good,' she says, 'because, you know, it would not be very polite if you didn't write back. It would be *im*polite is what I mean to say.'

On the train, she lifts his case onto the overhead rack and says, 'Mrs Kaplan will lift it down for you when you get there.'

She waits for him to take offence, to let her know 'I'm tall enough – I can take it down myself.'

But he says nothing. She puts the basket down on the seat. 'Now remember, don't you take your eye off that basket. Someone needs the space, you put it on your lap. Or lay it on the floor under your feet. Understand? And later, when you're all settled in, you give it to her, you say, "This is for you, Mrs Kaplan, to thank you for having me to stay" – you got that now? And be sure you let her know I made the apple pie myself but that I bought the strawberry one in the French bakery on Fifth Avenue. Well, I guess she'll see the name on the wrapper when she opens the box – everyone's heard of a place like that.'

The boy stands stiffly by the seat, his legs like two white stalks growing out of his canvas shoes and up the legs of his short pants. Away from the apartment, he seems so tall. Even with her propped up on high heels, they are almost on a level. Soon he will pass her out. After that, he will pass Harry out. When he first came to live with them, she thought he would never grow tall enough or flesh out enough to be able to fit into poor Jake's clothes. He'd been so small for his age then. But now? Look at him. Five minutes' wear was all he got out of Jake's clothes before she had to give them away to strangers. Too tall and still too thin, like she never feeds him.

She hands him a comic book, a candy bar and a bottle of soda. She gives

9

him an envelope with coins and five dollars inside. She tells him he needs to make it last for six weeks but that he should buy ice-cream for his new friend, Richie, or maybe take him to the movies or something.

'Be polite at all times – thank you, please, all that. And call her ma'am, unless she tells you different. She will. She's a very nice, down-to-earth lady – you know, for a lady. But just to show you know how to be polite. And remember, Richie's mom is also called Mrs Kaplan on account she was married to Mrs Kaplan's son. Say your prayers. No grabbing for things at the table. And eat nice. And, please, no lies. If you don't know something, you don't know. You don't have to make up an answer. You understand? Good. Because, you know, nobody likes a liar. Not even another liar.'

The boy sits down on the edge of the seat, the comic book over his lap and the candy bar and soda resting on top of it.

'You look tired,' she says. 'Did you sleep even one wink the whole night? You can sleep on the journey, you got a few hours – just take good care of that basket, okay?'

The boy nods.

'Well, that's it, I guess,' she says, 'and don't forget to send me a postcard. Or a letter, maybe. I love to look at your handwriting – you know that, so grown up that handwriting. It's only a few weeks but, still, it'd be nice to hear from you.'

The boy won't look at her. He folds the envelope of money and puts it into his pocket. He takes the basket from the seat and lays it on the floor under his feet. Then he turns his attention to the comic book.

She leans down, kisses the top of his head and lowers her voice. 'And no speaking German, huh? It's better, I told you. I'm not saying there's anything wrong with German – what is it but another language, after all? But, you know, it's just better you don't speak it, is all.'

His face is flushed and she can see now that his bottom lip has tightened downwards, like maybe he is about to cry. Something inside her wants him to cry, to throw his arms around her and beg her not to send him away. She thinks, If he does that, I'll keep him with me, I'll hug him so tight he won't know how to breathe. If he does that, I'll know at least that he feels something for me. I'll

10

hug him and say it's okay, honey, you can stay with me. You can stay forever and always and—

The boy shoves the comic back at her. 'I read this already,' he snarls.

She takes a step away. 'Oh yeah? Well, give it to Richie then. Or throw it away – what do I care?'

On the platform, she stands under the window of his car, craning to see in. But all she can get is a glimpse of the crown of his head. Her shoes are biting into her feet and she feels like she could throw up any minute. It is taking forever for the whistle to sound, the wheels to give their first chug. All along the platform, she sees other people well placed to say their goodbyes. Faces raised to the train and a passenger hanging out the window of a car, or leaning over the opened window of a door between cars, talking, laughing, holding hands, crying even. A sailor and his girl taking a last, long chew of each other's faces. She is the only one to stand alone. To have nobody on the other side of her farewell.

The boy is obstinate – she knows that – but still she hopes that before the train pulls away he'll come round. Even a small wave, even a peek out the window. Oh, but he is obstinate to his bones. On the way here when she suggested they stop by the United Nations building – never mind that the rain had come on and they didn't have all that much time to spare – he looked at her like she was dirt. A place she usually had to drag him away from. A place he loved. He had learned all about it in school, told them one evening at dinner in an unexpected outburst that had made her scared to blink in case the moment was broken. It was to be called the United Nations building, he announced, and the men inside would be in charge of the world so countries couldn't just go round destroying each other any time they felt like it. Oh no, the men in charge would not allow any of that. And every country in the whole world would have its own flag blowing in the breeze outside, even Germany, because his teacher, she said that's what it would be about, forgiving and maybe someday forgetting.

For weeks they'd been watching it grow out of nothing. He loved to look at the workmen crawl all over the concrete carcass, to count the empty sockets of the soon-to-be windows, take note of what had been added since last time round. It had become their thing, something they could do together, to go to the East River on her half-day from work and check on the progress of the United Nations building. And what did he do this morning when they got there but walk straight on by, leaving her trotting behind him all the way to 46th Street, where she'd had to make several grabs at his hand before finally she managed to catch hold of it.

A man comes into the car and begins to settle himself down opposite the boy. She watches the man push an odd-shaped case onto the rack, then fold his raincoat and bundle it on top. He sits down. She can see him take off his hat and smooth down his hair. He leans back and, bringing one hand to the window, begins tapping his fingers against the glass, nodding slightly as if he was listening to music inside his head.

The man catches her eye then looks away. The boy continues to ignore her. The man lights a cigarette and looks at her again. She feels her face grow hot. She begins to rub her stomach. The man will not associate her with the boy. He will assume she is looking in at him. He will think she is a crazy person who stands around looking in windows of trains. He will think she is one of those women who hang around terminals, picking up men for money.

~

THE BOY WATCHES Frau Aunt rubbing her stomach. He slides further down into the seat and now all he can see is the top of her head, her hand rising over it, once and then twice, like she's some kind of swimmer.

Behind him the black tunnel is waiting. Soon Frau Aunt in her blue raincoat will be a blue stain and then a blue smudge and then nothing at all. It will be more than six weeks before he sees her again. Or – if this is a trick to get rid of him – it could be forever. Even so, he will not wave goodbye.

He thinks of the letter that Richie sent with the photograph wrapped up inside it, Harry laying it out on the table so the three of them could read it together. The writing on the letter had been like a five-year-old would do, but the words were all grown up (I do hope you enjoy… I'm very much looking forward to…). It was obvious that Mrs Kaplan had told her grandson what to write, even if Frau Aunt had said that she was sure they were Richie's

12

own words and that he was probably just advanced for his age on account of his going to private school. 'And so what?' Harry said. 'They don't teach them handwriting in those fancy schools?'

He just loved it when Harry said that.

The photograph had been of Richie: Richie and a ball on a beach. At the edge of the photograph was a corner of a rug and what looked like a dog's two front paws lying on it.

He had not liked the look of the place. (And what sort of a name was that anyhow – Cape Cod? What was that even supposed to *mean*?) There was way too much sky behind Richie and a sea that looked like it was rising up just to bite down and swallow him up. He wished it would swallow him up because he didn't much like the look of Richie either. He thought his face was a mean-looking face and that the smile on it was phoney. He had stared at the photograph for a long time; he came back to it again and again and stared at it some more. But he still hadn't been able to find anything to like about Richie – not his hedgehog hair, not his striped T-shirt, not his mean, chubby face, not his bare foot pressing down on the ball and that look in his eye like it was a human head he was pressing into the sand and not just some old blow-up ball.

Richie is only part of the reason for being sore with Frau Aunt. Frau Aunt telling him to stop speaking German – that's the other part. It was unfair and untrue of her to say that. He never speaks German now. As soon as he went to live with them, he started to work hard to unlearn the language. And she knows that, too, because she was the one to unteach him. She took all his own words out of his head and put new American ones in there instead. Hours of sitting at the kitchen table learning and unlearning till it grew dark outside, and now he has mostly forgotten how to speak it. Even when he does remember a conversation, it's the meaning of the conversation he remembers and not the actual words that were used to make it. Hundreds of words he would have known how to speak when he came to America – some of them he maybe would have known how to read and even write down. Thousands maybe. Thousands and thousands of words and he'd really only held on to a couple of them and that was only as souvenirs.

*

The boy kicks the side of his foot lightly against the belly of the basket. He knows there is a special parcel at the bottom for Richie. When Frau Aunt tried to show him what she was putting in this parcel, he said he didn't want to know. He closed his eyes and refused to look. But she went right on ahead and told him anyway: a colouring book and a box of paints, a kit for making a model boat or maybe it was a model aeroplane.

He lifts the basket from the floor. The lid opens like a mouth as he places it on his lap, breathing apples and cinnamon on his face. And something savoury – like garlic, maybe. The last thing to go into the basket had been the box Frau Aunt had bought from the French bakery. *Tarte de fraises* had been written on the tiny flag sticking out of it. A Frenchman sold it to her, wrapping it so gently in waxed paper and then laying it in the box like it was a new baby or something. And Frau Aunt smiling up at him and saying oh what a beautiful wax paper and oh what a wonderful tart and oh what a lovely box to lay it in and oh what a charming ribbon, and then complaining about the price as soon as they left the shop and calling the Frenchman a thief and keeping it up until she suddenly decided they should take a last look at the United Nations building. And he knew what that was called – rubbing salt into the wound was what.

The train begins to growl. Growl and shudder and gasp. He feels several movements within a bigger movement, strong and at the same time clumsy. A bull or a bronco horse struggling to break out of a wooden pen. The man seated opposite turns a page of his newspaper, gives it a little shake then takes another pull of his cigarette. He crosses one leg over the other. The hem of his pants lifts when he does that. Small black spikes on white skin. The man's brown hat is on the seat next to him, a brown hat with a dip in the crown.

The boy knows the hat, knows that if you turned it upside down there'd be a printed crest on the stiff lining and that the lining would be stained with a greasy smear. He doesn't know how he knows this hat – Harry only wears caps and only in winter. But it's there anyhow, stuck to his memory, like all the other scraps of garbage that sometimes break loose and drift by.

Frau. That was one of the words he kept, though he didn't really know why. Frau and otherwise mostly numbers because he couldn't seem to forget how to count in German.

14

The train bucks. It gives a larger, more urgent gasp this time and the boy feels his knees slide forward. He stops them from falling further by digging his heels into the ground. Across the way, the man also lurches forward, cigarette smoke tumbling into the boy's face. When it clears he sees that the man has long fingernails but only on one hand and that there are more of those black hairs showing under the cuff of his shirt and sprouting around his wrist-watch. The hairs seem alive to the boy, like tiny insects growing out of the man's flesh. He hopes the man will keep his face behind the *New York Times* for the rest of the journey or, even better, that he gets off at the next station and takes his live-in colony of insects with him.

Outside the sound of whistles, one then another, then another again, slashing like swords against each other. The doors slap shut along the line. The boy hears his own heartbeat over them.

He lowers himself further down in the seat. Now, placing his hand on top of the cake box, he begins to push the ribbon until it falls over the shoulder of the box.

The train begins moving. Everything outside tightens up and slowly starts to retreat. He closes his eyes. He can see orange flickering through the skin of his eyelids. He feels his hands begin to shake. He can smell the strawberries from here, can already taste the unbearable sweetness of them curling into his throat and filling up his whole head. He makes a claw of his fingers and presses them into the soft, damp cushion of pastry and syrup and fruit.

Soon the tunnel will suck the train in, down, down into its long black gullet. Dead men will go floating by. Dead men and bits of old beds and drowning rats, struggling to stay alive. A woman stretched out with her face in the water. A fat man in a black overcoat who is swimming like a pig. If he keeps his eyes closed he will soon be asleep and will not need to see any of that. If he keeps his mouth full of pastry and strawberry, the sweetness will block it all out. Until the tunnel sets the train free again. Then the train and the man with the long nails and himself and all the people seated all over the train, or stumbling along car to car, will stop existing. They will be stuck between one place and another; they will be stuck until the train begins to spit them out, like pips, along the journey. When that happens, they can begin to exist all over again, but in some other place, a place they probably don't even know yet.

~

HE THINKS HE IS on a different train as he begins to wake. A train in Germany just after the war. He feels jets of cool air on his face and thinks they are coming through the bullet holes left by the strafers in the roof. Or maybe through the spider-web cracks in the windows that have not yet been mended.

He reminds himself to keep his eyes shut. Because that's what you do when you wake up among strangers in Germany: keep your eyes shut and pretend you haven't yet woken or that you're already dead. You do that until you've worked out what and who is around you.

He remembers those trains so well. Climbing on and jumping off again. Walking so long, walking and walking. Until the last train that took him to the big farm for making boys healthy again.

He imagines that he is on that last train now, sitting in a row of four or five boys. There is another row of bigger, older boys sitting across the table. He is the youngest of all the boys on the train, the youngest and smallest, and this is why they call him *die Runt*, or sometimes just Runt.

He is sitting on the end of the row by the aisle, where Frau Nurse can see him when he puts up his hand. Whenever he does this, the older boys elbow each other and snigger – 'Oh, look,' they say, 'the runt has put his hand up again, he wants her to take out his little winky for him. Does it stick up when she does that – takes out your little winky?'

Three of the big boys playing cards. The fourth big boy stuck into the corner at the window. But the fourth big boy never looks out the window, not once. He doesn't look at the cards or at the other boys, and when the drunk man stumbles into their carriage in a few moments' time, he will not even look at him.

He does not know the name of the fourth big boy; he does not know the names of most of the boys. Not even the small ones sitting beside him. Apart from Otto a few rows back, he doesn't know the names of any of the boys that have been placed here and there among the ordinary passengers. But he does

16

know the names of two of the card players: Bruno and Erich. Because that's something else you do when you find yourself among strangers in Germany – you learn, first, the names of the bullies.

The older boys will not allow the younger ones to play cards. Little boys are too stupid to understand cards, they say, little boys only spoil the game. But he understands the game all right. He understands it better, anyhow, than Erich who keeps making stupid mistakes and does not even know the difference in value between acorns and bells.

He knows the cards from watching the men play under the blue light. The blue light was in the big cave beneath the train station. What a stinky place that was. But there was another, even stinkier cave in the Tiergarten, next to the zoo, and that had a blue light too.

The big boys will not allow the small ones to touch the table and that's not fair because they don't own it. The table is stuck into the floor right in the middle and is supposed to be shared by both sides. Put one finger on this table, Erich has warned, and *clip*! We will chop it right off your hand.

When the boy turns around and kneels up on the seat, he can see all the way down to the back of the carriage and the other boys stuck here and there with their faces shy and also a little bored. Otto is squeezed in beside a big woman in a big brown fur coat. The woman is really a big brown bear who is wearing a blonde wig and red lipstick. He longs to tell Otto that so they can laugh till they ache. Otto is his friend. He knows him from the American camp where they both arrived on the same day but from different directions. They were put into the same section and then they became best friends. The big bear woman is fussing over Otto and stuffing him with cake. And there is Otto with his face turned to one side, trying to hide his greedy grin. On the far side of the aisle to Otto, Frau Nurse is reading her book with the English name on the front of it. Every now and then her face comes out of the book to check that her boys are behaving. My boys, she calls them, *meine Jungs*. Soon she will notice him kneeling up on the seat, and then her hand will start lifting and pressing back down – one, two, three times, bouncing a ball. But really it is only telling him he has to sit back down now.

When he sits back down and leans a little forward, he can see through the window the countryside moving past in the opposite direction. And the dark forest. And sometimes the small wooden train stations that are empty now that the war is over. And then the dark forest again. The train waddles right by the forest without a care in the world and then it waddles straight through the small wooden stations. He sees that the sky is beginning to darken and, in the distance, a broken bridge like a long arm with a hand that has been snapped off at the wrist. He sees other bridges too – some completely broken; others that have been put back together again with a strip of new wood or a slab of clean concrete and that makes him think of new patches on worn-out clothes.

He is wearing patched clothes. Clothes that are new, but at the same time old. All the boys wear the same kind of clothes. New and old. But they are not rags – nobody could say that about them. The big boys told Otto that the clothes had been cut out of dead soldiers' uniforms and that the jumpers had been made out of wool unravelled from socks that had been stiff with blood or mufflers that had been wrapped around the soldiers' necks when they died. Otto said, 'I could be wearing part of your father's uniform and you could be wearing part of mine.' He wishes Otto had not told him all that about the uniforms. Because up till then he had quite liked his clothes. They had a good clean smell and they kept him warm. Now he is a little afraid of them. It is such a terrible feeling to be afraid of your own trousers, to feel your own jumper could be some sort of ghost.

Through the window again, and the forest again, rags of old snow caught between branches and the spaces between the trees getting wider in places so that sometimes you can see the shapes of firewood pickers bent to the ground like black hooks. Or an old jeep with branches growing out through the windows. And then what first looks like rows of sapling trees, but turns out to be hundreds of wooden crosses stuck into the ground. Row after row, a red rag tied around the neck of each one.

Bruno springs out of his seat, and his face turns a dark, excited red, his eyes sharpen with light.

'Look – out there! Quick! The graves of the Ivans! Thousands of Ivans. Let's hope they are burning in hell!'

'The Red Army,' Erich says, 'they are not true soldiers like our fathers were. They are cowards – what they did to my sister and mother.'

'And what did they do to your sister and mother?' Bruno asks.

'What did they do? What do you think they would do? Raped them, of course! Raped them and raped them!'

'What does that mean, raped them and raped them?' he hears himself ask.

There is a small silence. The big boys look at one another and then:

A snort from Bruno, a burst of laughter from the third big boy and finally another snort from Erich. And then all the boys (except the boy at the window) laughing with their puckered faces. Pucker and snigger and snort and point. Even the younger boys, laughing, laughing, pretending to understand what's so funny.

'He doesn't know what it means!' Erich cries. 'He doesn't even know what it means! Oh, the poor runt. He knows nothing about sex, you see. Nothing. Isn't that so, Runt?'

He feels his feet jump and slap down on the floor as he stands to defend himself.

'You never said it meant sex. I know what that means, I do know what it means! I do. I do.'

Frau Nurse calling out from the back of the carriage, 'Quiet, please! Quiet or no supper for any of you.'

The drunken man comes into the carriage round about now. He knows him even before he comes in because he has already noticed his big, clumsy shape, bumping along through the train, slamming doors open and shut, stopping at seats to frighten the passengers.

The drunken man enters the carriage just as Frau Nurse is starting up the aisle. 'Quiet up there, please! Quiet, I said, or no supper for any of you!'

The drunken man is an old drunken soldier. He is missing one arm, the empty sleeve of his raggedy tunic tucked into its raggedy pocket. He stays by the door rocking on his heels. Then he shouts all the way down at Frau Nurse, 'Leave the boys be. They have been quiet long enough. You go back to where you came from, you American bitch, and leave our poor boys alone.'

His heart stops when he hears the drunken man talk this way to Frau Nurse.

He wants to jump up and beat him with his fists. He knows that all the boys feel the same way. They want to bite and scratch and punch and kick the old soldier. And all the men too, reading their newspapers and stuffing their pipes. And the women doing their knitting – everyone wants to hit the drunken man. But nobody does. Nobody moves. Not even a little finger. Not even to utter one word.

The drunken man sways up the aisle, singing his head off about the old rotten bones in the ground. Frau Nurse has to step out of his way. The drunken man goes down the aisle once, leaving his stink behind him. He turns and comes back up it again, bringing his stink back with him. The empty sleeve has slipped out of his pocket and now it is rubbing off the tops of the seats, the way Frau Nurse's cape does when she walks along the aisle.

He stops at their table, taking his time over each boy's face, spurts of noisy breath coming down his nostrils. And then he says, 'Look at them – just look! Little piglets off to the farm. Yes, that's right, that's where they are taking them. Off to the farm to fatten them up for the American market. Little piggy piglets.'

He turns then to the rest of the passengers, waves his one arm through the air. 'This… this is what their fathers died for. This here is what it was all for – so we could fatten up our little piglets and send them off to the *Ami* market. Am I right? Or am I wrong? Can anyone tell me that?'

Then he turns back to their table, sticks out his neck and goes, '*Kkrraw kkkrraww, eeek eeek. Sqweeeee*. Piggy, piggy, pigs.'

When he finishes making his piggy noises, he stumbles back out of the carriage.

After he leaves nobody speaks or looks at each other. There isn't a sound for such a long time, but for the sound of the train and the sniffly sound of Bruno crying.

The train pushes on. Before it gets dark the light turns purple. On the glass of the purple window, Frau Nurse's cape and the white of her dress and the smear of her pretty face, asking in her funny accent if Erich and Bruno would care to be her helpers in serving supper. The shape of them sidling out from behind the table. Sidling out, with their heads bent low.

Coming and going, boy to boy, silently handing out apples. First, the apples and then black bricks of bread and butter. Last, the small bottles of milk. And then Bruno and Erich sit down again.

Outside, a German night is rising out of the darkness, the small clumped lights of a mountain village or a chain of street lamps pointing the way.

Inside, a train filled with yellow light. How strange to see all those pieces of light so close together. How strange to see any light at all. To be sitting with the windows left uncovered as the train flies along with its big wings of black smoke. And strange, too, that people outside can look right in. At the rows of boys in the harsh yellow light, or the single boys seated here and there between ordinary passengers, in their clean but not new clothes. Shame-faced and silent, carefully chewing on their bricks of black bread and trying so hard not to look like little piggies.

2

HE OPENS HIS EYES, finds himself alone on the seat in the corner by the window. He is holding his head in one hand, elbow stuck on top of the basket for support. The man with the long fingernails has gone and in his place a big woman is snoozing. Her head lilts and flops to the rhythm of the train as if someone has broken her neck. He notices, then, the box from the tart is lying on the floor, red showing through white. He lifts the lid with the tip of his little finger and peeps inside – all that remain are a few pastry flakes and two or three clots of jelly.

It had only taken him a few handfuls to demolish the tart before he had fallen asleep. It had lasted just long enough to get him through the first tunnel, and as it is only the first tunnel that he is scared of, he guesses the tart has done its job all right.

But it was not much of a pie, not for the price. Frau Aunt had been right: the baker was nothing but a smiling thief.

His hands are sticky. His mouth grimed with oversweet fruit. His belly aches from greed and shame, and now dread too, as he thinks of how easily he could be found out. He screws the empty box into the shape of a bow and then heels it under his seat. He will say nothing about the tart – it will be as if it never existed. But supposing Mrs Kaplan writes to say thank you for the other gifts in the basket? (I did so enjoy the apple pie and the French pâté was quite delicious…) Frau Aunt would not be pleased when the strawberry tart got no mention. She would be sure to write back fishing for compliments. (I do so hope you enjoyed the tart… I so look forward to hearing how you enjoyed the… Thank you so much for eating the strawberry tart which came from that very expensive French bakery on Fifth Avenue.) Maybe it would be better if he got rid of the basket altogether? He could pretend that it was stolen by the man with the long fingernails. Or he could throw it out the window. Leave it in the washroom, even? But if he pulls the window right down, the lady opposite will be sure to wake up and if he leaves it in the washroom Harry's porter friend will probably find it and it wouldn't take long for him to figure out who it belonged to, and when Mrs Kaplan gets on in Boston, the porter might meet her at the door with the basket held out. He stands up and places the basket on the overhead rack as far away from his suitcase as it can go. He will simply forget the basket. Pretend that it just slipped his mind and he walked off without it. He won't notice till they get to Mrs Kaplan's house and by then it will be too late to do anything about it.

When he sits back down, he sees there's a stain on his pants. He sticks his finger into his mouth and tries to clean the stain off with his spit. He rubs it a few times but that only makes it worse. He takes his handkerchief out of his pocket and goes at it again. The stain spreads across his thigh. Now it looks as if he pissed in his pants. He pushes harder and harder into the stain. His head feels heavy and sore. He grows tired of trying to fix the stain, tired of trying to keep his eyes open. Tired of worrying about a stupid pie with a fancy French name. He edges back into the corner and places his head against the glass of the window. How soothing it is to rest his head against the cool glass, to feel the movement of the train grinding through his skull and into his brain, rocking his worries away.

In his mind, he finds Frau Nurse again. They are in the toilet of the train. And his feet. His feet are far off the floor, his pants looped round his ankles while his winky just lies there, like a small, fat maggot, doing nothing. He is torn between the shame of all that and the pleasure of having her long safe hands around his middle holding him up, the smell of her soap.

She says, 'I'm keeping my eyes shut, I can't see a thing. Now off you go. Give us a tinkle.'

Above, flickering bullet holes of light in the roof. And he is talking and talking, questions mostly, hoping the splash will come and go and not be heard behind the sounds of the train and the sound of his questions.

'Why is the light through the holes so bright – is the night over already?'

'We're going through a station. No more blackouts. Remember?'

'But not Berlin?'

'I've told you a million times, we are not going near Berlin.'

'So no big tunnels, Frau Nurse?'

'No big tunnels, I told you.'

'But the drunken soldier – Frau Nurse, why did he say you were American if you are English?'

'I am English.'

'But why do you work in the American camp then?'

'Because we are allies.'

'But allies – doesn't that mean people who want to kill us?'

'No, it means we are on the same side – like you and me, we are on the same side.'

'But what if there is another war – will we be on the same side then?'

'There won't be another war, I can promise you that. Now shh, shh, concentrate, there's a good boy – we can't stay here all night, you know. Christ, my ruddy arms are breaking.'

'Frau Nurse – guess what? A boy in my last camp said there are people buried under the gardens and parks all over Germany. And in the sea, dead sailors sometimes just bob up and start floating around. That's what he said.'

'Did he, indeed?'

'Yes. And, and, one time after a raid, I saw a dead horse and a man said the Americans killed it with a machine gun, poking out of the door of the aircraft, because Americans hate horses, you see.'

'What about the cowboys, then? They're American and they love their horses – don't they?'

'Oh, yes. The cowboys. Did the cowboys fight in the war? Oh, wait, Frau Nurse, wait, it's coming now I think, here it is now, oh yesss.'

He opens his eyes a fraction, looks at his legs reaching all the way down to the floor and his feet in their American sneakers. There is a sound of low American voices and he sees a woman's legs in pale stockings crossed at the ankle, polished shoes with a gold buckle and the hem of a daisy dress. He tilts his chin slightly and now, through the slit, there is a little bit more of the daisy dress and hands on the lap of it in white lace gloves. And past that, the leg of a boy, his feet in sandals, swinging back and forward under the seat.

He tries to keep Frau Nurse in his head, to stay with her and her lemon-soap smell; he wants to tell her everything he has ever seen and everything he knows. He wants to ask her question after question just to hear the sound of her voice.

Frau Nurse helping him to pull up his pants, then taking his hand and stretching it out under a flow of water. 'Water. Say it.'

He says it.

'Not Vvva vvva. *Wwwa* wwwa. Say it again. Water. Good. And again.'

'But why do I have to keep saying it again? And again?'

'Because you have to learn how to speak English.'

'Wwwa, waaa, water. But why do I have to speak English?'

'Because that's what they speak where you're going. And something else you have to do is to stop asking so many questions.'

'What questions?'

'All these questions about the war, for a start. You have to stop talking about soldiers and dead horses and guns – all that rot. Where you are going, they had no war. At least not at home. You don't want to go bringing it with you.'

'Bringing what with me?'

'The war.'

'But that's so funny! How can I bring a war with me?'

Frau Nurse lifting her long finger, tapping him in three places: his forehead and then his stomach and then his heart.

'You can bring it in here, and in here, and in there,' she says.

He opens his eyes another fraction. From the far end of the seat, a boy's voice begins to squeak. 'Look, Grandma, he's awake, he's opening his eyes!'

The daisy dress begins to move; a woman's face rises out of it and says, 'Well, hello, sleepy head, we were just about to wake you up! And now here you are, just in time for our famous sunset. I'm Mrs Kaplan and this young man here is my grandson, Richie. Welcome to the Narrow Land – that's what we call this part of Cape Cod.'

'Ask him, Grandma,' the boy squeaks again, 'ask him if that's his basket up there on the rack!'

He opens his eyes fully, turns his face to the window, finds that Germany has gone. Instead of black icy rivers and walls of dark forest, there are low, soft hills and wide open fields.

He looks back into the car, then back through the window. Everything he sees is rinsed in red light – the boy, the woman, the seats in the train, the hills outside, the little train station. Everything.

Mrs Aitch

1

HIS SLOW FOOTSTEP CROSSES the studio floor and from the kitchen she follows his progress. There is a tapping of brush handles against the wooden sides of the box, the rustle of squeezed-down paint tubes. Now the sound of his hand pushing jars and oil cans around on the back shelf. He is gathering the afternoon about him, making his choices.

Footsteps again; after that, a long pause. And she knows he is standing by the north window now, long arms behind his back, clasped at the hands like a bracket. She imagines him there, leaning into the window, the slight stoop at his shoulders that has lately become more prominent, the bottom lip stretched in concentration. And his broad, benign face staring out, patient as a fisherman. He is looking for his sky.

His mind running clear, nothing to clog or confuse it, and Saturday afternoon will have long since evaporated. And why should he concern himself with Saturday anyhow – almost three whole days ago for goodness sake! – when there are far more important things to worry about than a wife and her chewed-up heart.

The long-legged bathers from the house up the way may well get a second glance as they come tiptoeing down the steps for their afternoon swim. But he won't waste much time wondering how come they have changed direction since Saturday afternoon, turning right now towards Pamet Harbour instead of their usual left. Because he's forgotten all that, and how. How it was her neck put on the line, her face they laughed into, her spit-spraying words as she tried to explain: my husband, you see, doesn't like to be distracted, doesn't like people poking around on *his* beach, intruding on *his* private swim, blocking *his* light should he decide to paint or, you know, just stand for hours and gaze out like an imbecile at the sky. He is such an important person, you see, my husband. My husband. *My…*

She pulls her little ponytail tight to her head and opens the kitchen cupboard. Pretty cans all in a row: Canadian pea soup, Boston chowder, various species of beans, sweetcorn and peaches – enough to keep him going for a few days anyhow. From the scrapyard pile of dirty dishes in the sink, she pulls the can-opener free and places it where he can easily find it. She will not be needing it anyhow. She will not be eating. Nor will she be doing any of that other stuff either: cooking or cleaning or washing or worrying about what to serve next. Let him take care of himself for a while – see how he enjoys all that.

She moves to the kitchen table, positions her seat where, if she wants – and she may not even want – she can keep an eye on the studio through the gap in the door. Then she hauls her drawstring workbag from the floor and settles it, like a plump child, onto her lap.

They will have thought her crazy, the sunbathers. They will have made her a topic of their after-dinner conversations. Sitting out on the porch playing their records or swilling cocktails on the verandahs of other vacationers they have befriended along the way. Exchanging their little experiences, passing on their summertime tips – the best place to hire a boat, to eat striped bass, to find a reliable baby-sitter. And then, while relaying the little peculiarities of the region (the stick-thin girl who goes out walking alone at all hours of the night; the middle-aged couple necking behind the cold storage plant), someone may say, 'We found this crab on the beach, the biggest crab I have ever seen.'

Someone else will throw in, 'Speaking of crabs on the beach, we met this crazy old lady near ours—'

'You don't need to say another word, we know her. We know who she is! Oh, how hilarious!'

Pretty soon even the locals will know about the encounter – everyone will know; word will probably worm its way to Mrs Sultz in her sanatorium.

Crazy. Old. These are the words they will use to describe her.

She widens the mouth of the workbag and then sticks her hand into the soft

30

heap of rags inside. 'I may be crazy,' she mumbles, 'but I am not old. Sixty-seven is certainly not *old*.'

She had rushed down the hill too quickly, that was all. Arrived puffed out and frantically blinking, tears of sweat in her eyes. She had not even fixed her hair before flinging herself through the door like an irate dog tearing down to the beach, already barking. She had been so angry. Angry the way a bulldog gets angry for the sake of its master. But why? What did she have to be so angry about? Did she really care who did or did not lie down on their sand? Living here, in this hermitage on the hill, with hardly another house for miles around, should she not welcome the occasional human intrusion? In the evening, sitting on the bluff unseen, as she'd worked on her rug, listening to the sound of voices gusting up from the beach – had she not enjoyed all that? She ought to have befriended them instead of growling at them through her teeth.

How many times had Mrs Sultz advised her? 'It's not up to you to protect your husband from the outside world and you need to make your own friends, dear – you can't keep living your life through him.'

She should have fixed herself up first, then taken her time coming down to the beach, introduced herself without any fuss. Brought some little thing in her hand, maybe – cookies or apples. Not that there were any cookies or apples in the house. But still. She could have waited one more day, gone into Wellfleet in the morning and bought some cookies or – why not? – baked a cake. That chocolate number she made for his fiftieth birthday wasn't half-bad – a long time ago, but she could probably remember how to do it.

Hello, she might have said with a friendly (but not *overly* friendly) smile. I'm from the house back up there, thought you might like some… apples or cookies or… something.

She could have played with the dog first, talked to the children, bit by bit gotten round to the adults. But only staying a few minutes, mind – first time, anyhow – before climbing back up in a calm and easy fashion. Let him scowl through the window at her all he liked.

She might have been down there this very minute, sitting on a beach towel, drinking tea from a Thermos and helping pass round a picnic, involved in a conversation. A conversation! Talking about everything and anything under

31

the sun, the way only women can do. And she wouldn't just talk. She would listen too. She would *make* herself listen and not feel the urge to bombard them with her opinions. Of course she could do that. She would certainly not fall into the trap of talking and talking and talking – how had he so cruelly put it? Endless old-lady talking, *horreur vacui* – the fear of silent spaces. The pompous twist on his mouth when he said that.

And no, she would not have gone down there every day either. Two or three visits, that's all, just to break up the week. They were younger than her, of course, but they were not all *that* young – the eldest, the one who had said her name was Annette Staines, must easily be in her fifties. Besides, younger women often craved a little advice from a woman who'd seen a bit more of life. The way she had once been with Mrs Sultz, before the falling out.

After a while they would probably have invited her up to their house. Gradually she would have become part of the little group on the porch, her voice a strand in the mingle of sound that comes floating downstream from the Kaplan house each evening. Laughter and talk and music. She could be listening to their records up close, instead of having to guess at the snatches caught from the distance. Sinatra, Duke Ellington, all that other jazzy stuff. And later then, with the friendship starting to build up nicely – say a fortnight or so later – she could have invited them for tea. One of the days when he had gone sneaking off to Orleans or Eastham or wherever it is that he goes scouring for subjects. She could have said – oh, very casually, of course, as if it had only just occurred to her – 'Why don't we all go on up to the house – have tea or even lemonade? I have some peaches just begging to be eaten.'

She could have shown them the house. Then she could have shown them her paintings. *Her* paintings.

'Well, you're a dark horse,' they would joke. 'You never told us you were an artist.'

She would shrug it off like it hardly mattered, 'Oh, I don't like to cluck over my own chicks,' as she passed around the teacups. Or something along those lines.

She begins to rummage through the workbag, sifting through blues: Prussian, sky, cobalt. Midnight. Then a few strips of cardinal red. A half-dozen

32

greens in different hues. Too many blacks. Not enough white. A shortage of reds. Not so much as one scrap of yellow.

Oh, but who was she fooling anyhow. Even if she had struck up a friendship with those women on the beach, it would turn out the same as all the other so-called friendships she had struck up over the years. As soon as they found out who she was married to, they would lose all interest in her. And why would anyone be interested in her when he was looming like a skyscraper right behind her? If they are too shy to talk to him, then they want to talk *about* him. And so it would have ended, as it always ended, with her as the torch bearer leading the way; the stone they use to step across the water. The fool that climbs the orchard wall and brings back all the apples.

Two women, the older one dressed in a black bathing suit, the other in a tomato-red number. One boy and his dog. They had been coming every afternoon for a couple of weeks. Setting up their little camp of beach towels and stripy parasols, picnic basket and a big coloured ball. The dog leaving his turds lying around like Italian pastries in the sand, not even an attempt to bury them.

Then it was three women, one boy. The third woman, younger and stockier than the other two, carrying the basket – evidently the maid. By Thursday it was four women and a boy. On Friday, she thought they had left, but it turned out they'd only taken the day off. Because on Saturday, there were seven women, two boys, one dog and a man – the man and one of the women fully dressed: he in a butter-coloured suit, she in long pants and a big-brimmed yellow hat.

'They're multiplying down there,' that's all he said – or had to say. 'Every time I look, another one is hatched.'

By the time she had made it down to the beach, the man and the woman in the big yellow hat had moved off in the direction of Pamet Harbour. A woman in a polka-dot bathing suit and daisy swim cap was standing ankle-deep in the water. The regular boy was already in, jumping the waves with the dog, while the new boy, only noticed in shadow, was a squiggle somewhere in the background.

The eldest of them wore the black bathing suit. She stood smiling with her head cocked while she pushed tufts of hair under her bathing cap. 'I'm Miss Staines but please do call me Annette,' she'd said, even though she had expressed no desire to call her anything at all. Two other women were giggling on the sideline; one of them wiggling out of a sundress, the other spreading oil on her arms. The maid, Hispanic, was spreading towels out on the sand and did not even lift her head. But it was the middle woman – the one in the tomato-red suit, probably in her mid-forties, although not at all middle-aged – who had caused the trouble.

'We've been using Fisher's beach since the start of the summer,' she'd said, pulling a cigarette out from a pack tucked under the strap of her bathing suit. 'It's sort of become our spot, you know.'

'I think you'll find,' she began but then found she had difficulty expressing herself. Her breath had shortened, her concentration blurred, while Tomato Suit smoked her cigarette, brazen-eyed, a long strand of dark-red hair trailing out from under her swim cap and catching on her mouth.

She could remember muttering the words 'my husband', although she could scarcely recall what else she had said. But she must have said something because Tomato Suit came right back and said, 'Frankly, I never heard of anything so ridiculous.'

'Well, I'm sorry you find it so, but the fact remains—'

'My two friends drive down from Boston and would like to take a swim before driving back and now you're saying...'

The polka-dotted woman was now plodding back through the water. 'What's going on?' she said, as she came up to join them.

'She's telling us we can't use this part of the beach.'

'She's *what*?'

'She's saying it upsets her husband.'

'Oh, one of those, is he?'

'I'm trying to explain,' she said, 'I'm simply trying to—'

And then suddenly all of the women were standing around her. She was surrounded by bathing suits and legs, tight hairless heads in bathing caps, stretched, sneering eyes. Like huge insects about to attack. Her hand had started to shake. She felt a little spittle on the corner of her mouth but was afraid to wipe it away in case they noticed her shaking hand.

'My husband— The fact is… My husband, yes, that's what I mean. Whether

34

or not he is present, this space must be… My husband he needs peace in order to… This is *our* beach and *he* is—'

But Tomato Suit had laughed right in her face. A sharp, cruel little whip of a laugh. 'Well, how about we just take a short cut across to the next beach up there? It would mean crossing his eyeline, of course, for about thirty seconds each way. But do you think he could be persuaded to bear that? This husband of yours. This very important man.'

Gathering her nerve, she looked the red swimsuit up and down. 'You're new here,' she said, 'so you probably are not aware—'

'Excuse me, but we've been coming to the Cape for the past five years.'

'Not to this stretch of the beach, you haven't, and let me just say, we chose to build our house here for the privacy it allows. If we'd wanted to be with other people then—'

The oldest woman, the one called Annette, still smiling ear to ear, laid her hand on Tomato Suit's arm and took a step forward. 'I am sure you must know Mrs Kaplan, and this lady here is her—'

'Oh, yes, I know Mrs Kaplan, of course. Well, I suggest you ask her. I'm sure she'll be happy to put you straight.'

Still shaking, she began to back away. 'There are plenty of other beaches along here, you know. You just come down your steps, turn right instead of left, acres of beaches all the way up to Provincetown – you'll be spoiled for choice. Just not this one.'

Tomato Suit hunkered down, twisting her cigarette butt in the sand. Then, coming back up, whistled first for the dog, then for the children.

'Come on, kids,' she shouted, 'better get out of here quick, before she calls the cops.'

When she'd finally made it back up to the house, she could hardly breathe. He came into the kitchen to meet her.

'What did you say to them?'

She couldn't answer at once – there was no breath in her to make the words – and so she sat on the window ledge, her two hands pressed on her chest as if to hold her heart in place.

'What did you say to them?' he asked again.

'I told… I told them… I— hold on. Wait, wait. You know, what Mrs Kaplan… What she is *doing*… To allow… Such people! A piece of work. The one… The one in red.'

'You told them what?'

'I told them it was our… Our beach and they had no… No business, then I tried to tell them who… Who you were but of course they wouldn't… Listen. And how you… You needed your privacy. In case… in case you… You know, wanted to… Work. Or swim. Or… Or just walk and that if they wanted… Wanted right of way then—'

'You threw them off the beach?'

'Of course.'

'What the hell did you do that for?'

'Well, because— Because you wanted—'

'Did I say I wanted it? Did I ask you to do that?'

'No, but you didn't have to ask me. I knew.'

'You knew what exactly?'

'Well. That they were disturbing you. I knew.'

'In fact, they weren't disturbing me at all. I don't want to paint and I don't want to walk and if I care for a swim how is a handful of people going to prevent me? Look out there, there's a whole bay to swim in. And I tell you what I don't want more than anything else. I don't want my wife objecting to things on my behalf. That's what I really don't need right now – your constant meddling in my affairs.'

She does not want to think about what happened after that. And yet she can't help but think about it over and over – once she had caught her breath, that is, and had been ready to stand on her feet again.

After the fight, a sleepless night, or what was left of it. She had spent hers weeping on the floor of the tiny loft. He, of course, took the bedroom and probably snored through till morning. She smashed two of her favourite Mexican bowls against the wall, attacked him with whatever else came to hand: the bowls (why had she not smashed something of his?), a few books, the broom handle which he had torn from her hands and snapped in half over his knee.

36

Oh, but it was a dirty fight. Dirty and disgraceful. But at least she had given as good – no, better – than she had got. She had shown him meddlesome all right.

Still, she shouldn't have bitten his hand. But then, he probably shouldn't have dragged her across the floor. Even if he had been dragging her away from the window. The window she had threatened to smash with the broom handle – though God knows why she'd decided on that particular tactic. As if the window somehow was to blame for providing a view down to the beach and the sunbathers. And say she had managed to make a smash in it, say she smashed each and every one of its thirty-six panes. What difference would that have made? It would be repaired and returned to its former state. Whereas words – they can never be taken back. Words are the deadliest weapons: merciless, vicious, diseased. Cut them and pus would ooze out.

She pulls a square of cloth from the workbag, lifts the scissors and begins to snip through it in slow, even-sized strips.

This time, at least, she hadn't drawn blood. This time. This time, she had only nipped him. And she had told him, warned him: 'Let go or I'll bite. Let go or I'll bite. Let go of me!' Nobody could say he hadn't been warned.

But his hand all the same. His hand of all things.

Since then, the righteous silence. He has come, he has gone. He has disappeared for hours, sometimes in the car, sometimes on foot. And not one word has he thrown at her; not even goodbye.

She feels a clawing sensation on the floor of her stomach and bile in the back of her throat. She has eaten nothing since the fight. She got up the morning after and decided that's what she would do – eat nothing. Nor will she, until he apologizes or until she dies. But, as it's not in his line to apologize, she will probably just have to die. She knows she's a child to behave this way but it gives her something to hold on to. A plan – albeit a pretty pointless one.

For who is left to care now whether she lives or dies? And if one of these days he were to come home from one of his excursions and find she has melted into a few old bones in a dress on the floor – would he even notice?

A man is such an ungrateful creature. Oh, but he is also a creature of enviable self-control.

When she was a child, and even well into adulthood, she had often used the hunger weapon to punish or appease her mother. Poor Mother. As if things weren't bad enough already with both a dipsomaniac husband and son to contend with. And yet she seemed to take a sort of delight in it too – that story she loved to tell about her little girl's temper tantrums and the visiting friend who had warned: 'Better break that temper of hers.'

'I will do no such thing – she might need it someday,' had been Mother's response to that.

She had been three years old then, a puny little thing, and Mother had somehow already known that life for her would be a series of battles, big and small, in one long and never-ending war.

She believes now that her mother was wrong to encourage her temper. She believes now that she ought to have taught her control instead. If she had a daughter, that's what she would have taught her. Control. It's the reason a man almost always wins out against a woman. He wins, not because he's more intelligent or more likely to be in the right, but because he is far less likely to allow emotion to crack his resolve or fog up his brain. He wins because control allows him to keep his composure, and that, in turn, allows him to know the right buttons to press. No wonder she scratches and bites! Well, she won't ever allow that to happen again. She will show him something about control all right.

She begins arranging the coloured strips of cloth into little piles on the table and wonders who's feeding him now. For the past couple of days, he's only gone into the kitchen whenever she is out of it and she only knows he's there at all because the smell of coffee finds her on her perch outside or down in the basement or shut into the bedroom because, after all, there's not that many places for a body to hide itself in this house. Coffee and maybe toast. Yet she knows he is not hungry, that in fact he's probably better fed now than he is when they are the best of friends. He has found another table. When he goes out walking or when he drives into Truro – but no, he would have to go further than Truro or risk the locals asking after his wife (or worse, not asking at all, meaning they have guessed the reason behind his solo dining). So when he goes, wherever he goes, Provincetown or Eastham or maybe Orleans, and sits wherever he sits, in a quiet corner anyhow, red checked cloth or blue, and when, in his slow, steady manner, he cuts up the food and leans into the fork (pork chops and apple sauce, most likely, sweet potatoes too, probably, buttered corn and, why not, a spoon of creamed spinach), and a woman in the background wiping her hands on her apron asks if he needs anything more and smiles at the pleasure her food is bringing him, does he think then, I picked the wrong woman, I ought to have gone for a more wifey type – a woman who likes to have a kitchen around her, who doesn't mind the smell of cooking in her hair, the feel of a wet dishcloth in her hands. A woman who quietly comes into the studio and lays a snack plate down without disturbing the flow with a blast of senseless chatter. Does he long for a woman who would silently sit darning his clothes while he reads the newspaper? Who would never dream of intruding when he's in the middle of a conversation with other men, who would smother her own opinions at birth rather than contradict a single one of his? A woman who smiles instead of snarls. A yes-dear-no-dear-more-apple-pie-dear? kind of gal.

She pulls a few cloth strips towards her and shifts them round on the table, playing with them until she's formed a few letters: a white H, a Persian blue T and a rather clumsy M, sap-green.

Her name would be Nancy – no, Betty. A nice, no trouble, well-rounded sort of name. And she would be well-rounded too, buxom front and back to facilitate his every approach. Well, good luck to dear Betty and welcome to him. Welcome to spend her days waiting for a crumb to be brushed off his lap while he pulls his success around himself, a big warm blanket made only for one.

She presses the last letter into place then reads the sentence she has made with the rags. I HATE HIM. There now!

Before the falling out, Mrs Sultz said to her, 'You ought not complain about your husband so. What woman would not be glad of him? He's not a drinker, nor a womaniser, he can fix things round the house, for heaven's sake! What more do you want? Disloyal I call it, plain and simple.'

'Disloyal? Well, I don't know how you can say that, I'm the most loyal wife,

I do everything, everything, I sacrificed so much for him, you know, my career for one, my—'

'Be that as it may. But I sometimes hear the things you say right out in front of almost anyone at all, and I just, well, I just can't quite believe it, is all. You ought not.'

'But he infuriates me – you don't know what it's like, he's so... silent. I get so... lonely – and out here, with so few houses around. He doesn't care if he never says a word to any living creature. But I need, I need to express myself. I have things to say. I open my mouth and they just come flying out.'

'Well, write 'em down then. Write 'em down and keep them for yourself.'

She lifts her head from the table, takes a long, sneaky look through the gap in the door into the studio. His Norfolk jacket and his old duck-hunting hat have been removed from their usual hanging place at the side of his easel. And now she sees that he is wearing both as he steps up to the easel and reaches out to it. The easel blunders and falls into his arms like an awkward partner about to be led onto the dance floor. And a yearning comes over her – unexpected, certainly unwanted, but there it is just the same – for his large, strong hands, the bulk of him, the smell of linseed oil that comes from his naked skin. She imagines for a moment flinging herself on him, begging for forgiveness, taking his hands in hers, burying her face in them, yes, washing her face in his beautiful hands.

She bites down on her lip, lifts the scissors again, brings it down to the I HATE HIM sentence and trims the straggled edges of the letters. It occurs to her then:

If he is taking the brushes and the easel is going with him and he has spent that long a time guessing at the light – there could only be one reason. Could it be? After all these weeks of inertia and gloom, sarkiness and silence – could he be ready to start a new canvas? Is it finally about to happen? And if he is – and he certainly seems to be – taking it all outside, could he be returning to nature; could he actually be going to paint out? Paint out from the fact, as he likes to call it. A warm rush begins in her chest, until it dawns on her: if he is starting a new picture, he is leaving her out of the process. This will be her punishment:

40

exclusion. There will be no discussion. He will brook neither question nor suggestion, and any comment she may make will be left unanswered to die on the air. He will keep himself out of her way. He will go out as he has done for the past few days, make a start on his painting and when he comes back, he will take his spoils into his corner of the studio and turn his back firmly on her.

But first, he will come from the studio into the kitchen in his Norfolk jacket and his duck-hunter hat, and he will pick the car keys off the window ledge and he will go out the door without a word. And the thoughts of having to go through all that for yet another day: him coming into the kitchen and walking by her, looking right through her, as if she had died a long time ago, or as if she had never existed in the first place. She is a ghost without him. Or, worse than a ghost, she has never even been born. She will be left standing at the window, watching him trudge down the wooden steps with his bag over his shoulder and his folded easel under his arm.

He comes out of the studio and turns for the kitchen. Her hand swiftly disperses the letters she's made and scoops them into a single pile. Then she frowns over the rags, sorting through them as if she too has a purpose to her afternoon, her own choices to make.

He passes in and out of the kitchen and she keeps her head bent – she will not look up, she will not give him the satisfaction. She can hear him outside in the studio now, climbing the steps to the loft, a banging then, a tussle of sounds. He is pulling at something, struggling with something – what? What is he doing? She peeks as he comes back down the stairs, holding a canvas already stretched.

Yes. He is going out to paint, and yes, he is going to do it from the fact. How long is it since he has done that? And he knows how she loves it when he paints straight from nature. When he picks his scene and sets up in front of it and then the small miracle of him ingesting it somehow before, stroke by stroke, he allows it to re-emerge on the canvas, the same but utterly, uniquely different. He is going to do all that. And he is going to do it without her.

He comes back into the kitchen and passes behind her and now he is reaching for the car keys on the window ledge. She turns and looks at him: pale eyes in a tanned face, the face itself inscrutable in the blaze of mid-afternoon light.

'I'm coming with you,' she blurts, gathering her own bits and shoving them into the workbag. He makes no response, just goes back outside and continues to collect whatever he thinks he may need until he is ready to walk out the door.

She comes out behind him. 'If that's all right? I mean, if you've no objection?' she asks, trying to make her voice sound light and lacking in any fear.

He stops and turns and, for the first time in days, speaks to her.

'What do you want from me?' he asks.

'What do I—? Well, I don't want anything. I just don't, I don't want to stay here on my own again. Honestly, what a question…'

He opens the door, pins it back with his elbow and with his head gestures her through.

~

THEY DRIVE INTO AND through Orleans in silence. At the end of town, he turns up a wide side street and pulls over. He gets out and she watches his reflection pop in and out of the side mirror as he goes round to the trunk, takes something out and then walks away down the street. His long stride and the roll of yellow typewriting pages he uses for sketching, sticking out from his jacket pocket, the upward tilt of his head. And a memory of Gloucester slips under the door – the first time they had really spoken directly to one another without anyone else being present; the day Arthur had gone missing. And later, watching him walk up the sloped road through dappled light and a geometry of sea captains' houses.

And now a series of memories tries muscling in on her – again from Gloucester, their honeymoon days and early vacations, watching him work, wanting him so much that her legs could hardly stay up on their own. The relief to be able to feel that way at her age – a forty-year-old bride. But what good are memories to her now, hungry, thirsty and no doubt wanting to use the bathroom before very long, made to wait like a little chow dog at the barren end of a street on the edge of Orleans? He even left the window open a fraction at the top so little chow wouldn't suffocate and parked under the trees, too, out of the heat – oh, how considerate is he? Although the choice of parking probably had more to do with his beloved Buick than the wife he's left inside it.

She pulls the door of the glove compartment down and on the back of it lays a little heap of blue rags. Then, turning herself round on the seat, she inserts the workbag as a cushion between the passenger door and the small of her back. She lifts her legs, stretches them out to the driver's seat, unfolds the backing for the rug and begins to speak into the car.

'Just have to wait till it suits him to return, I guess. Well, that's fine. That's just fine, fine, *fine*.'

At least she can do that here, talk to herself in peace without having to hear him say, 'Your imaginary friend in there with you again?', and without her having to reply, 'Well, I got to have someone around here to talk to – don't I?'

She spreads the burlap backing over her lap and begins working on the top left corner.

'Took the keys too, I notice,' she says. 'Oh yes, we wouldn't want the simple little woman getting it into her head to drive off unsupervised. We certainly wouldn't want *that*.'

She pushes a rag through the backing and tugs it into position: push, loop, tug.

She lifts another strip from the pile and repeats the process. She does this a couple more times before it dawns: when he walked up that street, there was nothing in his hands. He was not carrying a thing, not even his oilskin bag. It could be that he's taking a walk, checking something out and that, in a few minutes, he intends returning, setting up in the back seat the way he used to do and painting something. But painting what? She peers up the street and then turns in her seat and looks backways. Houses, trees, macadam road.

'Doesn't look like there's much here,' she says out loud, 'but with him you never know…'

Push, loop, tug.

No oilskin bag, no canvas. Just the yellow sketch pages in his pocket. And why go to all the trouble of bringing them along just to leave them in the trunk – unless?

43

Unless he has no canvas in mind at all, and never did have – that's it, of course! There is nothing in his mind but a big blank screen.

A ploy, that's all it had been. Because he knew it would push her to give in and make the first move. He knows how much she loves to be there from the start – how could she have been so naive?

'Asking to come along was like asking forgiveness. I should have stayed where I was. I should have let him go and then packed a bag and walked into Truro, got on a bus. Left him. Yes, left him here and then collected my few things in New York and then left him again.'

Left him to the sharks and the grinning gallery owners; to the interviewers who want to drag out his soul and X-ray it along with his innards for all the world to see. To the empty promises and the stingy percentages. The cheap picture frames that squeeze the life out of his paintings before they're thrown any-old-way up on the wall. To the Park Avenue ladies looking to match up their wallpaper. I should have left him to all that.

Push, loop, tug, tug. *Tug*.

As she reaches out for another strip, her eye is caught by something across the street. A boy. He is sitting on the porch step of a house. A boy alone. He is bent over with his head resting on his knees. She cranes and sees that his face is buried in his open hands and that the hands are resting on his knees. She raises herself off the seat and sees now that the boy is rocking his head from side to side as if he might be crying. Poor boy, and such a pretty house – too pretty, maybe, with its pristine white clapboards and the hanging bowls of tamed flowers. Probably in some disgrace, left a smear on the bathroom mirror or footprints on the kitchen floor. A boy ought to be allowed dirty things up a little, to run wild and come home covered in all sorts. If she'd had a son, she would have— Well, who knows what she would have done, really. And who knows what sort of a sarky, twisted creature would have come out of her nature and his.

She looks down at the rug. The blue all filled in. The whole top section a gentle gradation of blue on blue. 'Quite lovely, if I say so myself.'

THE BOY COMES OUT of the house and notes a Buick parked across the street. He sits on the lower stoop where he can't be seen from the living-room and puts his hands over his face. Then he bends over his knee and presses into his eyes with the heels of his hands.

He presses until it feels like the wires behind his eyes can't take any more. Then he lifts his face and opens his eyes as far as they'll go. A surge of butterfly blobs and coloured streamers. Orange and silver, purple and blue. He follows their progress until the blobs begin to fade and fall away and the daylight comes back in again. And it's all back now: the stoop and his knees and the short paved pathway cut in the small, neat lawn and the white wooden gate in the white wooden fence. And the Buick still parked across the street.

Behind him, the voices of women; in his head, the shape of the room he's just left. There's Mrs Kaplan's voice coming from the yellow sofa and the voice of Mrs Grant, the English lady who owns the house, right beside it. From the big green armchair comes the voice of Richie's mother, who is called Olivia or ma'am. She is perched on the arm of the chair and sitting in it is her friend Annette, who doesn't like to be called Miss Staines. These two voices sometimes throw in with the others and sometimes just peck away together. On the bigger green sofa on the far side of the room, there's Richie's Aunt Katherine who says almost nothing at all. At first he thinks that could be because she's sick and her voice may be too weak to do any real kind of talking – the kind of talking the other women do, anyhow. But then he remembers that since he's been here he's heard her singing a few times, whole songs at a go, so being sick probably has nothing to do with it. The last voice comes from the high-backed red velvet chair just inside the living-room door. He doesn't know much about this voice except that it comes out of a stink of perfume, two sly eyes and a big lumpy face, and that it sure knows how to ask a lot of questions.

The Buick is parked under the trees and there could be someone inside it but it's hard to tell with the shadow of the branches hanging over it. Sometimes he looks and thinks he sees something moving, then next time he looks there is nothing at all. He knows it's a Buick anyhow because it's just like the one Harry's friend Vince used to drive.

Richie's mom lifts her voice and moves it out of range, and he thinks she may be going to sit beside Katherine, but then on the same long sentence her voice goes out of the room into the hall, snakes around and slides back in again. And he wishes she wouldn't always have to do that, keep moving around, because he likes to know where everyone is in a room and the only way he can do that, without having to stay in the room himself, is to pin them down by their voices.

It doesn't matter what the voices are talking about, it always ends in a muddle anyhow: the war in Korea and then Katherine's new shoes and the old lady who threw them off the beach the first day that he saw the sea. And now it's turned into a big discussion about Labor Day Weekend, when the men will be coming down and what should be done with them from the moment they arrive till the moment they go away again.

He doesn't really know who these men could be if Richie's dad died in the war and Katherine isn't married because Richie said she's too sick to have a husband, even if she's pretty enough to catch a hundred of them. They had to take her kidney out, was what Richie said, break her ribs to get at it. They smashed them with a hammer then the doctor just reached right in there and plucked the kidney out.

And no husband for Mrs Kaplan either because his heart gave out a long time ago when Katherine was still in high school. And it can't be Annette's husband if she's sometimes called Miss Staines. It could be the husband of Mrs Grant that they're talking about. Or Mrs Lumpy Face, if she has a husband, and he already feels sorry for him.

Across the street, movement inside the Buick catches his eye again, and outside it, all over its roof and down the side, shadows from the overhanging trees are dancing like black jigsaw pieces.

When Vince drove the Buick, he would come by on Sundays and take them out for a ride. And he liked that a lot. Harry would always explain to him before they got in the car exactly where they were going and what they would see on the way and what to expect when they got there.

And that was a good feeling, looking out the window at the buildings and then the sudden river. Harry pointing out the bridge as soon as it came into sight and Vince maybe telling them something about the bridge, like the name of it and who made it and how many workers died before it was all done. And then when he'd open his eyes, the bridge would be behind them. After that trees and grass and ice-cream and sometimes even a hot dog.

A few times, they went the other way, up to Central Park, and he didn't like that so much because they had to drive right back through their whole neighbourhood where the Sunday streets seemed so bare and lonely and you could notice only the bad things like the bits of garbage stuck to the kerbside and newspaper pages flapping along and an old lady sleeping in a doorway. And once Vince took them to visit someone in a house way past the other end of Central Park and when the man opened the door there was a whole family of negroes inside and Harry and Vince talked to the man in another room about union business and the woman made coffee for Frau Aunt and the baby sat in a steel crib the negro man had made with his own hands and kept throwing his rattle on the floor. But the two boys? The two boys who were around his age wouldn't play with him even though that's exactly what their mother told them to do. They wouldn't even answer him when he tried being friendly and then, one by one, they just snuck out of the room and the next time he saw them was through the window playing softball with a bunch of other negro boys, leaving him with nothing to do but, over and over, pick the rattle up off the floor and hand it back to the baby.

There's a jangling, tinkling sound coming from Mrs Grant's house, a sound he recognizes from Mrs Kaplan's house in Truro. It's the sound of the hostess trolley that her maid Rosetta pushes out from the kitchen to the back porch. He knows it's called a hostess trolley because one time when he was in Macy's with Frau Aunt there was a demonstration called the Joys of the Hostess Trolley, and this lady with a crazy smile pushed one through the crowd. It was loaded up with plates of cookies and cheese balls and the lady lifted the plates off two by two and went around saying, 'Please help yourself, please *do* help yourself, madam. Madam?' While a man at the counter spoke into a microphone and said nice things about the trolley. The man asked Frau Aunt if she wouldn't like to make entertaining a little easier for herself and Frau Aunt said, 'I don't need to make it easier because I don't do it in the first place,' and the other women standing around thought she was joking and laughed while Frau Aunt went red, right up to the roots of her hair.

Mrs Grant's maid looks like Mrs Kaplan's Rosetta and both of them are a version of Mrs Mendez, the Mexican lady who cleans the school, or one of those girls who work in the sewing factory near his apartment. Mrs Grant's maid seems a little more sour than Rosetta, who can also seem a little sour but she can be playful too – just a couple of days right after he arrived, she started this crazy pillow fight and it was the most fun ever, Rosetta laughing with her teeth as white as chalk, until Richie got one belt too many and started whining and then he let himself fall off the bed on purpose so he could have an even better excuse to whine, then Rosetta put her sour face back on again and told them go wash up before supper and leave her get on with her work.

He looks over at the Buick again. This time it seems certain that there is something moving inside it. A dog, maybe, or even a child. Something low-sized anyway. He is considering getting off the stoop and taking a closer look when he notices that the conversation in the house has taken a sudden twist and that his name is in there, right in the centre of it.

Richie's mom's voice: 'Novak, they're called Novak, I believe.'

And Mrs Lumpy's voice: 'And you say they live in New York – but where do they come from?'

'Mr Novak was born there, I believe. She may be from Eastern Europe originally, I think – I must ask my mother-in-law. Mother, where is Mrs Novak from, do you know?'

'I'm not sure, Olivia.'

'And how long did you say the boy has been with the Novaks?' Mrs Lumpy asks.

'Mother, how long would you say he's been with the Novaks?'

'How long what, dear?'

'How long would you say he's been with the Novaks?'

'Oh, let me see now. About four or five years, I suppose. He was one of the first batches but one of the last to be taken up. He was in the American camp for two years anyhow and before then – who knows? Mr Novak and his friend, Mr Roncati, they did so much work for us, you know, putting up shelves and fixing things. They were just wonderful!'

'Mother said he was a lucky boy, that without the Novaks he'd probably have been left behind.'

'Olivia! I said no such thing. I simply said that babies are always first to go, babies and the older ones with personalities before the, well, the older, quieter child. He was very reserved, you see, didn't mix so well.'

'Nothing changed there!' Richie's mom says.

Mrs Kaplan says, 'I like him very well.'

When he hears her say that! It makes him so happy, he almost feels like crying. But then Richie's mom says, 'Oh well, everyone knows, my mother-in-law, she likes just about everyone.'

'Now you're just being silly, Olivia,' Mrs Kaplan says. 'Why don't you help Mrs Grant instead? You could pass these out. Let me help too, Mrs Grant, please, I insist. Now, who'd like cream and sugar? Or lemon? Would anyone prefer lemon? Katherine, what about you? And do you know, Miss Staines, that Mrs Grant met her husband during the war when he was stationed in London – now isn't that romantic?'

'No, I didn't know that but, please, won't you call me Annette?'

'Oh yes, Annette. And tell me, Mrs Grant, do they really have this feast every afternoon in London? It's a wonder you ever eat dinner!'

Mrs Grant laughs and Mrs Kaplan laughs and then the cups and saucers laugh and all the stuff on the hostess trolley laughs and clinks and clatters and bangs like crazy.

When Vince took them out on Sundays, he sometimes brought his girl along but he always made her get in the back so Harry could sit up front and they could talk about baseball or work. The girl's name was Shirley and she didn't much like the back seat, crossing her arms and turning to the window and barely answering Frau Aunt when she said something about the weather, or that's a nice dress you're wearing, Shirley, or I sure like the way you've fixed your hair, Shirley. And when Vince said, 'Ladies and gentlemen we have reached our destination, Shirley wouldn't even smile, and as soon as they got out, she would hook herself onto Vince like she was afraid he'd float off in the air like a balloon, Harry said later, and not let go no matter what, not even to eat an ice-cream cone.

Frau Aunt said Shirley was way too thin and Harry asked him if she wasn't the skinniest girl he had ever seen.

When Harry asked him that, his head filled up with all these pictures. The pictures were of people who were way skinnier than Shirley. And some of them were lying down and some of them were just shuffling along on a road in the middle of nowhere. But he wasn't sure if they were real people or people who maybe just popped up in his nightmares and then stayed on in his head and so he just said, 'Oh yeah, the skinniest girl in the world, that Shirley.'

One time Shirley said, 'Why don't we ever go to Coney Island?'

'It's the lights, all that jerky noise, it reminds them,' Harry said.

'Reminds them of what?' Shirley said.

'We were told not to, that's all. Maybe when he's a little older.'

'What – are you kiddin' me? How old you gotta be to enjoy Coney Island?'

And Vince said, 'Knock it off, Shirl, just leave it.'

The day they went to see the negro family Vince didn't bring Shirley along. Vince said he didn't bring her because she'd only give him a hard time. She wouldn't have gone in the house anyhow, Vince said, and then he did Shirley's voice, 'Not in a million years am I goin' in there'. And if he'd left her in the Buick she'd still give him a hard time – 'Leavin' me out here on my own when God knows who coulda come along and slit my throat right open ear to ear'.

And they all laughed so hard when Vince did Shirley's voice and then Harry said, 'Vince, you gotta get yourself a trade-in.' And Vince said, 'Harry, I would, but it's a little late for that.'

Mrs Kaplan's voice comes out of the house again and this time it sounds a little frosty. 'No, as a matter of fact, we don't know his background, who his people were. We don't know any of that. And we don't want to know either.'

Mrs Lumpy's voice then: 'Really, Mrs Kaplan? You mean to say you don't know if he's a… well, you know?'

'But that's the whole point,' Mrs Kaplan says, 'to give the children a clean start, not have the past hanging around their necks. He's been five years here now and I really think—'

'Well, I don't know…' Mrs Lumpy says.

'Are you worried that he may be Jewish?' Mrs Grant's English voice asks.

'On the contrary, I hope he is. Because otherwise… well, we must ask ourselves – who is he? *What* is he?'

'All I know is that he is a child and I don't see that anything else matters.'

'Well, I'm sorry, Mrs Kaplan, but *I* do. What about the Novak family, don't they have a right to know? I don't know how they can stand it. I'd want to know – wouldn't you want to know? After what happened, what those people did. The *in*-humanity of it! It could be in the blood, you know. The Novaks ought to be told one way or another, especially *now*. Olivia tells me that Mrs Novak is—'

'Well, they can't be told one way or another,' Mrs Kaplan's voice rises up to say, 'because we don't *know* one way or another and, besides, a child is a—'

'Child. I quite agree with you, Mrs Kaplan,' Mrs Grant says. 'During the war, many of them were brought to England, poor defenceless kiddies that had been just left like stray dogs all over the continent to fend for themselves.'

'Thank you, Mrs Grant. And where is he, by the way? Richie, where—? I thought you were supposed to be taking care of your guest?'

Richie's voice comes up from the floor, dull and squashed from lying there, reading his comic.

'Huh? Oh, he's taken Buster for a walk.'

'I don't know why we had to bring that dog,' Richie's mom says. 'Richie wouldn't leave him behind. We had to stop twice on the way so the car wouldn't get it. I told him the dog was perfectly safe in Truro, but—'

'But will he be all right?' Mrs Kaplan says. 'He doesn't know Orleans. He's only been with us five minutes and we just let him wander off. Really, Olivia, what if he gets lost?'

'Oh, Mother, you could put that boy down in the middle of the desert and he'd find his way out.'

*

The boy slips sideways off the steps of the porch then sidles round the house to where the dog is patiently waiting with its long, wet tongue wobbling from its jaw. He unties the dog from the gate-post and takes it out on the street, sneaking round by the backside of Mrs Kaplan's automobile.

He glances over at the Buick and now it seems to be empty again. He crosses over the street to take a peek inside, but as he comes near, he sees there is someone inside it after all – a girl. A girl who appears to be reading a comic laid out on her lap and so he quickly bends one knee and veers away, then keeps walking towards a gas station on the corner at the end of the street.

The dog pulls him on. The sky is starting to haze over and the air is thick and hot and still. Two girls pushing bicycles at the far end of the street are screaming with distant laughter. At the corner, a whistling man at the gas station rolls a tyre across the forecourt. And then everything goes quiet. The dog continues to lead the way with its dainty paws and flouncy coat and nose stuck like a cone in the air.

At the corner the dog decides to turn left. But he's not so sure he likes the look of things down there, just a couple of automobiles crawling in and out of side roads and no one around apart from one tall man standing under the trees. The man is dressed in pale-coloured clothes and is wearing a beige hat and he's just standing there, staring up to a spot past this end of the street. The boy turns his head to the right and follows the man's gaze: a row of houses and then some stores and another few houses after that. A woman in a green dress comes out of one of the stores and stands under the awning, leaning out on one foot to look up the street. And he feels afraid for her suddenly and thinks maybe that's on account of the man under the trees. The man reminds him of someone. He doesn't know who – but someone dangerous, anyhow. He wonders if maybe the man is watching the woman in the green dress and if maybe he plans on killing her or he could be sending a signal to someone hiding in that automobile parked a little way up from the woman, and any minute now the door will snap open and someone will step out and grab her and stuff her into the back, and maybe the woman senses something terrible is about to happen and that's why she's leaning out that way and peering up the street.

A pick-up truck comes out of one silence, passes right by the woman and disappears into another silence. The woman goes back inside the store.

He takes command of the dog, pulling it across the street towards the row of stores. When they get to the other side, the dog relaxes. There's the tipping of its claws on the sidewalk and, somewhere in the background, the sly clicking of those creatures that Rosetta calls cicadas.

He stops at the store where the woman in the green dress disappeared. A dress shop. But he can't see the woman in there. Just two pretend women in the window, all dressed up like two big dolls. On the floor of the window, two empty dresses are pinned down into a sort of twist. Another two dresses are pinned in the same way to the wall at the side of the window.

He starts to feel uneasy again. Uneasy and a little sick in his stomach. He does not like the heavy silence, the deserted street behind him, the man standing under the trees up the way, the *crickcrickcrick*ing from creatures he can't even see. He does not like the dresses pinned to the floor, nor the image of himself blurred on the glass of the window with no eyes in his face.

He looks back up the road. The man is still standing there, and now it looks like he is writing something down in a yellow book, and he wonders how many more just like him could be hiding in the trees. He tries to be brave, the way Harry tells him to be brave when he gets this way: take four deep breaths, close your eyes and wait till it all goes away. But what if he closes his eyes and the man comes up behind him and if his eyes are shut he won't know to run until it's too late? And as for the breaths, he can't even manage one of those, never mind a whole four of them. All he can do is stand and stare in at the empty dresses.

A bell rings once, making him jump. And now the woman in the green dress comes out of the store.

'You'll lose your dog,' she says, 'if you're not careful.'

And he sees now that he's dropped the dog's lead and that the dog has gone trotting off towards the corner. He runs after him, catches the lead and brings the dog back. The woman has a pole in her hand.

'I was about to close up,' she says and waits for him to step out of her way.

She looks him over, then sticks the end of her pole into a steel bracket at the side of the window and starts making twisty moves.

'What's your name?' she asks and waits for him to answer.

'You don't want to tell me?' she says then. 'Well, that's fine, you don't have to if you don't want.'

'It's Richie,' he decides.

'You on vacation, Richie?'

'Oh no. I live here.'

'You do?'

'I live down there, my father drives a Buick.'

'And I thought I knew all the boys around here. Funny, I've never seen you before. Now why is that, do you suppose?'

'I don't know. Well, I've been in hospital for a long time.'

'Oh, I'm so sorry to hear that. How long a time?'

'I don't know – about two years.'

'Goodness, that is a long time. What was the matter with you?'

'I don't know,' he says, 'they plucked out my kidney, though.'

'Oh, heavens! You poor boy.'

'Had to smash my ribs to get at it. With a hammer.'

'Good Lord – a hammer!'

The woman finishes twisting the awning and then she smiles at him. 'Would you like some cookies, Richie? I have cookies I keep for the ladies. Cookies and lemonade. But as there weren't any ladies today… I'm afraid, I drank all the lemonade myself. But the cookies are still there if you'd like them?'

The boy nods and she disappears.

When she comes back out, she's holding a brown paper bag. 'You enjoy those, dear, and I hope you continue to feel better.'

'How come those dresses are empty?' he asks.

The woman gives a little laugh. 'What a funny question,' she says. 'Well, Richie, that's just the display. I only have two mannequins, you see, and the window is not that big. But those dresses, well, I hope they will be sold and some nice lady will wear them and then they won't be empty any more. Well, goodbye. Enjoy the cookies.'

She steps back into the store and then steps out again. 'And you be sure to tell your mom, now, if she needs a new dress…'

'Oh yes, I will,' he calls after her, 'I'll tell her soon as I get home.'

As he comes to the junction, he notices the man is no longer under the trees. He peers up the road and then back down it. He puts his hand over his eyes and squints down the street where Mrs Grant lives. The man is nowhere to be seen. The man is gone. He loosens his step, kicks a pebble onto the road and strolls on.

The dog stops for a sniff of a tree followed by another cock of his leg. He decides to sit down on the kerb and try one of the cookies. He opens the bag and sticks his nose in. The words *die Mandel* come up from his throat and settle on his tongue. 'Almond,' he says into the bag, 'almond, almond, almond.'

He gulps the scent into his throat. Then he counts the cookies. Six in all. If he eats one now and gives one to the dog that would leave four. He could eat one a night and that would keep him going till Saturday. But if he only had half now and half tomorrow and the next day and so on, he could make the cookies last a full week. But the terrible feeling then, when the week was over and all the cookies were gone. He takes another sniff and another few almond-scented gulps. But why worry about that now? It should be a cinch finding a few bits of food in a house like Mrs Kaplan's. In the meantime, where to hide these cookies? Under the bed and Rosetta or Richie could find them. In the bottom of his suitcase and they would go mouldy in the heat. What he needs is a box like the one Richie keeps in the drawer of his bedside table. At night he takes the box out and drops his stuff into it. Richie has never shown him what is in the box, but he has pretended to be sleeping so he could see the comings and goings from Richie's pocket to the box and back again the following morning. A pocket knife, a small rubber ball, a rescue inhaler, a candy bar usually and a few balls of bubblegum, maybe a few dimes or even a dollar.

He doesn't have any place on his side of the room where he could hide a box safely – there's only a big mirror on a stand and one narrow shelf over the bed. And even if he did have, how does he know he could trust Richie to stay away from it?

55

He could tuck the cookies into one of the wooden beams out on the veran-dah where the sea air would keep them nice and cool. But if the birds found the bag, they'd go pecking and plucking till it fell to pieces. A good hiding place, that's what he needs, as well as a box like the one Richie has that would keep them protected. Someplace away from the house – but not too far away – a place no one would ever dream of looking.

He runs his fingers through the sandy kerbside dust and thinks about all the hiding places back in New York, out on the roof or under the loose floor-board beneath the rug in his bedroom.

Today is Tuesday, Frau Aunt's choir night. Harry will be coming in around now, leaning over the sink, washing his hands right up to his elbows. Aunt Frau will be putting on her lipstick in the mirror, calling out instructions. He won-ders if Harry will bother having the boys over for cards now that he doesn't have to babysit, or at least not until the new baby he's not supposed to know about comes along, and he wonders, too, if they've already forgotten him.

He takes a cookie out and holds it up to the dog. The dog stares at him, waiting. He stares back at the dog, right into its close-set beady black eyes. 'Hey, Buster, know who I am?' he asks it. 'Know who I am, Buster?'

He teases the dog with the cookie, bringing it up to its nose and then draw-ing it back.

'I am the very boy, that's who. The *very* boy.'

He drops the cookie into the dog's open mouth; the dog snaps it back in one.

'Oh no, Buster. That's way too fast. You're supposed to make it last – like this, see?'

He pulls back and begins on his own cookie then, nibble by slow nibble, while he thinks again about Harry and Vince.

They stand the beer bottles out on the window ledge to keep them cool in the winter or in the sink stuffed with ice in the summer. A bottle of soda pop for him. A candy bar. The big glass ashtray packed out with cigarette ends.

Vince and two more of Harry's friends come by to keep him company – sometimes they play cards but mostly they forget and just sit in the kitchen, talking. They're supposed to put him to bed at a reasonable hour, but they always leave him till he is ready to drop.

It's his job to open the beer bottles, to light up the cigarettes and, when ten o'clock comes along, to take out the corned beef sandwiches Frau Aunt has left ready. And the men, they just sit there telling each other stories.

Sometimes Harry takes charge of a story with Vince adding bits or making corrections. Sometimes it's Vince who takes the story with Harry butting in. The other two guys don't talk so much, Frank maybe sometimes but Jim almost never – he just listens and smiles with his face getting rosier as the night goes on. But when it comes to the orphanage story, it's always Vince who takes charge. The orphanage story is his favourite – he waits all night and hopes they will tell it, and if they don't, he sometimes just comes right out and begs them to tell it, even though he's heard it a hundred times before.

Vince always begins: 'We used walk by that building every day on the way to work, every day. This would have been before your time, Jim. Every day and not a sound – you could hear your own footsteps walking along. Am I right, Harry? And then suddenly there's this one day when you couldn't hear yourself think. What a commotion! We didn't know what was goin' on – did we, Harry? It was like every seagull in the city had moved in there. *Cackcackcacksquawksquawk* – it was unbelievable, Frank, I'm telling you. That went on a few days until there's this evening on the way back to the subway – a different noise. What was it like, Harry?'

'Clocks.'

'Clocks. That's right, Harry. It was like a hundred clocks going *tick tock tick tock* in there, and not all at the same time either. So I see this woman across the street with her head out the window. What's going on in there? I ask her. In there? That's Truman's orphans is what that is. And I say, they sure know how to make enough noise, and she says, tell me about it, they're from all over Europe, it's like no two can speak the same language but they all like hearin' themselves talk. And what's that then – they turn it into a clock factory or somethin'? Oh, that? Ping pong, she says. Ping pong? What do you mean, ping pong? Ping pong – I'm tellin' you, the only time they shut up since they arrived is in the evening when they're over there whacking balls at each other.'

Then Vince will stop smiling and kiss the flat of his thumb before making a short, fast sign of the cross over his chest and Harry will look down at the table, and this means the sad part is about to happen: poor Jake.

'Poor, poor Jake,' Vince will say. 'Well, we won't talk about that now, but one day, about a year or so after he'd gone – you remember him, Frank, but I wish you'd known him, Jim, a great kid. A real tragedy. But anyhow, poor Jake, he was gone and Harry here, Harry says to me, she's never gonna stop cryin', Vince, she's never gonna get over the loss and she's too scared to try for another. It was me who got the idea – right, Harry?'

'That's right, but it was more than a year. A year and a half, maybe.'

'So it was. My apologies. What you gotta lose, Harry? That's what I said. A kid's just what she needs, someone to take care of, to pull her mind away from poor Jake. And so, we knocked on the door and we went in and there was all these kids running around like crazy, maybe ten schoolyards pushed into one. And Harry here. Harry, let me tell you, was very specific about his require-ments. Age, colour hair, height, personality – all that. And I'm thinkin' you're goin' about this the wrong way, Harry, you shoulda said a kid – any kid. And so I say, hold on, Harry, it's not a made-to-measure service here, you know, but the lady – God bless her – Mrs Kaplan, what does she say? She says, well, Mr Novak, it just so happens, I have the *very* boy for you. And that was this kid here – look at him over there, grinning with chocolate all over his face. What is he?'

And then Vince would beat his hands off the table and they'd all throw back their heads and yell it right out: 'The *very* boy!'

He hears someone whistle. A feeble sort of whistle struggling up the street. The dog hears it too and he just about manages to get on his feet and stamp down on the leash before Buster takes off. And now he sees Richie up there, leaning over Mrs Grant's gate. Richie has spotted him and is through the gate, running down to meet him.

He rolls the top of the cookie bag tight, sticks it down the back of his pants and pulls his T-shirt over it.

At the sight of Richie, the dog gets all excited, pulling against the leash and making little squealy sounds.

'Where've you been?' Richie whines, and then the dog whines back and Richie drops down on one knee, hugging the dog, stroking its muzzle and cooing into its ear while the dog licks Richie's face like it's an ice-cream cone.

'Are you okay, boy? Are you okay? Did you miss me? I sure missed you.'

Richie looks up from the dog and scowls at him, then he snatches the lead from his hand and stands up. 'You were only supposed to be gone five minutes. And how come you're always runnin' off anyhow?'

He doesn't answer; he moves around Richie and begins walking ahead of him. Richie and the dog fall in behind.

As they near the Buick, he sees the girl is still inside. He can't see her face, just a ponytail sticking out of her lowered head. The dog cocks its leg again, and while they wait for it to finish, Richie says, 'I hate these visits. These crummy tea parties. That Mrs Grant and her dumb little English sandwiches.'

He tries to work out what the girl is doing in there with her bobbing head and her elbow going up and down. Then he notices under the trunk, between the two back wheels, something glinting in the grass.

Richie says, 'I sure hope Mr Thompson doesn't come for the Labor Day Weekend party. He served with— with my— you know, when they were overseas, and he keeps asking me if I need to talk and, oh boy, not to you, I sure don't! And then there's Mr McCreedy who thinks he knows just about everything and spends his whole time making goo-goo eyes at Aunt Katherine. At least he won't be staying with us, which is something, I guess. He's married to the stout one – we're not supposed to call her fat but I don't think my grandma likes her too much. She's an opera singer and big deal to that is what I say. It's gonna be the biggest party seen around here for years, Mom says. All these servicemen and Captain Hartman will be coming too – he's some sort of a hero and I don't care much for him either, let me tell you – and, well, I wish I didn't have to go at all and that's the truth.'

The dog uncocks its leg, and begins sniffing along the stalks of the fence. And now, parallel to the Buick, he sees it's not a girl after all, but a small woman sitting sideways on the seat. She looks as if she might be talking to someone but he can't see that there's anyone else in there to talk to. The glint on the grass is sharper now. He bends to tie his shoe-laces and get a better look.

Richie says, 'Hey, what's that sticking out the back of your pants?'

'What?'

'There, look right there, a paper bag sticking out the back of your pants.'

'Oh, it's just some cookies.'

'Cookies? Why'd you stick them in the back of your pants – that's kind of disgusting, don't you think? Where'd you get them anyhow?'

'A woman gave them to me.'

'What woman?'

'I don't know, she just stopped and passed them out through the window of her automobile.'

'What sort of an automobile?'

'A red one.'

'You can't just take cookies from strangers,' Richie says.

'Why not?'

'You just can't, is all… But, hey, I know! Why don't we keep them for tonight? Eat them in bed or, or how about we sneak out and have a picnic on the side verandah? Eat them in the dark? What do you say? Wouldn't that be fun? One time, when I was little, Aunt Katherine and, and— Well, I went with her and my dad and some others for a midnight picnic. We went to the Highland Light – that's a lighthouse, in case you don't know…'

He steps out onto the road and takes a closer look. A rectangle shape. A box maybe. He begins to cross the road.

'Hey. Where you going?' Richie says. 'Come away from there. Come away *right* now.'

Richie drops his voice. 'Don't you know who that is? Don't you even recognize her? You don't wanna go over there. Oh boy, you don't wanna do that.'

The tin rattles when he lifts it. He holds it for a moment and then thumbs a little sandy dust off a faded label. The words Conté Crayons are written on it. He comes round to the driver's door and taps on the window. The woman's head flies up, her hand goes to her chest and her eyes first widen and then narrow. She climbs over to the driver's door on her knees and rolls down the window.

60

He stares at the woman and she looks right back at him for a few seconds then cocks one eyebrow at him. He pokes his hand in the window and hands her the tin.

'Where'd you find it?' she asks.

'Out there, just under the trunk.'

'Hope he has a pencil with him, that's all I can say. Hate to think of him wasting his precious time. Well, thanks,' she says, and moves to put the window back up.

Behind him, he can hear Richie's feet slapping up the wooden steps of the porch, then the slam of the storm door and a muffled 'Grandma – Mom! Grandma-Mom!'

He doesn't move, just stays there looking at her.

'So,' she says, 'nice weather we're having, wouldn't you say?'

He nods.

'And… how are you?' she asks.

'I'm fine,' he says, 'how are you?'

'Oh, I'm all right, I guess. A little hungry maybe. A little thirsty. But fine. That was a nice dog I saw you with earlier. My husband once painted a dog just like that and for a minute there… but of course it couldn't be. Unless it's a grandson. Or grandpup, should I say? But you know, back then you couldn't find a collie for love or money, just happened to spot one outside the post office one day and I kept it happy while he sat in here and slyly sketched away, got a beautiful dog out of it too – you'd think he knew it all his life! Now, of course, they're everywhere. Probably down to that movie, you know the one, *Lassie Go Home*.'

'*Lassie Come Home*,' he laughs, 'Come *Home*.'

The woman smiles back at him. 'That's right. The one with little Liz Taylor in it.'

'Yes,' he agrees.

'Of course, she's not so little any more – is she?'

'No, I guess not. What happened to the dog from your husband's picture?' he asks.

'Oh, he's dead and buried, I guess. That was the year the war started in

61

Europe. But your collie is young enough, I'd say. You don't have to worry about him, not for a long time yet.'

'Oh, I'm not worried. He's not my dog.'

'No?'

'I was just walking him. I don't really like dogs.'

'No?'

'I prefer cats.'

'You do? So do I! I had a wonderful cat once. Arthur. Oh, was he something else. I have a beautiful painting of him – I wish you could see it.'

'You called him Arthur?'

'And it suited him too. What's he called, anyhow, the dog that isn't your dog?'

'Oh, he's called Buster.'

'Why, that's a terrible name. Doesn't even make sense. He's far too elegant for that name.'

'Yes, I know. Sometimes they call him Buzz.'

'Ridiculous,' she says and begins shaking her head.

'They say – here *buzzbuzzbuzz*. Like he's a bee or somethin'.'

The woman laughs.

'And what about you,' she says, 'what's your name?'

'Me? My name, you mean?'

'Yes, your name, I mean.'

'Oh. Well, it's… It's Vince.'

'So what are you? Italian, Irish?'

'Em. Both, I guess.'

The woman opens her mouth to say something else but then her eyes spring away over his shoulder towards Mrs Grant's house. 'Oh no,' she mutters.

He turns to see Mrs Kaplan coming down the steps and then Richie's mom behind her and then Richie and the dog. He shoves his hand through the window again, this time with the brown bag on the end of it.

'What's that?' she asks.

'Cookies,' he says, 'you said you were hungry.'

She gives a little gasp and takes the bag from him.

And now Mrs Kaplan is right up beside them, her hands on his shoulders, moving him out of the way.

'Mrs Aitch!' she says. 'Am I glad to see you. Would you believe – I was thinking about calling on you tomorrow to say… Well, I heard all about the misunderstanding the other day and my daughter-in-law, Olivia – she'd like to apologize. She feels very badly about the way she spoke to you. Very—'

'I don't care much for apologies, not even when I'm on the receiving end of them, so why don't we just forget it.'

'Well, that's kind of you. Won't you please at least come in and join us for tea? Do you know Mrs Grant? She's from London and has recently come to live here with her husband, Alec Grant. He was stationed there during the war. And I was just about to say to her, to say, the only other person I've heard of round here who can put on an afternoon tea on this scale is— when Richie came running in to tell us you were here, right across the street. Now isn't that funny? We've been having a lovely time – please do join us.'

'Well, I'd love to but, you see, my husband…'

'Where is he?'

'He's gone looking for his sky.'

Mrs Kaplan shakes her head softly and dreamily says, 'Looking for his sky…? Well, I'm sure the boys won't mind waiting and telling him where you are.'

'Oh, I don't know, he'll be anxious to get home and get it down on a canvas – you see, if he doesn't act quickly… But you know, if Mrs Grant wouldn't mind, I could do with using her bathroom?'

'Of course, of course, please.' And Mrs Kaplan stands aside.

He leans on the hood of the Buick and watches her roll up her rag rug and then put it into a big, soft bag that she leaves on the seat along with her purse and the bag of cookies. He watches her again as she crosses the street between Mrs Kaplan and Richie's mother and thinks how much more like a girl she is than a woman, the way she just climbed out of the automobile and the way her little ponytail swings from one side to another as both women look down on her and try to hold her attention.

Richie's mom: 'I was just so tired that day, the heat, you see, and I…'

63

Mrs Kaplan: 'Now, if you won't stay and have tea then you must at least promise to come to dinner some evening.'

'And I had no idea,' Richie's mom is saying now, 'I mean Mrs Kaplan, my mother-in-law, she forgot to mention that it was your house and this is the first year I've used any of the beaches in Truro – my sister-in-law Katherine used to spend her summers in Eastham, you see, and I always went to her whenever I wanted to swim…'

'Even better, Labor Day Weekend,' Mrs Kaplan says, 'when we will be having an end of summer party. That would be wonderful. We are expecting half of my son's regiment to show up. And on Sunday, some of the men will go sailing – does your husband still sail?'

Richie's mom again: 'But, of course, Katherine stays with us now, and I can't tell you how embarrassed I was when Mother told me who your husband…'

Mrs Kaplan again: 'He could join them if he wished, I know they would be thrilled to have him as part of the crew, and of course, *you* too.'

'Oh yes, do say you'll come!'

'Of course she's going to come!'

He keeps hoping she'll look around so he can see what her face looks like from a distance. But in a few short seconds, the storm door has opened and the inner door closed and the house has swallowed her in.

When he turns round, Richie is peering into the passenger window, his hands shielding his eyes from the light. 'You gave her the cookies,' he whines. 'What you have to go and do that for?'

'She was hungry.'

'What?'

'Mrs Aitch, she was hungry.'

'Mrs *what*? Oh, that's not her name. It just begins with an aitch.' Richie tuts and glares at him. 'You know, the letter.'

'What letter?'

'The letter in the alphabet, dummy.'

He begins counting the letters on his fingers. 'Ay, bee, cee, dee, ee, eff, gee, aitch.'

Then he draws three big lines on the air. 'Aitch,' he says, 'aitch, aitch, aitch.'

~

AN HOUR LATER SHE'S back in the car, belly loaded up. Fruit cake, English scones and who knows how many cucumber sandwiches contribute to the ache. She had agreed to 'oh, all right then, maybe one cup of tea'. And then 'just the smallest slice of fruit cake, if you insist'.

But once she'd given in, the hunger of the past couple of days just sort of reared up and pounced and soon she was eating anything within an arm's reach. Having the time of her life too, laughing and talking and agreeing to attend some little party on Saturday night, and again to the garden party on the Saturday of Labor Day Weekend, which, why of course, her husband would be thrilled to attend (if they have a team of wild horses to drag him there, that is).

The light too frail now for working on her rug, she closes her eyes and tries for a nap. But she can't settle because wriggling away in the back of her mind is the usual worm of dread. Did she say too much? Did she listen enough? And what did she – or anybody else for that matter – say anyhow? There had been a long run at the weather, a commentary on all the stores in Provincetown. That new picture showing in Hyannis, recommended by one, dismissed by the other. Several titbits in between that she can't recall now. But had she made a fool of herself – that was the only question. And if so – by how much?

'Oh, as if they don't think you're a fool already,' she says aloud and then opens her eyes, 'sitting around till near dark waiting on your master's return.'

But then, one way or another, they had all been waiting for him: the boys watching out at the gate. The women inside keeping the conversation going, even the dog on the porch had seemed to have an air of expectancy about it, just like the dog in his painting. Back in New York, his agent would be waiting for a picture that is a long time coming, his sister too, waiting for her allowance and a kind word to be scribbled at the end of the monthly letter that he couldn't be bothered to write himself. Everyone waiting.

And now almost dark and across the road they have given up waiting. She watches the two boys and the dog, along with Mrs Kaplan and her daughter-in-law, Olivia, followed by her daughter, Katherine, and that Annette woman climb into Mrs Kaplan's automobile. And then she watches Mrs Grant and the opera-singer woman standing on the porch waving them off. The automobile slides by and there's the boy who gave her the cookies, face pinned to the side window, trying to catch her eye. The car disappears. And now the deserted street; the unbearable silence.

Until she sees him, coming down from the corner, his buff-coloured clothes pushing through the dark. And her heart starts to beat once more. He is carrying a brown paper bag up in his arms which he takes round to the rear then opens the trunk, puts it in and slams the trunk shut again. And now here he is, opening the door and sitting into his place.

Her hand begins to shake again. What if he speaks to her, what if he says, oh, come on now, let's stop this? Let's put Saturday night behind us, start over.

But he would never say that or anything like it, he never has. He always leaves it to her. If she was to wait for him to make the first move – why, they would still be on their first honeymoon fight. She asked him once: 'Why is it, any time we have a fight, I am always, *always* the one to make the first move?'

'I don't know,' he said, 'maybe it's because you are always, *always* the one to start it.'

She fights off an impulse to start another one right now, to say, what sort of a man leaves his wife waiting for over two hours, waiting till nightfall, hungry, thirsty (so far as he knows anyhow), without access to a bathroom? What sort of a man does something like that?

But she can feel his weariness beside her, the weight of it. She glances across at his face, drained and ghost-like in the street light, and she wonders: am I making him sick? Is it too much for him, all this worry about work, the lack of peace in his life, the bickering and fighting? When we were young we had such magnificent fights, such passionate reconciliations. And afterwards, at least for a while, the tender days of peace. But oh, my husband, we are young no longer and never again.

'I saw your cat.' Those were the first words he spoke to her, that day in Gloucester when Arthur went missing. Then he drew her a map of the town and she pretended to be grateful for it, even if she could have found her way round blindfolded and walking backwards. Playing up the ditzy female – anything to keep the ball in the air. It had taken him so long to say anything (it had taken

66

her no time at all to say far, far too much). Between them an appointment – you could hardly call it a date – had been arranged to go sketching together the following morning. And then watching him walk away. His height, the easy movement of him, the tilt of his head. And her heart.

She would give anything to hear his voice right now.

They drive by the gas station and turn the corner for the highway.

'You forgot your crayons,' she says and he says, 'Yes, I know.'

She lifts the tin to show him. 'A boy found them lying on the grass under the trunk. I guess you dropped them.'

'Yes,' he says, 'I guess I did.'

His voice so mild, she decides to continue. 'What's in the bag,' she asks, 'the bag you put in the trunk?'

'Supper,' he says.

'Supper?'

'I thought you could do with a good square meal. And so.'

'And so?'

'I'm fixing supper.'

'Oh,' she says.

'You sound a little disappointed.'

She says, 'Oh, but I'm not! Not in the least. No. Thank you, supper would be nice. Yes, very nice indeed.'

Venus

1

EVERY YEAR IT SEEMS to get a little tougher, a little less worth his while. An uphill trek with a knapsack of rocks on his back, a couple more rocks each time.

He drives along familiar roads, passes through small, clean-cut towns; follows the stretches that link them one to the other.

In the mirror, barren hills and scrub pine hills dip in and out of view, long tawny grasses wave him goodbye. Or there is the dark sway of cat's tails from a retreating pond. He tries uplands and lowlands, ocean side and bay side. He stands behind tourists and tries looking at it all through their eyes. He stands alone and watches the evening soften over Pamet Harbour.

And he sees nothing he hasn't seen before and feels nothing much either, unless a vague sense of loss in his gut.

He comes across scenes he has already taken, twisted, laid down, sold on. Scenes that once would have made his blood pound, caused his hands to sweat so much he could hardly keep hold of the brush. He drives right by – they mean nothing to him now. He is the office wolf strolling by the secretarial pool without a second glance.

There are moments, of course. Moments of hope as he enters a town, follows a hunch up a side street or takes another look at a grocery store in case he missed something last time round, or even the time before that. There has to be something. He pauses, gets out and walks for a bit, sometimes gets out and walks for a long time. He sizes up a store front, a shack, the porch of a house, figures out how it takes or even refuses the light. He crosses the street to see where it tucks its shadows.

At the twilight hour, he becomes less fussy and almost anything will do. The brow of a barn or the sudden peak of a roof through treetops will be enough to lure him down any old dirt road. The wheels struggle over inhospitable ground, the hedges claw at the flanks of his automobile, and he will be seized by the notion that this could be it now, this could – yes, yes, definitely – be and then… Then he finds, after all, there is nothing.

Come nightfall, he drives the rough sandy cart-road that leads to his house. In the headlights night insects perform their dance of disdain. The house glares down from its hill. His wife's small, anxious head appears in the lamp-lit window.

He takes his time putting the automobile to bed, slowly closes the door of the garage and makes the final trudge up the steps to his house: the hunter returned whence he came, empty-handed and empty-minded.

His wife, when she's with him, will point something out.

'Doesn't it make you feel proud?' she will ask.

'Not particularly.'

'It will hang forever on a wall, your signature beneath it – something you have created that nobody else could have created. And it doesn't make you—? I mean, how could it *not*?'

'I guess, I don't see things the way you do.'

'You don't love it? Maybe it's just as well we didn't have children. I mean, you create something and yet you don't even *love* it?'

'It? What do you mean by *it* exactly?'

'You know – that barn, this farm, that house – now immortalised.'

'Then I guess no, I don't love it.'

He doesn't tell her that when he finds it at first, then, yes, all right, he feels it. When he carries it in his head and silently waits for it to take form. When he shyly glances at the sketches he's made and feels the urge inside him. When it's there in his head coming out of the dusk. Then it's love all right. More love than he has ever felt for her, or any other woman.

She likes to come with him when he first goes out searching – so long as the search doesn't take forever. She calls this 'being at the conception'. She also likes to talk in the car, sit next to him asking questions. She likes him to respond. She will stare at him and twitch at him until he comes up with something, and so, mostly, he tries to oblige.

'I guess it's the idea that I love,' he says, 'you know, when it's in my head taking shape. But then…'

'But then? But then what? Tell me, *what*?'

'Once it starts to take… I mean, when there's more of it on the canvas than there is in my head and it's always less than I expected somehow. And the more I do, the more I kill it. Well, then all I can see is… decay, I suppose.'

'Decay!'

'Decay of an idea.'

She will squirm on the seat, her ponytail irately wagging. 'Oh now, that's ridiculous. I never heard such— Oh now, I won't allow you say that, I just won't allow it.'

When she does that, he remembers he loves her.

In the morning, she takes him outside and makes him walk all around the house.

'Look around you,' she says, 'all you see is beauty.'

'Yes, but not my kind of beauty.'

In the evening she does it again. This time pointing it out to him – that glow of late summer on the land all around them; that sunset melting like a coloured bulb into the sea; that sea like crushed aluminium.

He shakes his head. 'Nothing,' he tells her, 'nothing, nothing and more nothing.'

They go back in the house, fix supper, then sit in what he hopes is companionable silence. The radio on low, the sound of him turning a page in a book. She gently tugs on her rug. They are not tiptoeing around each other exactly, and are far from being on tenterhooks, but they are careful both not to disturb this peace, to make it last for as long as they possibly can.

On Tuesday night when they came back from Orleans he told her, 'I can't work with all this acrimony going on. I can't take any more of these fights.'

'You can't? *You*? Are you the only one here? And me? What about *me*? I'm

73

an artist too, in case you didn't know. I haven't been able to lift a brush all summer with all this fighting and—'

'All this shouting and accusation and provocation. I can't.'

'It hurts me just as much.'

'Yes, I'm sure it does.'

'More! It hurts me more!' she cried and then put her back to the wall and slid down onto the floor where she sat with her hands pressed to the sides of her head. 'After all these years, it's so repulsive, you give me no attention and now my heart, my heart it has withered with loneliness and that's why my paintings are born dead and that's why I can't bear to make another.'

When she talks like that, he can't remember why he ever loved her.

And yet he knows, too, how difficult it is for her, his morose silences; her yearning for a recognition that is never going to come. She used to call this being recognized in 'her own right' but he suspects recognition under any terms would probably do her now.

Sooner or later it will build up again: the disappointments, the recriminations, the outright blame. It will build up and break out. It's as if she has a box of snakes inside her hissing to get free; all anyone has to do is lean over and unclasp it.

For now, though, there is this quiet evening, the sea winds outside, the comforting smell of kerosene, the light of the lamp.

He waits for a moment, watching her still bent head, her deft hands moving beneath it.

He says, 'Would you like me to read to you for a while?'

She looks up at last, a tear spiked in one eye.

'I wish…' she begins.

He nods and says, 'I know, I know.'

~

SHE HUSHES HIM OUT of another nightmare, then rubs his back when he wakes.

'How do you know it was a nightmare?' he asks. 'And even if it was, how do you know I wasn't enjoying it?'

74

'You were in distress,' she says, 'now go back to sleep.'

'And if it happens again?' he asks. 'Are you going to wake me again?'

'I won't let it happen again. I'll keep guard, I'll fight off your demons. You know how ferocious I can be.'

In the morning, tight-eyed, pale-faced, she begins the day. 'When are you going to start something?'

'I don't see anything.'

'But then you're not really looking, are you – you're sitting there reading your newspaper. So tell me when?'

'When what?'

'When are you going to make a start?'

'I may go for a drive later.'

'Inertia and self-indulgence. I think you should start something. Anything. Now. Today.'

'And I think you should start leaving me alone.'

'What about Orleans? I thought you may have hit on something there the other day while I sat and waited – how many hours? You made sketches. The corner, the gas station, the awnings, a car. I *saw* the sketches.'

'I have made a start. But— Well, I can't seem to— Maybe. I don't know.'

'It's like asking you to dive into a bay of ice cubes, getting you to shift yourself. Have you taken your pills?'

'Not yet.'

'Well, what are you waiting for?'

'I'll take them when I'm finished reading this article.'

'Are they doing you any good?'

'What?'

'The vitamins, the Benzedrine at least – what do you think of them?'

'I think they have very nice colours.'

He pours himself a glass of water and goes into the studio where he stands facing the north window. He hates these dry days, the thought of yet another. He had come to regard this time of the year as his traditional drought of midsummer – a time to break up the fallow ground before starting anew. But these past few years the drought has run on longer and longer. Now it is late summer coming into early fall. Soon it will be mid-to-late fall. Then it will be winter. If January comes and goes it would mean a whole year without a thing.

He shakes the pills out onto the palm of his hand, runs his fingers over them: carmine, amber, the colour of jewels. For a while he thought they might have been doing some good, but that was probably down to his own wishful thinking. These days, he wakes up tired, goes to bed tired, stumbles through the intervening hours. The pills are useless coloured bits of glass but he whacks them back anyway: four steady gulps and they're landed.

He looks down at the deserted space that his wife a few days ago cleared of invaders and wonders about the woman in the yellow hat again. She was and she wasn't. One day, yes, the next day, no. She was tall enough anyhow, although a little too thin – at least he seems to remember there was more of her last year. Only once did she take off her hat and that was the second time he saw her down there. A brief show of long hair, swiping across her face like an Eastern veil, covering it. Then the hat had gone back on again. It was the wrong colour hair, he decided, although he couldn't be certain with the yellow hat and the beach behind it and the white light from the sea flashing all around her. If only she'd left the hat off for longer, sat down on the sand with her arms stretched out behind her then, face lifted to the sun so that her hair would come off her shoulders. He would have seen then if it was the same full-breasted girl. He would have seen her face too. Even at a distance, he felt sure he would recognize her face. But then again, the distance is all he ever had. He'd never been up close to her, except on the canvas.

A different woman sneaks into his mind then; a different woman, a similar long body. Slim and at the same time well-built. But that was so long ago, when he was young and in Paris. He had presumed he would know her face because he had painted it so often; he would know every strand of her hair. And yet, when it finally happened between them. His first time with a woman, that way at least. And afterwards, the shock – to think that he'd been walking around Paris with all that violence hidden inside him. Lying on her unmade bed – unmade even when she had led him to it, in late afternoon – and wishing

76

afterwards that she would fall asleep so he could study her in peace: the weight and curve of her hips, her uneven breasts, the slight dip at the end of her long back. But wanting, too, to touch her face, her hair, without seeming like an awestruck boy, which of course was exactly what he was. She'd asked him if it was his first time and when he'd blushed and said, 'Sort of,' she smiled and said she envied him.

Then she asked him what he was thinking. He said, 'Your face, it's not the same. Your face looks different somehow.'

'Because I look older?'

'No, it's just, I thought when I painted it that I knew it.'

'Ah, but you painted the face you wanted – this is the face I have.'

Her accent, the way the words rolled out from the back of her throat: 'ave, she had said. 'This is the face I 'ave.'

He passes his eye over the bay: the agitation of light on water, the tracks of dead seaweed along the empty beach. He stays until his mind begins to clear. Then he pulls his hat off the top of the easel.

'Where you going?' she says. 'Orleans?'

'No.'

'Not Eastham?'

'Maybe.'

'Why not go back to Orleans – try to get a hold on that picture?'

'Because I don't feel like it.'

'Well, if you're going to Eastham again, you can count me out. The plainest town on the Cape and you keep going back there. You've gone to Eastham every day for more than a week and nothing's come out of it. What on earth do you hope to find there?'

~

WHAT HE HOPES TO find is another lifeline, like the one he found this time last year when he'd all but given up. A bad year in general that had been, with little to show for it and all that sickness, and worry of future sickness, hanging over him. It had been early last September when he saw her, late October by the time he'd finished the picture. It had taken a little longer than he'd expected but then he'd wanted to keep her with him, keep her inside his head.

The day that he found her. He'd been driving around Eastham and turned in to a side street and there she was about a third of the way down. She was standing in the doorway of a house, a man standing on the threshold, maybe leaving or maybe hoping to get inside.

He'd driven by and pulled in further along the street. Then he walked back past the house. There had been a bush by the gate, tangled and dried up from the heat, a lawn, yellowed by neglect and the ravages of a long summer.

He could hear them as he neared the house: the man speaking low, the woman a little higher. He could hear the irritation in her voice. But it seemed it wasn't the man bothering her, but the heat, which she appeared to be taking personally. She was wearing long cream-coloured pants and a pale-blue blouse cuffed at the wrists. She was pulling at the sleeves of the blouse as he walked by the gate and he heard her say, 'I'm wearing too many clothes, this damned heat, driving me crazy. It's driving me *crazy!*'

He had walked on for a couple of minutes, then crossed the road to return on the opposite side, his head tilted as if he were searching for the number of a door. As he came closer to the house, he saw her lift her hands and put them under her hair, which was a whiter shade of blonde. Then she flipped it all up, holding it for a few seconds to the back of her head. He could see the damp patches of sweat stamped into her armpits and the outline of her long neck, the soft curve where it joined her shoulders. She dropped her hair and her face lifted upwards. The blue blouse. The light on her face. He couldn't figure out if it was pouring into her or pouring out of her. He thought she looked sanctified. Then he thought she looked the opposite. The light and the punishing heat, it did something to her that was beyond his understanding.

He couldn't hear the man's voice this time as he walked by, but he must have said something to her because next thing was she was yelling, 'Well, maybe that's because I can't sleep, maybe that's the reason! It's almost dawn before I close my eyes and almost high noon by the time I can drag myself out of bed.'

All he could remember about the journey home was that he had driven it far too quickly. The fifteen miles or so instantly disappeared from his memory.

He hadn't bothered putting the automobile away either, just abandoned it outside the garage, rushed up the hill and pushed through the door, pushed by his wife too, saying, 'I'm not hungry,' even though she hadn't asked if he'd wanted anything to eat. Next thing, he was in the studio, dragging his easel to the centre of the floor.

Behind him he had heard her cry out, 'Well, halleluiah! This house can finally live again!'

And so he had started. He laid it down: the street, the house, the figure of the girl in the doorway, the figure of the man alongside it with one foot on the step; the lawn, the gate, the tangled bush. A few days later, he had it all painted over in blue. Then he carried that around for a while, in his mind, painting and repainting it.

He knew he would need to see the house again but hadn't wanted to risk seeing the girl – she was already alive to him and settled in his head; he wanted to keep her that way. Instead, he did something he hadn't done since he was a kid: he made a heavy paper model of the house.

'Why bother with that?' his wife had asked. 'Why not just go back to the house and take another look?'

'I thought it might be fun.'

'Oh, so you're a fun guy now, are you?'

He put the house on the table to see what the light would make of it. He took everything else off the table and saw that the house belonged on its own. He thought about that for a long time. Mostly, though, his mind was on the girl.

He had his wife stand in a doorway and measured a few inches over her head.

She said: 'Why not leave her my height?'

He said: 'I don't see her that way.'

She asked: 'Is she a woman or a girl?'

He said: 'Both. She's both.'

When he'd finished he looked it over. He had taken the man from outside the house and the house away from the street. The house now stood alone in the middle of nowhere on a bed of burnt grass. The woman was standing in the doorway in the glare of high noon, her naked body covered in a blue sleeveless house-coat open down the front. It would keep her cool in that heat. It was the least he could do to show his gratitude.

Then he called his wife in to the studio.

She stepped back, she stepped forward. She moved to the side, she did plenty of grimacing and frowning. He could tell that she liked it and liked it a lot.

'Looks a little sloppy – her clothes, I mean?'

'Well, yes,' he said, 'but it's such a hot day.'

A whole year ago, that was.

If he could find her again this summer.

Once he thought he saw her on a crowded sidewalk. That had been in Provincetown a couple of weeks ago, on one of the days when he'd gone out on his own. As soon as he arrived there, he had regretted it and was in a hurry to get out of the overcrowded town away from all that noise and confusion. But he found himself stuck in slow traffic. A woman turned out of the Lobster Pot and began along the sidewalk. Edging along in the row of traffic, he'd watched the crowd suck her in and then release her until finally she had outwalked it. He was out of heavy traffic by then but he stayed with her, pulling in at the edge of town to give her a chance to gain a little ground. When she turned onto Snail Road, he followed. The height and shape of her, the size of her head. This woman hadn't worn a hat – her hair, bunned at the nape, more white than blonde: platinum. The right hair, but when she stopped to cross at the top of the street, it turned out to belong to somebody else.

And now there is the woman on the beach. He keeps changing his mind about her. She stands out from the others, a little aloof, but that could be because she is the only one to always be fully clothed. He saw her on the edge of the group, three or maybe four different occasions; and a couple of times more, he saw her standing on the top of the beach steps. Always she wore long, loose pants, full sleeves and a brimmed yellow hat. Maybe it was the similarity in clothes that had made him imagine it could be the same girl. Or it could have been nostalgia: a regret for an old lost love who happened to have a similar stature.

The girl on the beach never stays for very long. She had been there the day his wife had let loose but had left before the evacuation, walking away towards

Corn Hill beach with a man beside her. He didn't think it was the same man from the year before, the man who had stood on the doorstep – not that he could remember the slightest thing about him.

The idea of a muse. He has never really bought into all that. He hears talk of it from time to time but has always suspected it was just another way to chase or control a woman. He does not want one anyhow. He would not want that kind of responsibility. And yet, he feels a certain loneliness for her, this over-heated woman standing in a doorway on a side street in Eastham. He knows he is desperate; desperate as well as faintly ridiculous. But he can't seem to help himself. If only he could find her, it would be like it was around this time last year, when he'd been about to go under. He would turn a corner and there she would be, doing whatever she happened to be doing, sitting, leaning, swinging upside down from a tree. All he would have to do is reach over, grab on and pull himself out of the doldrums.

He drives out of South Wellfleet into North Eastham. At Nauset Lighthouse he stops to watch a man with a fancy-looking camera make a meal out of the scenery. He would like to hear the sound such a camera might make when it snaps off another piece of lighthouse, ocean, sky. He rolls down the window but all he can hear is the lurching sound of the Atlantic Ocean. The photographer leans back and then forward; he genuflects and then goes down on both knees. Finally, he lies down on his stomach, stretches his arms out over the bluff and gobbles up a bit more of the scenery.

He envies this man, his eager, greedy clicking, his unbridled hunger to capture so much and so quickly. The man gets to his feet and begins to move down towards the beach, making a few sudden turns before snapping again, as if he has caught something or someone in the act of following him.

When the man is gone, he reaches for a page from the sheaf on the seat beside him and then brings one hand to the safari pocket of his jacket to pull out a pencil. But he has to ask himself then why? Why would he want paper, a pencil – just what does he intend doing with them? He puts the paper back down on the seat, takes his hand away from his pocket, puts it on the wheel and turns on the gas.

*

In Eastham he drives in to the street and pulls to the kerb across from the house. The shutters are still closed. In one of the windows, the summer rental sign hangs from its string, askew. The tangled bush is still tangled, the lawn yellow and so much longer now. A weather vane on the roof of the neighbour's house gives a pirouette.

Through the windscreen, he stares down the snout of the car to the road's dull grey surface. He thinks maybe he should go back to New York. For the past couple of weeks, on and off, he's been thinking this way. But he has yet to find the energy or the courage or whatever it would take to face the inevitable discussion and argument and blow-up that such a suggestion would bring about. In any case, he can't be certain that he would do any better in New York. He misses it, though. He misses the sense of insignificance it brings to him. It has always done that much for him – rendered him insignificant. When he was a kid, overgrown, conspicuous and taking up far too much space, in the kitchen, in the school-room, even in the backyard. Too big and too awkward, that is, until he got off the ferry and began to walk among the wharves and the warehouses of lower Man-hattan, the buildings gaining in height the further along he went. He became free of himself somehow, diminished. He wants to do that now, to walk the streets alone at night in a downbeat neighbourhood. He wants the sense of peace that such danger always seems to bring to him. He wants to feel the insignifi-cance of the self. At the same time, he misses Monhegan Island. And Gloucester. And Ogunquit and, come to think of it, pretty much anywhere else he's been able to work throughout his life. Apart from this place – where he's already plucked and ravaged and carved to the bone anything that's worth the price of a canvas.

In Gloucester he felt sure on his feet. A seaworthy town. Sturdy and clean and bold. In Monhegan Island there were granite ledges, the climb up the rocky path to the headland spiked with danger. And he liked that too, being young and able to stand for hours, nothing to weigh him down but his wooden panels and his oilskin bag. Other painters before and behind him, the banter passing back and forward along the rocky pathway. And then each to his own little workplace. He misses all that: the clean-cut ledges, the belligerent surf, the blades of light on far-off boats. The pleasure of being with, and at the same time not with, people.

But he knows he's too old to go back to Monhegan Island to go climbing rocks to get at a subject, and that it's long over between him and Gloucester. And he knows, too, that if he misses New York now, as soon as he gets there he will think, If only I had stayed on the Cape something would have turned up, something would have saved me. At night he would close his eyes and long for the sea to shush him back to sleep; he would close his eyes and all he would see is long grass in pure light swaying, like so many heads of blonde hair.

He stays sitting in the car on a side street in Eastham, across from an empty house, even though he knows he's not supposed to stay sitting for long because it aggravates his diverticulitis.

'Sounds like fun,' he said to the doctor, the first time he heard the name – diverticulitis.

The doctor, unamused, had looked at him with his plain, clean face. The doctor knew better. He feels it burning him now, pinning him to the seat. But he can't seem to move or do anything to help himself. He can only sit in this stupor of despair. No, not even despair – despair, at least, would require a degree of energy.

He leans his forearms over the steering wheel and rests his tired head. I am finished, he thinks, everything that was inside me is no longer inside me. I am done.

When he gets home he goes down to the basement. He has a worm's eye view through the window, the glaze of sunset distorting the ground outside and spilling like watery blood into the basement's interior. He excavates a box at the bottom of a whole pile of boxes. Then he begins pulling books from it. A folded page falls out of one of the books. When he opens it out there's a letter written in his wife's hand. His eye follows the lines before he has time to think about it:

I know I'm lucky to have him, I know he is generally cheerful and toler-
ant and putting up with me and my tantrums and that he helps with all
I do in the kitchen. But it makes me simply too devilish a hyena to have
to cook at all. Time was I considered myself an artist, now I see myself

83

as a kitchen slave and no way out. No life beyond any fatigue and irritability while he—

The sentence cuts off; there is nothing on the reverse. He may have walked in and disturbed her and she had hidden the letter between the pages of a book and then forgotten all about it. He sees that the letter is written to a mutual friend, now deceased. If this is what she is writing to their friends what poison is she putting into her journal, he wonders, her *liber veritas*, as she likes to call it.

When he finds the book he's been looking for, he holds it and regards it uncertainly. It feels narrow and slight in his hand and yet he can feel the pulse of life coming from it. He opens it and for a moment the French words seem like tiny insects frozen onto the page. He flicks through and the words begin to adjust and translate into meaning. Then he opens the fly leaf and sees the once familiar handwriting there, steady, slanted, the ink not yet faded. She would be old now. Her hand perhaps no longer so steady. He touches the words, *souvenir d'aimitié*, the year 1922 and her name: Jeanne Cheruy. The first time he saw the inscription he had been hurt; he'd wanted her to change the word *aimitié* to *amour* but had been too bashful to ask her to do so. He knows now that, in a way, they can mean the same thing, although *aimitié* is perhaps the more endurable.

He doesn't hear his wife until she is halfway down the basement steps and her shape comes sideways out of the shadow. He drops the book back into the box and quickly pulls out another one.

'What are you doing down here?' she asks, her face through the crimson light.

'Just looking for this,' he says, lifting a sturdy volume to show. He begins walking towards her. 'And you – what are you doing down here?'

'Oh,' she says, 'I heard a noise and…'

She turns back around, begins to re-climb the steps and, stooping his head, he follows behind her.

2

ALWAYS, THE BOY EXPECTS the worst, his heart beating hard as he comes down the wooden steps and then runs bent over, keeping close to the edge of the beach grass. His hidey-hole will have been discovered. The camouflage cover he spent so long making will be broken up and dumped to one side. There will be someone inside. Or maybe someone has already been and gone, taking everything he has worked for and gathered and worried over for days on end, including his beautiful square tin box.

When he gets to the hidey-hole, his heart calms a little. The cover is still in place and there is no mark of an intruder, not even the tiny prong-print of one of those jumpy seabirds. He pulls the cover back, folds himself into it, replaces the cover and begins shovelling through sand with his fingers. At the first glimpse of the tin box his heart picks up speed and he begins to worry again. What if everything has rotted inside and a stench blasts out of the box as soon as he pulls off the lid? And all he can see are spiders running around in there or even tiny grey maggots crawling through the mouldy remains?

He lifts the box out, closes his eyes and, edging the lid away, brings his nose close to it and takes a cautious sniff. Apple and pencil lead, the smell of a school desk. He opens his eyes again. Everything just as he left it. And now he feels calm; calm and happy and safe.

He checks off each item: six balls of bubblegum, half a candy bar, a few salt crackers at the end of a twisted packet and one small green apple. His long page of paper is just as he left it, folded in four and, sticking out of the fold, a brown jigged handle. Behind that, held together by a rubber band, four pencils and a six-inch wooden ruler.

He empties out the pockets of his pants. A pack of Chesterfields with three cigarettes still inside; a small wedge of Swiss cheese wrapped in a strip of newspaper. He places these items into the tin then sits back on his heels and surveys his bounty. The cheese will have to be eaten soon or it will start to grow a white rash. Then it will dry out and go hard. Or it may just decide to skip all of that and turn straight to mould.

And now he worries that it's starting to get a little crowded in there – if this keeps up, he will need to find another tin box, or a bigger one anyhow. Rosetta will wonder what's going on. She gave the box to him because he asked if he could have it. He said, 'Could I have that tin box up there, Rosetta, when you're done with it, please?'

Rosetta climbed up on a chair, stretched her arm out and teased the box away from the top shelf. She rammed the tin into her belly and pulled the lid off backwards. She put it on the table and counted the few oblong shaped cookies that were left inside up to six. Then she gave *uno, dos, tres* to him and *uno, dos, tres* to herself.

'I done now!' she said and slapped him lightly on the shoulder with the heel of her squat brown hand.

She told him the cookies came from a place called Scotland – only Rosetta called it 'Sgoland'. A woman had sent it along with a bottle of Scotch whisky and a tartan shawl as a gift to Mrs Kaplan for finding her granddaughter during the war. She said the picture on the lid was of a woman. He knew she was kidding about that, and not just because of the gleam in her eye but because a boy in his school called McEwan had brought in a picture of his uncles on Heritage Day. They were all dressed up in skirts called kilts and one of them was playing the bagpipes. But he didn't say anything about that to Rosetta. He was enjoying listening to her speak, the funny way she used her words and that way she had of fooling around, and so he played along.

'I don't know, Rosetta,' he said, 'it sure looks like a man to me.'

'Nah,' Rosetta said, 'in Sgoland the women are bery, bery ugly, they wear their hair up skyscraper high.'

He pointed to the bagpipes and asked, 'So what's that thing she's carrying in her arms then?'

'Oh that? That is her baby. In Sgoland the babies are ewen more uglier than the women.'

And then they had both burst out laughing, spraying Scottish cookie crumbs all over Rosetta's nice clean kitchen floor.

He pulls one pencil out from the bunch and then takes out the folded page and the knife with the brown jigged handle. He pulls out the packet of crackers. He puts the box on his lap and, replacing the lid, uses it as a little table. He opens the page out. It is covered in forty-two small, even-sized squares: one for each day since he arrived here and for all the days to come before he gets to go back to New York. He licks the pencil and draws a firm X across the box that represents yesterday, then he counts the remaining boxes. Thirty days to go, nearly two weeks already past.

Some of those days he can hardly remember. They seemed to have slipped through the cracks in the floorboards as soon as he got out of bed. Mostly, though, it has been the other way round, the day crawling along like a snail and looking like it was never going to make it as far as nightfall.

He refolds the page and lays it aside. Then he takes out one of the crackers. He puts the cracker on the lid of the box and lifts the brown jigged handle. He weighs this on his hand for a while then sticks his thumbnail into the side of it and snaps the blade open. He cuts the cracker into even quarters. The last quarter falls to crumbs under the blade of the knife. He studies the three good sections and the one broken one. He sighs and says, 'Sorry, guys, looks like there's only enough for three today.' Then he begins mumbling down into his chest: *oh no, hey, that's not fair.*

'Shh, shhh,' he says, 'you want us to get caught? Now keep it down or you won't get any of –' he pulls an orange out of the back pocket of his pants and shoots it up – 'this!'

Then tucking his chin to his chest again, he allows the voices to cheer. Placing the globe of the orange on top of the box, he takes the penknife to it and scores four long nicks in its skin. Slowly, he opens the orange out, pulls off the segments and arranges them around the sliced cracker. A feast! The voices mumble their appreciation and he sucks contentedly on their behalf, until one of them blurts *'Danke schön.'*

He stops, looks warily from side to side and then, bringing one hand over his mouth, whispers into it, *'Bitte schön.'*

He helps himself to a second segment. 'But that's it for today,' he warns. 'No, I'm sorry, we got to make it last. We need to be *strong* now, come on – you know the rules.'

He looks at the knife and begins pulling out all the other metal pieces hidden inside the handle until it's lying there like a big brown beetle on the palm of his hand. He snaps everything back in place, except for the main spear. Holding it close to his face, he reads the engraving: *official boy scout knife.*

If he had a magnifying glass it would be easier to read, or maybe a flashlight or even a cigarette lighter. If he had a flashlight, he could come down here in the dark when Richie was sleeping. If he had a cigarette lighter, he could teach himself how to smoke. He could sit with Katherine on the porch at night and smoke cigarettes. He could stay with her until the record stopped playing music and was pointlessly wobbling around. He could hold the ashtray for her so she wouldn't spill any ashes, watch her hand glide back and forth. He could clean out the ashtray when she went to bed so that in the morning she wouldn't have to hear Mrs Kaplan say, 'Katherine! *Please* don't tell me you smoked all those cigarettes!'

He slips off his sneakers, makes a small gap in the camouflage foliage, draws his legs up to sit like an Indian and looks out. He rests a broken piece of cracker on his tongue and slowly pushes it around in his mouth. Then he begins to suck on one of the orange segments. It's his favourite thing to do since he got here, escape to his hidey-hole away from the house and all the rules he can't seem to keep hold of, and to get away from whiney Richie too. Richie and his sissy dog and his mom and her dopey friend Annette. Just sit back and make whatever he happens to be eating last as long as it possibly can, while he listens to and looks out at the sea.

Because he loves the sea now. The first time he saw it was the night he arrived, and he hated it then, the way it had looked in the dark from a distance, black and dangerous like the ridged back of some huge flesh-eating animal, the terrible sound of it gnashing and breathing. And lying awake until daylight sliced in through the shutters, not being able to fall asleep before then for fear it was coming to get him.

~

IT HAD BEEN DARK by the time they got to the house that first night, driving along a narrow road and hardly able to see a thing. No street lamps and no other cars. Just two long spears of light from Mrs Kaplan's automobile. All he knew for sure was they were somewhere in the middle of nowhere. And when they got out, it was a different sort of dark – not at all like the dark of the city. The sounds of invisible creatures all around, birds or frogs or crickets – tigers for all he knew.

They had to walk up a steep, broken pathway to get to the house, with Mrs Kaplan saying, 'Watch your step, boys, now watch your step!' And when she wasn't saying that she was going on about the beach and telling him how wonderful it was to have it right here in their own backyard. And then the house suddenly, like a house made out of shadows. A light popped out as they came closer and a porch lit up with an outdoor living-room on it: chairs and a table and a record player even, and then Rosetta coming down the steps to meet them.

Darkness again when Mrs Kaplan turned out the light and said, 'Well, good-night, boys, may the angels watch over you.'

She closed the door and the room disappeared, then Richie's voice in the dark. 'She always says that. As if we're four years old or something. As if anyone even believes in angels.'

Then Richie got out of bed and opened the door a fraction and light from the hallway elbowed into the room.

'You don't mind, do you?' Richie said. 'It's not that I'm scared of the dark or anything, it's just I like to know what's going on around here, is all.'

He was surprised to hear Richie talk that first night, because as they drove to the house he had said nothing at all, even though they were sitting together on the back seat. And at supper he had just sat there, darting sly looks at him from across the table. The only time he really spoke was when his plate was put in front of him and then it was: 'Ah, come on, Grandma, you know how I hate roast beef!'

Now he knows that Richie loves to talk in the dark, to talk himself round in circles until he's talked himself to sleep.

That first night it was: 'I don't like this house very much, if I'm to be honest. I think it stinks. Well, I guess it was okay for a while. The first year or so, but, well, now, I just think it stinks, is all. This year they'll be keeping the house on right up to the end of October. Can you imagine? An extra eight weeks or something stuck here. And no television set. You probably don't have one of those – I mean, I don't know, maybe you do. I'm not trying to say you're too poor to have one or anything, I mean, all I'm saying is we only have ours a couple of months and we only bought it because my mom, see, she got a cheque from the US army for, well, you know. Usually we go back after Labor Day but now? October. Oh well, what do I care, I'll be starting my new school in New Hampshire soon, in case you don't know. I don't suppose there will be a television set there either.'

He could hear Richie fidgeting in the bed and then the sound of him jabbing punches into his pillow. 'It's my Aunt Katherine, you see, she's the reason they're staying on. You'll probably meet her in the morning. Not at breakfast, though, because Grandma usually brings it to her in bed. And she probably won't go to the beach either. Or if she does it will just be for a little while. She used to have her own summer rental in a different town about ten miles from here and she shared that with two nurses she worked with in the hospital but then one of them went to Mexico and the other went and got married and anyhow Grandma needs to keep an eye on her now. The sun does something to her skin – I think it's to do with the shots Doctor Tom gives her or something.'

He threw another few punches at the pillow and then: 'It's one of the oldest boarding schools in New England, you sleep there and, and everything. You know what's the worst thing, though? About here, I mean? The way my mother always has to invite her crummy friends to stay, that's what. Why can't they get their own summer rental, that's what I'd like to know? Always hanging around and taking over the record player and acting like Buster is their dog and not mine and then going out to dinner in Provincetown anytime someone has a dumb birthday, like tonight with Miss Staines who is about a hundred and five or something, and… always smiling at everything while someone else picks up the cheque, and Aunt Katherine's not supposed to go out too much, see, she's pretty sick. They took one of her kidneys. Plucked it right out. Had to break her ribs to get at it. I don't know how. Maybe with a hammer. She's got this disease, and she could… She probably is going to… I mean, I wouldn't be surprised if she… It's like they're all waiting for her to— you know, just…'

But then Richie had fallen asleep before he could say what they were all just waiting for Katherine to do.

When Richie had gone to sleep, he looked around the strange room and all the things in it that he had never seen before in his life and he thought about some of the things that were missing. Like the black-lined design of the fire escape through the window and the lights of all the traffic rubbing off the ceiling or the general whizzbang noise of the city outside. The windows here were as long as doors and there were shutter things at the sides of them that Mrs Kaplan had unfolded and then closed over instead of drapes. On the far side of the shutters was a sort of porch that Richie had called a verandah, but smaller than the porch he had seen already on the way into the house. And he guessed that was where you would have to go if a fire broke out because how else could you save yourself in this house made of wood? Walls, floors, ceilings, stairs – the smell of it and the sound of it under your feet. There were two high, plump beds in this bedroom – Richie's by the door, his by the shutters – and all that floor in between, instead of his usual low, narrow bed tucked into the corner. Here the floors were bare – you could see every one of the boards, instead of the rug at home with red and gold flowers on it that Mrs Morgan had given to Frau Aunt when she moved out to Brooklyn. And there was a long mirror on a stand that his eye had been dodging since he first came in the room. On the wall, about a dozen framed pictures, all of them pretty much the same: boats and the sea and the beach and more boats and more sea and he didn't really see the point in all that if the sea and the beach they kept going on about was already out there, right in their own backyard.

There was a radio playing loudly down the hall and he listened to that for a while until, sometime after Richie had fallen asleep, he heard the sound of slamming car doors and then voices. The voices were coming from below his window. For a long time he listened to them. Voices and music on the record player and then the voices began to call out to each other – goodnight, yes, goodnight, Annette, dear. See you in the morning, Olivia. Yes, yes, see you then, dear, goodnight. Goodnight, Miss Staines, nighty-night, Mrs Kaplan. Mrs Kaplan, goodnight. Aren't you going up yet? No, Mother, I think I'll stay a while. Oh, please *try* to get some sleep. Oh yes, Mother, I will.

Then the radio down the hall stopped and the music down on the porch stopped, and another sound began to creep into the room. A gasping, wheezy sound that seemed to get a little louder every few minutes, like it was coming closer and closer. He pulled his pillow around his ears and turned away from the windows. On the wall above Richie's bed there were three slits of light – two long horizontal slits and one smaller one centred just beneath them. It looked like the face of a cat on the wall, with two long eyes watching and waiting to see what he was going to do next. He was torn between fear of the cat and fear of the huge creature gasping outside. But he knew the cat wasn't real, that it had been made by a light outside pushing through the shutters and throwing itself on the wall. All he had to do was figure out how to open the shutters and that would be the end of old sly eyes.

He slipped out of bed and, catching the long mirror by the shoulders, turned it to face the opposite side of the room so it could stare at Richie instead of at him. Then he opened the shutter and folded it over just as he had seen Mrs Kaplan do, only he did it in the opposite direction. He took a careful step outside. There was someone smoking on the porch below. He could see two bare lady feet on a stool, crossed at the ankle, and could smell the drift of the tobacco. A woman's hand came into view and made a flick at an ashtray on a small table beside her, missing her target. The woman down there didn't appear to have company and he had felt she wasn't reading either. Just sitting and smoking and looking out. He could still hear the monster gasping and wheezing. It sounded close and at the same time far away. He couldn't understand why the woman down there on the verandah could just sit there and listen to such a horrible sound. He tried not to see where it was coming from, but it was there just above his eyeline, wedged between a hill and a few tall trees, vast and black, glinting and slobbering only a short way from the house.

He stepped back in the room and jumped into bed.

The folded-back shutter gave a new picture now: a ladder thrown slantways across the floor and then up the wall before leaning a little way across the ceiling. He lay awake for a long time, looking at the ladder, over and over counting out rungs of light.

In the morning, he sensed somebody watching him. He opened his eyes into a blaze of sharp sunlight and there was Richie, all shiny and scrubbed, standing at the end of his bed with his hedgehog hair and a towel rolled under his arm. Richie, asking if he knew how to swim.

He squinted at Richie and said, 'Sure, I mean, maybe.'

Richie rolled his eyes sideways. 'Well, I don't know about that,' he said. 'I mean, I don't know how anyone can *maybe* swim. You either can or you drown. There's really no maybe about it.'

And so he had pretended to feel sick because that way he wouldn't have to go near the sea to find out if he actually could swim or not. And that seemed to work for a while, with Rosetta bringing him a tray with his breakfast on it, and then later a tray with his lunch on it, and saying that she was going to ask one of the ladies to take a look at him as soon as they got back from wherever they had gone for lunch. Until sometime in the afternoon, Richie's Aunt Katherine came in, sat right down on the side of his bed and put her cold hand on his forehead.

She said, 'I'll be back in ten minutes and if you're not up and dressed, I'm going to have Doctor Tom take a look at you.'

When she came back in the room, he was putting on his sneakers.

She led him out of the bedroom by the hand, and she kept his hand as they came down all the stairs of the house and only let go of it long enough to lift her hat from the table by the door, pat it down on her head, open the door to the porch, then hold it back for him.

A voice on the porch said, 'And where are you two sneaking off to?'

93

She said, 'Oh, you know, cocktails, we may go dancing afterwards. Don't wait up.'

The voice said, 'You be careful now, he looks a little dangerous to me.'

She said, 'Don't I know it,' and took his hand again.

She walked him up a small green hill made out of low-growing curly bushes. She let go of his hand when the path narrowed and then she was walking ahead of him. The ground began to change. The bushes fell away and now he began to see patches of sand between chunks of long grass. He could hear the long grass swishing and he could hear, too, the sound of the monster again, breathing easier than it had done last night, like now it was sleeping.

He couldn't really see anything, though, only her walking ahead, and a huge bare blue sky all around her, and the brim of her hat, and the fall of her brown hair resting on her back, and the slow, long way her legs had of walking.

And he thought again of what Richie had said about his aunt being sick the night before and decided that either he had heard wrong or else Richie, he was a liar.

His legs felt shaky when they came to top of the beach steps, his stomach full of knots. He could hear the sea now breathing right in his ear. She turned around to him, put one hand on his shoulder and twisted him to the side.

She was pointing to something in the distance – she was telling him to look. But he couldn't look: he was too afraid of the sea.

'There they are down there,' she said. 'See the dog?'

And he nodded yes, although he couldn't see anything because he wasn't looking: he was just keeping his eyes on her neck instead.

'And, look, there's Richie already in. There's his mom there in the red, talking to that man – see?'

She was so close he could smell her skin; there was a red patch of rash like a brooch on her neck.

'And that's Rosetta – look, there she is, kneeling on the blue towel. The other women are visiting – they go back tonight so you don't need to bother too much with them. Except Annette Staines, she's staying with us. See her there? There in the black bathing suit?'

And he nodded again and said, 'Mmm.'

94

She said, 'Who do you suppose that man is, talking to my sister-in-law?'

'Your sister-in-law?'

'Richie's mom – she's my sister-in-law. Richie's dad was my brother. Who do you think the man is? He's Doctor Tom. But we won't be needing him to take a look at you now – will we?'

'Oh no, I feel fine now.'

'And what do you suppose they're talking about down there, Doctor Tom and Olivia – Richie's mom? Can you guess – no? Well, I can. They're talking about me. Know how I know that?'

He shook his head.

'Because they are always talking about me.'

She straightened up, turned away from him and said, 'Come on, let's go.'

But he was too scared to follow; too scared to move at all. He clammed his eyes shut and stiffened his legs and grabbed on to the wooden railing.

'What's the matter?' she said. 'You're not scared, are you?'

'I don't know,' he said. 'Maybe.'

'But it's only the sea. Go ahead, open your eyes – just look at how glorious it is. Open them, I promise you're going to love it.'

He opened his eyes a little, and a pure white liquid poured into them. Then he opened his eyes all the way. And there it was, like who knows how many pieces of smashed diamonds bouncing around. And that was it, the glorious sea.

'It's really beautiful, huh?' she asked.

He smiled at her and she laughed right back, then she turned away from him. She sort of danced down the wooden steps like she was Ginger Rogers. She had one hand holding down her big yellow hat, the other touching off the wooden rail. Her clothes were blowing away from her limbs as if they were trying to make her float away.

~

NOW HE SITS IN his hidey-hole with his eyes softly shut against the late afternoon light. He can smell the orange on his own breath. When he opens his eyes and looks at the square tin box, the orange has disappeared leaving only its peel, all bitten and chewed in parts, teeth marks scraped along the white pith. The crackers, too, have all been eaten. There is a stickiness on his hands and a stinging sensation on his lips. He sees now that the piper on the lid is also stained with juice and that there is a thin crust of sand and crumbs stuck on the hills and the waterfall behind him. He feels a weakening in his chest, a feeling of shame.

'I am disappointed in you,' he says. 'I am disappointed in your lack of self-control. You are greedy and you are the worst kind of a thief – a thief who steals only for himself.'

He sits for a while, staring at his tin box and twisting and pinching the skin on the back of his arm. Then he takes the knife and places the point of it into the side of his palm and twists it. A small spurt of blood pops out. The juice from the orange enters the small hole in his skin and now it begins stinging like crazy. He counts to twenty. Then he puts his mouth over his hand and sucks the blood away. Better now, he climbs out of his hidey-hole and begins walking with his tin box towards the sea. There are gulls standing on a sand-spit, their faces turned to the evening sun. And he can see further along the bay, the curve of other beaches and on them, the shapes of people like bits of coloured paper, playing and swimming and running around, and he can see a huge boat stuck like an island of glinting steel in the water and other smaller boats zipping around it. At the end of the bay, there's a town squeezed onto the hook of land and he thinks about all the people hidden inside it, moving around in their houses or going in and out of stores or eating dinner or just walking along the streets. But here, on this beach, he is alone. There are only the four gulls staring at the sun, and they don't really care how long he stays. He could stay here for a long time if he wants. He could stay and then the lady from the Buick could see him and come rushing down the hill to throw him off her private beach. Then he would be able to see her again. He feels sure she wouldn't throw him off the beach, though – not after he gave her all his cookies. He feels sure that her face would change into a big smile when she recognized him and she would say, 'Oh, it's you!'

The sea is far out in the bay. It seems softer out there; the waves are hardly moving, only sort of winking on and off. He begins to notice something in the middle of them. Maybe a boat or part of a boat. He watches it for a few moments and now it starts to take the shape of a swimmer. A swimmer, all the way out there, with no one around to help or even to hear if they start to drown. He wonders who could be brave enough, and at the same time dumb enough, to trust themselves to something so strange as the sea.

He walks a few feet to a shallow pool, stoops down to it and washes his sticky hands and the trickle of remaining blood. Then he scoops water over his face and then over the piper on the lid, the mountains and the waterfall behind him. He pulls the end of his T-shirt away from his stomach, dries his face, then carefully dries and begins polishing the box. When he stands up and looks out at the sea again, he sees the swimmer is getting closer. He appears to be coming in a straight line towards him. He looks all around but sees no sign of clothes or a towel that he could have left on the beach. Yet the swimmer is definitely coming this way. He can see the movement of his head turning, the hand coming over his shoulder and down into the water. And now the swimmer's head rises right up, and next he is standing in the water up to his chest, and then his stomach. He is walking through the water, walking in this direction. The boy stares for a moment then spins round and, holding his tin box out in front of him, starts running as fast as he can. Now and then he looks back and he sees the swimmer still walking towards him, the tops of his legs moving up and down, his feet invisible in shallow water.

He runs over the tough wet sand, then the soft pale sand, then the grassy ledge, and now he is back in his hidey-hole, pulling the cover over and fixing it back in place. He opens the lid with a shaky hand, quickly drops the pocket knife in, the pencils and the page with all the days written on. He puts the lid back on, places the box back in the hole, scoops the sand over it, covers it up and pats it over. He puts on his sneakers and, ready to run, squats down and waits.

~

AS HE COMES OUT of the sea, he notices a boy standing on the beach watching him. He continues to wade through the water, thigh to knee, knee to shin. The boy is holding something in his hands, holding it out as if it's some sort of offering. He can't make out what it is, but it gives a single glint as the boy turns

97

away and begins to run. He watches the boy for a moment, his legs unusually pale for a boy so late in the summer, pale and thin and long, scrambling over each other towards the bushes. The word *grasshopper* comes into his mind.

He turns around and faces the horizon. The warmth of the sun on his face; the cool water slapping around his ankles. He thinks about walking back to the soft sand, lying down for a while and letting the sun do its work. But if he lies down, he will have to get back up again. And when he gets back up, he will still have to face the uphill trek to the house. Better stay upright, get it all over and done with – there will be time enough later to rest.

He presses both fists into his hips and begins doing the exercise the doc has shown him: five times, a pause and then five times more. But his spine doesn't feel in any way re-aligned. His spine feels, if not twisted exactly, then certainly off-kilter, as if it no longer has any interest in holding this body together. He feels a general all-over ache. Not the sort of ache he gets from standing too long at an easel – he wouldn't mind at all if it were that. But the sort of ache that makes him want to lie down and stay down.

He begins to get the feeling that his wife is watching him and wonders how that could be when he has just left her to go shopping in Provincetown and is not due to collect her for another hour. He looks back at the house, not so visible in full summer: the peak of the roof and the top half of the north window. Even if she was at the north window – and she couldn't possibly be – she probably wouldn't be able to see him at this angle. Not at her height. Although he knows she wouldn't mind dragging a chair across the room either and climbing up on the window ledge.

He stands longer than he is supposed to stand – the doc discourages this sort of thing, standing in cool water, swimming in the sea. Bad for the urinary, he says and then always seems keen to add that, oh, he has nothing against water, a good hot bath is fine – 'It's just the cold sea I'm against. A cold sea is no good for a man your age and condition.'

Yet it has been his way for such a long time: standing like this until his skin grows so cold that it feels as if it is lifting away from his body. A good stretch, then a long swim, followed by another stretch and a few more moments of standing in the water. Finally, a lie-down on the soft, warm sand.

The climb back up to the house has lately taken the good out of it. The doctor's orders had put the nail in the coffin. And yet, he is not quite ready to let go of it – not something he has loved all his life.

When he was a small boy he could see it through his bedroom window. He would stretch out his hand and believe he could touch it. It had seemed that close. Why could he not feel it – he used to wonder – why won't it allow me to feel it? He thought if he could just reach up to the window and open it down, he would be able to step right out and be there in the middle of it, splashing and floating and smothering himself in all that light.

They had an Irish maid then – young to be so far away from home, though he hadn't thought so at the time. Inclined to sarcasm, which had annoyed his mother but seemed to amuse his father. Mary – was that her name? Mary showing him how to skim stones on the water. That funny way she had of scolding him. 'You! You and your boldness, I'll cut your two ears off your head and feed them to the ducks.' Mary crying behind the kitchen door and him throwing his arms around her hips and declaring his love for her. Poor Mary – if that was even her name.

He had never been afraid of the water. His mother worried, calling him back in, the wind tossing her words around: 'I said, NOW! *Now-ow-ow.*'

No sense of danger, that's his trouble, she would say then, drying his hair with a compact aggression that hurt like hell. But he liked it too, her hand whipping the towel over his hair and his brain rattling round in his head, his forehead against her breast, the secret smell of her underarm – sweat and something sweeter. In later years he would tease her that his early baldness was down to her hair-drying technique.

And then there was the river – he was maybe eight years old by then, running downhill to it and being completely lost in the sounds and the smells of the Nyack boatyard, his father striding behind, calling out to him to slow down. But he couldn't slow down – the best he could do was run back now and then, a breathless pause, a hop and a couple of words before taking off again. Later still, learning to smoke with his school pals, blots of light on the underbelly of the bridge. Grasshopper. That was the nickname he'd had then: twelve years old and already six-foot tall.

He looks down into the water, his feet pressed into the flabby sand, the remains of a wave cuffing his shanks, the light dissolving them. Soon the tide will begin to turn. The waves will toughen up and become forceful. If he stood here long enough, they would eventually cover his head. If he thought for one moment that the sea would allow him to remain on his feet, he would gladly die here, covered in water. But of course, it wouldn't stand for that; it would knock him down, toss him around and, when it was tired playing with him, drag him out and dump him on the sand along with the rest of the debris.

He turns and, leaving the water behind, begins to walk back towards the house. As he does this he notices someone walking from the direction of Pamet Harbour. Another boy – a different one entirely. This one trudging wearily through the sand, arms dangling, face forlorn. As if it's the Sahara Desert he's crossing instead of a beach on Cape Cod. The boy signals as if he wants to say something to him and so he stops and waits.

The boy stops short a foot or so away from him. He's not sure if he's seen this kid before – a boy is a boy after all and they always look more or less alike to him. The boy is healthy looking, sturdy and tanned. He loudly exhales and in a pinched voice says, 'I'm sorry, sir, I know we're not supposed to disturb you and all that…'

The kid waits, heavily breathing and looking up at him in quiet dismay. After a few seconds he gets fed up waiting and lets it all out.

'You see, it's our guest, I've been looking everywhere for him and— we're staying in the house up there, in case you don't know. My grandmother is renting it for the summer and my mom, she's the woman in the red swimsuit,' he quickly adds, as if that somehow makes her famous, which of course it probably does. 'Well, he just keeps running off. My grandma, she's Mrs Kaplan, you know.'

He's about to say yes, that she came to tea at their house a couple of years ago, but the boy hasn't stopped talking: 'Well, sir, he's supposed to be here as a friend for me, but he keeps running off and I can never find him and he never wants to go anywhere or do anything much with anyone else except maybe my Aunt Katherine – he seems to like her well enough.'

'Maybe he just likes being alone.'

'Well, yeah, sure and that's fine, if my grandmother would stop saying, "Are you boys having fun? And what did you two rascals get up to today?" And, well, we're not having fun is the answer to that and we got up to nothing at all because I couldn't find him. Of course, I don't tell that to her or anything.'

'Why not?'

'Her feelings, of course. And she'd, well, she'd…'

'Try to make you have fun?'

'Well, yeah, something like that, sir.'

The boy waits, shifty-eyed, like a kid standing before a headmaster, and he wonders if he's supposed to formally dismiss him. Then he realizes the kid just wants to talk. 'It was him found your crayons, you know. He gave them to your wife.'

'Well, if I see him, I'll be sure to thank him.'

'And, sir, I wonder if, well, if you do see him, would you tell him that I've been looking for him just about everywhere and that supper will be soon and he's supposed to wash up before supper because usually he just, well, he forgets.'

'I'll be sure to do that.'

'Oh and my name is Richie, sir. You know, in case you have to tell him who it was gave you the message.'

'You're a very polite boy, Richie.'

'Oh. Well, thank you, sir.'

'You're welcome.'

Richie takes a few backward steps and then turns and walks for a few steps more before cutting loose and breaking into a run. He watches Mrs Kaplan's grandson run awkwardly towards the beach steps.

In the hidey-hole, the boy stays down. Through the gap in the camouflage cover, he sees Richie come down the beach, then he sees him walk past the hidey-hole and disappear from sight. He thinks Richie may have gone to the end of the beach and that maybe he's going to double back by the roadway. He is wondering if it would be a good idea to sneak out and get back to the house before Richie does. But then when he twists his head to look further out, he sees Richie's legs right beside the swimmer's legs, and he knows the two of them are talking even if he can't hear a word they are saying. After a couple of minutes Richie comes back into view, passes the hidey-hole and begins running up the beach again, back towards the house.

He begins to count to sixty. He will do that five times and then follow Richie back to the house. He is on the second batch of seconds, almost right up to *sechstag*, when a long shadow slants over the hidey-hole. He stops counting.

A man's voice, deep and slow: 'You can come on out now, he's gone,' it says; and then: 'And by the way, thank you for finding my crayons.'

The shadow slips away. Seconds later it comes back, this time shorter and more round. It bobs a few times as it begins to climb the hill over the top of the hidey-hole. It disappears for a moment and then comes back and bobs a few more times before disappearing for good. The boy stays folded into himself, his hands over his ears and his face scrunched so hard that it hurts. He stays that way until he's certain the shadow has gone for good.

He moves away from the boy hiding in the bushes and begins his climb homeward. He has not managed to get very far before he needs to take a rest. He turns and looks back at the Kaplan house, sees Mrs Kaplan's grandson is now halfway up the wooden steps. A woman comes into view at the top of the steps and waits there to greet the boy. He can't tell much about her from this distance, except that she is tall. She is tall and she is wearing a pale-blue full-sleeved blouse. On her head is the yellow hat.

The woman bends to the boy and draws him away. He stares into the space they have left for a few seconds more and then resumes his climb. He can hear the sea behind him and the wind all around him and the sound of his blood pushing against his chest.

Mercury

1

SHE IS WALKING THROUGH an art gallery. A typical city gallery of door-less rooms, one leading into the next. The rooms square, light-washed, high ceilinged. There is no one else in the gallery, which seems a little odd – not even a guard standing at a wall. And something else that seems odd – there are no paintings. Yet the rooms seem prepared for paintings; there are hooks along the walls and here and there a picture-light cradles an empty space. The hooks are unusual, she notes in passing; double-barred and the colour of old ivory, they are set right into the wall.

At first the light dazzles. But as she walks further into the gallery, it begins to dim. The rooms too are becoming smaller. She only notices this when she happens to turn and look back the way she has come. The gradual shift in size is apparent then, as if the rooms are nesting into one another. She can see all the way back to the first room and, beyond that, across a black and white tiled floor to the large double doors that divide the gallery from the street outside. There is a glimpse of the street through the doors' glass panels: part of a sign on the side of a truck, the top knot of a fire hydrant, a nun's veiled head gliding by. She knows the street somehow – the nun, the fire hydrant, the large red *& Sons* sign on the truck – yet can't recall standing out on the street, nor coming to the door, pushing it open and walking across the chessboard floor. But anyhow, here she is.

She almost misses the last room. Much smaller than the others, the entrance is narrow and low in the wall like the door of a cupboard. She has to bend her head and turn sideways to get through. When she looks in, there is complete darkness, but when she steps down into the room, a column of light breaks open and points itself into the far corner where a painting hangs. She knows this at once: it is her painting, from seed to completion – she was the one who brought it into being. She covers her mouth with one hand and with the other her heart. A small gush of tears comes into her eyes. It is the most beautiful painting she has ever seen. Oh joy, she whispers into her hand, oh joy, oh life.

To think that, after all these years, it has been here all along, trapped in the dark of a secluded room, waiting, just waiting for her to come find it.

She dries her tears with her hands, then dries her hands in her skirt before carefully placing them on the sides of the frame. She tries to ease it away from the wall, but the picture resists. She begins to tug at it. She tugs harder and harder. She stops pulling then and attempts to look behind the picture. But the picture is tight to the wall, and now there is a low growling noise coming from behind it.

The light in the room snaps off. There is a strange smell, an animal smell. In the dark the growling noise deepens. The sound of an animal that is angry and, at the same time, frightened. She hears the thud of a heart, feels something wet and slick on her neck and chest. For a terrifying moment she thinks the animal is slobbering on her, getting ready to attack. But then she wakes and finds that both the smell and the noise, they are coming from her, and that the sweat on her skin is her own.

She lies in the dark, her mind running over the dream, each detail vivid, apart from the one detail that really matters – the painting itself. She can remember the weight of it when she first tried to ease it away from the wall and how solid and cool the frame had felt in her hands. She can still feel the rush of love that had come over her when she first looked upon it. The sense of achievement. And, oh, the pride! But as to what was inside the frame – subject matter, paint, colour, light – all that has now gone from her.

She turns on her side and studies her husband's long, broad back, the pyjama stripes like broken bars in this light. She brings the flat of her hand close to his back and wonders if she will tell him about her dream in the morning. Her hand hovers for a moment, the heat that comes out of him like smouldering coal.

She imagines herself explaining it to him (And what do you know but… And then? And my heart so full of *when*…), the little grunts he would allow across the breakfast table until finally she asks, 'What do you make of all that?' A shrugged one-liner as he pushes his plate away: 'It was only a dream' or 'I don't see that it had to mean anything in par-tic-u-lar.'

Before returning to his newspaper or his book or his post at the north window for his usual morning scrutiny of all the thin air in South Truro.

She sits up in bed, pulls her pillow up behind her and sips water from a glass on the bedside table. He shifts his shoulder then, glancing over it, asks in a mumble if she is all right.

'Yes, yes, it's nothing,' she says, 'you go on back to sleep.'

She stares into the room. The closet doors, the chair, the bureau beyond the fog of darkness like land ahoy. The hulk of his coat hanging from an unseen hook, as though it's standing up on its own.

'Do you remember the bears in Yellowstone Park?' she says aloud. But already he's gone back to sleep.

She continues to sip on the water and, as she does so, comes to a decision: tomorrow she will pay a visit to Mrs Sultz. For weeks, she has been toying with the notion, and now it is final. Mrs Sultz, tomorrow – a Sunday visit – what could be nicer? And she will go alone, even if he offers to drive her there. He will be surprised by her refusal, pleased too – an uninterrupted afternoon is just what he needs right now, a chance to do some work on that Orleans picture. She will ask him to drive her only as far as the bus. At the other end, she can call a cab to take her the rest of the way.

Or she could drive herself there – and why in hell not? It's her automobile too – she has just as much right to use it as he does. He will object – that much is certain – and when he does she will neither fight nor reason with him. She will wait for him to go for a walk or to become immersed in his painting and beyond noticing. Then she will simply take it (leaving a note pinned to the garage door, of course, in case he gets it into his head to go calling the police).

For a moment she sees herself driving along the Old County Road. No one beside or behind her to bark out criticism or unnecessary directions (not so close to the ditch; not so middle of the road; truck coming up! Kid on a bicycle! Watch out for the bridge at the next bend). As if she were driving with her eyes shut tight. To be all alone on the open road, maybe a little radio music to keep her company – how invigorating would that be? Fields and trees and wild-flowers flickering by, and the window rolled down to three-quarter mast, the taste of salt air coming over it. And Mrs Sultz – she would be so proud of her.

'You drove here? All by yourself – *you*?' she would tut before saying, as she always does when utterly astonished, 'Well, now, isn't that *something*?'

All the way there on her own. How many miles to Hyannis – how many after that to reach the sanatorium, along how many back roads? And then all the way home again. The highway busy with day trippers at the fall of evening and the light fading before her on the road. And supposing the visit doesn't go so well? Driving home alone and upset – how many miles from the sanatorium to Hyannis, how many from Hyannis to home…?

And now she sees herself clinging to the wheel, waiting at an intersection to cross over the highway, twilight slipping into darkness and the Sunday evening traffic at this time of the year, headlights cat-swiping her eyes. Swipe after swipe while she waits and she waits…

She will ask him to drive her to the bus.

The important thing is to get there. To make it up with Mrs Sultz, spend an afternoon with her best, and only, truly honest friend. It is certain to be a nice sanatorium – Mrs Sultz is not poorly off. They will sit outside; garden furniture on a smooth green lawn. Iced coffee under a tree. She could tell her all about the dream. Mrs Sultz has always been interested in that sort of thing: the psychological slant, as she calls it.

She would tell her other things too: about the women on the beach, the boy who gave her his cookies, the invitations to the Kaplan parties – one of which is already past, the other yet to come. And how she had intended going to that first one, yes, even on her own – because she hadn't bothered telling him, knowing only too well what he would say. She had bought a whole basket of peaches to take along, had put on her lipstick, ironed her best dress. She'd been about to put the dress on, then go out and ask him to drive her there. At the same time, she had been prepared to walk should he fail to show willing. And then, at the very last minute, she had sat down on the side of the bed and couldn't seem to bring herself to stand up again.

But why? Mrs Sultz would ask her. Why on earth didn't you go? And she would be able to explain it somehow and know that Mrs Sultz would understand. She simply hadn't been able to face it. She was too tired: too tired to fight with him to come along, and too tired to go it alone.

She had always been able to speak frankly to Mrs Sultz – say things she wouldn't dream of saying to another soul on earth. Talk to her about the past, tell her things about her secret self. And she had known that whatever was said, and despite the falling out, Mrs Sultz could be trusted to take it with her to the grave.

But what if Mrs Sultz has turned, if she finds her like she found that old friend of her mother's, Mrs Neeson? Demented and sitting up in bed swaying like a swamp tree? And what if she doesn't recognize her? Or worse – if she *does* recognize her and, when she sees her standing there, stops rocking and starts yelling instead? Get that woman out of here, she is a liar. She lied about her age when she married and she lied to her husband. Get her out of here – she was not, I said *not*, a virgin when she married!

She ought not to have told her. It's just the sort of thing an elderly woman would pull out of the bag. Mrs Sultz was not like most women of her background but even so – there had been no need to go telling her all that. There had been no need to tell her a lot of other things too. Like her regret at not having a child. But she only told because Mrs Sultz had asked. Do you regret? It was during the war; Mrs Sultz had brought her clamming. They had been laughing at her clumsy first efforts and then, suddenly, the question. Do you regret?

She had said: well, my age may have been against me, of course. But my husband doesn't care for children, not one little bit, and we are both so dedicated to our work… Yes, but do you regret? She would never have admitted it to anyone else. She had barely even admitted it to herself until the moment Mrs Sultz had asked.

She looks around the room, neither dark nor light: dusk before dawn. She can see the mirror on the bureau now, her possessions laid out on top of it like grown-up toys. Her mother's jewellery case; the small rose vase that had belonged to her grandmother. The powder tin she'd bought in Mexico. The box that held a necklace he bought her, one long ago Christmas.

When she is gone, all will be gone. No one to say: this necklace was my mother's; my great-grandmother owned that rose vase. Her name gone too: both single and married, no one to carry the can on either side. His paintings, of course – they will last and bear his name. But paintings are not flesh and blood, they are not the sound of a voice, the expression in an eye. And besides, he won't be cold in the grave before they are reduced to commodities: buy-and-sell trophies for rich men's walls.

What would their life have been if it had all worked out differently, if there had been a child? An only child – there would have been time for only one. Still, the difference one child would have made – where and how one lives for a start. His mother would have died a grandmother; his sister would now be an aunt. An artistic child, it was bound to have been, both sides being so inclined. But plenty of children turn out to be duds and so often in this life the rules of algebra seem to apply: two pluses do not a minus make. Mrs Sultz and her late husband good and true both. Yet the son? Insolent face and avaricious eye, always on the lookout for—

She hears herself gasp as the memory hits her – of course, he is dead: Matthew Sultz is dead. He died in the war. A prisoner-of-war. How could she have forgotten that? Died before he had a chance to settle into his own particular manhood. They told Mrs Sultz he hadn't suffered – of course, they would always say that. God knows what sort of death he really had. And God knows what sort of a shrivelled up and mean little soul she must have to think such thoughts about a poor dead boy – a boy who gave his life for his country?

She feels the shame burning her face, the swift awkward beat of her heart.

She will not sleep now.

She gets out of bed, goes into the bathroom, washes her face and spends a long time and a lot of tooth powder cleaning the sour taste from her mouth. Soon it will be sunrise. She could go out for a walk and catch it in the act. She could watch it break like an egg and pour itself all over the sea and the sand and her hands and her body until she is standing like a gaudy trinket on the shore. She will wait for the light to pale out and purify, and then she will begin walking along the seashore to Ryder Beach, cutting home by the hogsback hills. She will be gone a couple of hours at least. (He will start to worry – and let him!) While she walks she will try not to think: to allow the new light of day and the sea to wash her thoughts away, the grass and the trees to brush the dirt from the corners. That way, she may be able to forget her mean thoughts about poor Matty while, at the same time, a space in her memory may be found for that painting from her dream to nudge through.

Back in the bedroom, she begins to gather her clothes. In the half-light his coat on the back of the door no longer looks like a bear. It is simply a coat – she can even make out the flecks in the wool.

She lifts the sleeve and rubs it against her face. Rough, dense, heavy, an outrageous expense when first he bought it – oh, but a coat that has proved itself over time. They had such a fight over it while packing to come here. He said, 'I won't need it, I'll be done before the weather turns.'

The coat, like the child in King Solomon's judgement, had been tugged between them; she'd flung it into the trunk, he'd pulled it back out again. Finally she wore him down – he sulked as far as the Connecticut Turnpike.

But she had known how it would be – a difficult recovery, artistically as well as physically. It was always going to be a slow summer and she had known, too, that he would die rather than go back to New York empty-handed. And now it was coming to summer's end with nothing to show for it, and this coat he had no need of in New York would soon become his best friend.

In Yellowstone Park, he'd been afraid of the bears. Mama bears taking a stroll with their cubs, other tourists feeding them picnic scraps through the half-open windows of their automobiles. She had longed to embrace them. Such a strange longing it had been, warm and at the same time lonely. A little like love. Love and loneliness and, again, disappointment. She'd asked him to pull over so she could pet the bears but he'd refused absolutely. And, yes, she had behaved like a child then, putting her feet up on the dash, knowing he would swat them off again. She had scratched his hand when he put it back on the wheel. Scratched and screamed at him, a long wordless scream. The shock on his face when she did that. Then came the tears, silent tears. She'd turned away from him, face to the window, overwhelmed by a sort of grief. After a moment, he had pulled over and switched off the gas. Then, taking her in his arms, he held her there until the tears ran out.

Embarrassed after her outburst, she said, 'I guess I was having a Lady Chatterley moment – you know, when she wept over the newborn chicks?'

'Newborn chicks are one thing,' he said. 'Mama bear – well, she's quite another.'

She sits down on the side of the bed, her clothes in a pile beside her, and starts to lift the hem of her nightie over her knees. He mutters.

'Whas madder – can't sleep?'

'I'm going out for a walk,' she says.

He lifts his head from the pillow, turns and blinks at her.

'Do you remember the bears?' she asks him.

'The Bears? No – who are they?'

'The Yellowstone Park bears – do you remember them?'

He turns away again, lays his head back down on the pillow.

'Remember, remember,' he says, 'why do you always have to remember? Look out at the stars instead. Or even better, go back to sleep.'

'There are no stars,' she says, 'it's almost morning.'

Then, letting go of her nightie, she climbs back into bed where she lays her face against the warm, damp patch on the back of his pyjamas and, in a moment, falls back to sleep.

When she wakes, he is already up and dressed. His pyjamas lying sideways on the chair and a smell of recent coffee on the air. The house silent but not empty – it's the wrong kind of silence for that.

She sees her clothes hanging off the side of the bed, her sweater on the floor, and she remembers her plan to visit Mrs Sultz then. She is not so sure about the visit now and has just started talking herself out of it when he comes to the doorway.

He stands looking at her for a few seconds while he screws the head of a brush into a paint rag. 'I'm going to buy a newspaper,' he says then. 'Need anything while I'm out?'

'I don't know – do we?'

'Groceries might be a good idea.'

'Fine.'

'Well, what should I—?'

'Whatever you like. Surprise me, why don't you? Just because I'm the woman – does it mean that I have to make all these decisions?'

'No, it's because you're the fussy eater.'

'So you say. Oh, if you wouldn't mind checking the bus times while you're out.'

'Going somewhere?'

'I'm thinking of going to Hyannis, since you ask.'

He looks at her, surprised and amused. And now, like it or not, she *has to* go to Hyannis.

'To pay a visit to Mrs Sultz,' she says. 'I was thinking if there's a lunchtime bus or a little later, I don't really mind once I'm there before three. You could check the return times too, so you'll know when to meet me.'

He nods and then says, 'Want me to drive you?'

'Certainly not! You better stay here and work on that picture, don't you think? But thank you for the offer. How is it coming along, anyway?'

He backs out of the doorway and she can hear his footsteps go first to his worktable, then into the kitchen and now cross the floor to the door.

She calls out after him, 'I said – how is it coming along?'

A moment's hesitation and then: 'I'm not sure that it is.'

'Well, what does your instinct tell you?'

'That it's a piece of tripe.'

'Oh. Can I at least see it?'

'No.'

'No?'

'Not yet, anyway. I want to leave it lie undisturbed for a while.'

And then the door clicks and he is gone.

*

She waits a few minutes before getting up and walking barefoot through the house. A dull sky and heavy clouded and now she remembers there was talk of a rainstorm. From the back window she sees the tail-end of the automobile turn at the gate-post and duck out of sight.

She comes back on her steps and stops at the easel. The easel is turned away, facing west towards the bay, so that if she wants to look at it she has to walk right in and around it. She does this and, now facing the easel, takes a few steps back and then stops.

He has it all down in blue. She moves closer to the picture and leans into it. Then, holding her index finger an inch or so from the canvas, she begins to trace over the lines: the oval of the garage sign, the vertical pole holding it up, the circles of the tyre display beneath it, the stop light with its three hooded eyes just behind it. She brings her finger across the street and continues to trace over the lines, straight and curved, rectangled and triangled. She tries to work it all out: the foliage along the horizon line, the thumbprint of an automobile heading into the vanishing point, the broad tilt of the road.

She turns to his worktable and begins looking through sketches, spreading them out, lifting one and then another for closer inspection. Treetops, shops, houses, stove-shaped chimney pot, canopies, garage sign, horizon line. Vanishing point.

She puts the sketches back the way she has found them and stays for a moment without looking at the picture on the easel. She finds she is unable to do that now, look at it face to face. Not because she is overwhelmed by it – which can occasionally happen – nor is she deafened by the clash of envy and pride, admiration and resentment – which can also happen. The truth is she has had her doubts about this picture right from the start. She sees nothing to fear and nothing to ponder in this rendition of an intersection at Main Street, Orleans. It is a bland picture, so far anyhow. No, worse than bland – it is dead.

She comes back into the bedroom, pulls her best skirt from the closet, lays it out on the bed and then fumbles in her mother's jewellery case until a silver brooch comes to hand.

*

The sky has darkened to a charcoal grey by now and looks about ready to rip wide open. As she comes to the window to take a closer look, her eye is caught by movement down by the garage. Two boys standing there. The boys appear to be having some kind of dispute: the taller stands square with his arms folded to his chest, the stockier one, in between stomping around, points up to the house like he's shooting an arrow. She comes outdoors, walks round the house and waits at the top of the steps.

The taller boy sees her immediately and drops his folded arms. The other boy turns and now he sees her too. They both somewhat reluctantly begin to make their way towards her. As they climb the steps, she starts to recognize them: Mrs Kaplan's grandson, and the taller is the boy who gave her his cookies. She can't recall their names and so she calls out to them.

'Well, hello, you two – and what brings you here?'

Mrs Kaplan's grandson increases his speed and, arriving a little breathlessly, says, 'Good morning, ma'am, I'm sorry to disturb you. I'm Richie in case you don't remember me. Richie Kaplan, you know. We're here because my grandma, that is Mrs Kaplan, she asked—'

The other boy rushes ahead of him. 'I've come to see Arthur,' he says.

'Who is—? Oh, you mean the cat, Arthur?'

'Yes, the cat.'

She feels the first smack of a large raindrop on the back of her hand and, wiping it away, looks at the sky.

She says, 'But he's dead.'

'I know *that*,' the boy says, 'but you said…'

'What did I say?'

'You said you'd love me to see the painting you did of him.'

And now she feels another drop on her arm, and the first rain stains on the wooden rail.

'Yes, I did say that – didn't I? Well, I'm glad you've come. And I'm glad it's only you two, after all. I looked down and saw two people hanging around the back of our garage and didn't know what to think!'

Mrs Kaplan's grandson's face shows a healthy blush. She can't make out if he's embarrassed or annoyed.

'He thought you lived down there,' he says. 'He wouldn't listen when I tried telling him – I mean, who lives in a gar—?'

'What in the world made you think that?' she says to the boy.

The boy looks down, pawing the step with his foot like a horse. 'It looks like a house, I mean with the roof and everything.'

'Pretty small for a house,' Richie says, rolling his eyes.

'Well, she's pretty small too.'

Richie turns and glares at him.

She tries not to smile. 'And who do you think lives here then, in this house?' she asks.

'That man,' the boy says.

'That man?' She laughs. 'Why, that's just what I call him sometimes – you know, in my head. That man!'

Another drop of rain, fat and cold, this time hits her right on the face.

'Don't you think you boys better come inside before the rain—?' she begins, and then it all rushes out like corn from a slit sack.

She turns and begins to run; Mrs Kaplan's grandson falls in behind her. When she gets to the corner, she glances back and the tall boy is still standing on the steps, rain streaming down his hair and face.

'What are you waiting for then?' she shouts back at him. 'You'll get soaked right through.'

'Are you alone in there?' he shouts back.

'Yes, there's only me.'

'Where's the man?'

'He's gone out. Come on, I promise, there's no one in.'

The boy nods and then runs in behind her.

They duck into the house and she slams the door, the rain pelting off it as if it's trying to get in after them. The sound of it bashing off the windows and walls, the roof.

Richie shouts, 'Oh no, all my clothes are wet!'

The other boy laughs and shakes his hair out like he's a dog.

'Oh, it's only summer rain,' she yells through the noise, 'won't harm you at all.'

Then the rain suddenly cuts out. And the house is quiet again. She goes into the closet and takes three towels out, throwing one each at the boys.

Richie pats his towel on his face and carefully dries first his hands, then his legs. The other boy swipes the towel over his face in one go and then drops it on the back of a chair. She takes her own towel and, much like Richie, closes her eyes and pats her face dry. When she opens her eyes Richie is pulling things out of his pocket and laying them on the kitchen table: a rescue inhaler, a pack of bubblegum and a small white envelope.

'At least *this* didn't get wet,' he says and begins shoving the envelope at her.

'What is it?' she says, now drying her ponytail.

'I don't know, ma'am, well, I sort of do – oh, I didn't look inside it or anything like that, but anyhow my grandma, she said to be sure to put it right in your hand.'

'They want you to come to a party on Labor Day Weekend,' the other boy says. He is staring around the house with his mouth wide open.

'You like the place?' she asks and tries again but fails again to remember his name.

The boy nods and then, pointing up at the loft, asks, 'What is that up there?'

'That's a loft.'

'It doesn't look like a loft.'

'Well, what do you think it looks like?'

'I don't know. Maybe where the preacher stands?'

'The preacher! Oh yes, we have one of those right here, let me tell you. Now, you wait here while I go search for Arthur.'

As she rummages through the loft she hears their loud whispers.

'Didn't anybody ever teach you anything about manners? Anything at all?' the Richie boy says.

'What'd I do now?'

'Staring at everything that way. And you're supposed to call her *ma'am* when you speak to her. And I don't think you ought to have said that thing about her being, you know, a small person.'

'But she is.'

She pulls the painting free from a pile-up of old canvases and, feeling giddy

117

suddenly, ducks behind the wall of the loft and pops the painting up over it, shouting: 'Miaow!'

The taller boy bursts out laughing and says, 'What are you now, Arthur, a Jack-in-the-box or somethin'?'

She takes the painting away and shows her own face. Mrs Kaplan's grandson is looking a little pained while the other boy continues to grin up at her.

She is on her way down the stairs from the loft when she hears the double click of the Dutch door opening and then Richie's voice saying: 'Oh hello, sir, I hope we're not disturbing you but, you see, my grandma, she—'

This is immediately followed by some sort of a scuffle and the sound of the door opening again followed by the click of it closing.

She hurries down the last few stairs. Richie is standing goggle-eyed and her husband, with two hefty grocery bags in his arms, is staring at the door. 'What was that all about?' he asks.

The boy is halfway down the wooden steps by the time she reaches the top of them.

'Hey,' she calls out, and then, as a name jumps out of her memory, 'Hey, Vince, come back here – where are you going?'

The boy turns for a second, a look of genuine panic on his face.

'Oh, now, don't say you're going to make me run after you – that would be too cruel of you, really, at my age!'

He turns as if to run again, but as he does, his knees seem to get caught up in one another and he stumbles, falls forward before coming to a twisted halt halfway down the steps.

She leans the painting of Arthur against a dry patch on the wall of the house, then hurries down the steps after him. The boy is hugging his knee, his eyes scrunched right back into his face. The knee, bleeding and badly scratched, is stuccoed in grit, there are more scratch marks along his shin, his elbow is skinned and the side of his forearm is also marked with scratches and beads of blood.

'Oh, you poor boy, oh oh. Are you all right? Oh, how terrible. Oh, Vince, what have you done? Can you get up? Do you think you can do that for me?'

He reaches out for the banister, but his arm is not long enough. She lifts her head to call her husband and finds him already coming down the steps with Richie close behind him.

'It's going to be all right now, Vince, my husband will carry you back up to the house and—'

'No!' the boy whimpers and folds himself over.

'Why, Vince, whatever is the matter with you?'

She looks back up at her husband and shrugs.

'Maybe it would be better if I were to drive Richie back to his grandmother's house,' he says. 'He can bring her back here.'

'Richie, would that be all right with you?' she asks. 'If my husband takes you back to fetch your grandma, I can stay here with Vince till you get back?'

'Vince? Well sure, ma'am, that would be fine, but the thing is, she's not there. Nobody is. Grandma and my mom went with Aunt Katherine to Doctor Tom's and then they are all having lunch with Mrs Grant, you know, the English lady, and even Rosetta, well, she had to go out too, left us to fix our own lunch and everything, or at least we have to fix it as soon as we get back from delivering this message.' Richie licks his lips and holds the envelope out for a second before lowering it again.

'What are we to do?' she says to her husband.

He comes down and sits on the step above the boy. The boy begins shaking his head in small rapid-fire movements. He stays sitting for a few moments without moving or looking at the boy and then he quietly asks, 'You know who this lady is?'

'Sure,' the boy mumbles, 'she's Mrs Aitch.'

'Mrs Aitch? Okay.'

'I told him, sir, that's not her real name,' Richie says, 'but he won't listen.'

'Well, in that case, I'm Mr Aitch, this lady's husband. Now, tell me, do you think Mrs Aitch is scared of me?'

The boy shakes his head.

'And do you think that's because maybe I'm not such a bad fellow after all?'

'I don't know, I guess…' the boy says.

'Well, the way I see it, son, you don't have much of a choice. We don't have a telephone and so we can't call a doctor. And we can't leave you on the steps out here, not with the rain about ready to start over. Supposing a hurricane comes? You'll be blown clear away. But what we do need to do is figure out if you're hurt – you know, in case you need to go to the hospital. Now, Richie can't carry you and my wife here, well, she certainly can't carry you, so you're stuck with me, I'm afraid. I can promise to be gentle as I possibly can, and as soon as we get you back up there and in the house, my wife can take over, check you out and fix you up – how does that sound?'

The boy, without looking at him, gives a small nod.

'I'm going to check a few things first,' he says and then puts his hand on the boy's leg, 'because if you've broken anything then we can't move you – you understand? All right, so how about this? And this? Okay, now, can you bend your knee, can you do that for me? Good, that's really good. You certainly are brave.'

The boy continues to rapidly nod his head.

'Okay, now, I want you to put your arms around my neck, that's it, good. And now I'm going to lift you up. All right? One and two and three. Here we go, that's it. Going up! All the way to the top floor. Now. That wasn't so bad, was it?'

The boy begins counting under his breath.

'That's it,' he says, 'you just keep on counting. By the time you reach a hundred we'll have you back in the house, sitting comfortably, and that's a promise.'

She watches him carry the boy up the steps. The boy like a young injured animal up in his arms. The delicate awkwardness. The knots of his bony knees and his thin legs hanging over the precipice of her husband's arms. The most robust part of him seems to be his injury, the dark patch of scratches and blood like a fabric on his skin. A fragile thing, a boy of that age – you only really notice it when he stops moving around. Her husband, though, is not fragile at all and appears to be a much younger man, suddenly strong and capable, carrying the boy up the steps. And the boy's head snug on his chest.

She recalls an evening, a long time ago, the first or maybe second summer in this house, when he carried her up the steps that way and it was her head on his chest. A beautiful day in September it had been. They had been out painting. He had left her to her own little spot and driven off to find one of his own. By the time he returned, the day had chilled into autumn. She'd only been wearing a thin cotton dress. He hadn't known the roads so well back then and had lost his way in the twilight. She was shivering, frozen right through. 'Even your hair feels cold,' he had said when he put his hand on it.

It seems funny to have shared the experience with a boy she hardly knows. To see his head lie where her head had lain, his legs dangle as hers had once done over her husband's strong arms.

She follows behind them; at the top of the steps, she picks up the painting of Arthur and hugs it to her chest.

In the studio, he places the boy on the high stool and she puts Arthur down and goes into the kitchen to put water on to boil. When she comes back, he is telling the boy about the first-aid course he did during the war. He doesn't bother to say that they both did the course, but that she was the only one to see it through to the end. He is holding the boy by the ankle and folding his leg back and forward.

'Just checking the hinges,' he says to her or the boy – she can't be certain. But in any case, they both seem to have forgotten that she was supposed to be taking over as soon as they got back to the house. She stands next to Richie and watches.

Her husband is now holding the boy by the elbow, moving his arm in and out. The boy is studying his face as if he's trying to memorize it. He stops doing that after a moment and begins looking at his surroundings: the easel, the work-table, the big window. Then he examines the high stool he is sitting on and, poking the cushion tied onto it, asks, 'How come there's a cushion tied on here?'

'Oh that? That was my wife's idea.'

'Why?'

'That's to make sitting more comfortable. I'm not supposed to stand for very long when I'm painting. But I always forget and stand up anyway.'

'How come?'

'How come what?'

'You're not supposed to stand?'

'It hurts when I do.'

The boy nods and looks around a little more, then he comes back to him and says, 'You said it would take a hundred seconds to get from the steps to in here.'

'How many did it take?'

'One hundred and seventy-nine.'

'Well, then I guess I owe you seventy-nine cents. A cent a second – that seem fair to you?'

The boy gives a half-grin and she feels a slight twinge in her chest.

'You stopped being scared of me now?' her husband asks.

'I don't know. Maybe.'

'Nothing broken,' her husband says, finally addressing her. 'I think he just needs patching up. A glass of orange juice, a few cookies. You like orange juice? I just brought some home. We don't have any ice-cream, I'm sorry to say, but we can get some when I drive you boys back. We can see my wife off at the bus stop first, if you'd like that.'

'Where is she going?' he asks.

'Hyannis, I believe.'

The boy looks over at her then. 'Why are you going to Hyannis?'

'Well, to visit a friend.'

'Do you have to go today? Can't you do it some other time?'

'Of course, I don't *have* to go.'

'So you'll stay?' he says, his voice bright and full of hope.

'Well, I suppose. Now that the rain appears to be starting again… Oh, I don't like the bus when it rains. You just can't see a thing out the windows – they get so dirty. And *stuffy* – my goodness. So, no, I don't have to go today. I can wait till tomorrow. After all, we have guests. The least I could do is stay and make them some lunch.'

Across the room, the boy sends her a smile and such a happy smile. 'Is she really your wife?' he says to her husband.

'Why – you thinking of proposing?' he asks.

'No. I just— Well, she seems a little young for you, is all.'

She laughs, claps her hands and says, 'Oh, you are the lambiest boy!'

As she turns to go back to the kitchen and fetch the hot water, she sees Richie standing there, looking a little dejected, the envelope still clutched in his hand.

'Would you like me to take that envelope now, Richie?' she asks, and he jumps to attention and hands it to her. She puts it down on the table next to the little bunch of things he left there.

'Do you suffer from asthma, Richie?'

'Well, yeah, I guess, sort of.'

'Oh now, be sure to remember your rescue inhaler, you might need it.'

He follows her out to the stove, talking behind her. 'Oh, I never use it really. Not for a long while, and not usually here – although sometimes in the fall – but mostly when I get it, it's in the city or if I get a chest cold and a few years ago after my father, you know, I had to go to a clinic in the mountains but no, not really. I should grow out of it soon, that's what my doctor says.'

'Oh well, that's good news.'

'My mom, though, she makes me carry it with me. You know, just in case.'

'Good idea,' she says.

'Oh yes, because, you see, when we were in the clinic, somebody died because they went out without their rescue inhaler and she gets scared since my— Well, you know, she just gets more scared about everything and makes me carry it.'

'Better to be safe,' she says and takes a bowl down from the shelf. She begins to fill it with hot water while Richie continues.

'And when I go to my new school next month, I have to take two rescue inhalers with me. One has to stay with the nurse and I keep the other, you know, in case I lose it.'

'Uh-huh,' she says and carries the bowl back into the studio with Richie at her heels. 'Yes, well, thank you, Richie, for giving me this invitation. Although, I should say we are not really partygoers. My husband doesn't like to stay up too late.'

123

'Oh, it wouldn't have to be too late,' Richie says. 'It's a day-time party. People will come and go all day. You don't even have to stay for supper if you're too tired. That's what Grandma said to Aunt Katherine, anyhow – you go lie down any time you want. Aunt Katherine is sick, you see, she gets awfully tired.'

'Yes, I know, your grandmother told me.'

'So if you're tired, ma'am, then—'

'Well, we'll see,' she says, glancing at her husband who has removed himself from the conversation.

She puts the hot water down on the worktable. 'If you could bring the first-aid box, please, Richie? You'll find it in the bathroom, right through there, just behind the door. Once we have Vince all fixed up, you can help me to make lunch, if you like.'

'Vince?' Richie squeals. 'Why do you keep calling him Vince?'

'Isn't that his name?' she asks.

'No, did he tell you that it was? Because, you know, sometimes he just— Well, I don't like to say it when he's hurt and everything.'

'Oh no, he didn't tell me a thing,' she says. 'I was mistaken, that's all. He just reminds me of someone I know called Vince – that must be what put it in my head.'

Her husband looks down at the boy. 'And what is your name, son?' he asks.

'Micha,' the boy says.

'Micha?'

'Michael, I mean – my name is Michael.'

THEY HAVE TO PARK at the end of a lane and walk the rest of the way to get to Mrs Kaplan's house. Mrs Kaplan's automobile is parked on one side, and there's another small convertible parked right behind it. She walks ahead with Richie. He follows behind with the boy in his arms.

The lane narrows and rises as they approach the house, a stand of red cedar trees on one side. The ground beneath her feet rain-damp and red, staining Richie's sneakers. As they reach the house, she sees a woman sitting on an upstairs verandah, the crown of her hat showing over the balustrade. Richie sees the woman too and begins to yell: 'Aunt Katherine, Aunt Katherine. He's hurt, Michael is hurt, he fell down all these steps and his leg is cut up and…'

Then Richie's feet pound up the porch steps; he flips off his sneakers and charges through the front door.

The woman on the verandah stands up, leans over the rail and looks down at her. 'Oh, hello,' she says, 'it's you again.'

'Well, yes, I guess it is…' she says.

'We met at Mrs Grant's house – a couple of weeks ago, am I right?'

She takes off her hat to show her face.

'Oh, why of course, you're Mrs Kaplan's daughter.'

'Katherine.'

'Yes, Katherine.'

Katherine smiles lazily at her, a pale, pretty face, long brown hair, tired-looking eyes as if she has just woken up or is about to fall asleep. 'My mother is inside—' she begins and then looks right past her and asks, 'Is he all right?'

She turns and sees her husband behind her, standing staring up at the girl on the balcony as if he can't understand what it is that she's asking.

'Michael, is he all right?' the girl asks again.

'Oh yes,' she finally answers on his behalf. 'He's a little stiff but no real damage. We fixed him up. He had a tumble, but there was no need for stitches or anything too terrible. I imagine he'll be back on his feet by tomorrow.'

'You look biblical standing there,' Katherine says, again looking over her head, 'you know, like Moses bringing his only son to be sacrificed.'

Again her husband doesn't say anything and again she speaks for him.

'I think you may mean Isaac. He was the one who sacrificed his son.'

'Oh yes, so he did! I'm always getting those guys mixed up.'

She gives a slow, lopsided smile and then moves away from the verandah and disappears through a French window into the house where Richie's voice is waiting.

Her husband begins to move again. The door to the house opens. Mrs Kaplan comes rushing through with a small Mexican woman fussing and clucking behind her.

IN THE MORNING, SHE sets out again to visit Mrs Sultz. He stands by the door waiting while she does a little last-minute fidgeting: hair, brooch on her blouse, now the interior of her pocketbook, coins – yes, dollars – yes, folded scrap of paper for the cab driver when she gets to Hyannis.

'You don't want to miss your bus,' he calls out to her.

She folds a sweater into her shopping bag and she rolls last week's copy of the *New Yorker* into the side of it, then the bag of crackers in case her stomach starts fussing on the bus, along with a box of chocolate candies for Mrs Sultz. Now the pocketbook where she can easily find it and, finally, a nest of four fat peaches, which she gently lays on top of the sweater.

'You don't want to miss it…' he calls.

She turns on her heel and comes out through the kitchen singing, 'Yes, yes, I'm ready to go, ready to go.'

'Oh!' he says when he sees her.

'Is that oh because I look so nice or because I really *am* ready?'

'Both, I guess,' he says, and with his hand softly on the small of her back, he steers her through the door.

He says it again as they come out of the lane onto the road where she suggests they could pick up the mail on the way to the bus. 'Well, if you're serious about catching that bus… I can pick the mail up on the way back.'

And again, when she suggests he might pull over when they get to Depot Road so she can see if that nice egg woman has managed to get her hens to lay: 'She'll keep you talking and what if the bus…'

They are coming up to the turn for Mill Pond Road when they see the two boys walking ahead. Michael, with his bandaged knee, limping a little while Richie, a couple of yards ahead of him, is plodding along on the end of the dog leash, the dog, on the other end of it, straining. And she thinks: poor Richie, everyone trying to get away from him, even his dog.

'Pull over,' she says. 'I want to ask about his leg.'

As they approach, the two faces turn – Michael's curious then pleased; Richie's startled then utterly confused.

'Oh, pull over,' she says, waving out at the boys.

'I am pulling over, just not here in the middle of the road – there's a verge up ahead.'

She sticks her head out the window and yells, 'There's a verge up ahead, we'll wait for you there.'

He pulls over and they wait for the boys to catch up. It's only then she notices, on the bend further up the road, Richie's mother and another woman sitting on a low stone wall, smoking cigarettes.

'That's her, look – no, don't look – sitting up there on the wall.'

'Who – who is it that I'm not to look at?'

'Richie's mother. Mrs Kaplan's daughter-in-law, oh, what's her name? I can't stand that I keep forgetting names – you know? Olivia! That's it, Olivia.'

'Yes, I see her now.'

'Has she seen us?'

'I don't think so.'

'Who's that with her – is it the other one? The daughter who's sick – Katherine, isn't that her name?'

'No.'

'Oh, it must be.'

'It's not her,' he says, 'and how do you know she's sick?'

'Mrs Kaplan told me. That day in Orleans. When you off were chasing that picture – when you abandoned me for hours.'

'Oh, we're back to that, are we?'

'I must say, I don't like her, I don't like her at all.'

'Who, Katherine?'

'Oh no, she's fine. A little tipsy, though, yesterday – didn't you think? No, I mean, Olivia. Richie's mother. And as for that friend of hers! On the make, if you ask me. Oh, I know she apologized and everything.'

'Who, the friend?'

'No, Olivia, of course. But it was the *way* she did it – or the reason, I should say. She strikes me as one of those women, you know, the vulture type. She wouldn't mind getting her shiny red claws into you, I can tell you that. Can't we just back up to the boys?'

'I can't back up here,' he says.

'Well, why not, for heaven's sake?'

'It's much too dangerous.'

'Well, can't you make a turn in the road then?'

'If I try that, they will definitely see us. Look, they're going to see us no matter what we do, so we may as well get it over with.'

'You're such an old stick – we could easily back up.'

'Or, I know,' he says, 'how about we slip out the door, crawl around to that field there, then edge along it Indian-style to the pond and wade back through it… That way, they'll never see us?'

'Oh, you are so *funny*.'

She turns in her seat and looks back towards the boys. Richie, red-faced, has stopped now and is pulling the dog with all his might, although the dog, head poked into a clump of roadside grass, clearly has other ideas. And now Michael, with a brisk and determined limp, is coming up the rear and passing him out.

'You know,' she begins, 'I think I may know why that boy was so scared of you.'

'You do?'

'He thinks you're a soldier.'

'I'm a little old for a soldier.'

'A German soldier – that's where he's from, you know, Germany. I bet he thinks you're an officer. I bet that's it.'

'Oh, so I've been promoted?'

'An SS officer. A Nazi. Well, why wouldn't he? You have the height, the right colouring – I can just see you in uniform.'

'That is not funny in the least,' he says.

'No, it certainly is not, the poor boy, going through all that just to end up with a neighbour who bears a remarkable—'

'Looks like we've been spotted by your friends,' he says.

She turns back around and, through the windshield, there's Richie's mother standing now, smoothing out the back of her dress with one hand and with the other giving a little wave. She sees now that the other woman is Miss Staines, taking a few last hasty pulls from her cigarette before twisting it into the stones on the wall.

'I think she may have been medicated,' he says.

'Who or what are you talking about now?'

'The girl, Katherine, yesterday. She's sick – isn't she? I think that's probably what it was.'

They come to the automobile like curious cattle: the two boys from behind, the two women approaching from the front. The boys – and she can't help being pleased by this – come directly to her window. As for the women – they make straight for her husband. Miss Staines holds back a little, while Richie's mother dives right in. He opens the door and stands out on the road with his 'Good morning, ladies.'

On her side of the automobile Richie is reciting a thank-you speech – for all the help yesterday, the pancakes for lunch, the ride home afterwards.

Whereas on the far side of the automobile it's 'Oh, I can't tell you what an honour it is to finally meet you. Very exciting – isn't that so, Annette? Oh, excuse me, this is my friend, Miss Staines.'

'Oh, please call me Annette,' she says and, shaking his hand, simpers. 'How do you do.'

Michael shoves his face into the window frame. 'Where are you goin'?' he asks her. 'Mrs Aitch, where are you goin'?'

'What? Oh, to the bus stop. I'm going to visit that friend.'

'Can we come too?'

'Certainly not, she's in a sanatorium. How's that leg doing?'

'Pretty good. It only hurts if I kneel.'

'Well, you'd better not say your prayers for a day or two.'

The boy laughs.

'Is that funny?' she asks.

'You're funny,' he says and puts his hand on her arm, startling her.

'We saw your retrospective in New York,' Annette is now saying, 'went up on the train specially and, oh my…'

Richie is still talking. This time it's about his grandmother and somebody called Doctor Tom who came last night to take a look at Michael's leg.

'Oh yes?' she says to Richie. 'Well, isn't that nice?'

129

'Thank you,' her husband is saying, 'kind of you to say so.'

'And I thought the best…' Richie's mother says. And, 'Oh yes,' Annette interjects, 'but my absolute favourite was…'

While Richie earnestly continues, 'And he said to Grandma that the dressing on Michael's leg was as fine a job as he'd ever seen and probably even better than he could have done himself.'

'Who said – your grandmother?'

'No! Doctor Tom, of course.'

'Oh yes, Doctor Tom, of course.'

Richie carries on – about what, she has no idea. Michael's hand, still on the sleeve of her blouse, has lifted a pinch of the material and is contentedly rubbing it between his finger and thumb.

On the far side of the automobile she can hear her husband's voice, polite and happy – why is it so happy? The long, flighty laugh of Richie's mother, the short, hoarse bark of her weather-beaten friend. And Richie's eyes still goggling and his mouth still moving:

'Excuse me, Richie,' she says to him and, abruptly turning away, leans across the driver's seat to call up to her husband. 'Shouldn't we be getting a move on? After all, I don't want to miss my bus, now do I?'

Olivia steps up to the open door, bends in with her sugar-sweet smile. 'I was just saying to your husband that we are so grateful for your kindness yesterday. If it wasn't for you both, well, I can't imagine what might have happened.'

'If it wasn't for us, it wouldn't have happened in the first place,' she says. 'The boys came to visit us – remember? To deliver the invitation.'

'Oh yes, of course. But, well—' Olivia laughs and then changes the subject to the weather – a topic she no doubt considers more suited to the wives of great men.

'Such a beautiful day and after all that rain! Though at least the hurricane didn't show up. But the rain, my goodness. Lying in bed last night listening to it, I felt sure we would wake to find the house floating like a ship out on the bay this morning.'

Olivia waits for her to laugh at the little joke – and let her wait, she thinks and stares her out. Olivia finally breaks and says, 'Well, we better let you catch your bus.'

She steps back from the door to allow the driver to lower himself in.

But Olivia is not done. She puts her hand on the top of the door and shows her girlish dimples. 'You are both heroes in our house, anyhow. I hope you know that.'

And they both look up at her standing there clutching the driver's door and it seems like neither of them can think of a thing to say.

Until Michael's head comes wriggling in through the passenger window and says loudly into the interior, 'Mr Aitch, can we come with you? Can we come wave Mrs Aitch goodbye?'

Richie's mother turns swiftly away from the door, both her voice and her step suddenly crisp, and makes her way round to Michael.

'Oh now, really, Michael! That's pushing it a little far – don't you think?'

Michael steps back from the window, his face full of sudden shame.

'After all, these good people had you boys for most of yesterday afternoon. You can't impose on people, you know – you have to *wait* to be invited.'

'Well, he's invited now,' she says, leaning the side of her head out the window. 'I'd love to have the boys wave me off – if the driver doesn't object.'

'No, he does not,' her husband says. 'Be happy to take them along. I have to run a few errands on the way home, but I can drop them off after that.'

She leans her arm over her seat and opens the back door. 'You heard him, boys, hop in.'

'What about the dog, Mom?' Richie says. 'Will you take him?'

Olivia takes the dog from Richie. 'I certainly will. We can't have Buster leave half of himself behind in this nice clean automobile. Bad enough he has your grandmother's car looking like a feathered nest. Honestly!'

And now she comes to the passenger window, billowing perfume in at her. The same perfume she would have billowed a moment ago at her husband.

'We really do hope you'll come to our party on Labor Day Weekend. My mother-in-law said not to force it, she knows how busy you are, but anyhow, I can't seem to help myself. It would be lovely to see you both there. It's my husband's anniversary, you see, and this is the first year that we will be celebrating his life rather than mourning his passing. If you can spare the time of course.'

'Well, now, that's very kind of you, but we're not here on vacation, you know, we are here to work! Both of us. I'm an artist too, as you know, and we have a lot of catching up—'

She looks at her husband, expecting him to back her up. But his eye, half-smiling, is on Olivia leaning in the passenger window. 'Oh, I'm sure we could manage an hour or so,' he says.

Olivia beams. Mrs Staines through the windshield beams. The boys climb into the back seat yakking like magpies.

'Oh, how wonderful,' Olivia says. 'Well, we certainly look forward to seeing you there. But, of course, we are sure to run into each other before then – the party's not for another couple of weeks.'

And then, gracefully retreating, she issues a sharp tongue click at the dog, who immediately comes to heel.

When she gets out, she sees the bus pulling in to the stop. She looks at her watch – ten minutes to go. Then she leans back in to him. 'Well, I guess I didn't miss it after all,' she says. 'I even have time to buy a newspaper. So you won't have to be stuck with me all afternoon – won't that be nice?'

'Please give Mrs Sultz my regards,' he says.

The boys get out of the automobile but he stays put. They walk, one each side of her, towards the newsagent's, Richie lagging behind when an elderly man greets him and again when a woman waiting to meet someone off the bus stops to ask after his grandmother. She walks ahead with Michael.

'How come the picture was all in blue?' Michael asks as they wait to pay for the newspaper.

'What picture?'

'The one from yesterday, how come he painted it all blue?'

'The painting on the easel? Oh, the real colours get added in later. He'll probably do them today.'

'And will he put the lady in then?'

'What lady?'

'The lady in the green dress. I saw her there.'

'You did? What was she like?'

'I don't know.'

'Well, what age was she then?'

He shrugs.

'Well, *who* did she look most like then – your grandmother or Richie's mom or even me maybe?'

'Oh,' Michael says, 'I get it now. She looked like Miss Staines – you know, Annette? She looked like her, I guess. Only a little shorter.'

'And what was she doing?'

'She came out of the dress shop and looked down the street like she was waiting for someone, then she went back in again – I saw her from the gas station.'

She pays for the newspaper and they come back out to Richie, who is standing near the stop watching the driver unload cartons and bags from the belly of the bus.

When they come up beside him she looks at Michael and says, 'When you go back to my husband, be sure to remind him about the lady in the green dress. Did you speak to her, Michael? Did you get to see her up close?'

'She gave me those cookies. And then I gave them to you.'

'So you did. And very nice cookies they were too.'

She puts her foot on the first of the bus's metal steps. 'Be sure to tell him she looked like she was waiting for someone. And you tell him that I said— I said that she belongs in there.'

She begins to climb the rest of the steps; behind her she can hear Richie say, 'Hey, I thought you said you got those cookies from—'

But then the bus begins limbering up and his voice is hissed away.

She steps onto the bus and, turning around, raises her voice against the sound of the engine. 'Remind him that he's to come collect me at seven-thirty. And you boys be sure to drop by again.'

'When? Mrs Aitch, hey, Mrs Aitch, when will we drop by again?' Michael yells and Richie pulls him by the tail of his T-shirt and he drops back from the step.

As she makes her way down the bus she can see them through the windows. First they are both waving like crazy, then Michael alone is waving while Richie begins to retreat. Now Richie has turned his back and is running out to cross over the street. As she passes from one window to the next, there are glimpses of Michael, waving, then looking over his shoulder, then waving again. Finally, there is one last uncertain wave before Michael turns and runs after Richie.

She finds her place. Sitting on the edge of the seat, she watches Michael climb into the Buick and, as it begins to pull away, the two boys wriggling like polecats in the back as they talk to her husband over the seat.

She settles into her place, puts the bag down at her feet and watches the rear of the automobile disappear into the street while she waits for the bus to start moving.

~

IN HYANNIS, AS SOON as she steps off the bus, a cab driver hurries forward to offer his services. He offers to wait for her too until she's finished her visit, but she decides it would be more prudent to let him go and have a nurse or someone call a cab later on when she's done.

'You should have let him wait,' the receptionist says as she walks her along the first corridor. 'His mother is a patient here; he could visit with her while he waits for you. And just so you know,' she adds with a sidelong look, 'he doesn't charge for the wait, not the first hour anyhow, and most people don't stay more than an hour.'

She thinks as they pass a pinkish room, where a woman sits rocking herself on a straight-back chair, they should put these people in rocking chairs, take the crazy look off them. And she thinks it again when her eye is caught by a man in a blueish room, until she realizes that he is rocking from side to side and a rocking chair would only serve to make him look even crazier than he already is.

And why do old people have to end this way anyhow – does life really have to be so unfair? Is this the best she can expect – a small room off a long corridor, the smell of medicated talcum powder on plastic sheets? But she is nervous

– she knows that – her mind rushing ahead of her, as it tends to do when she gets this way, as if bits of it are breaking away and bouncing off the walls. At the same time there is the whispering voice – what if Mrs Sultz refuses the visit, what if Mrs Sultz barely endures it, oh, what-if, what-if, what-if?

The receptionist hands her over to a nurse.

The nurse, she senses, senses her fear, and they are like two dogs, sensing each other along the corridor. 'You came by…?'

'Yes, yes, bus.'

'And a pleasant…?'

'Yes, most pleasant. Indeed.'

'But you're not from…?'

'That's right, New York but every summer…'

'Well, isn't that…?'

'Well, yes, it certainly is.'

The corridor is long and bright – rooms on one side, windows on the other, and all the rooms have their doors wide open, and through each open door, a window ledge, and on each ledge, a vase of flowers, quite possibly fresh, positioned – she can't help but notice – as much for the passer-by as the patient tucked in behind the door of his or her room. Pinkish for a girl, blueish for a boy.

She is passed on again to another nurse, short, fair-haired, young – so young, it's as if someone has bought her a nurse's outfit and she is playing make-believe. The nurse says, 'I think she's in the recreation room – would you like to come this way?'

And here they go again:

'And your journey was…?

'Yes, yes, by bus.'

'And then?'

'A cab.'

'Of course, a cab, was it Mr Walls?'

'I think so and, yes, I know I should have let him wait.'

Nobody recreating in the recreation room. Tables and chairs, a television set built into a cabinet with a spray of plastic daisies on top of it. A radio. A record player. Soft chairs and unopened board games. Shelves of books so clean they could be in a bookshop.

'Oh, she's not here!' the nurse says – and again, as if in a children's game – 'Oh, now, where could she be, I wonder? Hmmm, now let me see. She's not in her room, and she's not in the garden, and she is certainly not in the recreation room. Oh, wait now, I think I may know… Come, come – follow me.'

They are calling Mrs Sultz Enid in the sanatorium. Enid and honeybun and sweetpea. When they find her eventually, she is in the garden room, sitting by an open French window. The nurse walks ahead and announces her like she's just stepped off a cloud from heaven.

'Enid – look who's come all this way just to see *you*! Did you ever in all your days imagine such a *wonderful* surprise!'

Mrs Sultz laughs when she sees her, laughs and lifts both her hands and then reaches out with them to take one of her hands, which she cradles for a moment against her face and then kisses it twice and rubs it twice and says, 'Oh, how lovely, *lovely* to see you again.'

And she can barely hold the tears back as she says, 'I can't tell you how relieved I am. I was so afraid you wouldn't want to know me, after all this time, and I was simply awful to you, my dear friend. Please do forgive me – this tongue of mine, well, you know how I am.'

The little nurse draws a chair over so she can sit beside Mrs Sultz.

'Why don't I leave you girls to catch up with all the gossip? And I'll come back in a little while with a nice jug of lemonade. Enid just loves her afternoon lemonade – don't you, honeybun?'

Mrs Sultz, smiling so sweetly at her, cocks her head to the side, ready to listen. And so, she lets it all out, starting off with the cold she had a fortnight ago. 'And I meant to write you and say that I would come, no, to ask you, really, if you wouldn't mind my coming and, well, it was more than a cold, that colitis again, the pain's unbearable. Of course, I don't have to tell you, we had been fighting again. I try, I really do try but…'

Mrs Sultz bites her lip in sympathy and nods her head. And it is such a comfort to have their friendship restored. But she will not be selfish and try to make the entire visit about her particular woes.

'You do seem very comfortable here, I must say. And this room! All the plants and ferns and surrounded by all this glass – it's like we're sitting in a bowl of green light, it really is very—'

But then she begins crying again. 'Oh, I don't know what to do. I've been so, so unhappy. When I am ill, he is such a tender nurse. He never complains and I know he is not at all well himself since his surgery last February. He hasn't, you know— recovered in any way, in a way that a wife would want, you know?' she adds, lowering her voice.

Mrs Sultz says, 'Oh dear.'

'And so you see, there is no affection. Whatsoever. It's like if he can't have, you know, the full thing then he simply can't be bothered with any little thing at all. He barely speaks to me, is the truth. Unless we are arguing. Then he speaks plenty all right.'

She stops for a moment to blow her nose, Mrs Sultz looking softly upon her.

'I'm sorry. I really am. But it is just so hurtful to think of it – all the times I've gone rending him limb from limb because I am left out and have been left out for all these years. And you know I am *still* disregarded. By him, his peers, anyone we run into. Dismissed, swatted away. Shot down. I can no longer find any comfort in work. No. Not even that. And he doesn't seem to be able to work either, he has produced almost nothing, and to top all that I think— I think he may be in love with someone else.'

She puts her hands to her face, shocked to hear herself say it aloud.

'I have no idea who it could be. There are all these women around – I mean, let's face it, there are always women around a famous man – but he usually doesn't appear to notice. But I don't know. This time? I might as well say it now, I think it could be a woman named Olivia – that sound like a name to you? She's just the sort that might crop up in one of his paintings. Tall, buxom, dark-red hair… full of sass. Very Bette Davis, and you know how he feels about *her*. But harping all the way back to that woman in Paris I told you about. That cradle-snatching, Madam Cheruy, or whatever she called herself. Seducing young men with her gifts of poetry books and, and— Oh, I don't know what I'm saying,

I am so sorry, it's selfish of me, supposed to be visiting you and yet here I am all about myself. It's just sometimes, well, I feel— I feel like I've wasted most of my life, that's all. *Wasted* it.'

Behind her a delicate tinkling noise. The nurse has returned, holding a big jug on a tray, lemon slices and ice cubes shuddering inside it. She pulls her handkerchief out of her pocket and tries to do a hurried tidy-up on her face. The nurse lays the tray down on a cane table, pours a glass out and hands it to her.

'And what about you, sweetpea?' she says to Mrs Sultz. 'I bet you would like some lemonade?'

Mrs Sultz reaches out with both hands, takes one of the nurse's hands, draws it to her face, kisses it twice, rubs it twice and says, 'Oh, how lovely, *lovely* to see you again.'

2

KATHERINE CUTS HIM A piece from her pill. She is standing by the shelf over his bed and he watches while she catches a piece of her hair behind her ear, then closes one eye, leans in with the blade and says, 'Gotcha.'

She licks the top of her finger and presses it down on the tiny piece of the pill. She brings her finger down to him and places it into his mouth. 'This will make you feel better,' she says. 'This will take away all the pain.'

The shock when she does that. It comes down into his belly and then floats back up to his chest, his throat, his face – his ears even.

She sits down on the side of the bed and places her hand on his forehead. She says, 'You seem a little warm.'

She takes a hanky out of her bathrobe pocket and holds it up to his nose. 'Blow,' she says, 'don't be shy, that's it, give it a good hard one.'

He can feel her fingers through the hanky, the spurt of his snots against them.

'No more tears – huh?'

Behind the hanky, he nods to agree and she smiles and says, 'Thata boy.'

He almost tells Katherine the real reason for the tears but he is afraid the words he needs to explain it will make him sound nuts. He was crying anyhow, and maybe she was walking past the room or maybe she just decided to look in on him, but there she was suddenly, sitting on the side of his bed, her fingers stroking through his hair, and asking him all those questions: 'Can't you sleep, Michael? Has your leg started hurting again? Or maybe it's the storm, Michael – does it scare you? Have you been awake all this time, Michael, just lying here?'

The way she kept saying his name, and her voice sounding so slow and hurt. He could only nod at everything. Yes, my leg feels bad. Yes, I'm scared of the storm. Yes, I've been lying awake for hours and hours.

But he had been asleep for hours and hours. Until the rain woke him, anyhow. The rain and the wind that scooped it up and whacked it off the walls of the house. He had heard it sloshing around on the floor of the verandah and slurping from the eaves and the railing outside. And the awful sound of the house rattling every time the wind grabbed hold of it and started shaking it like it wanted to break every bone in its body. There was so much noise going on that he could barely even hear the sea. He could imagine it, though, going crazy out there, tossing and bucking and lifting its elbow again and again to fight off the wind, growling back at it. But he hadn't been in the least scared. He had liked the feeling of lying all cosy in bed while, outside, the storm and the sea fought it out between them.

Richie hadn't looked too scared either. When he turned his head to look across the room, there he was, lying on top of the covers in the long plank of light coming in through the open door. His arms straight down by his side, his mouth open wide like he was a dead person lying in a coffin. He watched Richie for a while and then, just when he turned his head back to his own side of the room, he saw the man looking in at him.

He had almost shouted out, Quick, quick, there's a man looking in the window! But as he pulled himself up into a sitting position, he saw the man wasn't looking in the window – he was looking out of the mirror. And he knew who it was then, the thin white face and black eyes, the familiar hole of his toothless mouth.

He remembered his knee then, the fall down the wooden steps the day before yesterday and how Mr Aitch had brought him home and carried him up all the stairs. And he remembered all the things that had happened the day after the fall, a day that had started out so blue and so beautiful, and Richie's mom saying he had to come for a walk to stop his knee getting stiff and not being at all pleased about that until the green Buick came along the road and he was so happy when he saw it. And then later going to wave Mrs Aitch off at the bus stop and the way Mr Aitch had listened to him when he came back to the Buick, delivering the message over the back seat about the woman in the green dress, and Mr Aitch buying ice-cream for him and Richie and telling them about the Pamet Indians as they drove home.

And then, coming back to the house just as the rain was starting to splat again and Mrs Kaplan saying he looked tired and that he ought to take a nap before supper but instead he had sat in the living-room with his leg up on a footstool while Katherine showed him her picture album. And that had been so nice, sitting there with Katherine showing him all the different times of her life and pointing to all the different faces she had since she was a baby and giving him the little story that belonged with each picture. He could have stayed there forever – if he hadn't suddenly passed out right in the middle of her telling him about a boat she fell out of one summer in Eastham.

The last thing he could remember was flopping around like a big fish out of water while Rosetta and Mrs Kaplan got him into his pyjamas. He knows now that he must have been fast asleep by the time Richie came to bed, which was how come he didn't do what he usually does – wait for Richie to fall asleep then get out of bed and turn the mirror to face the other way so the man could look at Richie instead of at him.

And it had been too late to do anything about it by then: the gummy man was already looking out at him and he was far too scared anyhow to get out of bed. And that had been the most upsetting part about it – the idea of the gummy man following him all the way from New York to here. And knowing, suddenly, that the man was always going to follow him, no matter how far he travelled and how long he lived. As long as there was a mirror nearby, the man would be able to find him. And that was the real reason he had been crying like a little girl, not because his leg had started hurting again or because he was scared of some dumb storm.

Katherine gets up and takes another pill from the box and pops it into her own mouth. She closes the box, then lifts the leftover half from his pill and takes that too, licking it off her finger.

'Was my sailing story really so boring,' she says, 'that it put you right off to sleep?'

'Oh no! I was listening but then— Well, I don't know what happened.'

Katherine laughs and sits back down on the side of his bed.

'You were exhausted.'

'I liked looking at the photographs you showed me when I came back from seeing Mrs Aitch to the bus. I liked that a lot.'

'Oh, that's nice,' Katherine says.

'Do you miss your house in Eastham?' he asks.

'Oh, it wasn't my house. And it wasn't much of a house either. A girl I worked with rented it every summer and a bunch of us would come down for weekends and take our vacation there. She got married and moved away.'

'Louisa?'

'That's right, Louisa. She married—'

'Jim. The man with the curly hair – right?'

'You *were* paying attention.'

'And you were a blonde then.'

'So I was.'

'Why did you stop being a blonde?'

'Oh, I don't know, it seemed like a good idea then. It just seems like a lot of trouble now. At least that's what I always say to people when they ask, but the truth is, after I got sick, well, I didn't really feel it was me any more...'

'Richie said you were a nurse. But I didn't see any pictures of you as a nurse.'

'Well, that's because you were asleep before we got to those,' she says and taps him on the nose with her finger. 'Are you feeling any better now?' she asks and he nods and puts his head back down on the pillow.

His arms and legs begin to feel light and he thinks about the time he was on a row boat with Harry on the lake in Central Park and lying back while Harry rowed and a feeling coming over him just like this one, like floating on water but without getting wet.

'Do you miss New York, Michael?'

'I miss Harry,' he hears himself say.

'You do? Hasn't he written?'

'He doesn't like writing. I had one letter so far but that was from my aunt – he just signed his name.'

'Well, why don't you write him?'

'I wouldn't know what to say.'

'Sure you would. You could tell him about what it's like here. About Rosetta and Richie and the beach and the dog and— I don't know. Tell him that you're getting a suntan and that your hair is turning blond and that one of these days you're going to be a knock-out.'

'A knock-out?'

'Yes, a knock-out.'

'Like in a fight or something? I don't know what you mean.'

'Don't worry, you'll soon find out.'

'Mr and Mrs Aitch – I could tell him about them.'

'You could. He may have even heard of him, of course. He's pretty famous, you know.'

'I used to be a little scared of him. But not any more.'

'I'm a little scared of him myself. He's a very impressive man. Good-looking too. You can tell him I said that. On second thoughts, don't – his wife wouldn't like it.'

'Why not?'

She reaches into her pocket and takes out a pack of cigarettes and a lighter.

'I'm just kidding you, Michael. Don't you know when someone is kidding you?'

'I don't know, sometimes, I guess.'

She puts the cigarette in her mouth and holds the lighter up to it; a flame stretches out and nips the top of the cigarette.

'Don't tell Richie's mom I was smoking in here.'

'Why not? She's always smoking.'

'Yeah, but not in the bedroom. Doctor Tom told her never in Richie's bedroom. And we must do whatever Doctor Tom says now – isn't that so, Michael?'

'I don't know…'

'Oh, and Michael, I don't think you should address the letter to Harry alone – you better include, you know, Mrs Harry, whatever her name is.'

'Frau Aunt?'

'Is that what you call her? Well, you better address the letter to her too. You

143

could hurt her feelings if you didn't do that. Wives are like that, you know – they don't like to be left out of things.'

'I don't know… a whole letter?'

'You can do it. Start tomorrow, write a little more on Tuesday, finish it Wednesday or Thursday and then on Friday I'll take you to the post office and we can mail it.'

'You mean it?'

'Sure. I mean it. Tell you what, I promise you this, every time you write a letter, I'll take you to the post office – is that a deal? I go maybe three, four times a week on the way to get my shot in Eastham. I could take you there with me. Starting to get a little sleepy now?'

He nods and nudges his head further into the pillow, a warm, light feeling up the back of his head like someone is tickling him.

'Katherine?' he says.

'Hmmm?'

'I like Mrs Aitch a lot.'

'Why's that?'

'She's— I don't know, I just like her a lot.'

'That makes you and my mother, both.'

'Katherine?'

'Yes, Michael?'

'Katherine?'

'Uh-huh?'

'Nothin', I guess. I mean, I don't know.'

She sits with him for a while and the storm quietens down; there's only the rain falling at its own steady pace, and the sound of the sea starts coming back in, like it is breathing big, slow sighs of relief. She smiles at him and he smiles back at her. She smiles at the wall and she smiles over at Richie. She leans back and sends a long spurt of cigarette smoke up at the ceiling; she taps the ash into the bowl of her hand and then she just melts away.

~

AND NOW THREE NIGHTS later he goes looking for Katherine. He wants to ask her to put him asleep like she did the night of the storm because, even though he turned the mirror right in to the wall, he still can't stop thinking about what and who is inside it. He wants to tell her, too, that he finished writing the letter to Harry and to remind her that she promised to take him to the post office with her tomorrow.

He pokes his head round the door of his room and sees, down the hallway, a stroke of light under one of the doors – her door. He makes his way down there, lightly knocks and waits a few seconds before knocking again, this time a little harder. He fences his mouth off with the sides of his fingers and pushes her name through the lock. He tries squinting through the lock, but the butt end of the key on the other side is blocking the view. He waits another few seconds and tries knocking again.

He thinks about going in there, walking right up to the bed and gently shaking her shoulder. He tries to imagine the picture that would make: her sleeping head turned sideways and the light of the bedside lamp on it and on her hair spread out all over the pillow behind it. Her long hand on the white sheet and the gold ring on her middle finger with two pearls stuck on it like two tiny eggs in a nest. On the bedstand: the book he saw her reading on the back porch yesterday, green cover with gold letters, or maybe one of those magazines from New York that she picks up in the post office and pulls out of a cardboard tube. The round box of pills would be on top of the bedstand too and probably a glass of water, just like the glass of water Mrs Kaplan leaves on the shelf beside his bed every night, a little white cloth draped over it to keep out the bugs.

Katherine, wake up, he would say, Katherine, oh, Katherine, wake up.

He was only ever inside her room once. That was the time Rosetta called out to him as he was passing one morning to ask him to go downstairs and turn off the stove. He offered to help Rosetta make the bed, just to stay a little longer in Katherine's room, maybe get a better look at her things. But Rosetta had said, 'No, you go, go, go, or ebrythin, it is ruined.'

Between stepping in and stepping back out of the room, there had only been seconds. But he had managed to take in a few things even so, repeating each name to himself as he went down the stairs and then pressing it down in his mind to make it stick. White bureau. Dark-pink silky coverlet. Lamp on the bedstand. Silver-framed photograph of a soldier. Cane chair with black cushion, white fluffy slippers underneath. Blue striped mat by the bed. A smell of flowers and honey and tobacco all over.

And another time, when he was on the way to bed, the door was open a little way and he could see, in the lamplight, Katherine sitting on the end of the bed facing an open window. He could see the trees outside turned black by the night and he could hear the field of long grass shuffling in the breeze. She had been doing something with her nails, her elbow moving in a way that reminded him of Mr Morgan when he was practising the cello before he moved all the way out to Brooklyn. Pink slip. White bedpost. Radio on small, round table, tall glass beside it with gold-coloured drink inside it.

Her room doesn't face the sea – he realized that night – she sleeps on the other side of the house, over the front porch and a little to the right. She is the only one to have a room on that side of the house – even Rosetta, in the basement, sleeps facing the sea. He had imagined what she would see when she stepped out on her verandah: the curved path that goes down to the parking space and the small sandy lane beyond that leading out to the hard blacktop road. The three big red trees on her right side and the two stubby trees to her left, and heading towards the sea on the bay side, the sloped meadow of long bleached grass. While in the other direction, away from the sea, the distant green and yellow hill with the one lonesome tree poking out of it.

Sometimes when she goes for her afternoon nap he goes round to the front of the house and throws the ball for the dog in the long grass. Or, if he can't get the dog without getting Richie too, he lies hidden in the grass and keeps guard. From there, he can see the approach to the house and the front porch, and he can see the little path that bends round to the far side of the house leading to the back porch that looks over the bay. He reads one of the books Mrs Kaplan put in his room. He reads about a boy called Jody and his red pony or he reads about Tom Sawyer, and every time he gets to the end of a page he looks up and knows that Katherine is up there, sleeping safely behind closed shutters.

The day after she gave him the pill, he found her reading the green book on the porch again. He wanted to ask her about the book – what it was called and what it was about. But he felt too shy to speak to her. He stood behind her for a while, hoping she would notice him and at the same time hoping she would not. She kept on reading anyhow, the brim of her hat shielding the words from his view.

And now here he is in the middle of the night, standing right outside her bedroom door, the letter he has written to Harry and Frau Aunt in his side pyjama pocket. He stays at her door, listening to the sleeping house and looking sideways now and then, up and down the hallway. If he goes in, he will need to be sure of his courage – it is not something to change his mind about halfway across the floor. He either does it or he doesn't do it. The last thing he wants is her waking up and catching him standing in the middle of the room. *He* has to be the one to wake *her*. That way, she won't think he's up to anything sneaky, like trying to spy on her or even steal something.

So he will open the door, step in and start moving and he will keep on moving until he is across the floor and standing right beside her. If she is wearing pyjamas – the sort of pyjamas Frau Aunt wears – then he will put his hand on her shoulder and give it a shake. If her arms are bare, and she is wearing the sort of nightgown Richie's mom wears, then he will probably be too scared to touch her. He will just say her name. Over and over, he will say it, for however long it takes her to wake. Even if he has to stand there until he hears Mrs Kaplan come whistling up the stairs with her breakfast tray, leaving him with just a few short seconds to get out of there and back to his own room.

He twists the doorknob in both hands, sucks in a breath and edges the door open a crack and then a bigger crack and now he can see all the way into the room. The overhead light is on but it takes him a moment to understand just what he is looking at. The room is a mess. There are clothes flung all over the floor and the top of the bureau looks as if someone has run a baseball bat through everything and knocked it all down. For a second he thinks that one of the heaps on the floor by the bed could be Katherine, that a burglar came in and hit her over the head before he started tearing the room apart. But then he sees, on the bed, her open jewellery case with all her jewellery leaking out of it, so he guesses it wasn't a burglar after all. Katherine is not here. She is not on the floor and she is not in the bed. Her pillow, blank and smooth, is about the only tidy spot in the room.

He stays with his hand on the doorknob, holding the door wide open, but he doesn't step in. There is something too shocking about being alone in her room under full lights surrounded by all of her personal things turned inside out.

The drawer of the bedstand is hanging open, pill boxes and bottles showing inside it. On the floor, a spread of letters and a dirty ashtray. A dark-blue sparkly gown is sprawled over the small table. One silver sandal on the cane chair. Bottle of liquor peeping out from the bottom of the closet. Carton of cigarettes. Underwear dropped on the bedside mat alongside the green dress she was wearing at dinner. Second silver sandal dangling by its heel off the end of the bedpost. He looks back at the clothes on the floor and notices a large bright-red bloodstain on the underwear. The stain startles him; it makes him worry that Katherine may be injured. But then bits from a half-remembered conversation come back to him: three older boys in a dark room whispering in German about the secret blood of women. He closes the door and moves on down the hallway.

Across whining floorboards and squealing stairs, he moves through the house. He switches on a light and the kitchen jumps out at him; he switches it off and the kitchen ducks down again. He feels his way along the kitchen wall, by the sink and the drainer, the icebox and the vegetable baskets, until he comes to the gap in the wall and the few narrow steps leading down to Rosetta's room in the basement.

He thinks that Katherine could be in there talking to Rosetta, as she had been one night last week when she had only been inches away from catching him with his hand in the icebox. But there is no light under Rosetta's door, and when he pins his ear against it, there is only the gentle sound of her on-and-off snore.

Back in the lobby, he looks through the glass at the side of the front door. Then he comes into the dining-room, turns left down the three wide steps into the L-shaped living-room. He walks up to the glass wall that looks out on the back porch facing the bay. The porch light is off, but the full moon is on. He can see Katherine's ashtray and Katherine's empty easy chair. And there's the tartan shawl she sometimes pulls round her shoulders and the slippers she almost never wears turned toe-to-toe on the floor.

He can see up the hill and, between the trees, a patch of the sea; the pale, greasy light the moon has spread over it. Behind him the room is reflected through the glass: the two low-backed sofas and the long cabinet with all the ornaments and books on top of it and the doors underneath it with handles shaped like seahorses.

He turns back to the room, switches on two side lamps and begins walking along between the sofas and the cabinets. He watches his reflection glide over the glass and thinks it looks like a ghost floating over a city. He does that a couple times more and when he tires of it begins opening the doors and drawers of the cabinets. There are all shapes of drinking glasses and bottles of liquor in there, linen napkins and small stacks of glass dishes. And there's a big ridged bottle like the one Richie's mom uses to shoot seltzer out of whenever she's making cocktails. There's a plastic container filled with small things in small bags. He slides it out and puts it on top of the cabinet, then he dips his hand in and turns it for a moment, the bags softly rustling and shifting around. He takes a packet of cocktail sticks out and puts it into his top pyjama pocket. Then he lifts a bag of peanuts and puts it into the side pocket of his pyjama bottom, next to the letter to Harry. He returns the container to the cabinet and, spotting a bag of pretzels at the back, slides it out and pushes it down the front of his pyjama bottoms, tightening the drawstring to keep it in place.

Before he leaves the living-room, he searches for Katherine's picture album. He finds it eventually on the floor beside one of the easy chairs. He puts the album under his arm, comes back through the dining-room and then into the lobby, where he switches on the lamp beside the telephone table.

He opens the album and begins flipping the pages, looking for pictures of Katherine as a nurse. The page falls open on a photograph he has already seen of two men in air force uniforms.

'Who's that?' he had asked her, pointing to the more handsome of the two and feeling a sudden cut of jealousy when she said, 'Oh, that's just someone I was going to marry.'

149

'What happened to him – did he die in the war?'

'Oh no, nothing like that, I just decided not to get married after all.'

'Why'd you keep his picture then?'

'Because the other man, the one next to him, is my brother Bill. Richie's dad.' She began stroking the face in the photograph with the flat of her finger. 'Poor darling Bill,' she said.

He turns another couple of pages and then finds the pictures of Katherine and the nurses. They are sitting on a rug on a lawn. And then they are sitting on a low wall outside a hospital. They are standing beside an army jeep and then they are standing in the snow with collection boxes in their hands. In each of the pictures there are at least four nurses. And in one picture, taken on the steps of a big grey building, there are three rows of them, all dressed the same, but he can still pick her out of each group, smiling at the camera with her hair bound up by a nurse's hat.

He flips back and forward through the album until he finds the photographs taken outside the house in Eastham. Katherine and her friends Louisa and Jim. Katherine looks so pretty in one of them. She is more than smiling, her shoulders bent over as if she's laughing so hard she could be knocked off her feet. She is wearing a summer dress that shows off her legs and her arms. Her hair is blonde and sleek and fat and sits like a white cat over one shoulder. They are standing at the front of the house by the gate – Katherine leaning over it, Louisa just behind with her arm linked through curly headed Jim's.

He wonders who was on the far side of the camera – was it Bill or maybe the man she decided not to marry after all, with his movie-star smile, calling out to them while he took the picture and saying something so funny that they all nearly died from laughing.

He worms his finger in behind the flimsy cover that keeps the picture in place, then he breaks the piece of tape that holds it onto the black page. He teases the picture away and, turning it, sees written on the back 'Eastham, August 1944' – two years before he came to America. He begins to shove the picture up his sleeve but then changes his mind – he doesn't want to crease or mark it in any way. He opens the telephone directory out and carefully lays it down on a page of M stands for Michael, where he can easily find it tomorrow. Then he closes the directory over and turns off the lamp.

He sits behind the door with his back to the wall. Here, he can see all the routes back to the stairs. If she comes in by the front door, he will see her. If she has the key to the back porch and comes by the living-room, he will see her too. Even if she comes in through the basement door, he will still see her as she passes from the kitchen to the passageway at the side of the stairs. The only way she will get past him is if she gets on a ladder and climbs up to her verandah. But he knows that's not going to happen.

Thin light from the moon on the floor of the hall. The shadow of the leaves from the trees wriggling on the wall. He thinks about the bedstand upstairs in Katherine's room, the open drawer hanging out of it with the little bottles and boxes of pills inside. He will count up to sixty. He will do that ten times. If Katherine hasn't come back by then, he will go up to her room and take one of the pills for himself. He will take the pill out and bite a piece off it. Then he will lie in his bed and wait for his body to start feeling light. Lighter and lighter until it almost disappears. When that happens there will be nothing to be scared of because there will be nothing to see and no one to hurt him. The room will disappear and the mirror will disappear along with the gummy man sitting inside it. There will be nothing left in the whole wide world. There will only be himself drifting along like a leaf on dark water.

THE FIRST TIME HE saw the gummy man in the mirror it was not long after he had come to live with Frau Aunt and Harry. He was on his way to the bathroom one night and had to pass the long mirror in the hallway. Frau Aunt and Harry weren't even in bed yet. He could hear them talking in the kitchen and the baseball man mumbling on the radio. He had screamed like a monkey when he saw the man in there. Then he ran into his room and hid under his bed bawling and shivering until Harry's strong arms pulled him out again.

The mirror was moved into Frau Aunt and Harry's bedroom. But that didn't mean that the man had gone away. He just started to appear in his dreams instead.

The dream sometimes changed. But one thing stayed clear – the man always crawled out of the hill and always ended sitting there staring at him.

The hill in his dream was more like a scrapheap, full of sharp angles and bits of things. In the dream he was looking at the hill through a window – the window of an automobile or it could be in a house too. There was nothing else on the road – a country road made out of fields and a couple of trees and a grey sky and, of course, the hill – and he was looking out the window when a man on a bicycle came along. As the man came closer to the hill, a voice started to call out. The man stopped and looked all around, trying to find the voice. Then he looked at the hill.

Hilf mir, Hilfe! Ich lebe, Ich lebe! was what the voice said.

From his window across the way, he listened to the voice and wondered why anyone would call out such a thing – Help me, help! I'm alive, I'm alive!

The man on the bicycle looked across the road to the window where he sat and shrugged as if to say – did you hear that? Do you have any idea what that could be about? And he shrugged in return. I heard that. And no, I have no idea.

The man laid his bicycle on the ground and went to the hill. After a couple of seconds he started digging with his hands. As soon as he started to do this, it became clear that the hill was made of dead people. Arms and legs slipping out of the heap. The man pulled his scarf up over his mouth and continued to dig. Then he started to pray out loud and now *he* was the one asking for help. My God, my God, help me. Help me. *Mein Gott. Hilf mir, Hilfe.*

After a while a gap appeared in the hill and two arms came through. These arms were alive. The man stopped his digging. He held onto the arms and began pulling. He pulled until the face of a man appeared. He helped the man to crawl out of the hill. When the man was out, the hill shifted a little as all the dead arms and legs and heads fell back into place. The man who came out of the hill was not like a man, he was more like a skeleton. A skeleton with the skin still on. The other man seemed like a giant beside him as he helped him to walk over to the side of the road and sit down on the kerb. The man went back to his bicycle, took a package and a bottle out of the saddle bag and brought them over to the skeleton. But the skeleton couldn't seem to take them. The man opened the package to show the skeleton – look, sandwiches. Then he pulled the cork out of the bottle. He took the scarf away from his face and mimed what to do with the sandwiches and the bottle. Eat – eat like this. Drink – drink like this. As if the skeleton had forgotten how to do these things. After a moment, the man gave up and, laying the sandwiches and the bottle on the ground, hurried back to his bicycle. The bicycle wobbled all over the road then, as if, for a few moments, the man couldn't remember how to ride a bike. The skeleton on the kerb started to cry. As well as tears, long spits were coming out of his mouth and snots out of his nose. As if he was crying with his whole face. He wiped his face with hands that were too big for his body. Then he lifted his face and looked across the road, straight in through the window.

After a couple of years, the mirror was moved back into the hall. He never told Harry, but he still saw the man in there, no older than he had been first time round, no fatter and no cleaner either. Still the same filthy face and torn clothes and dark eyes. Still the same black hole in his gummy mouth. But at least he stayed in the mirror and stopped coming into his dreams.

~

HE WAKES TO FINDS Katherine leaning over him in the lobby. He sees her bare feet first, then her ankles and, just above them, the hem of a huge coat she is wearing.

'What are you doing, Michael,' she says, 'lying there sleeping on the floor?'

'I was waiting for you,' he says and tries to get up.

She pushes the sleeves of the coat up her arms, reaches out and he grabs on. When she pulls him up, they both begin to sway.

'Dah, dah,' she sings, 'dah-dah,' and pushes his hand in and out, like they're doing the jive.

'Your coat's too big for you,' he says.

She stops singing and looks down at herself.

'Oh, this? Not mine. This is Bill's old air force coat, keeps me warm when I go out at night.'

'Where do you go?'

'Oh, you know, just out. To look at the stars. Howl at the moon.' She laughs and then says, 'I'm just kidding, Michael, I don't really *howl*. Come on, better get you upstairs. Were you sleepwalking?'

'No, I told you, I was waiting for you. I wanted to give you something. And I wanted to ask if I could have another piece of your pill.'

'What for?'

'To help me go to sleep.'

'You didn't look as if you needed much help to me, lying there on the floor. You know how long it took me to wake you?'

'But what about when I get back to bed – what if I can't sleep?'

'Then you can't sleep.'

She begins leading him towards the stairs and then stops. 'That was a once-off. To stop the pain, Michael, and because you were so upset. Don't you tell anyone either. You promise me?'

'I promise.'

'What did you want to give me?'

'A letter—'

'Oh, I hate letters. I don't want it. I hate letters, I hate telegrams, I hate any sort of message.'

'Oh no, it's not *for* you.'

She sways again and says, 'This coat is so heavy. I can't bear it.'

He waits while she frees herself from the coat. She lays it over her arms and then holds it out.

'Catch!' she says, dropping the coat into his arms. His legs stagger under the weight of it. 'What did I tell you? Heavy, huh? Give it back now, come on, give it here, *here*.'

Katherine is standing without the coat in a long nightgown with no sleeves in it, her arms so thin when she reaches out to take the coat back. He can see the outline of her legs through the nightie and her body beneath it, from her chest all down her stomach as far as the tops of her legs, everything darker as if it's been coloured in. She takes the coat back and kneels down on the floor.

'It belonged to my brother. Bill. This was his coat.'

'Yes, I know.'

'You do?'

'You just told me.'

She pushes the coat off her lap and leaves it on the floor. Then she puts her arms around him and squeezes him tight. He smells liquor on her breath and the sea on her wet hair. Her nightgown feels damp, and he knows then that she has been swimming and that the dark colour under the nightgown is her bathing costume.

'Michael?' she says and he feels the words creep out of her mouth and onto his face. 'Can I tell you a secret? Can I trust you with a secret?'

He swallows and says, 'I won't tell anyone. Swear, I won't.'

She draws back a little, frowns and then in a different voice says, 'Hey, what's that you got there?'

'Where?'

'There, right there.'

She lifts his pyjama top, tugs the bag of pretzels out from the waistband of his pyjamas.

'Pretzels! What else you got hidden in there, you sly little kangaroo, tucked away in your pouch?'

'Nothing, I swear.'

'Oh yeah?'

She begins to pat him all over. She takes out the peanuts; from his top pocket, she pulls out the cocktail sticks.

'Have you been *stealing*, Michael?' she says. 'Have you been—?'

'No! No…'

She bursts out laughing. Then she starts to tickle him, plucking at his stomach and poking under his arm and frisking him under his chin. 'Have you? Have you been stealing? Do I need to call the cops?'

She stops after a moment and says, 'What's the matter – don't you have any tickles?'

He stands shamed before her; his heart hurts. He pinches the inside of his arm to stop himself from crying.

'Oh, come on, Michael, who cares? No need to be upset. It doesn't matter. Here, take it all back.'

'I don't want it now.'

'Sure you do. Here, come on. You can take whatever you want – most of it gets thrown out anyway. Here, come on, take it. Take. Honestly, as if anyone even cares. In this house of plenty.'

'I don't want them!' he yells and pushes her away. 'I don't want anything from you, just leave me alone!'

She wavers a little, almost losing her balance, then she steadies herself, blinks a couple of times and, pulling the coat with her, carefully stands. She turns away, crosses the lobby, leaving him to watch the shape of her back grow dim as she climbs the stairs and gradually disappears into the dark and then all that remains is the clicking of the buttons on Bill's coat as she drags it along the floor of the hallway above.

3

SHE STANDS UP FROM the bench where she has been reading her book and looks northwards. There is a sense of something untoward nearby, a stillness. She turns and cocks an ear to the west then, closing the book between thumb and finger, walks across the bluff and looks down on the beach.

On the beach there is no one. Not as far as her eye can see. Not even the top of a head coming up along the curvature of the hill. There is only the relentless movement of beach grass and sandpipers. She stands for a while watching the long, slow waves bringing sea lettuce and weed to the shore. And now she begins to notice something else, another type of stillness. This time it comes from within. She has been noticing this feeling on and off for some time now – quite a few days, in fact – but, so far, has failed to put a name on it. If she had to locate it, it would be in the small pocket between the top of her rib cage and just below the bone of her breast. It is as if something has been added or maybe taken away. She is only ever aware of it at times like this – while watching the sea, or at night just before dropping off – such moments when her mind has quietened down.

She turns back to the house, tapping the book on her thigh as she goes to a tune in her head. She first heard this tune at the start of the summer – one of many that were carried along on the breeze from the Kaplan house. Now she hears it everywhere she goes: through the open doors of parked automobiles; through the kitchen windows of holiday rentals; blasting out from juke boxes in diners and drug stores. Small seasonal orchestras are playing it in clubs and hotels in Provincetown – a version that is a little tame for her liking but none-theless pleases her. A tune that even her husband approves of, which may be down to the fact that there are no words to it. Or maybe it's that little spike of danger that he admires. The tune is attached to a movie – they have seen the trailer and have heard people rave about it. She knows when they get back to New York the first thing he will want to do is go to the theatre to see it.

They will sit in the dark and look up at silhouettes skulking around a snowy Vienna while the music twangs all around them. But she will always associate the tune with the light of Cape Cod at the turn of another decade, the half-mark of a century, in this, the summer of her sixty-seventh year.

Coming back towards the house, she glances around in search of a stray shadow. But there is nothing to disturb the clean-cut lines of darkness and light: the print of the house on the crowberry patches; the ink flicks of the grass thrown against the white clapboard; the black stamp of a bedsheet cast from the washline onto the bushes. Not a wisp out of place. Perhaps it was, after all, just a cat.

She puts one foot on the step to go back indoors, then changes her mind and takes it off again. And now she begins to make her way round to the far side of the house, turning at the north-west corner. As she comes to the big studio window, she ducks and edges along beneath it. Then cautiously stepping around the slope of the bulkhead, she tucks herself into the small space beyond. She waits a few seconds before taking a peek round the edge of the house. A shadow on the top turn of the wooden steps slithers out of sight around the opposite corner. She pulls back. She waits for a moment before retracing her steps and coming back to the north-west corner, where she flattens her back to the wall. A needle of shadow moves into sight, inching across the ground like a big black hand on a clock. It stalls, then moves off again. The shadow begins to fatten out as it wings across the bluff. Then it starts to narrow again as it draws nearer to the house. Silently, she counts: one, two, three and—

'Four!' she yells, jumping out from her hiding place and pouncing, the book flapping down like a raptor on its prey.

Hands held like a helmet on top of a head. She slaps the book down on them, again and again. Then she beats it along the side of the body, which is now hunched to the ground and turned in to the wall of the house. She catches a knee, an elbow, the hands again.

'I caught you and I caught you good,' she yells. 'Now, what you have to say about that? You give in yet? You give in? Come on now, an answer is required, you better say something or else—'

But Michael can't say a thing; he is debilitated by laughter.

'Do you give in?' she demands and begins poking his ribs with her finger.

He snorts and squeals and tries to get up, but she beats him back down with the aid of the book and a few well-placed tickles.

'Do. You. Give. In? I'm asking you now and if you know what's good for you...'

'I give in,' he laughs, 'I give in.'

'Who is the victor?'

'You are.'

'One more time. Who is the—?'

'You are! You are!'

'Are you begging for mercy?'

'Yes, yes, I am. I am begging. *Begging!*'

'Thank heavens for that,' she says, sitting down on the ground beside him, 'because I've just about run out of gas.'

Michael straightens himself up and, with a few short laughs still coming through, waits for his breath to calm down. They stay in the shade of the house, sitting on the grass, backs to the wall.

'How did you *know* – how come you always just *know*?' Michael asks.

'Oh, I guess it's just another symptom of my all-round brilliance.'

'Well, I don't believe *that*!' he says.

'You don't? Well, how would you like another belt of this book then?'

'No! Just tell me.'

'If I do that then you will start to win and I'll be stuck making the tea.'

He smiles at her, then cranes at the book resting now on her lap. 'What book is it anyhow? Is it any good?'

'Oh, it's just some old French poetry book – you wouldn't much like it.'

'You bashed the cover in.'

She looks at the book. 'Oh yes, so I did,' she says and begins to get up, leaning her hand on his shoulder for support.

'It has to do with the shadows,' she says then, 'the reason I always win. You need to know how to read the shadows.'

'But how?'

'You live with my husband long enough and you know all about shadows. Someday maybe I'll show you.'

Michael opens his mouth to speak.

'I said some day – not now.'

Almost every day the boy comes to see her. It started after he took a tumble on their steps and now it is almost routine. She suspects he may come even when she is out. The days she went to Orleans with her husband looking for his sky, she found traces of him on her return – a sprinkling of sand on the doorstep and the mark on the window pane as if a hand had been pressed there while he peered in. And on some days he comes more than once. She will look out the window in early evening and see a quickening in the long grass or she will catch an incongruous shadow popping out from the side of the garage. But for some reason, the second time round he won't make himself known. He will hang around for a while and then disappear. As if he is on some sort of patrol and is checking to see that everything is just as it was when he left it earlier in the day.

The first time he came, he had Richie in tow.

He said, 'You told us to drop by any time we were passing.'

Richie said, 'I told him you didn't mean right away, ma'am, but he just wouldn't listen.'

Richie with his yes-siring and no-ma'aming and reminding them every few minutes how they weren't allowed to stay for too long and how they weren't supposed to go making a nuisance of themselves.

'He's such a silly old snoot that Richie boy,' she said to her husband after that first visit. 'I mean, some of the things he says! It's like listening to an old woman speak. Comes from spending too much time in adult company, if you ask me.'

'Oh, he's just trying to be good,' he said.

'There's being good and there's being a downright pain.'

160

'He comes from a background where children are taught to be obedient,' he said and then, sticking his head out from behind the newspaper, 'not something *your* mother would have bothered about too much.'

Richie came along two or three times after that. Then Michael started to come alone. The first time he did this, he stood on the steps waiting to be invited in, his face so worried and tight that she decided to have a little fun with him.

She said, 'What you want, you little squirt? Get out of here before I set the dog on you. Go on, get.'

'But you don't have a dog,' he said.

'I have my husband, don't I? He sure knows how to bark.'

When she said that Michael's eyes widened out, then he gave her one of his grins.

He was covered in sand. She held the door open while he toed it from his sneakers and brushed it off his legs and hands.

'What you do – crawl here?' she asked and he laughed outright and then barged by her into the house.

He is more at ease when he comes across her out of doors, as if they happened to run into each other and it is all her idea to invite him inside. And so, she tries to arrange it that way. She sits outside in the morning, and if he doesn't appear, she will sit out again in the afternoon. If she sees him through a window, she will wander out and busy herself until she happens to look up and see him there. If – and only *if* – her husband is not around the place, they will try to sneak up on one another. Loser – and so far this has always been Michael – gets to make the tea.

When he comes into the house, he stands feet square and shoulders slightly hunched until, bit by bit, everything about him loosens out and he forgets to keep looking over his shoulder. Then he will probably just blurt something out like: 'They said I should call you ma'am.'

'Whoever said such a ridiculous thing?'

'Richie's mom. Every time I address you, I'm supposed to call—'

'She said that? What did she say exactly?'

'"Now, Michael, we talked about this – a nice, well-brought-up boy will always address a lady as ma'am."'

161

And she laughs at his rendition of Olivia, the voice and expression of face.

'You can call me anything you like,' she says.

'Mrs Aitch is what I like,' he says.

'I've been called worse in my time, let me tell you.'

'Like what?'

'Oh, let me see. Mrs Moose. I was called that for a while.'

'But why?'

'Well, you see, somebody in a magazine wrote that my husband, he looked like a moose, and I got so mad about that he took to calling me Mrs Moose. He thought he was funny. Even drew a picture of it. He with his moose head wearing a suit, me with my moose head with lipstick, wearing a skirt.'

'Can I see it? Oh, *please* can I see it?'

'I'd have to root it out. Tell you what, someday when he's gone out and we're sure he's going to be gone for a few hours, we can have a good rummage in the studio.'

If her husband is home when Michael calls, then he takes a little longer to thaw out. He will sit on the edge of the kitchen chair answering a few polite questions.

'How is that knee, Michael – been giving you any more trouble?'

'Fine, sir, thank you.'

'Richie not with you again today?'

'He's too busy.'

'But you asked him along?'

'Oh sure. Maybe next time, that's what he said.'

But after a while, Michael starts turning the tables and asking a few questions of his own: 'That story you told us about the Indians burying the corn in Corn Hill and the pilgrims digging it up – well, how come the corn didn't rot if it was left there all that time?'

Or: 'How many pictures you done your whole life so far? How many you done so far this summer?'

Or: 'Mind if I ask you a question, Mr Aitch – I mean, sir?'

'Go right ahead, Michael.'

'If that's the sea out there in the bay but if it's the ocean back four miles over

162

the other way on Ballston Beach, and if the Cape is a peninsula and if a peninsula is really just a three-sided island, then where does the sea start, where does
the ocean stop and how are you supposed to know which is which?'

After a few such questions, her husband will tend to disappear. If they are in
the kitchen, he will go into his studio. Or he may go outside and sit on his
bench, his long, forlorn face looking hillward.

'What's he doin' out there?' Michael may ask. 'What's he waitin' for?'

'Maybe he's hoping one of the Indians will come over the hills and offer him
a ride back to New York,' she says.

And Michael's eyes will shine up and then he will say, 'Yeah, on the back of
one of their ponies.'

Michael often shows up not very long after her husband has gone out. And
she loves that he does this – as if he knows somehow that she's been left all
alone and guesses she might like a little company. She imagines him hiding at
the entrance to the Kaplan house, waiting to see the Buick drive by. Or ducked
in behind a bush on the beach waiting for him to go out for one of his walks. If
Michael has left by the time her husband returns, she doesn't always say that
he's been. She may mention it later or the following day in passing; she may say
nothing at all. She enjoys keeping it to herself, and she enjoys, too, knowing
that Michael is someone who wants *her* for a change, and not him.

Her husband says, 'The things you say to that boy.'

'What things?'

'You speak to him as though he's an adult.'

'What you expect me to do – go goo-goo at him? He is ten years old.'

'And I'm not sure either that you should encourage him to make fun of the
Kaplans that way. Nor do I think he needs to hear the sordid details of your
past life.'

'I'm just trying to get him to open up about himself. I tell him something,
he tells me something. And I don't see what is so sordid about it – all I did was
tell him a little about the drunks *père et fils*. Do him good to realize that sometimes a person is better off an orphan.'

'Ever consider he's the child, you're the adult?'

'Oh, I get it now.'

'Get what?'

'Yes, I get it all right.'

'What – what do you get?'

'You're jealous.'

'I am?'

'Jealous.'

'If you're going to talk nonsense—'

'Jealous that, for once in my life, someone likes me better than they like you.'

'Do you have to make everything into a competition?'

'Jealous.'

'Oh, suit yourself.'

'Jealous. That's it.'

'I'm going out for a walk.'

She calls after him: 'The boy sees something in me – and you, well, you're just another untrustworthy adult as far as he is concerned. Jealous, jealous. *Jealous*.'

When Michael comes, he sits on the floor like an Indian, his face turned up to her while she curls her feet under her on the chaise longue. She reads to him and then she hands him the book to read aloud.

She says, 'Slow down, Michael, for goodness sake, that's Robert Frost you got there in your hands, show due respect – when you read a poem you need to remember that each word counts for so much.'

If she's busy in the kitchen, he sits at the table and watches her move around. When he makes tea, they take it outside and sit next to one another on the step. She makes him laugh and he throws his head back. When he's really giddy, he does a double-kick with his long legs in the grass.

One day she takes him into the studio, turns the pages of the ledger that records her husband's work. She shows him the snapshot drawings her husband has made of each of his pictures and the notes she has made to go with them.

'This is a record of all his work,' she says. 'This is a very valuable ledger – we have to be so careful with it.'

She tells him how each picture was built and where it ended up. She spreads her arms to demonstrate the size and unscrews the lids of the little tubes to give him a sense of the colours he used. Michael kneels up on the chair and leans his elbows on the table. He holds his face with his hands, enchantment written all over it.

Another day, she takes him out for a walk and they come back with their arms full of goldenrod. She sets up two vases on the kitchen table and begins to paint. She talks him through each stroke of paint on each turn of petal, shows him where the light comes down on the vase. Then she hands the brush to Michael and says, 'Now, your turn – go ahead, paint.'

Michael takes the paintbrush and gives her a worried look.

'Start anywhere you like,' she says. 'How about that flower there – see the nice long stem on it, how it curves?'

He bites his lip and makes a slow green arc over the paper.

She claps her hands. 'Michael,' she says, 'I'll make an artist of you yet. Now go ahead, do another bit.'

Michael hands her back the brush. 'Nah, I don't want to.'

'But why not? You made a fine start.'

'That's only because you told me how to do it.'

'But we all have to be told, Michael.'

'Mr Aitch doesn't,' he says.

Sometimes they go for nature walks across the dunes, down by the swamp or through the pine scrub. She loves to teach him – a city boy – about the wildlife all around, to show him how to listen to the sounds of nature, how to hear beyond its silence.

'Michael,' she says, 'has anyone ever told you that you have remarkable visual recall?'

'No – is that good or bad?'

'Well, let me tell you this much: if any old witch thought they could pull a Hansel and Gretel trick on you they'd be sorely mistaken – I swear you would remember every leaf and branch in the forest and be home before her.'

'I used to know someone called Gretel,' he says.

165

'Who's that?'

'I don't know, I just this second remembered the name.'

After one of these walks, he curls up on the chaise longue and falls asleep. As she stands in the doorway watching him, the feeling comes on her again, under her breastbone, between her ribs. A feeling that is one second of joy, two seconds of grief. And she knows then: what has been removed is loneliness and what has been added is love.

~

SHE TAKES DOWN THE model of the house her husband built and places it on the table.

'He made that for a painting he did last year. It's a model house. Isn't it something? He's good with his hands, that's for sure. Know why he made it? So he wouldn't have to keep going back there; he could keep it here and study the light.'

'What light?' Michael says, peering inside it. 'I don't see a light.'

'The sunlight – the way it touches the house. See, how it comes in and hits it, here and here?'

'Oh yeah,' Michael says, 'oh yeah…'

She pulls down a few rolls of old preliminary sketches and uncurls them on the worktable.

'These are sketches he did for his Cape paintings. Let's see if you can guess where they are.'

Michael pounces on the first one. 'That's just by the Pamet,' he declares.

'Yes, it is! What about this one?'

'That's the dog who looks like Buster! Who lives there?'

'I don't know, nobody probably.'

'What about that one – where is the road going?'

'Nowhere.'

'Nowhere – but it's got to go somewhere!'

'Can't it just go on?'

'No! No, it has to *stop*.'

'What's the matter, Michael?'

'I just want to know where it stops. I just want. I just—'

'All right then – it ends at a swamp or a dump heap.'

'Which, though – a swamp *or* a dump?'

'A swamp then. It ends at a swamp.'

'Okay,' Michael says, clearly relieved. 'Good. How about that house there? Look, in that sketch – who's that man and that woman on the porch?'

'He made them up.'

'You mean they don't even exist?'

'That's what artists do, Michael, we make things up.'

'Oh, you mean you *lie*?'

'I suppose in a way we do. Now come on, we better start clearing up before he comes back.'

'Oh, but you didn't show me the sketches with the little model house in them. I want to see how it turned out. Can I just see those first? Can I, *please*?'

She finds the roll, spreads out the sketches and watches while Michael examines them, squinting at the colour notations, leaning right in to look at the woman.

'That's me,' she says. 'He always uses me as a model.'

'It doesn't look like you.'

'He made me taller, a lot taller. He changes things around you see and—'

'She looks more like Katherine.'

'Katherine? Katherine who? Oh, you mean Katherine Kaplan? I don't think so.'

'Oh, she does.'

'Let me see that.'

She picks up a head-and-shoulder sketch study. 'I don't see it, I'm afraid. I don't see Katherine there at all. There's no resemblance – even the colouring is wrong. Not in the least. And anyway, how could it be her? We didn't even know her till this year.'

She begins to re-roll the sketches. 'For once, you're wrong, Michael. Completely wrong.'

The boy looks at her sideways. 'Well, okay,' he says. 'I don't see why you have to get mad about it.'

'Who says I'm mad? What's there to be mad about? You're mistaken, that's all. Now come on, we need to fix everything back in place before he comes back and finds out we've been snooping through his things.'

She picks up the little house and replaces it on the top shelf.

'You need to push it back a little on the shelf,' he says, 'another inch over this side. No, no, that's not it, a little more. And that book beside it, turn that a little to the right. That's it now. That's *exactly* how it was.'

He hands her the rolled-up sketches and guides her as she puts them back.

'Well, I guess it can't be Katherine then,' he says. 'Maybe I'm thinking of the house she used to live in before. It had those funny windows stuck in the roof. I guess maybe that's what made me think of her.'

'Where was that?'

'I forget,' he says. 'I just saw it in a photograph.'

He straightens up suddenly, climbs down from the chair. 'Shh, you hear that? Quick, Mrs Aitch, I think I can hear him coming, he's coming.'

She stands at the window and looks out. 'There's nothing out there,' she begins and then the side of the Buick slips into view.

~

NOW THAT HE IS almost done with the Orleans painting and has nothing new on the go, her husband has taken to driving around again.

One afternoon, Michael sees him reach for the keys and says, 'Where are you going?'

'For a drive – care to come along?'

'And Mrs Aitch?' Michael says.

'And Mrs Aitch, of course.'

Michael sits up front between them; he sits with his hands under his knees and his knees tipping over the edge of the seat, his heels tapping on the floor. He looks from one to the other of them, then he looks out the window. He looks at them both again and can't seem to keep the grin off his face.

'You drive the Buick round New York?' he says.

'No, I leave it in Nyack.'

168

'Where's that?'

'Oh, not too far. About thirty miles or so. I put it up for the winter.'

'Don't you miss it?'

'He sure does,' she says. 'He misses it like a cowboy misses his horse.'

'Where do you leave it?'

'At the house where I grew up.'

'The house?'

'That's right, the house.'

'You mean you grew up in a whole house?'

'That's right.'

'A lovely house too,' she says. 'He could look out the window and see the Hudson River.'

'Why don't you live there now?'

'I prefer to live in New York and anyhow my sister is living there.'

'But if it's a whole house wouldn't there be room enough for everyone?'

'It's not always a question of room, Michael.'

'Oh. Does it have a front yard?'

'Front and back,' she says.

'I sure would like to see that,' Michael says, smiling at her.

If her husband wasn't with them, she would probably promise to take him there someday. If her husband wasn't here, she would probably name that day.

'You have to cross a big bridge to get to it, Michael,' she says, 'and you don't like crossing bridges, you told me.'

'I could shut my eyes real tight, the way I used to when Vince and Harry... and anyhow, I don't think I'd be too scared if you were with me, you know – if I could sit right in the middle of you, like I am now.'

There is a sound of the blinkers clicking. The nose of the Buick points at the turn for the Kaplan place.

Michael turns a worried face to her.

'You can't do that,' she says to her husband.

'Why not?'

'You already invited him to come with us.'

'And he *is* coming with us,' he says.

169

He pulls over behind Mrs Kaplan's automobile. 'I just thought Richie might like to come along too. I'm sure Michael doesn't mind going up to the house and seeing if he can find him and inviting him along.'

He turns to Michael. 'Why don't you do that, and better tell his mother or grandmother or, or…'

'Katherine?' Michael suggests.

'Yes, any one of the adults, that you are both invited to come with us to Provincetown.'

'Is that where we're going?' she asks as they watch Michael race up to the path. 'Are you onto something? I thought you wanted to finish the Orleans picture first.'

'Oh, I think it could rest for a few days; all it needs really is a sky.'

'You have something new in mind?'

'I don't know. There is a house near the monument – I'd like to take a look at it. The window, anyhow. Later we can take the boys for a soda or ice-cream or whatever it is that boys go for these days.'

They sit in the afternoon stillness for a while, her husband leaning his elbow out his window while she leans a little out hers.

'I still say that if Richie wanted to see us he would have come along with Michael,' she eventually says.

'Well, that depends,' he says.

'On what does it depend?'

'On whether Michael told him where he was going.'

'Oh, I'm sure he didn't just sneak off.'

'And I'm sure you're right – but in any case, I don't want to leave the Kaplan boy out.'

When Michael comes back Richie is with him, Richie's face bright and happy. Michael moves to go round to the passenger door and climb between them again on the front seat, but her husband reaches back and pushes the rear door open. 'In you both get, boys,' he says, making it quite clear that he expects Michael to sit in the back. She catches Michael's eye as he climbs in and gives him a reassuring nod.

Then Olivia appears. She stays at a distance, holding the dog by the collar. She is dressed in beach shorts and a sleeveless blouse; her hair, whipped up and sitting on the top of her head, looks like a big lugworm casting. She is standing with one hip raised.

Her husband calls out the car window: 'We'll have them back in a couple of hours – if that's all right with you?'

'You take as long as you like!' Olivia laughs with a gaudy smile and a little wiggle of her shoulders.

As the wheels nudge into the gravel and her husband reverses back off the lane, she takes a look at her own legs, turning them a little and slyly lifting the edge of her skirt. She is pleased to note: Olivia's legs might be younger than hers, and Olivia's legs might be considerably longer and more tanned than hers, but Olivia's legs are most certainly not, not, *not* in any better condition.

In Provincetown, Richie and her husband fall into step a few yards ahead and she walks with Michael behind them. Richie appears to be doing all of the talking, which is no surprise, but she can tell that her husband is listening attentively to him. He even stops walking for a few seconds while Richie's earnest profile explains something to him. Then they start moving again, slipping through a gap in the traffic and leaving herself and Michael further behind.

On a busy Bradford Street, they wait at the kerb until a bus driver stalls and waves them across. Michael takes her hand as they cross the street. She has not held a child's hand since her days as a teacher, and even then, it was always a much smaller hand and the owner was usually a little fearful in her company. She has not held any hand at all, come to think of it, apart from the hand of Mrs Sultz, recently, and she would just as soon forget about that.

Her first impulse is to drop Michael's hand and push it away. But she manages to keep hold of it, and then she gets used to it, and as they walk under the elms and past the white houses, it begins to feel natural.

She says, 'I stayed in an inn here one summer, you know, with my mother. And Arthur. One of the best vacations of my life I would have to say. It was called the Gingerbread House then of course and—'

'How come I've never seen you in New York?' Michael says.

'Well, I don't know,' she says, a little put out by his interruption. 'It's a pretty big place, you know.'

'It's not so big, not when you live on the same end of it, like we do.'

'When you put it like that, it does seem funny. We may have passed each other and just not noticed.'

He cocks his nose. 'I would have noticed you, I think. I would have noticed him for sure,' he says nodding to her husband, now a good distance ahead.

'Well, you could hardly miss *him*,' she laughs.

Her husband puts his hand on Richie's shoulder as they cross the street and now they are standing at the church railings.

'Can I still come visit you when we go back to New York?' Michael asks. 'I could sleep over, you know, if the new apartment that Harry finds is far away, so I wouldn't have to worry about getting back or anything. I don't mind sleeping on the floor either – I can even bring my own blanket. I could help you make tea and I could go to the grocery store and maybe we could go visit the house in Nyack some…'

She sees now that Richie's head is bowed and that her husband is taking his handkerchief out of his pocket and handing it to Richie.

'I'm sorry, Michael, what were you just saying?' she asks.

'Nothin',' he mutters then pulls his hand away from hers and sticks it into his pocket.

On the way back to the parking lot, they stop in Marty's Diner.

'You find what you're looking for?' she asks her husband as they stand at the counter waiting to be seated. He replies with a non-committal downturn of his bottom lip.

When they are seated she notices that the rims of Richie's eyes are raw.

She leans across to him. 'Is everything all right, Richie – has something upset you?'

Her husband takes the menus from the waitress and passes them out to the boys. 'Oh, a fly got in his eye, is all,' he says. 'Isn't that so, Richie?'

Richie nods and dips his face behind the menu.

~

A FEW DAYS AFTER the trip to Provincetown, Michael is helping her pull weeds from the grass patch at the side of the house.

She looks at the big bag of weeds he has filled and says, 'Oh, well done – you darling boy.'

'Why do you say that?' he asks. 'Why call me a darling boy?'

'Well, because I like you.'

'Why do you like me?'

'All sorts of reasons.'

'Tell me.'

'Because you come visit and you laugh at my little jokes and you help me do things I don't want to do, like this weed-pulling business. And because, well, we're friends, aren't we?'

'Oh yes,' he smiles.

'We have many things in common.'

'We like cats,' he says.

'Yes, that is very true.'

'And we both like tea!'

'Yes, that's another thing.'

'And the United Nations building. Maybe we could go see it together some time – you know, when it's all finished and the windows are in and everything?'

'Well, yes, we'll see. So tell me, what else do we have in common?'

He thinks for a moment and then: 'We don't like Richie.'

She stops weeding and sits back on her heels. 'What a thing to say! Of course we like Richie.'

'No. We don't.'

'Well, you must speak for yourself, of course, but you can't go round telling people who they like and don't like.'

'Why not, if you know it's true?'

'Why on earth would I not like poor Richie?'

'Because he's always whining and he's always running to his mom and snitching on people.'

'Well, I don't know anything about that. And I don't know what's gotten into you either. To say such a thing. You can't possibly know who I like and don't like.'

His face heats up and he looks hurt. 'You didn't want him to come with us to Provincetown the other day,' he mumbles.

'Now, that's not at all true, Michael. I just didn't want to *force* him to come. As a matter of fact, I was going to ask you to invite him for tea tomorrow afternoon.'

'Why?'

'What do you mean why? Why does anyone invite anyone to their home? I want him to know he's welcome. I'm going to write a little note – you can give it to him later. I hope to see you both tomorrow afternoon at four.'

'You don't send a note to me every day. Why not just make him tea if he turns up?'

'I mean a proper tea, not just a cup. Everything laid out nice, you know, a cake-and-conversation event – it's a while since we've had one of those in this house.'

'Sure, I'll ask him, I'll give him a note too if you want, but I *know* you don't like him.'

'Nonsense,' she says and, climbing back onto her feet, lifts the two bags of weeds and takes them round to the side of the house. Then she goes inside to the bathroom and washes her face and hands.

A few minutes later she comes back out with the note and Michael has gone.

Neither Michael nor Richie shows up the next day. There's no sign of Michael again the following day. In the end she tells her husband about the incident.

'Do you think I ought to go over there and see if he's all right?' she asks as they finish off the apple pie she had baked for their little tea party.

'I think you should leave it alone,' he says. 'He'll come back in his own good time.'

'I just don't understand it – I mean to say, we didn't have a fight or anything, I just told him…'

'What did you tell him?'

'Well. I suppose I did tick him off for saying that about Richie. I mean, I couldn't allow him to talk that way – what do you think?'

'I think he's a kid who looks on you as an equal. I also think he's probably a little more unusual than most kids his age. If you want I can call by tomorrow morning and check on him.'

'Oh yes, if you would? But maybe wait till tomorrow afternoon, give him a chance to call by in the morning. Tell him… tell him… Oh, I don't know what you could tell him, really.'

'Don't worry, I'll figure it out.'

The next morning she finds Michael down on the beach, hunched over a shallow pool. He is playing with pebbles and shells; the pebbles built up on one side, like a miniature Irish wall. He is arranging another pile of pebbles to add to his wall and, as she comes closer, she can see he is counting these out, pointing his finger at one following another and pausing to refresh the count in between. Michael is turned the other way and seems to be completely absorbed in his task. He doesn't see her come up behind him, which surprises her, as he's usually so alert. She can't see his face, but she can hear him now, counting aloud. His voice sounds a little off key and she realizes then that this is because he is not counting in English.

'Hey, Michael,' she says, and his head comes up, startled and embarrassed as if she has caught him doing something shameful. She decides not to make any mention of their little spat, or his failure to show up for tea.

'Nice collection of sea pebbles you got there. You going to make something with them – a house? A fort, maybe?'

Michael shrugs. He kneels up and, with his right hand holding his left arm, looks down at the pebble wall.

'What language was that you were counting in?' she asks.

He doesn't answer but begins rubbing his arm and keeps looking at his collection of pebbles.

'You know, my husband, he sometimes counts in French, usually when he's upset. One time, we were at this funeral – a dear friend of ours, she had died – and everyone was crying, even the men, and there he was whispering to himself, *un, deux, trois…* counting, I don't know what – the tiles on the floor, maybe. I could only hope people thought he was praying.'

175

'I'm not upset,' he says, 'and it wasn't French.'

'Oh. Well then, I suppose it was German?'

She waits but he doesn't say anything else.

'That's all right,' she says, 'it's none of my business anyhow.'

He shrugs again and says, 'I don't know.'

'What – you don't know if it was German?'

'I guess. I mean, sometimes it just sort of happens.'

'But what a wonderful gift it is – to be able to speak another language. It makes one look at the world in a different—'

'Who is one?'

'Excuse me?'

'You're always saying "one feels this" and "one knows that", but I don't know who you're talking about.'

'Now, you know very well what I mean. It makes *you* then, it makes any *one*, look at the world—'

'Well, that's funny because my aunt, she says people don't like to hear German spoken, so I don't know what you're talking about.'

He sounds angry. Angry at her or the aunt, she can't be sure which.

'She may be right. It is only a few years since the war, after all. But I must say, I don't mind hearing it – after all, German Jews spoke it, didn't they? And they still speak it, I presume.'

'How would I know?'

'All I'm saying is I think it's just nonsense to go punishing an entire language!'

'Yeah, well, not everyone is like you, are they, Mrs Aitch?'

'No, I don't suppose they are.'

The boy is scratching his arm now, his fingers clawed into it. 'She's not my real aunt. I'm adopted.'

'Well, yes, I know that.'

'She's having a new baby – I suppose you know that too?'

'No, as a matter of fact, I didn't know that – why would I?'

'They didn't tell me about it; too busy figuring out how to get rid of me.'

She pushes his hand away from his arm.

'Stop that, Michael, you'll hurt yourself,' she says, 'and I'm sure that's not how it is. They probably just want to surprise you. When you get back you'll have a new baby sister or brother. Now what could be nicer than that?'

'That doesn't even make sense,' he says and glares at her. 'I'm adopted, I told you.'

Then he stands and moves away from the pool over to the soft sand. He drops on his knees and starts combing his hand through the grains. She follows and sits down beside him.

They sit in silence, looking out at the bay, watching the traffic of boats and yachts. 'It's like Union Square out there,' she says, 'so much traffic. Since the war – this time of the year, anyhow – well, it's gotten you can hardly see the water for all that show. Who do you suppose owns it all? And look at that yacht! Big as the Ritz! They say it belongs to that Woolworth girl. Hope it makes her happy, that's all I say.'

Michael bends his toes into the sand and says nothing.

'Are you sure about this baby?'

'I'm sure! Ask Richie's mom if you don't believe me – she knows. I heard her tell it to that singer woman, you know the one with the lumpy face, that day in Orleans in the English lady's house.'

'You heard her say it?'

'Yeah, but I already knew. They think I don't hear anything in that apartment, but I do. At night when they think I'm sleeping, I hear a lot of stuff.'

'Oh well, some people can be a little silly about these things. They prefer to wait a while before telling everyone. Would you like to come up to the house for a while, Michael? We could have some tea and talk about it?'

'I can't,' he says. 'We gotta go get haircuts. For the party on Saturday. It's like the president is coming or somethin'.'

'Knowing Mrs Kaplan, I wouldn't be at all surprised,' she says.

A light breeze lifts Michael's hair. 'I guess you could do with a haircut,' she says. 'It is getting a little long.'

She reaches out to touch it. Michael pulls back from her hand.

'I used to teach boys,' she says, 'a long time ago, of course.'

'I didn't know that.'

'In New York.'

'Where in New York?'

'Oh, you know, different schools. I taught sick children for a while. I mean, really sick children who probably never got well again. And I worked in the Hebrew Orphan Asylum too. What I'm trying to say is that if you need to talk—'

'You think I'm a Jew?'

'I have no idea.'

'A boy in my school, Jerry Newport, showed us pictures of all these Jews comin' out of those camps. So you think that's what happened my parents?'

'I don't know, it's possible. Look, I only mentioned the Hebrew school because I happened to teach in it and most of those boys were orphans and this was well before the war so that had nothing to do with it. I was only, you know, trying to say that I might understand how you—'

Michael cuts her off. 'Well, I'm sorry but I'm not a Jew. I know that. My father was a soldier, he died in the war.'

'How do you know that?'

'I don't know, I just do.'

He gets up, flicks the sand from his hands and starts walking away from her.

He walks for a few yards and then breaks into a run. Then suddenly he stops, turns, gives a big, happy wave and yells back to her, 'Hey, Mrs Aitch? See you at the party!'

'See you then, Michael,' she hears her voice cry out.

4

HE GETS UP EARLY to read. Most mornings, he manages an hour or so before his wife begins to stir. If she's still sleeping when the hour is done, he may attempt to work. If it happens to be one of those days when the studio seems more like a place of incarceration, he will put down his book, close the door behind him and go out for a walk.

When he reads, he opens back the Dutch door to let in the morning air. He sits into his chair, puts his feet up on the chaise longue, keeps the coffee pot close to hand. Then he opens his book. And he is a fly on the wall at someone else's party. It's the same reason he has always enjoyed going to the movies.

His wife usually starts talking as soon as she stirs. He hopes today won't be one of those days. Sometimes she will start even before she opens her eyes.

She may say something like: How's the weather doing out there?

Or: You know, I had the *strangest* dream last night.

For the past few days, the first words out of her mouth have been in the form of a question – the same question: 'Do you think we might get any news from New York today?'

He will usually respond.

Calling out from the kitchen or studio, or coming to stand in the doorway of the bedroom, he may say: Looks about the same as it did yesterday.

Or: Dreams are supposed to be strange.

For the past few days, though, it has been the same answer: 'It's hard to get hold of anyone in New York this time of year; he's probably closed up the gallery and gone on vacation.'

When he reads at this solitary hour, there is a calmness around him, a suspension of time. The pain in his lower gut lifts, contentment appeases him. It is only when he moves his position, or maybe reaches out to refill the coffee cup, that his eye will be caught by the light. He will notice, then, the latest stain left by the sun on the surface of the room. Each time he happens to look up, the shape of the stain will have changed, the intensity of light will be altered, from the first chrome yellow stripe on the floor to the last wedge of white through the open door. And he will be aware, once again, that the axis is turning, that even at this hour of the morning, the day is already moving towards death.

He recalls Harry Sterner, a reformed drunk who used to drop by his father's store from time to time. The only thing he missed about being a drunk, Harry used to say, was the suspension of time – a whole day would stop so long as he was prepared to walk into a bar and surrender himself to the bottle.

He has experienced this feeling himself from time to time – not through booze but through work: some paintings more than others; some paintings not at all. But for him it has always come in short spurts, the peace dissipating the moment he steps away from the canvas. Apart from that one summer, the summer of endless rain when he decided to accept defeat, give up looking for a subject and put away his brushes. He took to working on the house instead, building things – the bench, the lawn chairs. He mended window frames and shingles, painted the exterior walls. He fixed and replaced whatever needed fixing or replacing. The pleasure of straightforward work, work that had felt sure in his hands. The ending already in sight before he had even started, and the knowledge too that the outcome could only be an improvement. He surrendered himself to each task. The days disappeared. Time suspended. The best months of his married life; the most peaceful, anyhow.

I should have been a carpenter, he had said to himself more than once that summer, I should have been Joseph instead of the guy on the cross.

At the start of this summer, he was reading only Montaigne. The old copy that used to belong to his father. He has given up on that now. No matter that he misses Montaigne as he would miss a dear friend, no matter that his essays have always had a settling effect – how many times in the past has he found himself nailing down an idea for a picture after an hour spent in his company?

He would like to open the essays right now, remind himself of what the little nobleman had to say on the subject of time. But he is afraid it will set him thinking about his father again. At first he thought it was the essays that were making him feel this way, written as they were out of grief for Montaigne's dead father. But he soon came to realize that it was the book itself – his father's name narrowly inscribed on the flyleaf in ink now rusted with age. All he had to do was hold the book in his hands and after a moment everything would darken. He would be pulled down by regret for the life his father did and did not have. Phrases of pity and pain passing through his head for the rest of the day – poor Pops, poor old Dad, poor Father. Poor lonely man furtively reading Montaigne under the counter like a schoolboy who is too clever for his teacher.

His father dead almost thirty-seven years and mostly forgotten, until this summer, this particular re-reading of Montaigne. Now it seems that every time he closes his eyes he is waiting. He is not sure why this should be – fear of his own death, maybe. But always, he imagines him in the store in Nyack – never at home and never out of doors. Six days a week behind the long counter, late nights catching up with paperwork. He sees him standing there, dwarfed by bolts of cloth and pull-out drawers stacked like mahogany bricks into the wall. Or he sees him walking through the store between the long, polished counters, knick-knack baskets laid out on top and the boxes of gloves that had frightened him as a small boy – skins from amputated hands, a delivery boy once told him.

Everything about his father was modest: his walk, the back of his head, his small, low-hung ears. And he remembers a day when he was six years old, catching his father push the bolt over the door and turn the *Sorry, We're Closed* sign to the street, even though it was only four-thirty in the afternoon. And then watching him come back into the dim-brown air, his head breaking through the single shaft of sunlight that had been rolling down from an upper window. And how surprised he had been to see this – his father's head break and scatter the gold-specked dust – and thinking even then, at only six years old, how unusual it was to see his father disturb anything at all.

Mrs Watson rapping on the door outside, then clicking angrily on the window with a coin and he (closing his eyes as he hurried past the amputated hands) running into the back office. 'Mrs Watson's outside, Pops – can't you hear her outside, banging to be let in?'

His father lifting a shushing finger to his lips before returning to his copy of the essays hidden in the folds of a large commercial ledger. While out on the street Mrs Watson continued to bang and click and almost knock the door down.

He is eight years older than his father was when he became a dear departed. He has passed his father out. He was young to die – he should have gone on a little longer, worked a lot less, enjoyed his life a lot more, stretched out with the sun on his face, reading Montaigne in broad daylight.

And now the Verlaine has gone missing. A few days ago he had an inclination to read 'La Lune Blanche' again in the original and went looking for the book in the basement. He searched one box after another but couldn't find it anywhere. He had been, and is certain still, that he had slipped it into the green box the evening he came back from Eastham when his wife had caught him off guard. He had shoved it down between Eliot's essays and a bunch of old copies of *Life* magazine. It had been foolish to hide it from her; it had been inviting suspicion. But he hadn't wanted her sticking her oar into his little moment of nostalgia. Nor did he want her reading the inscription, saying the name in a derisive way or being sarcastic about words that were once so dear to him. He emptied the boxes out and went through the books one by one. But the Verlaine was absent. He did not, and will not, ask if she has seen or taken it – even if he knows she has done both. Let her cherish her jealous intrigues; the book will reappear when she finds something else to carp about.

And so he is down to the last Frenchman in the house: the *Journals of André Gide*. He found it in a book store on Fourth Avenue, in the second-hand section – even though it looked as if it had never had a hand laid on it. He likes going to this store to browse or buy, but only when his wife is not with him. The woman in charge is, herself, a walking library – if a book is not in the store, it's on a little shelf inside her head. She is also a Francophile. He enjoys talking to her about books, about France, about anything really and knows that if his wife were with him he probably wouldn't get a word in. The bookstore woman spent two years in Paris round about the time he was first there, although of course

182

they never met. On occasion they have slipped into speaking French in a jocular fashion – the way non-native speakers tend to do. She had always seemed to him to be the easy-going, broad-minded sort. But she showed her teeth when he brought this book to the counter and asked if she was familiar with Gide.

'No,' she said, 'and nor will I ever be. If he ever came in the store, I would throw him right out that door.'

He was both shocked and amused by her attitude, the bitterness of the words she spat out. French thug. Pederast. A man of violence and deviance. A disgrace to the title of Nobel Laureate.

He turns another page and smiles to himself. Who would have thought he would have gotten along so well with that type of man?

He hears his wife get out of bed, the pat of her feet across the bedroom floor and on out to the bathroom. She calls his name. He doesn't reply. Just this page, he thinks, just till I get to the end of this page, this last drop of coffee.

And now the background movement of water: a trickle followed by a robust flush, a few feeble splashes as she washes her hands and then the pat of feet again.

Just to the end of this paragraph, he thinks. Let me just finish this paragraph.

And now she is calling out to him, something about flowers and something about the weather and this is followed by a long tutting complaint about the hordes of invaders choking up the streets of Provincetown.

Another few seconds, he thinks, just another few seconds in Marseilles, with this man who doesn't mind cutting himself with the blade of his own honesty.

But she is back to the flowers again: 'And so once you've collected them, then you could—'

'I'll be just a minute…' he calls, hoping she will wait there and find something else to do.

But she does not wait. Her voice, nearer now, says, '*Flowers.*'

Over the frontier of the printed page, he sees her shape caught in the shadow of the doorway.

'What flowers?' he asks.

'The flowers I ordered for Mrs Kaplan, of course. You were with me when I ordered them!'

'The party is not until tomorrow.'

'Yes, but I'm thinking Provincetown? Tomorrow? I mean, can you imagine?'

He looks at her blindly.

'I'm trying to tell you something,' she says, 'and I wish you wouldn't look at the clock any time I begin to speak.'

'I wasn't aware I had looked at the clock.'

'It's like I'm at the shrink or something, paying on the hour.'

'This is not going to take an hour – is it?' he says.

'You have to go to the florist and much better you go today, that's all I'm saying.'

She comes into clearer focus now, her hands on her hips, nightgown crumpled in the front, her hair sticking up as if it's squirting out of her head. Like a precocious child, he thinks, who finds herself constantly exasperated by the stupidity of grown-ups.

'What are you grinning at?' she says.

'I wasn't aware—'

'Oh, would you please stop saying that!'

He puts down the book. 'Now why don't you just tell me what you would like me to do?'

She pauses, takes in a small breath and – 'Well now. I would like you to go to the florist's and pick up the flowers for Mrs Kaplan. You can do it when you go out to collect the mail.'

She turns to go back into the bedroom.

'I wasn't thinking of going to the post office today.'

She spins around, her face pained and worried.

'Oh, but supposing—?'

'I told you what he said – he said not to expect any news before the end of the summer.'

'But it's that now. It is the end of the summer *now* – don't you think? Monday is Labor Day – I mean, if that's not the end of the summer, I don't know

184

what is, unless we're expected to wait until the green has drained out of every leaf on the Cape!'

He knows that if he refuses to go now, she will only push him to go later. And if he refuses later, she will go by herself. She will go, even if she has to crawl every inch of the way.

'I'll pick up the mail, then I'll go get the flowers.'

'Thank you.'

'Think they'll stay fresh till tomorrow?' he asks.

'Oh, I'm sure they'll be fine.'

'The humidity – I mean.'

'The humidity?'

'You're going to have to take them out of the bouquet, put them in water and pack them up again tomorrow.'

'Oh. Oh yes. Oh goodness. I never thought about that. What am I going to do now? Unless we leave them in the basement – but no, that won't do either. In the afternoon, you can't breathe down there – they'd only suffocate. And if I open the windows, a cat is sure to—'

'I could drop by Mrs Kaplan on the way home, leave them for her then.'

'Oh, but *I* wanted to give them to her.'

He closes the book, lets his feet down on the floor.

'Fine, we can both go.'

'Oh no, no, I don't want to go there today, not like this.'

'You could always put on some clothes.'

'Oh, now, that's not what I mean, you know it's not what I mean. I want to go when my hair is washed and I'm all fixed up for a party. Never mind, I'll figure it out.'

He stands, puts the book back on the shelf and walks across the room.

'You do that,' he says over his shoulder, 'and be sure to keep me informed.'

He pulls the easel away from the wall and turns it to face into the room. The Orleans picture sits patiently waiting. He studies it for a moment, neither satisfied nor dissatisfied. All feeling he had for this painting left him with the last few touches of light: to the curve of the pump stand, the hood of the automobile

185

coming out from the side road, the final tip of light to the woman's green dress, all the better to broaden her rump.

His wife calls out to him: 'Oh, I know! I know *exactly* what we can do.'

'I bet,' he mutters.

He has gone back to Orleans a couple of times, searching for the right sky. He may give it one more try. If the sky isn't there, he will just have to root one out of his memory.

'Are you listening to me in there?'

'Certainly, I'm listening to you in here.'

A late summer sky before dusk, that particular lustre and yet the dark trees. The sky would alter from here to here. Paler there and then, from the sign to the cruciform of the telegraph pole, less so. Until just above that, he would need to add—

'What I mean is… You drop by the florist, ask them if they can deliver first thing in the morning. I can't believe we never thought to ask them to deliver! No, on second thoughts – not a good idea to deliver in the morning. They will be far too busy at the Kaplan place getting everything ready for the party and may not even notice the flowers, never mind who sent them. And after all, we do want them to know who sent them! Let them deliver this afternoon just to be certain. Write a card as if it's from both of us. No, wait, I can write a little note now – why not? And *you* – you can give it to the florist to attach it to the bouquet. I can use one of my fancy mauve notelets – you know, from that set I bought when we were in Wyoming? Yes, that's what I'll do. I'll do it right away.'

Her voice is happy and girlish as she rummages for a pen and her fancy mauve notelets with the matching mauve envelopes. He knows she is looking forward to the party, to meeting new people, taking part in the various pockets of conversations throughout the house and the garden. All that he so dreads, she so enjoys. But besides the party, there is something else – the prospect of the letter coming from New York. And he worries now that she may go broadcasting news she hasn't yet received, nor is likely to receive, in order to give herself some standing among her fellow guests. As if hoping for something will make it a fact. She is buoyed by hope, always has been. It is something he both admires and pities in her. Her ability to suspend everything on that one little sliver of hope. As long as she has it, she is happy – it doesn't seem to make any difference how many times it has dragged her down and left her for dead. She will get back up eventually, screaming for blood – usually his. Until it's time to start hoping again.

~

WHEN HE PULLS OVER at the post office, he sees Mrs Kaplan's grandson sitting on the stoop at the far end of the building with his dog by his side. The boy, with his elbows on his knees, the cheeks of his face puckered up in his hands, is busy watching two men string outdoor lanterns above a paddock across the street.

He gets out, walks down to the boy and says, 'Looks like you're not the only ones to throw a party this weekend.'

The boy starts, then, squinting against the sun, looks up at him. 'Oh hello, sir,' he says and begins to get up.

He holds out his hand to tell him to stay where he is, but the boy is on his feet and ready to report for duty.

'Oh, I hope we have outdoor lanterns too, sir,' he says.

'I'm sure you do, Richie.'

'We got plenty of flags though. All sizes.'

Richie has a chocolate stain around his mouth and there's an empty wrapper on the stoop which the dog noses into for a few seconds before coming back to his master. They stand, all three, watching, across the street, a man in dungarees hammer a wooden dancefloor into place.

'So – have you lost him again?'

'Excuse me, sir?'

'Michael – have you lost him again?'

The boy looks away and then pulls his dog's head into his hip and begins stroking its mane. He doesn't answer for a moment and then: 'Well, I don't know, I guess so. But I don't care any more – as a matter of fact, I wish he would just go on home.'

'I thought you two got along just fine?'

'Well sure, we do when we're with other people, like you and your wife. But…'

187

'But what?'

'Well, I mean, there's not much point having a friend if they don't want you as a friend, is there? I mean if they keep running off every time you turn your head for more than half a second or so.'

'No, I suppose not. So, are you here alone?'

Richie takes in a breath and then: 'Well, they're all busy at home, getting ready for this party, and the automobile wasn't there but my grandma, she was, and so I thought Katherine— You see she usually collects the mail on her way to Eastham. But she's not here yet and she hasn't been because I just went in back and asked. And Michael, she sometimes takes him with her to mail the letters he writes to his— I mean to the Novaks, I guess, and this whole bunch of friends he claims to— Well. And so I thought—'

Richie stops talking and takes another breath.

'You thought Michael could be with her?' he suggests.

'Well, yeah. Maybe.'

'I see. You need a ride home?'

'Oh no, thank you, sir. I'll just wait here for Katherine. She's probably gone to get her shot first. She's sick, you know.'

'Oh yes, I heard.'

'I don't know much about it. Nobody tells me anything, except maybe mind my own business. All I know is she has to get one every day. Sometimes she goes into Eastham and sometimes Doctor Tom, he comes to her. Friday it's always Eastham.'

Richie takes another breath.

'I'm just in the way all the time in the house anyhow. My mother— That's what she said.'

'You sound a little short of breath – the humidity getting to you, Richie?'

'Oh no, sir. It's the grass, they cut the grass for the party, you see. But that's okay, it passes. I took my— my rescue inhaler this morning so. And I'll be seeing some sort of specialist soon. My mom, she says, I can't— I can't start school until I do. But you see, we couldn't get an appointment until a couple of weeks away so I'll be late back to school. So now I'm stuck here because she says the sea air does me good.'

'You don't like it here?'

'Sure, but I was all ready. Ready to go to my new school next week. I was all packed and everything. All my new stuff and— She thinks it's making me nervous, the idea. The whole idea of going, you see, and so— She wants me to wait. Well, I don't know. We got all these special tags with my name on them. Rosetta and my mom, they, they sewed them on. Except, of course, for those hard things that wouldn't take a needle, like my shoes and books and my luggage obviously. They wrote my name on those in special ink. So I wouldn't get in trouble for— for losing anything. I'm always getting in trouble for losing my things, you see.'

'Yes, I see. Would you like me to get you a soda or something, maybe an ice-cream?'

'Oh no, thank you, sir, I'm not really allowed to have anything between meals. My luggage is new too. Colorado brown. That's the name of the colour.'

'That's a good name for a colour. Good colour for luggage too.'

'Thank you, sir, it is. And, and it's the oldest boarding school in New England, you know. My, my— well, you know, my family they all went there too.'

'Your dad, you mean?'

'Well, yeah, sure. Him too.'

Richie stands with his arms straight by his sides, looking down at his feet, while the dog sniffs around the edge of a trash can by the fence.

'Well, I guess I better go see if we got any mail,' he says. 'Be sure to let me know if you change your mind about that ride.'

'Oh, I won't, sir. I mean, I will let you know but I won't need the ride, thank you. So what I mean is—'

'That's all right, Richie, I understand.'

Then Richie sits down on the stoop again and the dog leaves the trash can to come join him.

~

THERE IS A SOLITARY car on Castle Road, a Pontiac Sedan if he's not mistaken. He watches it from his vantage point above the spur in the road where he pulled in a few moments ago after picking up the mail. A postcard and two letters, one of which is now burning a hole in his pocket. He had decided to get out and walk a while. He had a mind, then, to go over the open hills, wander through the pines, see if he could find the old smallpox cemetery he happened across a couple of years ago, sit down on a stile and read the letter there. But after a few short minutes of walking uphill and getting mobbed by insects, he grew tired and hot and decided to come back on his steps.

Now on the slope of the meadow, he takes off his jacket, flattens the grass back with his foot, before sitting down on it with his knees drawn up and his arms hugged loosely around them. He watches the Pontiac drive past the far side of the trees along the curve of fence line far below, its silver body like a hemming needle, stitching in and out of view. When the Pontiac stops showing itself, he takes off his hat, lies back with clasped hands holding the back of his head.

He can hear the sound of the firing practice coming from the army camp at Wellfleet, and when that takes a breather there's the broken sound of a carpenter's hammer coming from the east – possibly the same hammer that was nailing the outdoor dance floor into place back in town. He wonders if Richie is still there, his bland face watching out, and if his stomach flips every time he catches the glint of an approaching automobile.

He hopes that was the Kaplan Pontiac he saw below and that one of them is in it – Katherine or anyone at all who could put that poor kid out of his misery. He reaches for his hat, lifts it up, closes it over his face like a lid and thinks about the letter in his pocket, the familiar writing of his old friend on the envelope.

The week they left New York, he'd brought his wife's pictures to the gallery. Four of them in all, although they had felt like the weight of forty as he pushed up Fifth Avenue with them and manoeuvred them through the door. Even when his friend took them from him and laid them out along the wall, he could still feel the weight of them in his hands. The pictures were old – years old in the case of two of them – and he had felt sure his friend must have seen them before but he decided not to mention anything about that.

'I hate to ask you,' was all he said, 'I really do, but I just thought if you could try – you know, to get them a nose in somewhere.'

'I understand, I'll do whatever I can.'

'Obviously, she doesn't expect you to take them or anywhere else like this place but maybe, you know, if you could use your influence…'

'Yes, I know.'

'One of the smaller galleries. Just to be part of something, you know.'

'Yes, of course.'

'We'll be heading out to the Cape in a couple of days' time.'

'I can try. That's all I can do.'

'I can't tell you how sorry I am to lay this at your feet.'

'Please, don't apologize again, I know how it is. I'll write and let you know what happens at the end of the summer. Just have a good time, okay? Relax, take care of yourself, your health. And try to get a little work of your own done, all right? But, hey – don't overdo it, we don't want you getting sick again.'

They had said a fond farewell, shaking hands and patting each other above the elbow. There had been no comment passed on the pictures themselves, although he had seemed to feel them glaring reproachfully at him as he turned to go out the door.

Afterwards he had to drag himself back down Fifth Avenue, weary in heart as well as step. He thought of all the times she had put him in similar predicaments, forcing her work on visitors: gallery owners and journalists who had called to see him, even their friends and lesser acquaintances had been pinned down. Humiliation sucking the air out of the room, which she alone appeared not to notice. The slightest bit of praise turning her head, the smallest success filling it up with entitlement. And then wanting more and more, until it seemed that nothing would be good enough save a room dedicated to her work in the Met. Then, when inevitably it didn't all work out, blaming the world: women-hating men; women-hating women. Forgiving the world then and blaming it all on him instead.

He had been bitter and hurt all the way back to the Village, had even stopped off in a bar and had a drink to soften the edges. Although all that had succeeded in doing was to add to the already sour taste in his mouth.

When he came home without the pictures, she was ecstatic; she threw her arms around him and begged to be told. 'What did he say? Tell me everything he said! Tell me everything *you* said.'

'He said he'd try. I said thank you.'

'Did he say he liked the pictures?'

'Well, you know he never says much.'

'But did he look pleased?'

'Well, you know, sometimes he's hard to read.'

'But he wouldn't have taken them if he didn't like them – right? Oh, come on now, you know I'm right?'

'I'm sure you are right.'

He did not mention that they avoided eye contact for most of the conversation; that they had rushed through the words, just trying to get them out of the way. Except for the parting moment, when he had paused to look straight into his old friend's eyes and saw in there all the pity he needs to see for whatever remains of his life.

When he wakes noon is sounding over the valley. The vertebrae of his spine feel numb – as if stuck into the ground. Drowsy, he lies for a while remembering himself as a boy waking on days such as this after dozing out of doors, the way he used to scare the hell out of himself. He would give himself two minutes to get up – if he didn't, his spine would start knitting into the ground and, soon after, his flesh would turn to clay. His hair, changing from fair to green, would grow like grass. He would be drawn right down, further even than the coffins go. He would stay there until roots began to grow out of him and he would eventually be pushed back up through the earth, this time as a tree. One of those trees he used to spend so long looking at through the schoolroom window, gnarled, multi-armed and unmistakably human, and he could imagine watching askance as his parents walked by, waving his branches at them and trying to get them to hear his voice: Mama, Pops, it's me; it's your son.

He lifts the hat off his face, blinks against the sharpness of light and then, as it clears, notices a hawk overhead. He watches for a while the red tail of the hawk turning in slow, easy circles. Then he sits up, rests his elbows on his knees and plucks a strand of leggy grass out of the ground. Dragging it through his fingers to clear it of its fluff, he begins to chew on the stalk. He stays at this for a moment then suddenly draws the envelope out of his pocket, slits it open with the length of his finger, pulls the page out and reads. When he is finished, he holds the letter down between his knees and sits for a while. He can smell the sea from here, the faintly female odour that comes off it, and can hear the increasing drone of weekend traffic coming up from the highway.

He rolls the letter into a paper golf ball and flicks it into the long grass; then he does the same thing to the envelope it came in, rolls it and flicks it away where no one is ever likely to see it, unless maybe the hawk.

~

ON THE WAY BACK from the flower shop, he waits to pull over to the gas station. A bunch of local boys, some of them carrying blueberry tins, stream past the front of his automobile, pushing each other. He thinks of Richie and Michael, how restrained they are compared to the Huck kids you see around here, with their blueberry-stained grins and fishing expeditions and softball games that are anything but soft. As one woman said to him last week in the post office, 'I have two sons – this time of year, I forget what they look like.'

The afternoon has filled up with weekend visitors. A group of teenage kids crowd around the weather board. Through the door of the grocery store, a long line of shoppers. Hot faces loading up car trunks with provisions before heading out to their weekend billets, and voices coming in at him through the window as he waits in line for the pump: howling babies and squabbling children, and high-pitched mothers who put their best accents forward in front of all these strangers. The usual old boys sit in the sun with their backs to the gas station wall, smoking and spitting and pretending they don't notice a thing.

He gets out, waits for his tank to fill, taps the nozzle a couple of times and is reminded that he needs to use the bathroom. He goes round to the cabin at the back of the store, catching sight of Richie on the way. Richie, still sitting on the stoop behind the post office, just as he left him maybe as long as two hours ago. The dog, at least, has had the sense to find some shade and go lie down in it.

As he waits to pay for his gas, two local men at the end of the counter discuss the week's poor fishing yield as if they have just come through a personal tragedy. And ahead of him a man is telling a woman that his son has been recalled to service. 'A place called *Kor-ee-ah*,' he explains. 'Can't say I ever heard of it till now.'

'Oh my,' the woman says.

'I thought they were done with him by now. I mean, he was lucky to get out alive last one – he may not be so lucky again. Wife's expectin' too, you know, early December, first born.'

'Oh my,' the woman says again.

He drives out of the gas station and turns back to the post office, then pulls over close to where Richie is seated. Not that the boy seems to notice. He is clutching a candy bar that he has stretched to the limit, bringing his head down at intervals to take another long suck from its twisted toffee peak. An empty bottle of Coke stands on the stoop beside him and there's a colourful strew of candy wrappers at his feet. He rolls down the window and waits a moment. Across the street, the lanterns are strung up, the dancefloor is in place and a man drags a stack of chairs backwards across it. Two women follow behind, one of them carrying a large plate with a full ham on it, the other shooing flies away from the ham with a dishcloth. The women are laughing and yelling.

'Oh, stop, Martha, please stop making me laugh or I swear I'm gonna drop this brute right on the ground.'

Richie quietly chuckling at the scene, as if he is watching a movie.

He thinks of that afternoon in Provincetown again, when Richie burst into tears. He still feels bad about it and maybe a little responsible.

The boy, in his peculiar, meandering way, had been telling him about some man he didn't much care for – a captain who had served with his father – and at the same time, he had been telling him about his Aunt Katherine and a fight she'd had with his mother. He seemed a little put out by something, maybe the fight, maybe the man – but he had not seemed particularly heartbroken or sad. Until out of nowhere he asked him, 'Do you miss your father, Richie?' That did it all right: the kid just broke down.

He gave him his handkerchief and, as he handed it over, all the boy could say was, 'Please don't tell anyone I was crying, sir, please don't let anyone know.'

He had no idea why he had asked the boy such a question – it was not his way to intrude on the private feelings of anyone, let alone a child. Since then, it has occurred to him more than once that he asked the question because he wanted Richie to answer it and he wanted him to answer so he could hear himself say, 'I miss mine too; lately, I just can't seem to stop missing him.'

He leans out the window and calls to Richie. 'I think maybe you waited long enough – don't you?'

Richie stands up again. 'Oh, I'm sure she will be along soon, sir. She's probably gone out for lunch with Doctor Tom and she has to pass this way to get home.'

He gets out, opens the back door and slides the bouquet of flowers out, then brings them round and puts them on the passenger seat.

'Come on, son,' he says, 'I'm taking you home now.'

'What about the dog?' Richie says. 'What about his hair all over the seats? My mom, she said—'

'Don't worry about the dog, the dog will be fine. Come on, in you both get. Yeah, you too, Buster – in. That's it, in you go, right in.'

Richie is silent on the way home but at least his breathing is quieter. Or maybe he just can't hear it over the dog's competitive panting. He plans on leaving them both at the end of the path leading to the house and giving the flowers to Richie to deliver to his grandmother. But when they get there, Mrs Kaplan and Richie's mother are unloading groceries out of the trunk of the Pontiac. Richie's mother turns when she hears the wheels on the gravel and stands for a moment, one knee of her bare leg pushed forward, holding a tray of lettuces like she's a cigarette girl.

'There you are, Richie!' she says as soon as they come to a stop. 'We've been looking all over for you. Where did you get to? Running off like that on such a busy day. Mother, look, it's Richie – at long last.'

She puts the tray of lettuces back into the trunk and begins towards the car.

And now Mrs Kaplan turns, puts down her tray and makes her way over, dusting her hands off. He stands out to greet her.

'I hope you're not here to tell us that you're not coming tomorrow, that you've changed your mind?' Mrs Kaplan says.

'Oh no, nothing like that. I just ran into Richie here and—'

Richie climbs out but the dog stays put. He notices Richie drop the twisted candy bar and heel it out of sight under the automobile.

'I was waiting for Katherine at the post office,' Richie says.

'You were *what*? Katherine is back hours ago and she didn't go to the post office today. Really, I don't know, the crazy ideas you get in your head. And on a day when we could do with all the help we can get.'

'You told me I was in the way.'

'What? Oh, you really are such a silly boy. And where's Michael? Isn't he with you?'

'No. I thought he was with Katherine.'

'Oh, honestly, Richie.'

Richie's mother then turns to him and smiles apologetically. 'I'm so sorry to put you to all this trouble.'

'Oh, no trouble, really. I was going to drop by later anyhow to deliver something, so I may as well do it now.'

He dips into the car and slides the bouquet out.

'Oh, what lovely flowers!' Mrs Kaplan says.

'I'm afraid the florist was too busy to deliver today or even tomorrow, so I thought I'd bring them myself.'

'Well, I'm very glad you did. Now, you must come up the house. Have a drink or something.'

'Oh, I think you're quite busy enough as it is,' he says.

'I'll make use of you, don't you worry about that,' Mrs Kaplan says. 'I could do with a little help moving a few things, to be honest. We had a man helping us earlier, but he seems to have disappeared. Goodness knows where. And I know nothing about him, you know, except that his name is Robin.'

'Yes,' Richie's mom says, 'and now he's just bobbed off!' She laughs at her little joke, then stops and swallows apologetically.

'I'll be only too glad to help you out,' he says.

He walks ahead with Mrs Kaplan, the flowers up in his arms. Mrs Kaplan is talking about the war in Korea and how the world is going crazy all over again. She seems well informed on political matters and so he listens to what she has to say. At the same time, he can't help hearing Richie and his mother walking behind them.

'But I took it this morning,' Richie is saying.

'Well, you better go right up and take it again, and lie down for a while. The last thing we need is you getting sick. And Richie – your new sweater. Know where I found it? No? I bet you don't. Well, on the beach is where, lying there like some old rag nobody cares a hoot about.'

'I'm sorry, Mom, I guess I must have left it there when I went swimming.'

'Well, you guess right because it hardly walked there on its own, now, did it? And what's that all over your face, would you mind telling me?'

'Nothin'.'

'Nothin' – my eye! Now we talked about this, Richie. You know we did. You're getting a little tubby and you don't want to be known as the tubby one in your new school, now, do you?'

'Oh, Mom, why do you have to keep saying that word? You know how much I hate that word!'

'You better lower your voice and behave yourself. Your father's friends are coming here and I don't want—'

'You mean Captain Hartman is coming! Well, I'll go up to my room and I'll stay there too, Mom. How about that? Then you and Captain Hartman can go off together to Hawaii or someplace like that.'

Then Richie runs past them with his red-faced mother marching closely behind.

Mrs Kaplan pauses, looks at him and gives a small smile. 'Poor Richie,' she says, 'he just can't seem to get it right.'

As they come to the house the maid is coming down the steps of the porch, a big tin bucket in her hand.

'Don't say he's been at it again, Rosetta?'

Rosetta holds her nose with her free hand. 'Oh yes, ma'am, he sure has.'

Mrs Kaplan puts out her hand and touches his sleeve. 'Careful,' she says, 'it's still a little soggy there under the junipers, and not all down to rain, I'm afraid. Buster has turned this whole area into his own private bathroom. I think we're going to have to put some sort of little fence around it, otherwise people's shoes will be destroyed. Maybe I'll ask that man Robin – if I ever find him again.'

Mrs Kaplan walks across the front porch and calls back to the maid. 'Rosetta, when you're finished there, would you mind taking those beautiful flowers and finding a home for them, please? I'll see you on the back porch,' she says to him and then disappears.

He stands with the flowers and waits for Rosetta to finish slopping the soapy water around the base of the tree. She puts the bucket down and comes to him, taking the bouquet and cooing over it, as if it's a baby she is lifting out of his arms.

He remembers then: 'Oh, one moment, please, Rosetta, there's a note. My wife gave me a…'

He looks through his pockets but all he can find are the remaining two items of mail he collected earlier from the post office.

'I can't seem to find it.'

'Oh, that's okay. Mrs Kaplan, she knows,' she says.

'My wife was very particular about that note.'

'Maybe you leave in automobile?'

'I'll go take a look.'

The dog is still sitting on the back seat when he gets there. He stands at the open door and says, 'Come on, time to go. Home, boy.'

The dog wags a thin tongue at him, but otherwise stays put.

'Come on now – beat it.'

He searches through the interior with the sound of the dog's panting in the background. He looks under the seats a second time, then down along the inside of the doors. He goes round to the trunk, opens it and looks in there. He comes back around and looks in the glove compartment.

'Unless you're sitting on it, are you, Buster?'

The dog looks away. He comes round to the back door, stretches his hand through and takes the dog by the collar and begins to pull. But it's as if the dog has been nailed to the seat. He goes round the other side with the intention of pushing Buster off the seat and out through the door. But then a long, searing whistle comes flying down the pathway; the dog's head lifts and in a second he's off the back seat and cantering off in the direction of the whistle.

He picks the envelope from the seat, straightens it out and plucks the dog hairs away from it.

There is nobody around when he gets back to the house. He stands on the porch step wondering what to do. He decides to go home, taking two steps down. And then he decides to stay, taking two steps back up. He crosses the porch and goes inside.

The lobby is better stocked than the florist's in Provincetown, with baskets of flowers and round-headed one-legged laurel bushes standing around in ceramic pots, and he pities his wife's offering back in the kitchen with Rosetta trying to make the most of it. He can hear a few disconnected piano notes somewhere and goes looking for their source.

The room is large and built on an L-shaped, three wide steps leading from one section to the other. He steps around boxes and stacks of folded card tables and garden chairs leaning against the walls. He comes down the three steps to the bay side of the room, with one glass wall and glass doors in the centre of it opening out onto a porch.

Over to the side, a man is bent over a piano, tuning it. All along the centre, a wall made of beer and wine crates. And standing on a big wooden table, pinning a string of bunting to the wall, is Katherine.

She is barefoot and tall, even taller than he had allowed, and he would like to know what her exact height is but of course would never bring himself to ask. He will just have to wait for an opportunity to stand beside her and work it out for himself.

'I hear you could use an extra pair of hands,' he says. 'I mean, your mother, she said—'

'Has she been bullying you into helping?' Katherine says without moving her head to look at him.

'Not at all. I'm very happy to help.'

'Liar!' she says, and glances under her arm for just a second and gives him a quick smile.

She pins another flag into place and now she is asking him something.

'I'm sorry?' he says.

'Michael – have you seen him?'

'Michael? No. I haven't seen him. Richie is here, though. He's gone upstairs with his mother.'

'Yes, I know, he sneaked down a while ago and asked me to whistle for his dog.'

'That was you? Well, that was a very impressive whistle.'

'Thanks. He's upset because he thinks Captain Hartman is trying to steal his mother.'

'I see.'

She brings her hand down from the wall, puts it on her hip and shakes her hair a little. 'Know what you could do, though? You could take those boxes over there and bring them to Rosetta in the kitchen.'

She turns her voice to the piano tuner but she keeps her eyes on him. 'Say, Frank, you ever come across a Captain Hartman? Walt Hartman?'

'The clarinet man? I sure did, baby.'

She laughs and says, 'He's not being fresh, not really. He calls everyone baby. He'll probably call you baby too, if you talk to him.'

'Well, I better not talk to him so,' he says.

He is aware that he has a fool's grin on his face and so he makes an inquiring gesture with his arm towards the boxes.

'The first two, right there. She'll give you a box to bring back with you. That's all we do around here, send boxes back and forth from the kitchen.'

He goes over to the row of boxes and bends his knees to the first one, dreading the first lift and bracing himself for a jolt. He is relieved and only slightly disappointed when it turns out to weigh hardly anything at all.

When he comes back from the kitchen, Frank is playing a tune on the piano and Katherine is still on the table. This time she is dancing, her bare feet gliding from side to side, her brown hair across one shoulder.

For a second he sees himself walk across the room, put his arms around her hips and lift her off the table. He imagines her sliding along his body till her feet touch the ground, and he sees himself then dancing tight to her, barely moving, hardly covering any ground at all, but dancing just the same.

If I was Picasso, maybe, he thinks, Picasso or one of those other European guys. A different man, anyhow, in a different sort of world.

He raises the box that Rosetta has given him. 'Clean glasses and napkins,' he says, 'and candles for when the sun goes down. She says.'

'For when the sun goes down…' Katherine sings and across the room the piano player laughs.

He lays the box down on the floor. Then he goes back and lifts another box destined for the kitchen. He can see her ghostly shape shift and sway on the big glass window. Colorado brown, he decides, is the colour of her hair.

WHEN HE GETS HOME, it is almost dusk and she is taking in the washing.

'You took your time!' she says.

'Is Michael here?' he asks.

'He just left about ten minutes ago. Went by the beach – why?'

'Was he long here?'

'Well, yes. And I was glad of his company too. He arrived shortly after you left – how did it go at the florist's?'

'I already delivered them.'

'But I thought—?'

'They wouldn't deliver. Too busy today and even busier tomorrow.'

He goes into the house.

A moment later, she follows him, arms full of laundry. She drops the pile on the chaise longue.

'Well? Anything interesting in the mail?'

'What? Oh no, nothing, just a postcard from the library and an inventory from February's show.'

'Nothing else?'

'I'm sorry.'

'Never mind. Maybe after Labor Day. As you say, the whole of New York is closed down this time of the year.'

She plucks a sheet out of the pile and begins shaking it out. He steps over, takes the end of the sheet and together they straighten it out, then fold it over, once then twice.

'They're going all out at the Kaplans',' he says, 'got a piano player and everything, name of Frank. He calls everyone baby, it seems. Mrs Kaplan asked me to help her out – that's what delayed me. She loved the flowers, by the way.'

'Oh, good. You didn't lift anything, I hope? You know you're not supposed—'

'Just a few glasses and napkins, knocked a couple of nails into a couple of walls. Nothing strenuous at all.'

She takes the folded sheet and puts it on the table, then she comes back and picks out another sheet and they begin again.

'I ran into Richie today,' he says. 'Matter of fact, I ran into him twice. I don't think it's at all true what Michael says.'

'What does Michael say?'

'About him not wanting to come here.'

'You don't?'

'No, I think Michael does, in fact, sneak off behind his back.'

'Oh, I see.'

'Richie,' he begins, catching the end of the sheet and stepping away.

'What?' she says.

He steps back to her. She takes the folded half from him.

'*What?*' she says again.

He turns his mouth down and shakes his head.

She lets the sheet slip through her arms and waits.

'I don't know,' he says, 'but I think he may be the loneliest person I have ever met.'

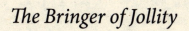

The Bringer of Jollity

1

ON THE BACK PORCH stoop, Michael stands picking his nose. It's the morning of the big party and he is first out of bed. He has been watching daylight push out of the darkness. He has been sniffing the dark smell of the sea. And now, as the sun spreads over the bay, he waits for the grackles to show.

There is a light south-westerly breeze. He knows which direction it is coming from because one day, a couple of weeks ago, Mrs Aitch gave him what she called a short lesson in orientation. Seagulls face into it, cows turn their tail ends to it, your face will tell you the rest – that was how the lesson began. Now every time they meet, she says, 'Hey, Michael, know which way the wind blows?'

He knows. North is from Provincetown and south is from Wellfleet. East is over the Atlantic side where the sun nudges up from the ocean each morning. West is the bay side where Mrs Aitch said it flops down at night and pulls the covers up over its head.

Today the breeze is chilly as well as light. The weather is beginning to turn – Mrs Kaplan said so when they were all out here last night and she brought Katherine an extra sweater.

And Richie's mom had sighed. 'You can feel it now, evenings and mornings, no matter how warm it is during the day.'

And then Frank, the piano man, said, 'It's making its first move towards winter.'

When he said that, Katherine and her mother gave each other this quick-fire look and then turned their faces away like they were afraid of something. He couldn't see Katherine's face, but he could see Mrs Kaplan's and for one terrible second he thought maybe she was going to cry.

But then Frank stood up. He touched the back of Mrs Kaplan's chair as he passed by, patted her on the shoulder and went inside. The floor had been cleared to make way for the party and hardly anything was left in the living-room at all, just two long tables that had been turned into a bar and, on the other side of the room, a big low-backed piano turned sideways that Frank had brought all the way from Boston in a truck. All over the floor were stacks of folded tables and chairs waiting to be brought out first thing this morning and straightened out on the grass. He could hear Frank's footsteps crossing the living-room floor, the slight drag on one foot, and then Richie's whisper in his ear that Frank lost half his leg in Sicily. And then you could hear the music coming out of the house onto the porch.

At first, just a few loose tinkles and nobody seemed to know the song, but then Mrs Kaplan put her finger in the air, the way she does sometimes like she knows something is coming. She began nodding her head to the music. 'What question is he asking you, Michael?' she said.

But he had to wait for another few notes to join up before he could say, 'He's asking if I'd like to swing on a star.'

'Good boy!'

In the living-room the piano man rolled the notes round and round and the tune melted away and a different tune took over. Richie's mom took a swig of her cocktail, closed her eyes and said, 'You would think he was playing two pianos in there.'

And Annette sucked her olive like a lollipop and said, 'Isn't it simply wonnerful…?'

After a while the tune came back to 'Swinging on a Star' and Mrs Kaplan said, 'Do you remember, Richie – do you remember how you used to stand on the kitchen table and sing that for us – how you used to do all the actions, your little face so serious?' And Richie said, 'Ah, come on, Grandma – I did not.'

Richie's mom stuck her fingers up out from the side of her head and went *hee-haw*, *hee-haw* and Mrs Kaplan laughed and Richie's mom laughed and Katherine laughed and Annette laughed and even Richie laughed. Everyone laughed except him because he didn't know what was supposed to be so funny about a little kid standing on a kitchen table singing, and anyhow it was a

Kaplan story that had happened a long time ago, when Richie's father and grandfather were still alive, and had nothing got to do with him. And then a few seconds later Captain Hartman arrived and Richie wasn't laughing so much after that.

He takes his finger from his nose, looks at the small bogey sitting on top of it, like a baby snail pulled out of its house. He glances around for somewhere to hide it, then moves away from the step and wipes his finger on the side of Katherine's full ashtray. He takes one of her lipsticky butts, draws the bogey into the middle of the stack and buries it there among the ashes. Then he puts the butt on the edge of his lip. He feels a lightness in his chest while he does this; his legs heat up; his wrists feel sort of weak. The lipstick had been on her lips, the cigarette in her mouth; the snot up his nose. Now the cigarette is in his mouth. He closes his lips around it and sucks. But the taste of old ashes is sickening and he throws the butt back in the stack and swipes his tongue several times across the back of his hand.

He decides to think about Katherine. Usually, he waits till he gets to his hidey-hole where he doesn't have to worry if he gets a little excited or talks to her out loud. But he won't get there today – not after he promised Mrs Kaplan he would stick around and help whoever needs help, starting with Mr Aitch this morning, when he comes early to take out all the tables and chairs.

He sits on her seat, puts his feet up where her feet are usually put, lays his head back where her head is usually laid. He lifts her shawl and rubs it along his face. Then he presses it down on his lips.

The night he yelled at Katherine in the lobby, he had to grab his face to stop himself crying as she went up the stairs. He pulled so hard on his cheeks he thought they were going to tear off like broiled meat in his hands. When he finally got the nerve up to go back to his own room, he got in bed and cried himself dry. Next day, he was so worried about running into her that he waited till Richie had gone downstairs and there wasn't a sound in the upstairs part of the house. He planned on sneaking right out, going to his hidey-hole and then, when he felt better later, going on to see Mrs Aitch. He had no intention of going in for breakfast anyhow, seeing them all in there looking up when he walked in the door, Katherine in the middle of them, probably telling them that he was the worst sort of thief and everyone suddenly remembering the little things that had gone missing: Richie and his scout's penknife, Rosetta and her jar of peaches, Mrs Kaplan and her silver nail scissors, and Richie's mom going, 'So that's where my *Ladies' Home Journal* got to!'

As he sneaked down the corridor and past her bedroom, he could see through the half-open door. He had to stop to take a second look because he just couldn't believe it. The whole room was all smoothed out, apart from one blur in the bedclothes where she had been sleeping. No clothes on the floor, no shoes hanging by their heels off the furniture; no photographs, no ashtray spilling out on the rug. No blood. Nothing. It was as if he had dreamed the whole thing up in his head. Then as he walked down the hallway and turned to go down the stairs, he saw Katherine just ahead of him. Everything inside him jumped, like he'd gotten an electric shock or something. He was about to turn back, hide in the closet – jump off the verandah if he had to. But it was too late, because she'd seen him already.

'Oh, hello, you,' she said and waited for him so they could walk in together. 'I'm so glad I'm not the only late worm this morning.'

She took his arm as they went in the door and sat right next to him at the table. She put a pancake on his plate and a squirt of maple syrup at the side of it. When he found the courage to look at her, she gave him one of her half-winks. At first he thought she was feeling sorry about last night and was just trying to be nice to him, but then he thought maybe it had nothing to do with last night because Katherine – well, she didn't act like she remembered anything about any of that.

He rubs the lower part of the shawl against his leg; the fringe is thick and feels like little fingers tickling his bare skin. Then it starts again. The soft heat crawling into the tops of his legs. He knows this feeling and wants nothing to do with it. He does not want to feel this dirty way about Katherine again; he does not want to have those pictures open out in his head or to end up crying with that terrible feeling in his chest, like he is going to die of a pain he can't put a name on.

He pushes the shawl away, sits up and looks out at the bay.

But he can't see the sky. There's a thick, pale fog on the bay blocking his view. He leans in some more, worried now that the grackles will sneak in behind the fog, meaning he won't be able to tell Mrs Aitch that he saw them and he wants so much to be able to tell her, to let her know that he took the trouble to get up just after dawn for that very reason.

She told him all about the grackle bird when they were out for a walk one day, that it is mean and stubborn and nothing but trouble. It plucks the farmers' corn seeds out of the land. It eats the eggs of other birds and it doesn't mind eating smaller birds or mice either – 'Oh, but it loves the taste of a nice juicy field mouse,' was how she put it, 'the way you and me, we love the taste of a nice juicy steak. Black, spindly legged, crazy eyed, they are not much to look at. When they get together the noise they make would split your ears right open. There is nothing to endear them to man and it's no wonder that the collective noun for them is plague or annoyance.'

And then, lifting her chin and clasping her hands like she was about to start singing a hymn or something, 'Oh but, Michael, when they take off, when they fly over the sky just after dawn and the early sun tips over their backs and the rich, deep colours begin to lift, sapphire and emerald, and oh, oh… as they move across the bay in long, loose lines, well… it's as if one is looking at the threads of a heavenly tapestry.'

When he first got to know Mrs Aitch, he used to feel like laughing right in her face whenever she talked that fancy way. But after a while he got to like it. And when one day at lunch Richie started to mimic something fancy she had said, he wanted to punch him right in his dumb fat face.

Richie's mom said, 'Well, yes, she does sometimes sound a little stagey, I agree, but it's not your place to criticize grown-ups.'

And then, of course, Annette Staines had to have her say. 'Oh, come on, Olivia, the boy is quite right. Honestly, she's probably one of the most pretentious people I have ever come across. I mean, just pin me to the wall and bore me to death, why don't you?'

In his hidey-hole, he cuts figures out of magazines. He cuts furniture out for the rooms. He keeps them safe in some of the envelopes Mrs Kaplan gave him.

Each room has a separate envelope and so has each cut-out person. He keeps all the envelopes in a green canvas bag he found one night in a chest under the stairs.

In his cut-out world, Rosetta is his friend, Mrs Kaplan is his grandmother, Mrs Aitch is his mom. It should really be the other way round, because Mrs Aitch is probably older than Mrs Kaplan. And Mrs Aitch could probably be his friend too, because he talks to her more than he talks to any other person.

He takes the furniture out of the envelopes and arranges it into the shapes of rooms, then he takes all the cut-out people and moves them around his pre- tend house. Once he cut out a Frau Aunt figure holding her secret baby. She knocked at the door and the cut-out Rosetta hopped along to answer it.

'I'm sorry, ma'am,' Rosetta said. 'No one here is that name. And can I say, that is a bery, bery ugly baby you have there.'

That day at lunch when they said those things about Mrs Aitch, he put down his fork, stood up from the table and began to walk away.

'What do we saaay?' Richie's mom said.

'I don't know.'

'I don't know...?'

'I don't know, ma'am.'

'We say, "May I be excused?" That's what we say when we leave the table before everyone else has finished eating.'

And he felt himself go red and his throat swell up, so that he couldn't say, 'May I be excused?' even if he had wanted to. He wouldn't have been able to get the first word out without choking. So he just kept walking.

'Well!' Richie's mom said, all shocked like it was the worst thing she'd ever seen in her whole life, a boy walking away from a table without saying, 'May I be excused?'

But Katherine. Katherine, she said, 'Oh, leave the kid alone, why don't you, Olivia? He's supposed to be on vacation.'

In his cut-out world, Katherine is his wife, and not just because she is beau- tiful. Turn a page in any magazine and no matter what other woman is there – Ava Gardner, Elizabeth Taylor – he doesn't care how much they smile up at him, Katherine will always be more beautiful. But more than that, she sticks up for him like no one else in the world has ever stuck up for him. And that is why he will always love her best.

The first time he got that fire in his belly about her, he was in his hidey-hole pretending to kiss her. He felt the tingles so much stronger than usual, shooting right up through his body. He closed his eyes and began rubbing himself and it felt so good pretending to kiss her and feeling the tingles getting stronger and hotter from his belly all the way down and in his legs all the way up. But then everything changed and he could hear German voices in his head – voices laughing and talking – and Katherine disappeared and he was inside a house in the middle of the night and there was a woman whispering, Micha, Micha, and pulling him out of his nice warm bed and shoving him under it instead. He was a little boy. And he could see the hands pushing him under the bed and covering him with a blanket. But he could not see the face. He could hear voices, though – a man and a woman overhead; the man grunting and the woman making smaller noises and the mattress above his face bulging through the diamond-shaped cage, and he was saying, '*Wer ist der mann?*' Who is that man? The taste of dust, the stripes on the mattress and the woman's voice – a voice he knew and yet didn't know – saying, 'Shhh shhh. Shhh, Micha, shhh.'

~

THIS MORNING HIS WIFE is up unusually early. He can hear her walking around the outside of the house even before he opens his eyes. Then he hears her firing up the tub. After that, he hears nothing at all.

'You all right in there?' he calls from the bedroom while tying his shoe-laces. 'I said, are you—?'

'Why wouldn't I be?'

'You seem a little quiet, that's all.'

'Why, you want to talk about something?'

'No, no. You go right ahead, enjoy your swim. I have my letters to write.'

His wife used to take care of such matters. But after she threw the Kaplans off the beach, that all changed. Their fight was over; they were discussing peace terms and he told her he was tired of her making decisions on his behalf, throwing people off the beach, responding to his letters with little or no consultation. And he was tired, too, of having to chase her letters with letters of his own in an effort to straighten things out.

He said: 'It makes me seem effete and you seem a little crazy, all this chopping and changing of minds.'

She said: 'I may be crazy but you're bone lazy – you can write your own damn letters in future.'

And now, it would seem, he is stuck with the task.

He takes his coffee over to the table, looks down at the stack of letters received over the past couple of weeks that are still awaiting his response. The word *tedium* blinks on and off in his head like a neon sign.

He selects a few from the pile: two people to thank; three invitations to refuse; one death to console; and his sister.

His sister cannot be put off for too long. She will need her allowance and he can't very well send a lone cheque with no word attached. He never knows what to say to her now but as children they communicated so easily. They would finish each other's sentences, at night draw pictures like comic strips and slip them under the doors of one another's bedrooms. He would hear her already laughing as he sneaked back to his own room. When he went away to camp he would write her long, funny letters. It cost him no effort to do so and brought him great pleasure. Now, he might as well be out in a snowstorm, chiselling the words into stone. He decides to put his sister on hold for the moment and to start instead by responding to the letter that came yesterday from his old friend in New York. He takes an envelope and puts the address of the gallery on it. Then he places a page over it and begins to write:

Old friend,
There is no need to apologize. I know only too well that you did whatever you could do, and for that I am eternally grateful…

Fearful suddenly that she will get out of the bath-tub and come silently behind him to look over his shoulder, he rushes to the end. A few short, warm lines, a promise to pick the paintings up when he gets back to New York, a joke about breaking the news to his wife and his chances of being alive next time they meet. Then, hurriedly, he folds the letter into the envelope and slips it into his inside pocket.

He continues with the gallery assistant who worked on his retrospective back in February. He writes the word *Dear* but forgets her name now, although it's only been moments since he read her signature. He does remember that her title is Miss and that her name begins with A.

Dear-Miss-A has certainly taken trouble over the list, dividing it into columns of title, date, sale price and final destination. He takes the list into his hand. As he runs his eye over the titles of the paintings, a series of images swing in and out of his mind: a woman sitting in her underwear on the side of a bed; then a blast of white water; now the side of a building cowed by light.

At first glance the list appears to be satisfyingly long. But when he lays it down on the table and runs the blunt end of his pen slowly over it, it becomes less impressive. He thinks – is this a whole life now? Or most of a life anyhow. Even if I live another ten years, the rate I'm producing, the list isn't going to grow all that much longer. Maybe it's not going to grow at all, maybe the Orleans painting will be the swan song – that's it then, thank you, folks, and safe journey home...

His wife calls out to him: 'I got up early.'

'You certainly did.'

'Couldn't sleep so I thought to have a long soak now, then a little breakfast, then back into bed for an hour and go back to sleep so that I'm fresh for this afternoon – what do you think?'

'Good idea,' he says, even though they both know the chances of her falling back to sleep are less than none – she is up now and will fidget and fuss until it's time to set off for the party.

'That was a hint by the way.'

'What was—? Oh, I see. Would you like me to fix you some breakfast?'

'Oh yes!' she says and he can hear the water swoosh joyfully as she goes under.

He shifts the letters about and finds the name of the gallery assistant peeping shyly out from beneath the edge of an income tax bill. Miss Arnott. Miss A.

Arnott. He can't remember her face but can imagine her neat hands ruling out the lines, transcribing the information, squeezing it into the columns. He probably never met her – they come and go so quickly these days. Nobody wants to make it their life's work any more. He recalls a blue-eyed Kentuckian who came to sit by him one night at an opening, breath tinged with cheap wine, calling him *sir*. A few months off her retirement and she told him, 'I dreamed my whole life of working in a New York gallery, sir, let my fiancé go and everything. And what did I get? Varicose veins and lousy pay. A boss who never learned the meaning of the word appreciation. Conceited artists who look right through me. And, sir, the paintings that are coming in now, you wouldn't believe! Some of them I don't know which end up they're supposed to hang.'

He writes: 'Dear Miss Arnott, I'm writing to tell you how much I appreciate all your hard work…'

From the bathroom, he hears a slap of water, the occasional spurt of a hot top-up. He finishes the letter for Miss Arnott, then writes the same RSVP three times – unfortunately we won't be in New York on that date – and can't help feeling a touch of glee as he does so. He decides to maintain his good humour and postpone the letter of condolence for another day.

He comes back to his sister. Holding the cheque-book in his hand, he flicks back through the stubs and wonders how she is doing now. The one and only visit she made to Truro left relations between them strained – even when they were alone, driving back to the station, neither could seem to find a word to say beyond goodbye. The row had been between the two women – he had nothing to do with it, had refused to take sides – yet both had ended up despising him.

He cannot even think of how to begin the letter. Dear? My dearest? Sister of mine?

He pulls a cheque out of the book and signs it. He holds it in both hands for a moment, then reaches out and takes a sheet of yellow sketching paper from the pile further along the table. He begins to make a sketch. It turns into a drawing of his wife and himself in a boxing ring, mitts raised. Beneath the drawing he writes: 'Well, I guess we're having another swell summer here on the Cape…'

He folds the drawing, puts it with the cheque into an envelope and regards the pile still waiting on a response. He pushes this aside, then lifts the small bunch of letters that are ready to go to the mail and slips them into the inside pocket of his jacket alongside the letter to his friend. He gets up and goes out to the bathroom.

Through the crack in the door, he sees his wife's head resting like a duck on top of the water.

'I'm just going to have a shave, then I'll fix your breakfast and then I'll be going out,' he says.

The duck flies up. 'To the post office?'

'Yes, yes and then I'll be going to—'

'Where? Where? Where will you be going?'

'I told Mrs Kaplan I'd drop by this morning and help her out with a few things.'

'Oh, you did, did you? And what about me?'

'You need help with something?'

'No, but…'

'I'm going to shave in the kitchen,' he says. 'The light's better in there.'

He steps into the bathroom, takes his shaving kit off the shelf.

'There's hours to go before the party,' he says. 'I won't be very long.'

'Fine, just don't you forget about me! Because I don't want to be late, I don't want to miss any—'

'Don't drown in that now,' he says and goes out to the kitchen.

Her voice follows him out. 'Oh, and by the way, I'm driving today.'

He stops.

'There and back,' she adds.

He takes off his jacket, puts it on the back of the chair. Then he sets up the coffee pot and comes back to the bathroom door.

'Did you just say something to me there?' he says. 'I didn't quite—'

'Yes, I certainly did. I said I want to drive. There and back.'

'If that's what you want…'

The water rocks back then forward and the duck is up again: 'Oh now, what's that supposed to mean, "If that's what you want…" Why are you saying it in that tone?'

'I know how you dislike driving in the dark, that's all.'

'You think we're going to stay that late? You think you're going to want to?'

'Looks like it's going to be quite a party. You should hear the piano player. They've cleared out the living-room for dancing.'

'Oh? Well, even so, it's only a short drive. I can manage.'

He nods, says, 'Of course,' and then he goes back to the kitchen.

He hooks the mirror onto the clasp of the window, softens the soap and creams it across his stiffened jaw. It occurs to him that what she really wants is for people to see her arrive by car, behind the wheel, driving. To be like the Kaplan women and countless other women around here. He has a vision of her edging up to join the end of a line of automobiles. The parking attendant Mrs Kaplan has hired politely guiding her in; he will be wearing white gloves, probably. Bumper to bumper, every inch of space precious today, and then the smashing sound as she hits the rear of the automobile parked ahead of her, and the crunch as she backs into the one right behind.

He makes a long swipe with the razor through the soap and regards his own pale eye gravely. He thought they were over all that by now: the question of her driving. He thought the incident earlier in the summer had put paid to it. On that occasion, she had wandered into the middle of the road just as a pick-up truck was coming round the corner. He had had to pull the steering wheel out of her hands, veer it into the side and allow it ram right into a post. But better a post than the front of a pick-up truck. She had refused to let go of the steering wheel – had insisted she'd been in the right. He tried to prise her hands off it and, when that didn't work, he tried pulling her out of the seat. One pull and she slid right off and landed halfway out the door. People in a nearby restaurant looking out the window, appalled. After that he swore there would be no more fights about driving. That he would let her drive if that's what she wanted. Sooner or later, she was bound to kill one of them. He didn't always mind which one of them it would be.

He pats his face dry, cleans and tidies the shaving equipment and unhooks the mirror. Then he puts on the coffee pot and begins to set the breakfast tray.

'I want to drive,' her voice declares.

He turns and there she is, a thin beige bath towel pulled around her: a raw shrimp wrapped up in pastry.

'Yes, I understand.'

He can feel the air stiffen between them.

'Don't think you can stop me,' she says with that gunslinger look in her eye.

'I have no intention of stopping you.'

'Because I want to,' she insists, 'and we agreed that whenever I wanted—'

'And I said fine. Do you want your breakfast tray in here or will I put it by the bed?'

'Put it anywhere you like, just don't you forget who's doing the driving.'

MICHAEL PINS HIS EYES to the fog. It is beginning to lift from the bottom up, like a curtain in a movie theatre. He can see just below it, a band of sea water that makes him think of a band of Christmas lametta. The fog turns to mist and the mist becomes wispy and the sky grows wide and the sea wings out. He leans forward a little more, hopeful once again for a sighting of the grackles.

But then noises begin to come out from the house, distracting him: a thud, then a few creaks long and short, and now the sound of somebody whistling.

He sits up, puts one leg out and begins to lean away from Katherine's chair.

He recognizes the whistling. It belongs to Mrs Kaplan. She always whistles when she brings Katherine's breakfast tray and he has heard her whistle at other times too, when she's alone in her study or outside pulling at things in the garden. She whistles as good as Harry whistles on his way home from work, or any other man he's ever heard down on the street.

He goes to the big glass door and presses his ear to it, following the trail of the whistling as it comes down the stairs. He waits to see where it will go next, into the kitchen or maybe out here. But the whistling cuts off even before it reaches the lobby and he has no sure way of knowing where Mrs Kaplan has gone or will go next. He hurries back to Katherine's chair, throws the shawl on the end of the seat and begins smoothing out the head rest. A few piano notes trot out behind him, one a little higher than the other. He goes back to the glass door, this time peering right into the room. He can see Mrs Kaplan standing at the piano. She is wearing a long purple bathrobe and her hair is all bunched up in pin curlers. The notes play again, about seven in all, and then, as if she knows he's standing there, she turns suddenly and looks straight at him. She comes smiling across the room, tugging a bunch of keys from her pocket.

She fidgets with the keys for a while, looks up at him and makes a face as if to say – so many keys, why do we need so many keys?

Her reflection leans into his reflection. His reflection passes through hers, and it is like they are both standing underwater staring at one another. Everything stops for a couple of seconds, then the room behind her starts filling up with people. Hundreds of see-through people, standing there in one big blurry crowd. Ghosts. He thinks, they have got to be ghosts.

And it comes to him then that you don't need a war for people to die. Sometimes they just die, the way poor Jake just died. One day Mrs Kaplan will die and then she will be a ghost. And one day he will be a ghost too. But Mrs Kaplan, she will have melted back into the crowd long before it is his turn to stand on the far side of the glass. He feels a small twist in his chest at the thought of it. His mouth tightens up, ready to cry. And now she is looking at him, frowning. Her eyes look worried but then suddenly they lift and now they are staring at something way over his head. Through their shared reflection, he sees a long, dark scribble move over the glass and edge into the sky. He spins round and looks up. But the grackles – if it was the grackles – are already out of sight.

The door slides opens. There is only Mrs Kaplan in the living-room. Mrs Kaplan and the piano standing sideways with one wing raised and the long tables covered in white cloths with rows and rows of bottles standing along them, glinting.

'Michael! And I thought I was the only one up at this hour. I hope I didn't scare you.'

'Oh no, I knew it was you. I heard you whistling.'

Mrs Kaplan laughs. 'And now you caught me in my robe with my hair in pin curlers. My mother would not be pleased. She was against my whistling, you see, thought it would stop me from getting a husband. Actually, it turned out to have quite the opposite effect. My husband, well, he swore he fell in love with me because of my whistling ability. And as for the pin curlers… I'm sure you won't tell a soul. How did you get out here by the way?'

'Through the kitchen door.'

'Oh, I must have forgotten to lock it. I've only recently started locking up the house at night and I still forget how many doors there are in this place – have you been up long?'

'A little while.'

'Excited about the party?'

'I don't know. Are you?'

'A little nervous.'

'But why?'

'Oh, I'm afraid I may have overdone things. It is one of the many reasons I miss my late husband – he stopped me from overdoing things. But who knows: it could go the other way and maybe no one will turn up, and we will be left eating finger food – as Olivia somewhat unappetisingly calls it – until long after Thanksgiving.'

'Mr and Mrs Aitch, they'll come.'

'Why, they will, of course, and that will be party enough for us, Michael. Tell you what, why don't you and I go in the kitchen and have a little breakfast before the whole house is up and about? We hardly ever get a chance to have a little talk on our own – do we?'

'No, Mrs Kaplan.'

'I'll put the coffee on and you can beat the eggs. We're going to need a good breakfast inside us. Because, you know, once this place begins to fill up…'

In the kitchen, Mrs Kaplan is looking through cabinets like she has never been in this room before, opening and closing doors, frowning at everything she sees.

'I notice you're becoming quite the letter writer now,' she says from behind the door of the icebox, and he's glad she's in there and can't see his face redden up.

She comes out with a butter dish in one hand.

'Well, I admire you, I must say. How many have you written this week?'

'I don't know, six, maybe seven, I guess.'

'Well, that is quite a lot. And have you heard any news from home, I wonder?'

She goes to the pantry and he can see the back of her head move up and down, then side to side.

'A couple,' he says, 'my aunt, she wrote and Harry signed his name at the bottom. But I haven't had anything in a while. I guess they've probably moved to their new apartment by now and won't bother writing again.'

'They wouldn't move without telling you, Michael. Those are good people you have taking care of you, you know.'

When she turns back round she's smiling and there's a big box of eggs in her hands.

'Do you remember me from the orphanage, Michael?'

'Sort of… I don't know.'

'Do you remember when you first arrived there?'

'I'm not sure.'

'What about before then – do you remember any of that?'

'No. Not really.'

'Well, all I know is that when you came to the orphanage you were a very shy little boy and I'm certainly glad to see you have so many friends now. And that you stay in touch with them too. It's important to do that, I think. To stay in touch with our friends. You know, some of the people coming today are girls I went to school with, oh, a hundred years ago. Girls!' She laughs and rolls up her eyes. 'One of them will soon be a great-grandmother – can you imagine? Although she was a few years ahead of me, of course,' she says and gives him a little wink, exactly like one of Katherine's little winks.

'I tried to get Richie to pen pal a couple of times, a boy in Hong Kong and another boy in France – both Americans who lost their fathers in the war. He wrote once or twice but the boys didn't reply or maybe it was Richie who didn't want to keep it up – anyhow, it didn't work out for whatever reason. And how about your friends – do they reply?'

'Well, I don't see how. I don't give them the address.'

'You don't – why not?'

'Well, you know, because they could be too busy to write back and maybe they wouldn't have the money for envelopes and all. And anyhow, I want to wait till I get back to school to hear all the news.'

'Oh, I see,' she says.

She pulls a large fork from the drawer then stands in the middle of the room, looking around. 'The bowl for mixing eggs,' she says, 'now, what does Rosetta use for mixing eggs?'

'She keeps it up there – look, on those shelves beside the stove,' he says. 'And look, on the shelf next to that is where she keeps the big copper pan.'

'Oh yes, so it is!'

She comes back to the table, places the bowl and the box of eggs in front of him. Then hands him the big fork.

'Get cracking!' she says and they both laugh.

She stops laughing then and puts her finger in the air, tilting her head towards the kitchen door. She goes to the door, pushes it open with her foot, and he hears now what she has already heard: the sound of the telephone ringing.

'I'll be right back,' she says and the kitchen door swings shut behind her.

He counts the eggs in the box and it comes up to twenty-four. He doesn't know how many he is supposed to break but decides to deal with them one at a time – crack, beat and then go on to the next one. He will just have to hope Mrs Kaplan comes back before he has gone too far.

Sunlight on one half of the kitchen, through the big window it flints off the sea and puts a glow on the wood of the beams and the floor and the table. It makes him think he is in a ship on the ocean. He looks out at the sea and rocks himself from side to side to make it feel real. The clock inches towards six forty-five.

It seems funny to be standing here, an egg in his hand, the bowl placed before him on the table. Frau Aunt would never allow it. He could lay the table and take down the trash, maybe dry the dishes once in a while or serve the sandwiches on choir night to Harry and his pals – but that was about it.

The egg feels precious in his hand. Fragile and at the same time tough. He's not sure what he's supposed to do with it, so he pictures Frau Aunt and what she would do in his place. He taps the egg on the side of the bowl. But the shell doesn't crack. He gives it another whack, and this time it falls apart in his hand, its insides slobbering down the side of the bowl and all over the table. He takes the shell with him over to the trash, phlegm dribbling out on the floor. Then he picks a cloth up and tries to clean the table off. But the egg's guts are stuck to the cloth. He spends a few moments rinsing it out. When he's finished doing all that, he looks at the clock. Another five minutes gone past. He hears Rosetta move around the basement but she goes out the other way and doesn't come into the kitchen. The sun twitches on the icebox handle; it swirls round a big tray of cocktail glasses that are waiting to be taken out; it zips up the wall and nips the side of the copper pan that Mrs Kaplan forgot to take down from the shelf. And he thinks: when I'm grown up I'm going to live in this house. I'm going to stand in this kitchen and pretend I'm on a ship.

He pulls a knife out of the cutlery drawer and starts over. This time, he manages to get through the shell, pulling it apart with his fingers, and it all falls down into the bowl. He takes the fork, stabs it into the perfect yolk and flicks it around. He picks up the next egg and does the same thing.

The first time he asked Mrs Kaplan for an envelope it was for Harry and Frau Aunt. She gave him one envelope and two sheets of paper.

'If you bring your letters to me when you're done,' she said, 'I'll see that someone takes them to the post office.'

'Oh, that's all right, ma'am. Katherine said I could come with her whenever she goes and that way I can mail them myself.'

It was only when he said that to Mrs Kaplan that he realized: the more letters he wrote, the more often he would get to go to the post office with Katherine.

He could be sure then of sitting beside her in the Pontiac and talking to her on the way to the post office, and maybe she would take him to Eastham with her when she went to Doctor Tom's for her shot. And he could look at her all he liked while she drove along; her hands on the wheel and her leg sticking out from the gap in her skirt and her beautiful face and her hair and all.

After that, he wrote so many letters that Mrs Kaplan ended up giving him a whole block of writing paper and a half box of envelopes. 'There now,' she said, 'that should keep you going a while.'

At first he used real names, names of boys in his class, although he didn't mail the letters to them – mostly because he didn't know anyone's address, and even if he did actually send one to a real boy, what was he supposed to say?

After that, he made up a few names to go with pretend addresses; whatever came into his head at the time. He tried to keep it to five or six letters a week and nobody seemed to notice. Except maybe Richie.

Richie said, 'How come you never said anything about all these friends back in New York before?'

'Because it's none of your business.'

'But you don't have to write them now, do you? I mean *right* now?'

'Yes, I do.'

'You're supposed to be here to keep me company, in case you didn't know, not so you can keep running off or hiding away to write letters.'

'Is that so?'

'Yeah, it is so. I could have had the two Westin boys from Hyannis instead. I mean, they're bullies and all, but at least they don't keep running off. What are their names anyhow?'

'Whose names – the boys from Hyannis?'

'No, your friends in New York. What are they called?'

'What's it to you what they're called?'

'I'm just not sure I believe you, is all. To tell you the truth, I think you tell an awful lot of lies. Some people would call you a liar.'

'And some people would call you a big ugly fat-head who can't find any friends of his own.'

The boy stands at the kitchen table breaking and beating eggs and thinking on and off about the letters he wrote. He breaks one egg and then another, until he has a bowl full of thick bright-yellow paint. He waits for Mrs Kaplan to come back. He waits until he hears the rest of the house moving around and Rosetta talking to someone out front of the house and the sound of truck doors slamming at the end of the lane and the stamp of the delivery men's feet over the ground as they carry the party up to the house.

~

HE PARKS THE BUICK out on the road, manoeuvres himself around a delivery truck and comes blind to the house, juniper leaves cutting up the light and throwing it in his face. Past the cedar trees, his sight begins to clear and now he can see Rosetta on the porch signing for deliveries to the left and the right of her, like a movie star doling out autographs.

'Oh hello, sir,' she says and beckons him on through her little fan club. 'So early! Go right in living-room, I go pull the boys out of bed.'

He hoists the hammer and a piece of trellis under one arm and falls in behind two delivery men: one of them carrying a crate of wine in a pair of hair-coated arms; the other having a much easier ride with a sack of dinner rolls over one shoulder. He glances behind and two more of them are coming up the rear, carrying stacks of flat, white canapé boxes. In the house, the delivery men turn left for the kitchen; he turns right for the living-room.

The room is deserted, the glass doors have been pushed all the way back and he can hear an odd pulsing sound out on the porch. He walks over the bare floors, aware of his echoing feet. Then he continues out to the porch and stands for a while regarding the sloped lawn and trying to figure out the various pegs that have been dunted into it. The pulsing sound continues. He moves along the porch and finds a gramophone player where a played-out record is still spinning under the needle. The cover of the record lies on a chair. He picks it up and studies it for a moment: an eerie pink and blue depiction of outer space, one lone figure, old and bent like some sort of Merlin, struggling to stay upright against the power of the surrounding planets.

Footsteps tip along the wooden floor and now Mrs Kaplan is beside him.

'Are you familiar with *The Planets* suite?' she asks.

'I believe I heard this particular recording on the radio a few years back. Stokowski was conducting it.'

'Oh yes, we heard that broadcast too! It's a favourite of Katherine's. Mine too, I must say. Although the other ladies find it a little dreary. What about you – did you like it?'

'Very much so, yes.'

He puts the record cover back down on the table. Mrs Kaplan smiles. 'I can't tell you how grateful we are for your help,' she says. 'Tell me, what do you think of our little lawn?'

'Very pretty,' he says.

She picks up a full ashtray and frowns. Then she smiles at him again and asks, 'And what's that you have there – a hammer?'

'Yes and I brought this.' He lifts the folded trellis to show her. 'I thought of a solution for the cedar, a way to curtail the dog from…'

'Using it as a latrine?' she suggests.

'I thought if I put this little piece of fencing around the tree—'

'Oh, but didn't you see on the way in? Robin has already fixed something up. And besides, we decided to send Buster off on a little vacation to Province-town for a day or two.'

'Robin? Oh, so he showed up then?'

'He certainly did. But he seems to have disappeared again. You see those little wooden things out there on the lawn? Well, he's placed them so the tables can stay steady – see the way they get bigger as the slope descends? Now isn't that clever? He is slippery, no doubt about that, and I certainly hope his wife has an easier time than I've had trying to keep hold of him, but… he is clever. Anyhow, he has put something over Buster's latrine – a sort of platform, I guess – so even if anyone happens to stand on it… But thank you anyhow for being so—'

'Oh, that's quite all—'

'I hope you didn't go to too much trouble?'

'Oh, not in the least,' he says.

The hammer and trellis feel too large in his hands and seem to be growing heavier. He looks around for somewhere to put them, decides to leave them down at the side of the porch steps and slide away from them as quick as he can.

'So…' Mrs Kaplan begins, 'what we need to do now is—'

Rosetta comes out from the house calling.

'Mrs Kaplan, Mrs Kaplan, Michael, he is gone. His bed is empty.'

Mrs Kaplan covers her mouth. 'Oh no, poor Michael.'

'Oh, is nothing to worry about, I'm sure, Mrs Kaplan. You know how he is.'

'No, no, Rosetta. I mean poor Michael because I left him in the kitchen about an hour ago, beating eggs. We were supposed to be having breakfast together and then the telephone rang and after that, well, I forgot all about him and went upstairs to get dressed.'

He follows the two women into the kitchen, where they find Michael happily laying the table. The piano player is by the stove, loading eggs from a big saucepan onto a row of plates. A man wearing a cotton khaki shirt with the shoulder loops of an officer on it is seated at the table. He begins to stand when he sees Mrs Kaplan, but she waves him back down again and speaks over his head.

'Oh, Michael,' Mrs Kaplan says, 'I am so sorry but with everything going on…'

'That's okay,' Michael says and smiles at her. 'I'm helping Frank and Captain Hartman. We're going to have eggs and toast.'

Mrs Kaplan is about to introduce him to the officer when the door pushes in and Richie and his mother appear. The officer is on his feet again. Richie's mother flutters a look at him, then turns to the piano player at the stove and says, 'Frank! Whatever are you doing?'

'I came in looking for coffee and the kid here was beatin' eggs enough to feed an army. And, well, I was once part of an army and my good friend, the captain here…'

'Walt,' the captain says.

'That's right,' Frank says, 'Captain Walt here, he's still part of an army and so… we volunteered to help him make – and, of course, eat – 'em.'

'Of course,' she laughs. 'Think you could stretch to another couple of plates?'

'Plenty for everyone,' the captain says and stands back to offer her his chair.

'Mr Aitch – you want some?' Michael asks. 'I beat them and helped cook them and all.'

226

'I've already had breakfast but thank you, Michael,' he says. 'They look very good.'

'Now why don't I make us some toast to go with that?' Olivia says.

'We already have toast,' Michael says. 'Look, I made a whole heap of it.'

'So you did, Michael,' she says and begins to position herself to sit down on the seat Captain Hartman is holding out for her. 'Richie, sit down next to me.'

'I don't want to.'

'Wouldn't you like some eggs?'

'No, thank you.'

'You need to eat breakfast, Richie.'

'I said I don't want any.'

'We don't want to waste the eggs, now, do we?'

'Give them to Captain Hartman then. I'm sure he'll be glad to take any leftovers.'

A long moment of silence, then Richie's mother stands and, face ablaze, takes a few brisk steps in her son's direction. But Mrs Kaplan gets in first, taking hold of Richie's shoulders and turning him towards the door.

'I think we can start moving those tables and chairs outside now and you can help out, seeing as you're not hungry.'

She pushes Richie through the door, calling back over her shoulder, 'If you're ready, Mr Aitch?'

'Oh yes,' he says. He nods at the captain, and then at Frank who, like himself, appears to be holding back a grin. Then he follows Richie and his grandmother outside.

He takes a couple of chairs out to the lawn and unfolds them, while Richie's grandmother gives him a talk in the dining-room. He catches the words 'your father' then 'I mean it now, Richie' and then 'I'm beginning to see what your mother means – the sooner you are among boys your own age'.

He doesn't hear a word out of Richie.

When Richie comes out of the house, his face looks puffed out and his eyes are red. He pretends not to notice, unfolds another couple of chairs and then says, 'Well, I guess if you're not hungry, we could make a start on the tables.'

227

'Oh but I am hungry, sir,' Richie says. 'I didn't eat supper last night and now—'

'Why not?'

'Well, I didn't want to, is all. I mean, it was Mexican supper and I really like that – Rosetta sometimes makes these tacos when we're having informal.'

'You're having what?'

'That's what my mother calls it, having informal. Not sitting at the table. Like an indoor picnic.'

'Oh, I see.'

'We have it on the porch, which is both inside and outside in a way, of course, but anyhow, Rosetta wanted to have a clear kitchen for today and the dining-room is all emptied out and she makes the best Mexican food ever and I was looking forward to it and then *he* arrives and suddenly we have to pull the table out again and it's got to be served inside and she sneaks upstairs to put stuff on her face—'

'Stuff?'

'Yeah, you know, make-up stuff.'

'Oh, I see.'

'While my grandmother has to go find a room for him and he just expects—'

But Rosetta comes out before he has a chance to say what Captain Hartman expects from his grandmother. 'Excuse me, sir,' she says, 'would you like some coffee?'

'Sure – thank you, Rosetta.'

'And would you like a little something with it?'

'Oh no, thank you, coffee will be fine.'

'You sure, now, you wouldn't like little box of cereal or something?'

'Cereal?'

'Yes, you know, the ones in little boxes.'

He begins to understand. 'Oh yes, Rosetta, actually a little box of cereal would be very nice.'

'And the toast – you want that?'

'Well, why not?'

'How about some peanut butter on the toast, you like that?'

'I don't know, do I?' he asks then looks at Richie who now has a gleam in his eye.

~

WHEN HE GETS HOME, she is waiting at the door still in her bathrobe.

'Well?' she says.

'It's pretty busy over there.'

'Did we get any mail?'

'Mail? Oh no, I mean, I didn't have time to go to the post office.'

'You didn't? But why not?'

'I thought I'd call by the Kaplans' first, get that over with, and then I got waylaid – you know how it is. I can go tomorrow.'

'It's not open for collection tomorrow. It's not open till Tuesday. It's Labor Day Weekend, in case you hadn't noticed.'

'I'm sorry, I forgot.'

'And what about your sister's cheque?'

'I'm sure she'll be fine if it's a day late. I mean, she's not living by the seat of her pants or anything.'

'That's a fine way to talk about your own sister. I suppose Olivia had you running around.'

'Olivia?'

'Yes, Olivia, slithering around the place in her little shorts, flapping her eye-lashes at you – which are not real by the way.'

'Oh, well, that's certainly good to know.'

'Flapping and fluttering and admiring every little thing you do, telling you how wonderful you are.'

'I hardly even saw Olivia. For a couple of seconds in the kitchen, that was it. Fully supervised.'

'So you say. And I just hope that you didn't push yourself too far trying to impress her, that's all, because if you strain something or give yourself a heart seizure…'

He goes into the kitchen, pours himself a long glass of water and stands in the doorway.

'Shouldn't you be getting dressed?' he asks.

She looks away. Pulls her ponytail and then tightens her arms to her chest.

'Something the matter?'

'No.'

'Good. Now, do you want to tell me about it?'

'The party – if you must know. All those people. The thoughts of everyone crowding around you while I just sit there like nothing. A no one!'

'Oh now, that's not true.'

'Bees around honey. While I'm just the weed that's been plucked out and thrown on the grass, forgotten. I'm just—'

'I don't want people crowding around me, you know that.'

'Want it or not, they crowd around. Maybe if you included me once in a while, they might notice I exist. Threw me an occasional crumb. But you won't do that, will you? Won't even bring yourself to say – "You know my wife, she's an artist too."'

'Oh, come on now. I always introduce you.'

'I don't even expect you to say "she's a fine artist" or even a mediocre artist. Just a plain old artist – that would do. Some kind of acknowledgement, a reminder that I do in fact exist. I wouldn't mind if your so-called friend had bothered to write. That is, if he ever did show my pictures to anyone. But no, too busy, I suppose, with his own big, important gallery and his real artists, his real male artists, to bother touting someone like me, a mere woman.'

'You know he's not like that.'

'Oh, they are all like that. You are all like that. All he had to do was find me one small wall in the lowliest gallery.'

'I'm sure he's done his best.'

'Well, why not write then? If only he'd – well, I could have had something to say – you know? Even just to be able say my work will be showing in such and such gallery some place, any place, as part of an exhibition or something. As it is, I have nothing. I can't work, I can't—'

'I wouldn't go making anything up now,' he says.

'You think I am really that pathetic? Well, that's nice to know, really nice to know that I have a husband who thinks so very highly of me.'

He stands looking at her from across the room and he thinks: this could be the moment to tell her, now that she's all fired up. Get it out and over and done with. But if he tells her now, they won't be going to any party. They will stay here instead, hours and hours of fighting ahead. And for once, it's a party he wants to attend. Yesterday afternoon and again this morning – he had enjoyed all that. Movement and sound and voices around and yet nobody demanding a thing from him as long as he rowed in and did his bit. He had liked having the two boys running around helping him out. And Mrs Kaplan bringing a tray, the banter with Frank and Captain Hartman too, while they stood around in the shade drinking iced lemonade and eating Rosetta's cookies.

And looking up now and then to see Katherine flit by a window or hearing her voice shout something friendly from the doorway or down from a balcony. He liked not having to say too much, but making someone laugh when he did. And the feeling he used to get as a younger man – of being part of, and yet not part of, something.

'Maybe we should just skip it,' he says. 'That's perfectly fine with me.'

She turns from the window and looks at him for a moment.

'Oh, you would like that, wouldn't you? Well, no, you can't have it. We are going. And anyhow, I don't want to disappoint Michael.'

She turns from the window and looks at him and he goes back into the kitchen and empties, then rinses, his glass.

'Whatever you want,' he says, 'I am happy to do.'

In the bedroom she sits at the mirror and begins fixing her hair.

He says, 'Place is crawling with people up there.'

'Don't say the guests have arrived already?'

'No, but there's a few servicemen wandering around. And a lot of catering staff.'

'What are they wearing?'

'Who – the servicemen or the caterers?'

'The Kaplans, of course! Oh really, now, do you have to be so funny all the time?'

'I don't know, they didn't tell me.'

'You mean you didn't notice.'

'No, I mean they didn't tell me – they weren't dressed for the party. As I was leaving, there was talk of Richie and Michael getting spruced up for the occasion – I heard the words bow tie being mentioned.'

'I would have thought Richie loved to wear a bow tie and get himself all scrubbed up. Michael, of course, would be more—'

'You may be underestimating Richie. He is his own man, let me tell you. He got snippy over some air force captain by the name of Hartman – I gather he's a suitor of the mother.'

'Richie did – really?'

'Pretty impressive it was too. I mean, he cut right to the bone. I'm going to change into my suit now. I'll tell you all about it as we walk along.'

He sees her hands drop away from her hair as he turns to the closet.

He takes a dark-blue shirt. 'What about this, with the white linen?'

'Excuse me, but did you just say we were walking?'

'Oh, I'm sorry, I meant to say – it's very tight for space up there and Mrs Kaplan, she asked if we wouldn't mind leaving room for all the out-of-towners. I said I was sure you wouldn't mind.'

'She asked, or you offered?' she said, standing up.

He takes off the jacket he is wearing, hangs it in the closet and pulls out his linen suit.

'Bit of both, I guess. To be honest, I couldn't really see any way out of it.'

She stands up, glares at him, then pushes past him to get to her closet.

He opens the Dutch door and she walks under his arm.

'You look very nice,' he says.

'Well, I don't know. I'm sure by the time we walk down there, my clothes and hair will be stuck to me.'

'If you like, we could take the car down as far as the road – we could park there and you could drive, of course, if you want.'

She looks up at him a moment and then, 'No, no, that's all right. But thank you anyway for suggesting it.'

ROSETTA SAYS: 'MICHAEL. YOU fly like the hare when you take the drink orders and fly like the hare when you find for the guests some place to sit. But you walk like the tortoise when you take their drinks out and you walk like the tortoise when you bring the dirty glasses back in the kitchen. *La Tortuga y la Liebre* – we call it the T and L way. Of course, you don't really go so slow as the tortoise or so fast as the hare – but you know what I mean.'

And Mrs Kaplan says: 'Two whole dollars for a few hours' work and all you can eat, plus tips. You knock off around seven when the main crowd is gone, then you can join the rest of the party for supper – now, Michael, can I say any fairer than that?'

Mr Aitch has just left to go pick up Mrs Aitch and the lawn is all laid out so beautiful, he could stand there just looking at it all day but for Richie who comes puffing out of the house and starts pulling on his T-shirt and dragging him away. 'They're here, we need to go hide someplace. Come on. Come on, they're here, I'm telling you.'

'Let go of me. Who's here – what are you talkin' about?'

'I'm warning you now, you better have nothing to do with them.'

'Who?'

'The Westin brothers. They are not nice people.'

'Not nice? Will you stop that, always talking like a girl.'

'I'm not talking like a girl… I'm just saying— shut up, here they are now and, oh noooo – they're with my mom.'

When he looks up he sees two boys with slicked-down hair, dressed in blue shirts, cream pants and white shoes. All he can think is he's never seen two bigger goody-goodies in his whole life.

Richie's mom is behind the boys, a hand on each one's outside shoulder. She guides them forward, takes a big breath in and says, 'Well, now, look who I have here. This is Michael, he's all the way from New York, and Michael, these two fine-looking boys are Peter and Martin Westin from Hyannis. And of course, you both know Richie.'

The boys ignore Richie and stare at him while Richie's mom goes on: 'You know something? Something I just remembered? There's a lady who needs some hot dogs tested. Do you think you fellas could help her out? She's in the house right now. So you go up the porch steps and through the hall and her name is—'

'I know where the kitchen is,' Richie says, 'and I know what Rosetta's name is too.'

'I know you do, Richie, I'm just having a little fun here.'

'Fun – is that what you call it?' Richie says.

'Well, why don't you bring your guests in then, smarty-pants, and let them have their hot dogs while I go get dressed? And I want you two back upstairs in thirty minutes to get changed.'

'Ahhh, come on, why do we have to get all dressed up?'

'Well, you can't go to the party like that! Goodness. Don't you want to look as fine and handsome as Peter and Martin here?'

Richie pounds his feet up the steps and into the house. And one of the boys says, 'Thank you, ma'am,' and the other says, 'Oh yes, thank you so much, ma'am.'

And then the four of them go in the kitchen.

Rosetta tells them, 'Forget it if you think I make hot dogs now. I already told that lady, hot dogs come later and they not my job anyhow. Now, go, get out of here before I take out my gun.'

'Well, what do we do now?' the one called Peter says with a phoney yawn while the other one starts clipping pebbles off the wooden platform Robin has built round Buster's toilet tree.

'How am I supposed to know?' Richie says

'How are you supposed to know? How are you—? Hey, Marty – how is he supposed to know?'

'Because he's the smarty-pants,' Marty says and the two brother start laughing like donkeys.

'Hey, where's your dumb dog anyway?' the one called Marty says then.

'He's not here and he's not dumb,' Richie says, his face getting fatter and redder by the second.

'He's not? Oh, I'm sorry. Has he learned how to talk?'

'I didn't say he could talk.'

234

'Well then, what do you mean he's not dumb?'

And the two Westin boys start laughing again.

'I, I… I'm going inside.'

'Your mom said you were to entertain us,' Marty says.

'Say, is it true she was a pin-up girl?' Peter asks and then Marty gives a long wolf-whistle.

'You better shut up right now,' Richie says.

'Or what? You'll tell on me like you did last time? "Mommy, Mommy, Peter and Martin were so mean to me."'

Richie says, 'Come on, Michael, I told you what they were like, didn't I?' and then he begins to walk back towards the house. He stops at the front porch steps. 'Are you coming or not, Michael?' he demands.

'You the new dog, Michael?' Peter says.

'No.'

'You answer when he snaps his fingers, is that it?'

'We need to get changed for the party,' Richie says.

'You wanna show us where the beach is, Michael,' Marty says, 'while Richie goes back to his mommeeee?'

'You can find the beach yourselves,' Richie says. 'It hasn't moved since last time you were here. Just go round the back of the house, in case you've forgotten, and there's a path going up a hill and—'

'We want Michael all the way from New York to show us,' Peter says.

'Well, he can't show you – he has to come with me. Isn't that right, Michael?'

He stands at the edge of the pathway and looks over at Richie. He can tell by his eyes that inside he's begging. And he almost gives in. But then Richie's eyes go hard suddenly and he says through his teeth, 'You better come with me right now, and I mean it.'

The other two boys have already started walking away but they stop when they hear Richie talk to him that way. He keeps looking straight at Richie and, at the same time, he says to the brothers, 'Hold on, I'm coming with you.'

He passes the two Westin boys out. He walks ahead of them round by the trees and up the sloped pathway. He leads them through the wall of beach grass and doesn't stop until he gets to the top landing of the wooden steps. He can hear the sea now, feel it fill up his nostrils, blast into his head and push down his lungs into the rest of his body. And now he can see it, jumping with white light and reaching back as far as his eye can go.

'There's the beach,' he says when the boys catch up. 'You just go down the steps there; you can use them as a marker to come back up when you want.'

'You not coming with us?' Peter says.

'I got things to do.'

'You hear that, Marty? He's got things to do.'

'Oh yeah?' Marty says. 'Like what?'

'Like mind your own fucken business or I'll slit your throat open ear to ear.'

He tries to walk as slow as he can, back through the long grass until he gets to the top of the hill. Then, when he is sure he is out of their sight, he starts to run and can't seem to stop, he feels so happy and proud of himself. He runs down the hill and through the trees. He runs round the tables when he gets to the garden; he runs round the chairs and benches. He runs up the porch steps and back down them, waving at Frank and Captain Walt by the piano through the big open door. He runs around to the front of the house, jumps up on the little platform Robin built and, lifting his arms up over his head, calls out Katherine's name. He waves his arms at her when she peeks through the French doors of her balcony. He brings his arms wide, jumps off the platform and veers them like the wings of a plane through the wide patch of high grass at the front of the house. He slopes his arms up and down as he flies himself along like a playground see-saw all the way round to the back of the house. He flies himself parallel, left to right, right to left. He can see Frank stand up and come to the porch to watch him. Then he flies down to the trees, turns back round and, facing the house, flies straight at it. His heart swells up like a loaf in a hot oven; he feels every drop of blood in his body pressing against his skin. He wants to wrap his arms around the house, rub his face off the porches and windows and walls and doors and every plank of wood, every pane of glass that went into the making of it. He wants to bury his nose in the grass outside and eat it like he was a horse. Because he loves the house and everyone in it – even, just for this one little moment, Richie and his mom and her stupid friend Annette. He loves all the people who have yet to arrive for the party. And the faraway people too, like Harry and Frau Aunt. Vince he loves more than anyone else for letting him hear that 'mind your own fucken business' line one card night when he'd had too much to drink and for saying that 'throat from ear to ear' thing when he was fooling around about leaving Shirley in the automobile.

But above all, he loves himself for remembering those lines at just the right moment and for knowing how to shove them, one after another, right in the faces of those two white-washed pansies from who-cares-Hyannis.

2

AND AFTER ALL, IT turns out to be a very pleasant walk. The zest of summer still on the air, the roadsides plush with wildflowers that don't yet know their days are numbered. The air honeysuckle-sweet, if a little too heavy handed for comfort. There is the thought, too, to keep one going, that at the other end of this really very pleasant stroll a party is waiting. And what could be nicer than that – a garden party at the start of an Indian summer?

She stops for a second, touches his arm and, 'Listen,' she says, 'do you hear?'

'What?'

'Music – now isn't that nice?'

'Music?'

'Yes, music. A brass band it sounds like – oh, never mind.'

They are not the only ones to arrive by foot; ahead of them, a young couple moves shyly along, and further down the line, a group of three servicemen, and, when she looks back over her shoulder, other small groups and a few single stragglers are drifting up from the south end of Fisher Road. All spit and polish. Hats, gloves and the bits in between. It's like going to Sunday church in the country, summoned by a brass band instead of bells. She considers sharing this thought with her husband but one glance at his face under the shade of his hat, like something carved into the side of Mount Rushmore, and she decides to keep the thought to herself.

As they come closer to the turn-off, her eye is spiked by a glinting mass of parked automobiles. Brow to tail up along the embankment and all the way down to the end of the road towards the entry to the beach, and there's more of them squeezed into the parking space at the end of the lane that leads up to Mrs Kaplan's house.

'I hear it now,' he says, 'a brass band – is it a little off key?'

She takes his arm as they come off the lane and, falling in behind another two couples, they make their way around the side of the house.

She still feels it. That small spark of pride whenever she walks into a gathering on his arm. People know who they are – of course they do – but what pleases her more today is that, even at their age, they can still cut an interesting figure. He, handsome and tall in that Panama hat, the blue of the shirt in the blue in his eyes. And she – petite though she may be – can still hold herself straight and has not run to fat like many a younger woman she could easily name. And as to her clothes, well, she can only hope she has made her best effort, struck the right chord between—

'It's definitely off key,' he says.

'What?'

'The band. It's definitely—'

'Oh, really now, must you start complaining already?'

'Who's complaining?' he says.

And now here they are suddenly, standing on top of the incline at the side of the house, the party going on all around and below them in the dip and further out even, on the hill that rises towards the sea.

There is a touch of the county fair about the proceedings. Red, white and blue flags looped from the porch of the house and along upper balconies and again from tree to tree. People standing around or sitting at tables or on car robes laid out around the edges of the lawn. A few old men throwing horse-shoes at a stave stuck into the ground. Men in uniform strolling around with their hands in their pockets. Children and hot dogs and lumps of buttered corn. Bottles of Coke and bottles of beer and summer punch in vessels as big as fish tanks. Out on the bluff, city visitors stand ankle-deep in broom crowberry and, further out again, up to the hip in long grass, gazing out at the sea. And nearby, a young mother sits on the grass feeding ice-cream to a fat-legged baby.

The rumble of friendly conversations, an occasional flitter of cautious laughter. On the porch, a small band of red-cheeked Cape Codders are blasting 'Swanee' to kingdom come.

And it's all very nice – if a little more provincial than what one might have expected from Mrs Kaplan and her crew.

She wonders which way to turn. If she leaves it up to her husband, they will be still standing here on this spot when the stars come out and it's time to go home. And that, she thinks, is her one criticism of garden parties – the fact that there is no warm-up time. The interval between leaving your coat and broaching the room does not exist. A person simply has no chance to acclimatise to the surroundings. At an indoor party your hostess will certainly notice and then introduce you to someone compatible – but here? You just come round the corner and there you are! Right in the thick of it, conspicuous even to the fat-legged baby, who is most definitely looking this way, and nothing to do but stand here with your sullen-faced husband, looking like some sort of gatecrashers or, worse, a pair of nobodies that have been invited on sufferance.

A tray appears beside her. In the blare of sunlight she can barely make out a small head behind it.

'Do you have any water?' she asks it. 'You see, we walked and I'm really quite—'

'Water? Ma'am? You want water?'

She now sees, at the far side of the tray, the young girl who helps out in the grocery store, a child, in fact, who could be no more than twelve years old.

'Is that you, Thelma?'

'Yes, ma'am, it is.'

'Well, if you wouldn't mind getting me some…'

'Oh yes, ma'am, of course, I'll get it right away.'

Her husband takes a glass from the tray.

'What is it?' she asks.

'Some sort of wine, I imagine,' he says and takes a sip.

Behind them a woman is talking about her son: 'Took up with a girl working at the Chowder House this summer. From Boston. Well, you know what they're like… husband-hunters, that's why they come out here. She's gone home now and he's been moping ever since.'

'Oh, it's so important they meet the right girl,' another woman says. 'One little mistake and, well, the pleasure is short but the price is long, I always say…'

She turns to glance at the two women. The larger one, in a bright-pink dress, is holding a cup of punch close to her breast; the other, clammy in a green shiny suit, is evidently the one with the mopey son. A man standing between the pair is staring hard at her. She is about to turn away when he gives her a smile and then dives on her as if he's fallen overboard and she's the one in charge of the rope.

'Oh, hello, so nice to see you again,' he says. 'You're a friend of Mrs Sultz, if I'm not mistaken. We went clamming together once – during the war.'

'So we did!' she says.

'On Ballston Beach, I believe?'

'So it was.'

'And afterward, Mrs Sultz, she showed you how to make clam jelly.'

'So she did!'

'And how is Mrs Sultz?'

'Oh, she's very well.'

'I hear she's in a nursing home out Hyannis way.'

'Well, yes, that's true, I saw her recently and—'

'Heard she's not doin' too good at all.'

'Oh no, she looked the picture of—'

'Up there, I mean,' he says and prods the side of his head.

The woman in green looks her up and down and asks, 'Where are you folks from?'

'New York, we have a summer house here.'

'A rental?'

'Well, no, as a matter of fact. We built it. This is my husband.'

She reaches out and begins to draw him in, if only in the hope that he might scare them off. The woman in green glares at him and demands to know, 'How many miles is it from New York to here?' Then she looks away and, lowering her voice gleefully, says, 'Oh, look, there's Mrs Childs now. Her daughter is married to a state senator you know.'

'About four hundred,' he says.

'Excuse me?'

'Miles. From New York city.'

'You poor man, you must be exhausted,' she says and rushes off towards the senator's mother-in-law, pulling Mrs Sultz's friend behind her.

'You say hello now to Mrs Sultz for me,' he says. 'You be sure and tell her I said she's to hurry on and get better and come on home where she belongs – though I don't suppose that's ever gonna happen.'

She turns back to the spot where they started. 'I wonder where that girl is with my glass of water,' she says.

From her elevated position, she has a good view of the party. She sees Richie and his mother standing behind a table under the locust trees. A man in uniform comes up to the table and reaches into his back pocket to take out his wallet. And now another man beside him appears to be reaching into his jacket. Richie holds out a big white box and they both take what looks like an envelope from it. A few seconds later Richie is holding out a big brown carton and the men drop the envelope in. Then Olivia buries her head in a book and writes something down. As one of the men steps away, she sees an Uncle Sam banner hanging off the lip of the table. She says, 'I think this is some sort of fundraiser.'

'What is?'

'The party – oh, we might have known!'

A woman's voice behind her says, 'That's right – for Mrs Kaplan's Orphan Fund.'

It's the woman in pink, left behind by Mrs Sultz's friend and his odious wife.

'Do you have any money with you?' she says to her husband out the side of her mouth.

'About two dollars.'

'Two – is that it?'

'I changed suit and forgot—'

242

'Well, that won't do, that won't do at all.'

'I'll write a cheque and drop it by tomorrow.'

'Oh yes, I'll tell her that.'

'No, don't say anything. Don't make a thing of it, I'll just...'

Another two men are standing by the table now, talking to Richie. Annette approaches and comes round the back of the table and takes over from Olivia. Olivia moves off and begins to meander hip first, through the crowd.

'She'll think we're terribly stingy.'

'Oh no,' the woman beside them intervenes, 'it's not like that at all. You make a donation if you want. Most locals don't bother, or they mean to and then they just sort of forget. You see, they only hold the table open for a couple of hours. And you don't have to use the envelopes – you can just throw fifty cent in a big black bucket if you don't have much money.'

She gives the woman a curt smile and edges around to the far side of her husband. This time she whispers, 'Just the same.'

She looks up at him and notices under the brim of his hat that he is looking carefully into the crowd below, his eyes moving as if they are following someone.

'I can drop it by tomorrow,' he says.

'I? I? What is all this I? Maybe I would like to come too, you know.'

'Then please do.'

'Or maybe you'd prefer to come alone. That way you could ogle Olivia without me breathing down your neck.'

He looks at her slowly. 'If we're going to have this, I'd just as soon go home now.'

'We are not going home. We are staying here. I'm going to have a little fun for once in my life. Oh, where is that girl, before I die of thirst.'

'I'll get it for you,' he says.

'No! I don't want to stand here on my own. I'm coming with you.'

'I'm still here,' the woman says, her big head appearing round his far shoulder. 'I'll be glad to keep you company.'

'I won't be a minute,' he says and then he is gone.

She watches as he makes his way through the crowd. The woman in the

243

big pink dress is talking to her, telling her a story about her cute little grand-daughter. The woman moves as if to open her purse and she thinks: if she goes rummaging in there and comes out with a photograph, I'm going to scratch her eyes out. But the woman is just readjusting herself to take another sip from her punch.

'You're welcome to a sip of this if you're thirsty,' she says.

'I don't drink alcohol.'

'Oh, me neither,' the woman laughs, 'unless they're givin' it out for free…'

There is a few seconds' pause. Then the woman says something about hop-ing to get home in time to listen to some soap opera on the radio.

'Never miss it,' she says, 'sure hope I make it. I'm relying on your friends the Atwoods to give me a ride.'

'Who?'

'The people you go clamming with.'

'I went once. Years ago. It hardly makes us friends.'

And now, as the woman starts to relay the plot details of the radio show going all the way back to episode one, she is brought to a swift decision. She cannot and will not stand here waiting for Olivia to find her husband so she can pour herself all over him while this odious woman in her big pink dress bleats at her. She cannot and will not abide being stuck with the party bore. But that, of course, is exactly what he is relying on – her standing here for hours, expiring of thirst, talking to a woman in a big pink dress. He forgets that she has been invited here on her own merit because she knows this, even if he doesn't know it: Mrs Kaplan likes her. Mrs Kaplan may even admire her. And why wouldn't she? They are both women of independent minds. She does not need him in order to be able to enjoy herself; she can do it well enough on her own, and so she will – to hell with anyone who tries getting in her way. The band stops playing; the woman bleats louder. She cuts her off midstream and says, 'Would you excuse me, please?'

'Well sure,' the woman says, her voice suddenly small and childlike.

She wanders slowly across the lawn, edging around the small groups, scraps of conversation catching on her ear.

'What a nice party. Yes, it is a nice party.'

'And how do you know the…?'

'I gotta tell you, the sewage on that beach, well, it is a disgrace…'

'You think we need another war right now? You really think that?'

'Used to sail with the late Mr…'

'No, no – you see, you gotta smear it with butter first and then…'

Her plan is to come to the edge of one such conversation, stand there until she finds a space to throw in a line. But the groups are tight and the conversations dull. She is thinking about going into the house, trying her luck in there, when Michael appears right beside her. 'Am I glad to see you!' she says.

'I saw you first!' he cries. 'I saw you first!'

'Yes, you did. My turn to make tea next time.'

'You like my bow tie?'

'You look very smart. And happy – you're obviously having a good time.'

'I've been pretty busy,' he says.

'Have you indeed?'

'I've been helping Captain Hartman and Frank and Mr Aitch too; this morning, we laid out all these tables.'

'It looks wonderful, Michael.'

'And I tied all those flags to the tree – Mr Aitch held the ladder.'

'Well, isn't that nice?'

'And I've been bringing drinks to people and finding places to sit for everyone and—'

'Could you find a place for me, do you think?'

Michael looks all around and then, taking her by the hand, draws her over to a table, a bench on either side of it.

There's a space on the nearest bench; she stands at the end of it for a shy moment, about to ask if they would mind her sitting down, when Michael butts right in. 'Sit there – look, right there. Go ahead, nobody minds.'

Everyone smiles and makes welcoming sounds and a man in a grey suit shuffles up to make room.

Michael says, 'Can I get you anything, ma'am? That's what I'm supposed to say,' he explains.

'Well, I would dearly love a glass of water.'

'Anything else, Mrs Aitch – somethin' to eat maybe?'

'All right, something small. Why don't you surprise me?'

'I know what you like, Mrs Aitch.'

'Just be sure you don't forget the water. You know,' she says to the man across from her, 'it is almost impossible to find a glass of water at a party any more. I mean, a plain old glass of water. Ask for a snazzy cocktail and that's no problem. But water? Forget it. Bring back prohibition, I say.'

There is a purl of good-humoured laughter and now names are being flung at her: Joan and John from Connecticut and Clarence and Dick from Virginia and Doris from someplace else, along with one or two others down the line that get lost on the way up the table.

And what a nice party this is, she thinks, settling in, what nice friendly people. I may stick with them for the duration, I may very well do that.

The one called Doris smiles at her from across the table. 'We were just talk-ing about the races tomorrow. I was telling this gentleman—?'

'John,' the gentleman says.

'I was telling John that he ought to stick around for the yacht races.'

'Oh yes,' she says, 'it is quite a spectacle.'

'Not for me,' he says, 'can't stand the water or anything got to do with.'

'But isn't that a marine pin you're wearing?' the man in the grey suit asks.

'Why do you think I can't stand the water?' John says and he laughs and they all laugh and then they stop laughing and look at each other, and for a moment it seems that nobody knows what to do now.

Until the brass band begins to play again. A few bars of something she is just beginning to recognize but then abruptly it stops and there's Olivia, in a long red dress, coming onto the porch, clapping her hands and asking every-one to do the same: 'A big hand, a warm hand for the somethingsomething-blabla drum and bugle baaand.'

The woman next to Doris leans over (Joan, did she say her name was? Joan or Jane?) 'Isn't she pretty?' she says. 'Used to be a fashion model, you know.'

'No, I didn't know.'

Olivia continues to yell at the crowd: 'And in a few moments we will have

Sergeant Frank Berrio on the piano and Captain Walt Hartman on the clarinet. The dance floor is all rigged up inside – thank you to Robin, if he's anywhere about? No? Well, anyway, he's done a wonderful job and if anyone feels like dancing, please just come on in and go right ahead.'

'Yes, before she married Bill Kaplan,' Joan or whatever her name is continues, 'she used to model in a big department store in Boston. I think she may have been in a magazine too. I mean, you can tell, right? Just look at that dress… and her figure!'

'Red certainly seems to be her favourite colour,' she says and turns her attention to the rest of the table in hope of a different conversation.

'I lived there when I was a young man,' the man in the grey suit is saying to the woman sitting on the far side of him.

'Me too,' the man sitting opposite says, 'spent my bachelor years there.'

'Are we talking about New York?' she asks.

'Yes, we are. I lived there too,' a woman down the table says, 'before I was rescued by this man here and moved out to Providence. It was a very lonesome time, I must say. I would *not* wish to go back there.'

She opens her mouth to join the conversation but Michael is beside her now holding a plate of apple pie and ice-cream.

'Why thank you, Michael,' she says. 'And thank you again,' she says as he lays a carafe of water beside her and then runs off.

She lifts the carafe to the company and she gives it a little kiss. There is a soft ruffle of laughter as she takes the glass off the top of it, fills it up and takes a long pull of water.

'But if we're talking about New York,' she says, 'let me say, I loved my single life there. I didn't know it at the time but I would rarely be so happy. My friends, my interests, my whole— well, I guess, my creative self. I was a teacher there for some time, but really it was where I learned to be an artist, you know. I lived all over the city. Once I had a tiny room near the Plaza hotel and not far from the New York Athletic Club. I shared it with a girlfriend. The fun we had! Hanging out the window watching the swanks on one side, the hunks on the other…'

She laughs, delighted by the memory, but when she looks around, the faces are looking blankly at her except for the man who was a New York bachelor, who gives her a knowing little smile.

'Oh, but of course, it was all in innocence,' she mutters, pulling the spoon from the ice-cream and looking down at it, ashamed suddenly although she can't think why.

Joan or Jane moves in again, this time addressing the woman on the far side of the man in the grey suit. 'We were just saying how pretty Olivia Kaplan is – I was telling this lady – Mrs Aitch, did I hear the boy say?'

'Yes, that's what he said all right, but it's not actually—'

'I was just telling Mrs Aitch that Olivia was a fashion model before she got married and we were sighing with envy at that figure and her dress, oh my goodness.'

'You may have been sighing, but I certainly was not,' she snaps and immediately regrets it.

'Oh, well now,' Joan says and looks demurely into her glass of punch. There is silence for a few seconds and then a woman down the way leans out and says, 'But isn't your husband the famous artist?'

'Yes, we are both artists – although of course I don't claim to be famous. Nor, might I add, would I wish to be.'

The woman down the line says, 'But you must enjoy living so close to Provincetown. All those art galleries and, well, really a very artistic little town.'

'Sunday painters most of them,' she says shortly, 'I'd hardly call them artists,' and jabs the spoon back into the ice-cream.

Clarinet notes bounce out from the house and couples start getting up from tables or crossing the lawn hand in hand to go indoors to dance.

A man sitting on the bench opposite leans behind Doris to ask Jane or Joan to dance, leaving two gaps on the curve of the bench like two missing teeth in a mouth.

The man in the grey suit next to her says, 'Well, I guess New York is more suited to you artistic folk; galleries and so forth – it must be very interesting.'

'Oh, people always think that,' she says, 'but the New York art scene is very superficial, let me tell you.'

'That so?'

'Oh yes, we don't really bother with it, despite every day getting cards inviting us to an opening of this or that – the "Come see me dance! Come see me dance! brigade", that's what I call them.'

'You're invited to dance shows?'

'What? No, no, of course not! To art exhibitions, openings and—'

The man looks away, waits a moment and then invites Doris, who has edged to the end of the bench, if she would like to dance. And now all that remains on the two benches is one very old man at her side and a pair of whispering teenage girls on the other.

She breaks the pie crust with the side of the spoon and lifts a piece to her mouth. Her throat feels as if it has shrunk somehow and the pie is too cumbersome to negotiate it; she just leaves it sitting there on her tongue. Through the porch she can see the sway of summer dresses as the piano and clarinet bid them to Begin the Beguine. And she recalls a winter's day in New York when the snow was falling and the same song came on the radio. He laid down his brush suddenly and came to take her in his arms and dance her around the studio. She had nearly fallen down on the floor with the shock! And so light on his feet, firm in his grip – for a man who claimed not to dance. She would love to dance now. She would love if he would come and find her and take her away from this appalling table. Something catches her eye and when she looks up she sees the woman in the big pink dress standing alone under the trees. Their eyes meet, then quickly slide off in opposite directions.

She swallows down the pie, takes a drink of her water, then gets up and goes in search of her husband.

~

HE LEAVES HIS WIFE talking with a large women dressed in pink and begins towards the house. Halfway along the incline, he stops. Down on the lawn there is perpetual movement. The tables he had earlier set out, the chairs he unfolded and carefully placed, the benches he tottered behind or before, are all beyond his recognition now. This morning they had been scrupulous in form, precise in the shadows they cast. He had stood for a while to admire the scene, had even dared wonder if, maybe— But that scene no longer exists. It started to die with the first footfall of the first guest, and now it has been obliterated.

The light quivers. It darts through Mrs Kaplan's guests, driving them on from group to group, from house to lawn and up along the two little pathways that lead to the bluff overlooking the sea. Only Richie stands still. His round sunburnt face over the orphan-fund table, like a coin suspended. And there is another, equally still, somewhere over to his left. He draws his eye up to the skyline then back to the roof of the house, down along the slope of it, into the dark mouth of the porch, where he finds her leaning against a supporting column, dressed in all-white. Richie and Katherine and himself. Three static points on an equilateral triangle. A frenzy of light and movement between them. Ruthless light of mid to late afternoon.

He feels a quickening inside him, at the same time a glint of something in the back of his mind. Richie's flushed face, the table with the black bucket on it, Katherine all in white, long and lean in the frame of the porch. He needs to hold onto all of that without looking it straight in the face. To be inside and outside of it; absent and at the same time present. Like looking sideways into a room through a mirror. Boy in his youth; woman in her prime; man facing into old age. The image comes into his head of the *Planets* suite record cover, the Merlin figure trying to stay upright. He thinks: Mercury. Venus. Saturn, the bringer of old age. Light before dusk through a mirror.

A voice calls up to him. It calls again and now he notices the neck of a bottle crane towards him.

'Like me to freshen your drink, sir?'

He turns his eye seaward, pretends not to notice.

The voice speaks again: 'Sir, it's from France.'

He turns and frowns. 'France?'

'Yes, sir, the wine. I understand it's from France. Pre-war. There's a few bottles set aside. Mrs Kaplan, she sent me over to ask if you'd like—?'

Behind him he hears the mirror crack, shatter and fall away. He nods and holds out his glass.

Moments later, he is passing through the crowd. He pauses to return one or two greetings, pretends not to notice one or two more, all the while keeping her white silhouette in his vision. Katherine on the bank reeling him in. Never was a fish such a willing victim, so happy to have the hook struck through, to taste the blood of his own death in his own mouth.

He negotiates each obstacle – guests grouped together, a flock of small children, the corner of a table, a Pisa tower of dirty glasses tottering on a tray. Each time, she comes into a clearer focus: the long white slant, the brown hair, the stillness. He imagines himself walking right up the porch steps to her, lifting a section of her hair, the weight of it in his hand, leaning in and then whispering into her ear, 'I want to paint you and when I'm done painting you, I want to do things to you that I don't have the words to describe.'

Overhead, the sound of a small plane. He lifts his head and watches it struggle through the smudge cloud. Something comes out of nowhere and lands on his arm. He looks down and sees a gripping hand, looks up and sees Olivia.

'And where do you think you are sneaking off to?' she enquires. 'I have so many people just dying to meet you.'

'I was just…'

She smiles a tilted smile and waits, as if she is expecting something meaningful to emerge from his mouth.

He clears his throat. 'I was just going to get a drink.'

'But where is Michael? He's supposed to be helping out. Really, that boy!'

'That's quite all right,' he begins.

She lifts her hand and beckons a waiter. 'Will you freshen this up, please?' she asks. He is about to explain that he is looking for a glass of water for his wife, but by now the waiter has filled up his glass and disappeared. Olivia standing next to him, talking and smiling. He takes a long sip, then another. A man cuts in then, takes Olivia's hand and kisses it. The man looks at him and says, 'Mind if I borrow her for a few moments?'

And he says again, 'That's quite all right,' while the man, still holding her hand, pulls a laughing Olivia away.

At the side of the porch steps, a drinks table has been laid out. He waits his turn. A man in his sixties, dressed up like a soda jerk, is serving drinks and jokes in equal measure. A bunch of young girls coo and cackle as he rips the caps from soda pop bottles and teases them about which one will be married first. A man with a personality. The type that usually irritates him. But not today. He is one of those guys himself, suddenly, boyish and full of swagger, showing off for a girl who is probably not even looking this way.

'I got beer and I got punch,' the man says. 'You want somethin' stronger you gotta go in the house – don't worry, I won't tell a soul.'

'What about something less strong?'

'Oh sure. I got lemonade and root beer.'

'How about water?'

'Water – who comes to a party to drink water?' the man asks.

'My wife does.'

'Sure she wouldn't like some lemonade? Or how about a nice glass of soda?'

'Water.'

'Sweet enough, eh? Don't answer that, don't answer it. I know how sweet they can be – I've been married myself for thirty-eight years.'

'Congratulations.'

'That's one way to put it. For plain old water, I'd say the kitchen is your safest bet.'

He sees the shape of her as he turns away from the table and it's still there when he puts his hand on the wooden rail of the porch. But somewhere in the moment between removing his hat and climbing the steps onto the porch, she has disappeared. As if the sight of him has scared her away. Her big yellow hat sits on the end of the chaise longue; there's an unlit cigarette on the lip of an ashtray. On the other end of the porch, the brass band battles on, and on the far side of the trees, the small plane appears to be hovering over the bay. He stands and finishes his drink, then he takes out his handkerchief and pats the sweat back into his big bare head.

In the living-room, a group of servicemen have gathered by the bar. At the far end of the room, Frank is leaning on the piano reading a newspaper. He crosses the room. Frank puts down the paper and shakes his hand. He is about to put down his empty glass when a waiter comes up beside him and now his glass is no longer empty.

'Just waiting here for the boys in brass to knock it off,' Frank says, covering one ear with one hand and grimacing. 'Then the good captain and myself will be on duty – if you're the dancing type, do drop by.'

'I'm not,' he says and moves off towards the kitchen, 'but thanks for the warning.'

On the way into the kitchen he is nearly knocked off his feet by a large tray loaded with bowls of ice-cream. He stands back and waits for the danger to pass, then carefully edges into the room. He can't see the sink for the number of people. The long table in the centre of the room has turned into a conveyor belt of ice-cream bowls and large plates of apple pie. He stays in the background, drinking his wine and watching the activity, then he turns his attention to a tray on the window ledge where two black flies are mooching through the aisles of canapés, and he wonders if one is aware of the other and if their paths will ever cross. It occurs to him, then, that he may have downed the wine a little too quickly and thinks he should probably train himself to drink like other men, or better not drink at all.

When he looks up again, the ice-cream bearers have gone from the table, and there is Katherine at the sink washing glasses. He makes his way over to her but Mrs Kaplan nabs him just before he gets to the sink.

'Oh, I'm so glad you've come. But where's your wife?'

'She's outside talking to someone; she's sent me to fetch some water.'

'Of course. Now let me see where… ah yes!'

Mrs Kaplan pulls a carafe off a shelf, leans across her daughter at the sink and fills it with water and slips away. Katherine looks over her shoulder at him, nods her head at the glasses on the draining board and says, 'My hands are wet.'

He picks up a glass, then a dishcloth; he turns the glass over, twisting it into the cloth.

'We've run out of glasses,' she says. 'There are way more people here than anyone can remember inviting.'

He nods and twists the glass some more.

'I've broken two already and the party's hardly started.'

'Two what – hearts?' he hears himself say and is embarrassed as well as surprised by his clumsy effort.

She gives a small, puzzled laugh, glances at him then turns away.

Her hand pulls another glass out of the suds and lays it on the drainer.

'I could dry these while I'm here if you want?' he says.

'Don't you have to bring water to your wife?'

'Oh yes. That's right, I do.'

He puts the glass down and is about to do the same with the dishcloth when Katherine pulls her hands out of the water and shakes them. Then she turns round and, lifting the end of the cloth he is holding, begins to dry her hands in it. They stand for a moment facing each other and he thinks she is five nine; maybe eight. Then he thinks how easy it would be just to lift his hand a little, reach out and touch her.

Mrs Kaplan comes back up beside them; Katherine drops the dishcloth and turns back to the sink in a movement swift and furtive that fills him with a ridiculous sense of hope, as if the past forty years have never happened, as if he is a man in his twenties who doesn't have a wife outside waiting for a glass of water.

'Could I ask you,' Mrs Kaplan is saying, 'if you wouldn't mind, that is, to take this last tray of ice-cream and apple pie out to the boys at the bar – you know, in the living-room? And maybe Frank and Captain Hartman might like some too.'

Mrs Kaplan hands him a large tray, the carafe of water for his wife in the centre of it. She takes the glass from the draining board and slots it over the top. He glances over her shoulder at Katherine. He sees now that she is not dressed in white after all, that her dress is in fact, olive green. She looks at him, a glint in her eye as if something is amusing her. Although he can't be sure about that either. He can't be sure of anything when it comes to Katherine.

He is passing the bowls out and enjoying a little banter with the servicemen when Michael comes in and rushes across to him. 'Can I have one of those, please?' he asks.

'I'm sure you could, Michael. You want one for Richie too? I think I just saw him standing behind a table out there.'

'Oh, he's not there now, he's gone off sulking.'

'He is – why's that?'

'He didn't want me to go to the beach with these two boys from Hyannis but I went ahead anyway and he got sore… Then when his mom sent me to help him at the orphan table, he told me get lost and called me a sneak.'

'Oh, I see.'

'But I didn't sneak off at all – I just showed them where the beach was and came straight back here. Anyhow, the ice-cream's not for me, it's for Mrs Aitch.'

'Well, in that case, I better say yes. I was just about to bring her this water.'

'Oh, I can do that too, if you want.'

Michael takes a bowl and the carafe from the tray, spins around and disappears.

A man standing beside him says, 'That your grandson?'

'No, not even my son.'

'He looks a little like you, I was going to say.'

'I don't have any children.'

'That's a shame,' the man says somewhat bluntly, then leans over and begins inspecting the few remaining bowls on the tray.

'I'm staying at the Anchor and Ark club,' the man says. 'I'll be staying there until Tuesday.'

'I hear it's a nice place,' he feels obliged to say, even though he's never heard a word, good or bad, about it.

'It's okay. One place is much like another when it comes down to it.'

'I suppose.'

The man holds the bowl and looks down into it. 'You don't have just plain ice-cream?' he asks. 'I mean, without the apple pie underneath?'

'No, no, I'm afraid not. But I could get you some, I'm sure.'

'I couldn't ask you to do that. Maybe your grandson? Oh, I forgot he's not your grandson.'

'No. No, he's not.'

'I don't have a grandson either,' the man says. 'I don't even have a son.'

He notices, then, that the man is wearing a small blue button wreathed with gold and white at the centre: the button given to a serviceman who has lost a son in the service. They stand looking at one another for a second and then

255

the brass band cuts out and Olivia's voice comes in from the porch. There is a sound of applause like a sudden rainfall and then, in a moment, Olivia is speaking again.

He thinks about Katherine back in the kitchen, the colour of her dress and the raw look of her hands when she dried them, as if they had been stuck in hot water for some time. She could not have been on the porch. But where had the white silhouette come from? A trick of the light? Some sort of mirage? It could have been anyone standing there. It could have been no one at all.

'I don't mind in the least,' he says to the man, 'getting you a bowl of ice-cream from the kitchen, if that's what you would prefer.'

The man looks morosely at the ice-cream, thinking it over. His eyes are damp when he looks back up at him. 'Nah,' he says, 'I don't think I'll bother after all.'

~

SHE CATCHES SIGHT OF him standing in the shade of a tree with Mrs Kaplan and two others. 'Slow Boat to China' is oozing out of a clarinet and she can see Katherine on the porch dancing with a very old man. Behind her, through the open doors, couples foxtrot in and out of view.

His head is bent to Mrs Kaplan, attending her every word, and there are two others standing there, equally enthralled. A shyness comes on her as she approaches, as if she will be intruding on him in his little group, and she finds herself hoping that he will glance up, see her and welcome her in. But it is Mrs Kaplan who notices her first and, although she doesn't stop speaking, she does give her a pat on the arm by way of a greeting and steps aside to make room.

'Well, I was expecting Billy when we moved to Mexico you see,' Mrs Kaplan is saying to the couple standing with them, the man wearing dark glasses, the woman wiry and with a complexion like a date palm, brown and cracked.

Mrs Kaplan breaks off here to say to her, 'We were just talking about our mothers and I was saying how much I regretted the fact that mine never got to see her grandchildren.'

'She died before they were born?' the man in the dark glasses asks.

'Oh no, not at all. We were living in Mexico on account of my husband's work, you see, and every few months or so I would say, "I'll be home for a visit this summer or next Christmas," and of course, two years go by and, well, you know how it is. I came home for her funeral – by then I was expecting Katherine – and I stayed on, simply refused to leave the house where I was brought up – a house, I may add, where I was not particularly happy. My husband had to change jobs and move back to Boston. I'm going to be honest – Mother and I, we weren't all that close, but even so I was haunted by a sense of guilt for years after. Still, I suppose we all have such regrets.'

She opens her mouth to say something about her own mother, how close they were, friends in fact, and the loneliness that had followed her death, but the first word is hardly in her mouth when her husband jumps in ahead of her: 'My mother never saw the house – here in Truro. That was something I've always regretted.'

'Well, of course his mother wasn't well enough to—' she begins to explain before he cuts across her.

'She was perfectly well. The visit was postponed and then it was too late, simply.'

'Oh now, that is a shame,' Mrs Kaplan says. 'I'm sure she would have liked the house.'

'She would have approved, yes,' he says.

'Well, we don't know that for certain,' she says. 'His mother could be quite diffic—'

Again he cuts in on her: 'She was very encouraging that way.'

'Well, now, that depends,' she says, 'I wouldn't agree necess—'

'I know I would have enjoyed showing it to her.'

Mrs Kaplan gives him a sad little smile and then glancing over at the porch says, 'Would anybody mind if we went over and joined Katherine for a while? She can't be in the sun and it's a little confining for her. I'm sure she would enjoy the company.'

Katherine is sitting down, her feet up on a chaise longue, the soles of her bare feet turned towards them. The old man she was dancing with is now pushing someone else around the dance floor. She crosses the lawn with Mrs Kaplan.

The woman with the brown face is walking behind them, hand in hand with the man in the dark glasses. When she glances back she sees her husband has been waylaid by Michael.

'My friend Lilian,' Mrs Kaplan says, 'and that's her youngest brother, George. He lost his sight fighting in the Pacific, you know, and Lily takes care of him now. He doesn't say much but seems content enough.'

She waits for Lily to catch up, then hooks herself onto her arm. 'Now, Lily here, she will tell you that she is a gardener but really she is a horticulturist and a botanist and a great explorer of forests and swamps and jungles and—'

'And my friend here,' Lily says, 'is a great exaggerator of my abilities.'

'She can make anything grow,' Mrs Kaplan declares.

'Except money.' Lilian smiles and both women laugh loudly at what is obviously an old and favourite joke.

She waits for the women to stop laughing and then says, 'Could you excuse me, I need to go to the bathroom.'

'Of course,' Mrs Kaplan says. 'Why don't you use mine? It's at the top of the house, end of the hallway. Go right through the bedroom. That way you won't have to stand in line.'

The way he just blurted it out! It had felt like a slap in the face to her and now, as she follows Mrs Kaplan's directions up the stairways, she can still feel the sour sting of it on her cheek. To imply that she had been somehow at fault. Sixty-seven years old and still a mama's boy and the mama not even alive! To do it, too, in front of strangers. He who could barely say good morning to someone he didn't know well for fear he might give something away. Mrs Kaplan may not have noticed, but the blind man and his sister certainly did. The blind man's chin going up; his sister's eyes going down.

At the top of the last flight, she stands and looks down a long, dusty hallway; three doors on the left, one on the end facing her. She comes to a door that is slightly open and takes a peek in, thinking it could be the bathroom. But it turns out to be a room with Richie in it, sprawled belly first on the floor, his raised foot swinging metronomically behind him. He is holding one of those brown US army Victory envelopes with the stamp of a fighter plane on the side of it. There are a few more of them on the floor beside him – old letters from his father probably. For the first time, she feels sorry for the boy, hiding himself away in a room at the top of the house to read his father's old letters, on today of all days.

She decides to leave him alone and steps back out into the hallway, where she remembers Mrs Kaplan said that in order to find the bathroom she would need to pass through her bedroom at the end of the hallway.

Sitting on the toilet, she leans her elbows over her knees and looks around Mrs Kaplan's spartan bathroom, the beehive window, the bath-tub flecked with rust, the sponge still plump with water. She feels a strong urge to pee and yet nothing is forthcoming. She tries to relax, not force it or think about it. She listens to the sounds outside the house. The volume has increased, the voices now louder, the laughter more carefree and robust. There is the nasal sound of the clarinet asking 'Why Don't You Do Right?'

All she had done was postpone the visit. The house not ready five minutes when he wanted to drive all the way to Nyack to bring his sister and mother back here. All she had asked was that they enjoy their first summer in their new home without having to cater and kowtow to his family; without having them look down their vespid snouts at all that she held dear.

'Isn't that why you designed it as a one-bedroomed affair?' she had reminded him. 'So we wouldn't have to put up with an endless parade of visitors?'

'Two people do not make a parade, and my mother and sister after all—'

'Yes, but don't you think she is a little old for all that travel?'

'We can take plenty of stop breaks on the way.'

'I'm not going all the way back to Nyack!'

'They can come on the train then – we can pick them up in Boston.'

'I'm not going all the way to Boston!'

'I can do it alone.'

'You need to work now. You don't want all that disruption.'

'You mean you don't want all the bother.'

'All I'm saying is that now might not be the best time and I don't mind writing a nice letter and telling them so.'

'She is not getting any younger.'

'Oh, there's plenty of gas in her yet.'

'They can have our bed, we can sleep in the loft.'

'No, no, that will not do.'

'They can stay in Wellfleet, I'll find a hotel.'

'No, no. Far too expensive this time of year.'

'You won't even have to cook.'

'I said NO! And I mean no, no, no.'

Finally, it comes trickling out, an insipid little effort and after all that trouble and all those stairs. By the time she gets back down, she'll want to go again. She waits for it to finish dripping into the toilet then wipes herself, rearranges her clothing and slowly washes her hands in Mrs Kaplan's sink.

And then what did she go and do, his mother? What did she do but pull the ultimate stunt. She died! Yes, died before she ever had a chance to see his precious house.

'His precious house,' she says to her reflection, 'which, by the way, my uncle's money paid for!'

She looks at herself for a moment then, closing her damp hands over her face, whispers: 'I said no, I said no, no. No.'

~

HE IS STANDING ON the lawn talking to Michael about lobster traps when Mrs Kaplan comes over and introduces two boys. Michael, without looking at the boys, mutters, 'I already met 'em before the party,' and he knows then that these must be the dreaded Hyannis boys.

'We were just talking about lobsters,' he says.

'Oh, I see,' Mrs Kaplan says, 'thinking of doing a little lobster trapping?'

'No, but I want to know how the trap works,' Michael says.

'And I couldn't really tell him,' he says, 'apart from the fact that the lobster can find its way in, but can't seem to find its way back out.'

'And I don't understand why it can't figure that out,' Michael says. 'I mean, if he can get in, why can't he get out?'

'That's how it is sometimes, I guess,' Mrs Kaplan says and Michael blinks at her. 'I mean, sometimes it's easy to get ourselves into something and later we can't seem to find our way out – oh, would you listen to me, preaching at a party!'

'I have a pet lobster,' one of the boys says.

'Well now!' Mrs Kaplan says.

'I call him Major Ursa.'

'Well, that is an unusual name,' Mrs Kaplan says, 'but then I guess a lobster is not a usual pet.'

'I called him after the constellation,' the boy says, 'you know, the stars.'

'You are interested in the stars then?' Mrs Kaplan says. 'Richie, you know, used to be a terrific star-watcher when he was younger. It was something his father very much enjoyed and he taught him all—'

'I asked for a telescope for Christmas,' the boy says, 'but I didn't get one. I wanted to look at Major Ursa.'

'But shouldn't it be Ursa Major?' Mrs Kaplan asks the boy.

'Yeah, but I wanted him to sound like a soldier too, because that's what he is, kind of.'

'My brother rescued him,' the other boy says. 'His claw was hurt and he fixed him up and now we're training him to fight.'

'Oh look,' Mrs Kaplan says, 'here comes your mother – I think she may be looking for you.'

'Come on, boys, time to go,' a blonde woman with a pretty but harried face says and is duly ignored by the boys.

One of the boys tugs on his sleeve and looks up at him, a little wild in the eyes. 'He's going to fight to the death. That's why he's a major,' he says.

'Well, I don't know about the soldier part,' he says to the boy, 'but in the outline of the constellation, I suppose, there is a certain lobster resemblance.'

The boys' mother begins to pull the boy away. 'I hope they're not being a pain in the neck.'

'Not at all, they were telling me about their lobster,' he says.

'My lobster – not his. He's just helping train it.'

'Not that Major again! I swear, one of these days, I'll throw him in a pot of boiling water.'

'You do that,' the owner of Major snarls, 'and you'll go in right after him.'

He expects the mother to clip the boy, but she appears not to mind or at least not to have noticed the impertinence.

'We're having a head to head fight,' the other boy continues, 'Major and this other lobster that a boy in our school owns. His lobster is German but Major, he's definitely American.'

'How do you know he's German?'

'He looks like it. He's a kind of grey colour like the German uniform and he's got a really mean face.'

'I see,' he says and tries not to laugh.

'They're gonna fight to the death.'

'So your brother said.'

'But won't you miss poor Major if he dies?' Mrs Kaplan asks.

The boy's mother puts her hand on his arm; he shrugs it off.

'I can get another one. He's a soldier, that's what they do – isn't it? They fight and then they die. Just like Uncle Pete. I'm called after him – he was a hero, you know.'

His mother says, 'There's your father now. You better start moving or you'll be next one to die. Look over there – see him waiting. And you know he doesn't like to be kept waiting.'

'I'm so sorry we have to leave early, Mrs Kaplan,' she says, 'but we're going to Kenneth's family for Labor Day and— Come on, I said! I swear... We had a wonderful time, though, and I hope you made pots of money for the fund. Marty! I'm telling you now, get movin'.'

'We haven't counted it yet, but we will be letting everyone know.'

'Say thank you now to Mrs Kaplan for the lovely party.'

'Thank you, ma'am.'

'Yes, thank you so much, ma'am.'

'I'll walk with you,' Mrs Kaplan says. 'I'd like to say goodbye to your husband. How is he doing?'

'Still not sleeping too good. I mean, there's nothing wrong with him on the outside but you know...'

As they walk away, he can still hear the mother scolding the two boys while carrying on her conversation with Mrs Kaplan.

'Shame we'll be missing your speech but, you know, if we don't get on the road— Peter! You hit your brother like that again and I'll—'

He looks at Michael and they both start to laugh.

'They're the two boys Richie doesn't like.'

'So I gathered,' he says.

'I don't blame him neither.'

'No. Still, their lobster sounds like an interesting character.'

'Mrs Aitch says not everyone has to like everyone.'

'That is very true.'

'Otherwise, she says, we'd all be going round grinning at each other like fools,' Michael says and then bursts out laughing. 'I think that's really funny. I don't know why, I just think it is.'

'Well, sometimes, my wife, she's a funny lady.'

Michael says nothing for a moment and then: 'I… I, I try to like Richie more. I really do. But…'

He looks at Michael, is about to say something about Richie needing a little understanding on account of losing his father. But then he reminds himself that this kid has lost everything: family, home, identity even.

'Oh, I think Richie is fine. I think you will grow to like him in the end. It happens that way sometimes.'

'His mom doesn't like me,' Michael says then. 'I know that for sure.'

'Oh now, that can't be true.'

'Oh, but it is. And I know why too. It's because I'm German and Germans killed her husband and, well, I can understand that. I think it's kind of fair, really. I mean, I don't know – maybe.'

'It's probably best not to dwell on these things, Michael,' he says.

'Well, I don't know. It just comes into my head sometimes and there's not much I can do about that – is there?'

'No, I don't suppose there is.'

They stand quietly for a few seconds watching the crowd move over the lawn and then he lays his hand on Michael's shoulder. 'Come on,' he says and begins to lead him away, 'let's go inside, see if we can't find something cold to drink.'

SHE SEES HIM AS she comes downstairs from the bathroom. He is touching his lips and chin, the way he does when he's talking to someone who makes him nervous. Craning her neck into the living-room, she sees that someone is Olivia. Annette and Katherine are also there, along with another couple.

'Oh, come on, you can tell us!' Olivia is saying as she comes close to the company. 'No need to be coy. Oh look, here's your wife, she'll settle the bet now.'

'What bet is that?'

'He won't tell us what his favourite painting is,' Annette says.

'He won't?'

'Says he doesn't know,' Olivia says, stamping her foot like a child. 'Now, how could he not know?'

'How indeed?' she says.

Olivia turns to the couple standing there. 'This is Mrs Aitch, she's bound to know.'

'My name is not Mrs Aitch,' she says to the man.

'No?'

'It just begins with—'

'It's Mrs Aitch in this house. The boys say so and the boys—' Olivia stops as she notices that Michael has just stepped into the company. 'Michael – can I help you?'

'I just came up to ask Mrs Aitch if she'd like to listen to Mrs Kaplan's speech with me.'

'That's not for another fifteen minutes – people haven't even finished dessert yet. Now, scoot, Rosetta will need you in the kitchen.'

'She told me to take a break.'

'Michael. Please do as I ask…' Olivia says with a little exasperated laugh.

Katherine says, 'Oh, he's fine, Olivia. And shouldn't we be outside with mother anyhow? She'll want us with her before she starts.'

'Oh. Oh yes, of course. Let me get another drink first.'

'I'll get it for you, honey,' Annette says. 'I'll bring it out to you.'

Olivia smartly downs the dregs in her glass and hands it to Annette.

'Does anyone know where Richie is?' Olivia says as Katherine takes her arm and draws her away. 'Michael,' Olivia calls over her shoulder, 'would you please go find him?'

And then, taking another step, she calls out over her other shoulder, 'When you are finished taking your break, of course.'

She lifts an eyebrow to her husband, then looks back at Michael.

'I think I know where Richie is,' she says. 'I won't be a minute.'

She climbs back upstairs and down the long hallway. Richie's door is closed over but she can hear him inside singing to himself.

She taps at the door and calls his name; there is a sound of fluster on the other side.

'Are you all right in there, Richie?' she asks.

The door opens and Richie's nose sticks out through the gap.

'Oh, hello, Mrs Aitch. How did you know I was here?' he says.

'Well, it's your room isn't it?'

'No, it's not. I mean, Michael and me, we sleep on the first floor. I just come up here sometimes when, well...'

'When you want to be alone? I understand. We all need time to ourselves.'

She looks over his shoulder. On the floor of the room is a comic book and a bottle of soda. The army Victory envelopes are no longer there, although she sees what could be a small heap of dollars peering out from under the comic book. Money his father's friends have given him, no doubt, as if money is any sort of substitute.

'Why aren't you at the party, Richie?'

'I'm just taking a little rest.'

'Well, I think your mother may have been looking for you. Your grandmother is going to speak soon and I'm sure they would like you to be there.'

'I'll be down soon.'

'Michael is down there, too.'

'Well, sure he is, with his new friends.'

'What new friends? He's alone as far as I can tell.'

'Those Westin brothers, and I'm sorry but I don't like them very much.'

'You don't?'

'No, as a matter of fact, I happen to think they are nothing but bullies, that's what I think.'

'Well, that's not so good, is it?'

'Doesn't seem to bother Michael, though – he doesn't mind being their friend. He went off to the beach with them and just left me behind.'

'Oh, I'm sure he was just being polite. Anyhow, he's not with them now. Why don't you come on down with me? People will be leaving soon. And you don't want to miss your grandmother's speech.'

'Where's my mom?' he asks.

'She's around. She's with Katherine, I think.'

'And Captain Hartman?'

'Who?'

'Doesn't matter.'

'Come on, Richie, let's go down – what do you say?'

Richie mulls it over while he chews on his bottom lip. Then he nods and, carefully closing the door behind him, falls into step beside her.

When they come outside, the porch is crammed with people and Mrs Kaplan is about to start her speech. She pushes Richie ahead of her and begins repeating, 'Excuse me, excuse me, we'd like to get through, please.'

A man makes tutting noises at her and another woman shushes her. There is laughter all around and then a heavy silence as Mrs Kaplan begins to talk about her son. She finds a dent in the crowd and, taking hold of Richie's arm, she pulls him through and now they are on the far side of the porch, standing at the side of the top step.

'Bill Kaplan, my son, Olivia's husband, Richie's father and Katherine's brother, he gave his life for this country. For the past few years we have mourned him on this, the day of his anniversary. But six years on from his death, we have decided, instead, to celebrate his life.

'We loved Bill and Bill loved us and we must remember that love does not go away – the love we feel for those we have lost, and the love they gave us while they were here, stays with us always.

'And so to all of you who have lost loved ones, be it through war or accident or illness or old age, let us raise our glasses and make a toast. To absent friends.'

Mrs Kaplan lifts her glass and people are lifting their elbows; even those who don't have anything in their hands are raising an invisible glass to absent friends. She can see her husband's profile straight ahead of her as he looks up at Mrs Kaplan and, next to him, she sees the crown of Michael's head moving around and popping up and down as if he is searching for someone. She is about to wave at him when she hears Mrs Kaplan's voice say something about a very special boy that she would like to call up to the stage. She feels Richie stiffen and get ready to move.

~

MRS KAPLAN IS CALLING out his name. She is calling it right out in front of everyone while he is standing there listening to her speech.

At first he didn't know it was his name; he was sure she must mean someone else. And he'd been busy watching all the glasses go up and listening to the voices mutter *absentfriendstoabsentfriendsabsent* and wondering if there was anyone else in the crowd like him who had no absent friends to toast – or none that they could remember anyhow. And he'd been busy, too, looking at all the faces looking up at Mrs Kaplan making her speech on the porch. Shiny faces with soft smiles and little laughs until she said the thing about her son Bill and then the mouths went down and the tears came out even from eyes belonging to soldiers and other men. And he was keeping an eye on Olivia and Katherine up on the stage, standing behind Mrs Kaplan, and he was wondering why Richie wasn't there with them, and he was keeping watch for Mrs Aitch and worrying that she was missing the speech. And that's why it takes a few seconds for him to realize that he is the Michael she's talking about.

He looks up at Mr Aitch standing beside him. Does she mean me? he asks with his eyes, but Mr Aitch is looking over to the side of the house and he looks too and there are Mrs Aitch and Richie standing side by side. Richie with his mouth dropped open and a look of shock on his face.

Rosetta gives him a small shove in the back. 'What are you waiting for. She want you to go up there.'

'You mean me? She means me?'

'Sure she mean you – who else? Now go, hurry, hurry.'

And when he looks up there is Katherine's hand calling him on and Mrs Kaplan's voice saying, 'Is he here? Yes, Michael, come on up here, come on up, no need to be shy, come on, let these good people see you. That's right, we are all friends here.'

He can hardly feel his own legs move as he makes his way through the smiley people and he can hardly believe his own eyes when they all stand out of his way and make a little path for him to walk through.

Mrs Kaplan puts her arm round his shoulder. 'This boy,' she says and then takes a breath and begins again, 'This boy is a shining example of the good work done by our fund. This boy, Michael Novak. And who has honoured us by being our guest these past few weeks. Now Michael, I'm sure, doesn't even remember this. But when he was a little boy at the end of the war in Europe, he was rescued by the American Red Cross. He was sick and undernourished and very, very frightened and had been that way for… we don't know how long. He had to travel halfway across Europe before he could receive treatment and often it didn't look as he would make it. For more than two years that was his life. But thanks to Mr Truman's directive he was brought to the United States and adopted by a fine hardworking family, the Novaks, who unfortunately can't be here with us today. When Mr Truman wrote his directive on displaced persons, he finished with these words: "This is the opportunity for America to set an example for the rest of the world in cooperation towards alleviating human misery."

'Please bear this in mind when I tell you that our work is not yet over. But it is worthwhile work and must be continued. This boy is testimony to that. An American boy, with an American future. So on behalf of Michael, and on behalf of countless other boys and girls who are recovering from the effects of a terrible war, we thank you for helping us to help them. And one more thing before I let you go back to the party.'

Mrs Kaplan turns away from him and opens her arms to take a parcel from

Frank. Then she turns back round and says, 'Michael, this is for you,' and places the parcel into his arms.

'It's a kite,' Mrs Kaplan says, 'that you may always fly high, Michael. But it's a kite that you have to build yourself, and this is significant because the aim of our fund is to ensure that our orphans grow into independent American citizens who learn how to build their own lives and to elevate themselves so that they can be a real and valued part of this fine country of ours.'

Mrs Kaplan starts clapping at him. Then the whole party is clapping. He stares into the crowd and first sees, taller than anyone else in the crowd, Mr Aitch.

But Mr Aitch is not smiling and he only gives two or three claps before his hands go down again. Then he looks across the way to Mrs Aitch, who isn't clapping either, and now he sees that Richie is no longer standing beside her.

HE DECIDES TO GO someplace quiet and smoke a cigarette. It's not something he makes a habit of, but when he does smoke, he prefers to do it alone. He has a mind to go round by Mill Road, observe the pond life as it gears up for nightfall, have his smoke there, then get back to the party in time for supper.

As he comes round by the front of the house and down the path, he sees quite a few people are already leaving the party. A group of air force men, recognizable even out of uniform, are loudly discussing a dance in Provincetown while all around families, with long roads ahead, struggle with contrary children. Down the path and out on the road he sees a large woman in pink who looks vaguely familiar leaning on the hood of an automobile and peering anxiously in his direction. He goes off the idea of Mill Pond and instead turns left. Pulling a cigarette from the pack as he goes, he follows a tangled path upwards. When he gets to the top of the knoll, he finds Frank already in place, smoking and looking out on the bay.

'Is it always this calm?' Frank asks, taking out his lighter and snapping it under his nose.

'Oh, it has its moments,' he says, accepting the light. 'You managed to pull yourself away from the piano, I see.'

'A friend of Mrs Kaplan's wanted her son to play Brahms. I couldn't bear listening to the little twerp. He knows where to put his fingers – conservatory kid, you know – but empty in here.' Frank sticks his knuckle into his chest and grimaces disapprovingly. 'Good speech, don't you think?' he then adds.

He takes a pull from the cigarette and nods.

'She's quite a lady, that Mrs Kaplan. They ought to come up with a medal just for her. All those kids, what she did for them. Of course she's not so active these days, but I guess she needs to be with her daughter right now. Tough days ahead.'

'I didn't realize it was all that serious,' he says and turns his face away.

'They're not holding out much hope. Talk about bad luck – first her son and now? One gets a bullet, the other cancer. A lady like Mrs Kaplan. Say, you need another spark for that, you seem to be gone out there?'

He looks down and sees his cigarette has failed. He lifts it back up to his lips and the lighter snaps again.

'What I wouldn't give to walk out here of an evening and see this spread,' Frank says. 'You live round here?'

'Just up the beach there.'

Frank turns to look and then stops and says, 'And who's this little lady, I wonder? Seems to be in quite a hurry like someone is chasing her.'

He turns and there his wife is, arms wide, feet juddering down an adjacent dune. 'That's my wife,' he says, 'and she always seems that way.'

She comes up beside them, nods at both and looks out over the bluff.

'That is one eye-smacking sunset,' she says and Frank laughs.

'You're the piano player – right?' she asks him then. 'I like the way you play.'

'Well, thank you, ma'am. I was just saying to your husband here what lucky people you are.'

'How's that?'

'To have a view like this under your nose – I mean, you just walk out here and all this is just waiting for you.'

270

'Lucky about the view. I don't know about much else.'

Frank smiles again, as if he thinks she is joking, then he says, 'That was a nice speech – don't you think?'

'No, as a matter of fact, I don't.'

'You don't?'

'I was disappointed by it. I might say, shocked. Putting Michael on display like that. I don't know why they don't just make a commercial and show it in the movies or on the television and be done with it.'

'I'm sure it wasn't meant—'

'Whether it was or not, the fact remains. And hardly any mention of Richie.'

'Richie?'

'Well, of course! After all, he was left without a father. His suffering may not have been quite so... well, dramatic, I guess, but even so...'

He notes the way Frank is staring at his wife's mouth, as if he can't believe what's coming out of it and can't wait to see what's coming next. But she's turned to the sunset now and for a moment has nothing to say.

Frank clears his throat. 'I have to say, ma'am,' he begins.

'Don't you just love this,' she says, smiling at him, 'the way the sun swells up and then seems to burst? As if it is bleeding all over the world. A few short seconds of looking at this, and the whole day – even the worst of them – seems worthwhile somehow.'

Frank plucks on his jaw and nods at her.

On the way back down the hill, Frank leads the way along the slender path. His wife is in the middle and he, a little less nimble on his feet than the other two, is coming up the rear. She stops halfway and turns to him.

'I suppose you want to go now?' she says.

'No,' he says.

'We've been here quite a few hours already.'

'Sounds like you're the one wants to go home.'

'Certainly not! You know how I love a party.'

'Well, that's good because Mrs Kaplan has asked us to supper.'

'And you said we would? So you're having a good time then?'

'It's a nice party.'

'Well, I hope I'm not stuck sitting with a bunch of drips, that's all I have to say. Earnest housewives and stuffed shirts are all I've met so far. Does anyone round here ever read a book or look at a painting or have a clue about— about anything that matters?'

At the bottom of the hill, they turn back towards the house. Frank stops and lifts his hand behind his ear. 'Hear that?' he says. 'A party with no music. Better go do something about it.'

Frank puts his hand on his wife's arm and pats it fondly. 'See you later, I hope,' he says.

They stand for a moment, watching him go.

'Well, here we are,' she says, 'just you and me, wrapped in a veil of blue twilight. It might be romantic except...'

'Except?'

'Except you can't wait to get away from me.'

'Oh now, that's not true. Actually, I was going to say – about Mrs Kaplan's speech.'

'Don't worry, I'm done criticizing for one evening. I know it's a tough day for them – I'm not completely lacking in sympathy, you know.'

'I was going to say, I happen to agree with what you said to Frank. I didn't like the way Michael was put on the spot either. And I take your point about Richie too.'

'You do?'

'Yes, I do.'

She looks away for a moment and then comes back to him. 'Well, isn't that nice to know? Pity you were too disgustingly timid to say so in front of Frank.'

And then she turns and marches away from him back into the house.

AT THE SUPPER TABLE she is shooed in beside an elderly lady who shouts, right in her face, that her name is Mrs Dutra and that her daughter is babysitting the Kaplan dog in P–town. Olivia is steering three more elderly ladies down her direction when Mrs Kaplan comes out of nowhere, laughing and talking to three young women dressed in wide-skirted flowery dresses: a poppy, a marigold and a rosebud. Within seconds they are fluffing their flowery dresses into place as they seat themselves right across the table from her, their faces all freshly repainted for the next phase of the party.

'Well, I wouldn't go near P–town the next couple of days,' the marigold says, 'all those crowds! Between the pleasure boats coming in from Boston and the daytrippers. Thousands expected, I hear. I'd just as soon spend Labor Day catching up with my ironing, thank you very much.'

A man further down the way leans out. 'Oh now, you're far too pretty to spend the day ironing,' he says and the young women replies, 'Mr Hatton – does your wife know you go round dishing out so many compliments?'

'Oh, she don't mind long as I keep the best ones for her,' he says and there is an outburst of giggling from the three young women. Another man down along the opposite side pokes his head out. 'Is that Beth Greene I see down there?'

'Beth Maxwell now,' the poppy smiles, 'I've been married going on three years, Mr Bax.'

'Three years! Any little chicks yet?'

Beth shakes her head.

'You oughta married my boy. He's got two of 'em. Twins, you know. And I wouldn't be surprised if there's another on the way.'

The smile drops off the girl's face and she lowers her eyes and begins pulling on the skirt of her poppy dress. She feels sorry for the girl then and decides to pipe up.

'Not everyone thinks children are essential to a happy marriage. It's a very old-fashioned attitude, if you ask me.'

'Maybe you're right,' Mr Bax says, 'but it's a waste of time otherwise. If you ask me.' And then he pulls his head back into the line.

She is about to whip back when Beth gives her a pinky smile. 'I'm from around here,' she says, 'but my friends, they're from Concord. We're best friends and our husbands – they're out there at the bar – they're best friends too.'

'How very convenient,' she says.

There is an awkward pause until Mrs Dutra announces that she will be eighty years old tomorrow. Oohs and ahhhs and general congratulations are sent from all sides of the table. The woman beams with pride and then, before her beam is quite done, she says her grandson was killed in action right along-side Mrs Kaplan's son. 'The very same day,' she says, 'oh yes. A different country, though. Bill Kaplan died in Italy, I believe. My grandson in Germany. Sam. Sam Leighton. On account it was my daughter's son, you see.'

A small subdued round of condolences and then the sound of plates being passed along the line and the gurgle of water pouring from a large jug and the hiss of a released bottle cap.

'Do you have a washing machine?' Mrs Dutra asks her after a moment.

'No, I do not,' she says.

'My granddaughter, she got one the other day. That would be Sam's sister. She married one of the Martinsons. Out of Chatham, you know.'

'Oh, I couldn't live without my washing machine,' one of the flowery house-wives says and the other pair nod in eager agreement.

'I'm all for the modern convenience,' Mrs Dutra says, 'but in our day, it was different – isn't that so?' she asks and looks straight at her, as if she too is eighty years old and as if, too, housework has been her reason for living.

'Oh, I deplore housework,' she says, 'kitchen and laundry especially – those, I tend to avoid. I think it's the worst thing an artist can do.'

'You're an artist?' Mrs Dutra says clapping her hands. 'Oh, how exciting!'

The housewives look peeved and so she continues: 'The kitchen is just about the worst place a woman can be – whether or not she happens to be an artist. I think the same applies to any woman with half a cup of pride. Spend time in the kitchen and you'll be kept there. I see it all the time, women who slave after their husbands – husbands who have little or no time for them, I might add. You step in the kitchen and you'll stay there. A kitchen slave for the rest of your life.'

She glances at the three young women across the way: one face flamed up; the other cast down; the third biting the corner of her lip and glaring into the distance. She feels sorry then and slightly ashamed of herself for trying to demean them by demeaning their lives. As if their lives won't already be tough enough. But for now, they are young women in freshly ironed flowery dresses with robust bodies and hips ready for child bearing. As if I am above them, she thinks, but I am not above them. I don't have what they have. I don't have that kind of power.

A short while later she sees her husband come in with Mrs Kaplan and another middle-aged couple in tow. In a matter of moments Mrs Kaplan has reshuffled the cards again and now Mrs Dutra has been moved and a new couple are on one side of her, Michael on the other, while her husband, placed across from her, sits in the middle of the three sulky housewives.

But the new couple beside her just couldn't be nicer. 'We used to live in Greenwich Village,' the man is saying, 'oh, a long time ago. We lived there for about two years.'

'Two years and three months,' his wife says. 'Shared bathroom, rattling windows. I can't tell you how much I miss it. How long have you lived there?'

'Oh, forever. I lived there even before I was married – I lived in a little apartment on the top floor… now you talk about a shared bathroom!'

'But you loved it!' the woman says.

'Oh, always.' She smiles.

She does not tell the woman about the lonely nights there; or the time she was sick with influenza and saw not a soul for a whole miserable week; or the time she held an exhibition of her work and nobody came. She does not mention any of that.

At the far side of the table, coming down this way, she sees Olivia's red dress and Olivia's hand serving out pieces of chicken. Annette is approaching from the other end with a big bowl of potato salad. Michael, beside her, is banging his knees impatiently together. She introduces him to the couple.

'My name is Gloria,' the woman says, 'and this is my husband, Arthur. We're spending the weekend in Provincetown.'

'Mrs Aitch had a cat named Arthur,' Michael declares a little too loudly, so that everyone around lifts their head.

'That so?' the man Arthur laughs.

'Yes, she took him on vacation to Provincetown, they stayed in the Gingerbread Inn. She said it was the best vacation of her life.'

Across the table one of the housewives bursts out laughing.

'Now, I was just kidding, Michael, when I said that.'

'No, you were not,' Michael insists.

'I was, Michael – just a little. No, Gloucester, I would say, was my best vacation. Let's go back there sometime,' she says to her husband. 'What do you say?'

'I say, what for?' he says.

The three flowery dresses turn their perfectly coiffed heads to look at him. Now Olivia and that awful Annette stop serving and look at him too. All are looking at him. She looks at him herself. Please do not let me down, she thinks, not in front of all these women. Please not here.

'Well, we were so happy there,' she says, the words out of her mouth before she can stop them. 'What I mean is, it might be nice to see it again.'

'I'm happy right here in Truro,' he says. 'I was happy in Gloucester too. We had our honeymoon there,' he explains to the couple. 'We had a fine time.'

Then he turns back and smiles at her. At. Her.

Take that, she thinks. Take that you three little flowery witches and take that Annette and anyone else who happens to be listening. And Olivia – you above all – take it, right in the kisser!

She looks across the table to one of the flowery dresses.

'What's your name, dear?' she says.

'Me? Oh, I'm Barbara, ma'am.'

'Would you mind passing me that basket of dinner rolls, Barbara?'

IT'S ALMOST DARK WHEN he finds her seated in the corner of the kitchen, surrounded by women, Mrs Kaplan included. Katherine is standing. There are two younger women standing alongside her. They are facing into the group, backs to the room, which is why they don't notice that he has come in and is standing just behind them.

He can't hear what his wife is saying. There is the clatter of post-supper dishes and the bicker of Spanish as Rosetta settles up with staff who have been hired by the day. It is often the case when he finds himself in a noisy room – the sounds seem to gang up on him, and all he can get is a big noisy blur.

His wife's little group appears to be keen; it leans in and listens to her. He is thinking about slipping away and coming back later, when he sees Katherine's elbow extend and nudge into the side of the girl next to her. The girl's shoulders begin to shake. And now Katherine's shoulders are going too.

For a moment, he thinks – or at least hopes – that his wife may have said something amusing, but none of the women seated around her appear to be laughing, and so he has to accept that Katherine and her friend are laughing at her. And now the third young woman joins in with a comment delivered behind the shield of her hand.

That in any given group she will sooner or later find an enemy – usually another female – he has come to expect; she has always irked people, rubbed them up the wrong way, frequently insulted them or swiped back at an insult where none had been intended. But until now it hadn't really occurred to him that she would be seen as a figure of fun.

He feels a sense of disappointment that he can't quite pin down – in Katherine or in his wife, or maybe in himself.

Katherine turns away from the group as if to hide the fact that she is laughing. As she turns, she sees him standing there and the smile drops from her face in an instant. She looks bereft as she steps away from the group, towards him.

'I was looking for my wife,' he says. 'I take it that she is here?'

Katherine nods her head rapidly, the way a little girl might do after being caught misbehaving by an uncle whose high opinion she is in danger of losing.

Her two friends sidle away and Katherine, too, steps aside. He moves closer to the group and now he can hear, and hear all too well.

'I can tell you this much, there is a boycott against the female artist. They elbow me out of the way, but I'm a tiger in my own right and simply won't be shoved aside.'

'But it must be so frustrating for you,' a woman's voice says, 'all that work and no reward. When I was singing in Milan, you know—'

'Actually, I'll be exhibiting next year – possibly even before then.'

'Oh, where? Do tell us, we can come along!'

'I don't like to say anything yet, not till I have signed on the dotted line, which I expect to do any day now. I'm a little careful that way when it comes to my exhibitions. But I'll be sure to let you know.'

He clears his throat and the women look up. His wife's shamed face looks elsewhere.

He addresses Mrs Kaplan: 'I just wanted to ask if it would be all right to take Michael and Richie down to the beach to do a little stargazing?'

'What a wonderful idea!' Mrs Kaplan says.

'Now all I need to do is find them,' he says.

'I'll track them down,' Katherine's voice says from somewhere behind him.

He thanks her without turning around and says that he'll wait for the boys outside.

He crosses the lopsided garden, past deserted tables and a few upturned chairs. He is the only thing moving outdoors, apart from a single red ruby of a live cigarette at a far-off table. There is the sound of someone unseen clattering empty bottles into some sort of container. He comes to a hill that leads to the beach and takes the first few steps along its beaten-down path.

When he looks back, the house appears to be rooted into a dip. The upper floors are in darkness, as is the north gable leading round to the front entrance. From the opposite gable, a slash of yellow light shows from the side of the room where the party is taking place, and the rest of the room glares out from the porch through the open doors. It looks like a house with no glass in the windows; the sort of windows that could belong in one of his paintings.

He can see Captain Hartman mixing cocktails and Olivia, a little unsteady on her feet, leaning out of a dance to take a sip from a glass left on the side of the table. The man she is dancing with is polite, patient as he waits for her to come back to his arms. He recognizes him now as a man called Grant who spent the war in London. He had enjoyed a conversation with him earlier about the trip he had made to London himself when he was a young man. It was daylight when they had struck up that conversation and they were standing at the north end of the house, the side that is now in darkness. Already it feels like a memory, something that happened a long time ago. He feels tired suddenly, tired enough to lie down under one of the tables and sleep the sleep of the dead.

The group from the kitchen begins filing into the big room, Mrs Kaplan and Rosetta at the rear, carrying trays of coffee cups. From this distance the sounds remain independent: laughter and chattering voices, an undertow of piano music. He takes a few further steps up the hill and now the sound of the sea begins to take over, the dull slur as the tide sucks it away. The dry grass crunches under his feet and there's a whiff of rot on the air. He is beginning to regret the whole idea of taking the boys to look at the stars. The sea knows it, the crickets know it, the low bushes and the grass know it: the party is almost over.

He stops and looks back down the hill. The red cigarette top has gone along with its owner, and three shadowy figures are now coming like ghouls from the north end of the house.

He comes back down the hill to meet them.

'Well, here they are,' Katherine says and the boys run the last few feet to him. She hesitates a moment before asking, 'Would you mind if I, you know, tagged along? If I wouldn't be in the way, that is?'

If she wouldn't be in the way. He had planned on giving his full attention to the boys, to muster up whatever schoolboy knowledge he has managed to retain of the night sky, its map of stars and scraps of legend.

There will be the vault of the sky; the vast belly of the bay; the acres of flat beach; and the ever restless grass. In the whole of that, she will not take up much space. But she will be all the space he is likely to feel.

He says, 'Not in the least,' and steps back to allow her in.

Richie pulls out a flashlight and hands it to him. 'You're the tallest, sir, so you should hold this and walk behind us.'

He switches the flashlight on and holds it up. One behind the other, they fall into line and he follows into the flimsy path of light.

On the beach, he turns the boys northwards and begins to trace out the Big Dipper. Richie has it in a second and seems to know all about it.

'Well, why don't you tell Michael how the name came about?' he says.

'He doesn't want to know.'

'I do too!' Michael says.

'Well,' Richie says, 'it's to do with the slaves.'

'What slaves?'

'Before the Civil War was won, the slaves, see – they had this cup with a long handle and they dipped it into a barrel of water and drank out of it and...'

While Richie speaks he is aware of her silence, two maybe three feet behind him. He knows she is waiting for him to turn and say something to her, maybe step away from the boys to have a few words.

'But where's the lobster?' Michael asks.

'What lobster?' Richie says.

'The lobster called Major.'

'He means Ursa Major,' he explains to Richie, 'the two brothers from Hyannis – they called their lobster after it.'

Richie makes every show of being astonished by such stupidity; he flops his arms and heaves out a sigh.

'Everyone knows that the Big Dipper is also known as the Great Bear,' he says, 'not lobster. Boy, I knew they were dumb but...'

And now Richie launches into the story of Ursa Major, and for the first time since he's known him, he hears him talk about his father and how he taught him the way of the stars. 'There's the nose, see, and just there is the tail and if you follow that line you come to the paws. It's a bear, anyone can see that.'

'Oh yeah,' Michael says. 'Oh yeah.'

He thinks now might be a good time to turn and say something to her but he finds himself invigorated suddenly by the boys' voices and the smell of the sea and the fact that she is there, standing behind him, silently waiting. He finds himself taking off with his own Ursa Major snippet – the story of Zeus, a half-remembered story of love and jealousy that his own father told him when he was a boy.

'There was a woman and a boy, her son. And Zeus, he was a god and he fell in love with her.'

'Where was the boy's father?' Michael asks.

'That I don't know.'

'Maybe he was killed in a war or something?'

'Possibly. There were plenty of wars then too. But in any case, Zeus was not free to marry. He already had a wife. And she was pretty jealous. She was going to kill both mother and son and so Zeus, to save them, turned them into bears.'

'How they get in the sky?' Michael asks.

'Oh, he grabbed them by the tail. He was strong, you know – those gods usually are. And he swung 'em around and swung 'em around and then… And then they landed plonk, plink right next to one another up there in the sky.'

'Do that again!' Michael says.

'What?'

'That swinging thing – do it again.'

He bends his knees and rotates his arms.

'Plonk, plink, right up there in the sky and that's why their tails are so long.'

The boys roar and he hears Katherine laugh behind him.

'Richie – why don't you see if you can find the Little Bear now?' he says and takes a few steps back to her.

They stay in silence for a while, watching, or pretending to watch, the boys running up and down scouring the sky.

He can see her face clearly enough when he happens to glance at it, by the light from the yachts at anchor, and the light on the distant hook of Province-town, and the big round lamps of parked automobiles further up the beach.

She says, 'I love it down here at night.'

'Is that what you do – come down here at night?'

'Most nights. Well, I can't come here in the day…'

'I understand.'

'Funny thing, I prefer the beach at night now. It's not like before where I could read or just look at people.'

'So what do you do?'

'Oh, I just sit here and look out. Sometimes I swim. Sometimes I drink.' She laughs a sudden laugh. 'Sometimes I drink quite a lot.'

'But not tonight?'

'No, not tonight. Nor today either. Today is for my mother. I didn't want to spoil it. And, well, sometimes I can do that, if you know what I mean… when

281

I drink. I can spoil things. What about you? Do you come down to the beach much – at night, I mean?'

'I've taken a midnight swim a few times. But not in a while. I walk some-times just to look at the stars. Though October is a better month for that – drier sky, you see.'

'You ever paint them – the stars, I mean?'

'Oh, I'm not crazy enough for that.'

She smiles and he smiles back at her.

'I'm going to go back to the house now and I'll probably go straight to bed.'

'I'll walk you to the steps,' he says.

His hand goes out once or twice to take her elbow where the slope in the beach or the yielding sand unsteadies her step. But each time, just as he is about to do so, she seems to steady up of her own accord.

She doesn't speak again till they are back at the steps and then: 'I just wanted to say I was sorry about laughing at your wife, you know?'

'Sorry you were laughing or sorry I caught you?'

'Well, a little of both, I guess.'

'I'm sure it happens more than I realize.'

'Oh, please don't say that. I already feel bad enough.'

'Let's just forget about it now.'

'I'm ashamed,' she says, 'because, well, she's an easy target. You don't like me saying that?'

'No. No, I guess I don't.'

She puts one hand on the rail of the steps and waits a couple of seconds and then says, 'Look, I know this sounds a little crazy, but… well, I wanted to let you know that I'm down here most nights. And that I wouldn't mind having a talk with you sometime.'

'Well, yes, that would be nice,' he says, as if the thought of it doesn't petrify him.

'The thing is, I can't talk to my family any more. It's not that I want to discuss anything too gruesome, but we seem to be so busy avoiding certain subjects that we don't talk about anything at all. I feel – and of course maybe I'm wrong – that I could talk to you. Am I wrong?'

'I don't know, quite honestly.'

'Forgive me, I wasn't always this direct. But I don't see the point in wasting time any more. It's no big deal – if you're here some night, it would be nice to talk to you, that's all I'm saying.'

She takes one step and then turns back to him.

'Well, goodnight,' she says. 'I hope I see you soon. Here or in the house or on the road. Or wherever.'

'Yes,' he says, 'I hope so too.'

He sees his arm go out in the dim light, his hand reach towards her arm – to do what, he isn't sure – but then Michael's voice roars out.

'Mr Aitch! Mr Aitch! I can see it! I found the Little Bear!'

He looks back and sees the silhouette of Michael jumping up and down.

'Goodnight, Katherine,' he says and watches her for a moment move further up the steps, till she is beyond the light. He wonders what he thought he was going to do when he pulled her arm back – fold her into his arms and kiss her?

My mother was right, he thinks, I spend far too much time at the movies.

He turns and comes back to the boys, his voice rolling along the beach to them. 'Where, Michael? Where did you see it? Don't lose it, now, keep your eye on it. I want to see it too.'

THROUGH THE OPEN DOORS, she sees a ball of light coming down the hill like a falling star, and then a white trail widen out from it, touching the locust trees at the edge of the garden and misting over a back row of uncleared tables. There's a dark, spider-like movement of limbs beneath the light, alarming her for just a second before the light snaps off. And there is her husband suddenly coming towards the house with the two boys beside him, all three laughing and talking, Michael throwing the flashlight from hand to hand. And I always tell people he doesn't like children, she thinks. I always say that.

Olivia has just started her party piece, singing 'You Do Something to Me' and giving it the full Marlene Dietrich treatment while the men all around drool, the opera singer's husband barely able to keep his tongue in his mouth and the servicemen who have just rolled in from a bar in Provincetown trying to keep their wolf whistles clenched back out of respect for Mrs Kaplan. Only Captain Hartman seated nearby appears to be less than enamoured, his face immobile throughout, apart from that slight twist of disapproval at the mouth.

When her husband comes in, the boys are no longer with him. He takes the nearest available chair at the end of a vacant row. She watches him as Olivia brings the song to an end. But her husband – although he is staring in the general direction of Olivia – is not looking at her. And that look on his face – a sad sort of longing.

She leans a little to the side to see whoever or whatever is making him look that way. Then she sees Katherine, standing by the door where she must have lingered after saying goodnight a short while ago – probably to hear Olivia's song. Applause breaks out all around her although it feels like it is happening right inside her head. Katherine standing, one elbow bent, looking slantwise up at the light, and she wonders what if? What if all along it wasn't his lust she needed to fear, but his pity?

She looks again at Olivia smiling and bowing behind her luscious hair, her long, strong legs pushing out against the flimsy red cloth of her dress, and there is her husband applauding and grinning like a moron and she thinks: Oh, it's you, all right, Olivia. It has to be. When she glances back at the doorway, Katherine has gone and now her husband is tiptoeing rather clumsily in her direction.

He leans over her seat and looks at her and she has to wonder if he is a little bit tipsy.

'You ready to go yet?' he asks.

She nods, then stands and begins to walk away from him.

'Where are you going?' he whispers quite loudly. She sees now that his eyes are glassed over – he *is* a bit tipsy.

'Have you been drinking?' she asks him.

'I had a couple earlier on. Do you mind?'

'Not at all. I'm just going to say goodnight to the boys.'

She wanders through the house looking for them. Unnoticed, she passes small leftover groups along the way: four young men sitting on the stairs and the three flowery housewives squeezed into the window seat outside the guest bathroom talking and laughing to two other women. She pushes the kitchen door open and there is another small group seated at the kitchen table, working their way through a hill of dollars and totting up sums. She comes back through the lobby.

The air feels heavy on her face as she comes out of doors. In the windless night, there is the sweet, woody aroma of the juniper tree mixed with something a little less pleasant, and she has to wonder if maybe some of those army boys got tired waiting in line for the bathroom.

A man and a woman come from the side of the house away from the party, the man elbow-steering his wife.

'What about that taxi guy?' his wife says. 'Call any old time, it says in the newspaper, and then his wife bites my head off when I do.'

'It's almost midnight.'

'Any old time is any old time. And now we're going to miss the fireworks in Provincetown.'

'We can see them better from the beach right here.'

'I don't want to see them better, I want to be, you know – in it. Right in the middle of it.'

The couple steps into the darkness of the path that leads down to the parking space and the road outside. She is thinking that when the time comes to leave she will ask Michael to guide them with the flashlight down that gnarled, narrow pathway as far as the road, when she hears singing coming from the house. She is immediately struck by the purity of it. The man and the woman feel it too; they stop and turn, the man letting go of the woman's elbow and now putting his arm round her waist.

She had not liked the opera singer the first time she met her in Mrs Grant's house in Orleans and had not warmed to her any more this evening, not even during the conversation that had taken place earlier in the kitchen when she had agreed with her several times. She had not liked her pushy manner, her way of confiding in her. Her mother would have described her as a woman whose face is her misfortune. But more than that, she found it a snide face, the sort of face that took pleasure in the pain of others, the gleam in her eye when she had told her all about Katherine Kaplan's illness. And now, here she is, singing 'O mio babbino caro' with a voice that would make you believe in God.

She feels the tears coming up from her throat. Oh, to have such an undeniable talent; a talent so strong that there would be no need to rely on the opinion or approval of others. To open your mouth and hear it pour from you and to know – how could one not know? – that you had been truly blessed.

After the aria, she exchanges a goodnight nod with the departing couple. Then she turns back to the house. As she comes up the front steps, she sees Michael, bent head the colour of corn under a fall of yellow light that is coming from a small window beyond the front door. He is alone and sitting on the floor of the porch, body parts of a kite all around him, an instruction sheet spread out under the light. She has a mind to ask him something about Katherine and the phtograph he mentioned but then she hears voices coming through the small porthole window. The voices of the flowery housewives. Twirls of cigarette smoke coming out along with their voices as if the window is a rounded mouth.

'Well, answer me this then, Beth, does she ever, I mean ever, stop talking? I wouldn't mind that so much, it's the subject…'

'You mean herself! But I pity her, Mary Ann, no, no, don't laugh, I really do.'

'Oh no, I pity him! Imagine having to put up with that, day in day out.'

'I guess she is just trying to be somebody, you know, trying to be important. And she *is* old. My grandmother, well, she can get a little crazy too, you know.'

'Oh now, everyone knows that your grandmother is a lady. But as for her – I mean, just who does she think she is, judging people and criticizing their lives. She is truly awful and so false, too, in the way she speaks. I felt like saying, Oh excuse me – are we in Paris now? Honestly! Slipping in those little French phrases any chance she gets.'

'Know what I heard? I heard she has these jealous rages. Mrs Sultz over by Beach Point, she told my mother.'

'Jealous of what – her husband? I think it's disgusting, a man of that age.

286

And something else I find, well, distasteful, I guess, is the way she talks about his work like they are her babies or something – I mean, did you hear that: "He sires them and I christen them." Sires them!'

'What a thing to say!'

'Will you two hush? Here's Mrs Kaplan. I wouldn't like her to think— Oh, hello, Mrs Kaplan, yes, we are just coming in now.'

And then their voices and their cigarette smoke are sucked back in through the window.

For a second she tries to tell herself that it is a coincidence and that they are talking about somebody else, some other person Mrs Sultz happens to know. But when she looks up and sees Michael, standing now a couple of feet away, the bones of a kite in his hand and a look of horror on his face... She turns away from him abruptly and walks back down the steps and around by the side of the house.

She stands in the garden among the empty tables and chairs and looks into the back of the house. The first chill of fall is on the air and the big glass door has been closed over. The moon, like a shy child, showing half of its face behind a door.

She can see her husband standing with his back to the piano and Frank seated behind him on the stool, arms folded, listening attentively. He is reciting something. She can see Michael has gone into the living-room and is sitting on the floor and the opera singer and her husband on the couch behind him. She can see two of the flowery housewives sitting prettily on straight-back chairs. And let it be 'La Lune Blanche', she thinks, let them hear him speak French – maybe then they will realize that French is the language of artists, that in their house it is practically a second language. She hurries back into the house.

But it turns out to be 'The Wanderer's Song' he is reciting – and in English, too, which also surprises her, as he usually recites this in German. Olivia and Annette are curled up, each to one end of a sofa, Olivia's ears up and her tail forward, smoking with all the drama that one cigarette can allow. And the whole room in thrall, hanging on his every word.

He is coming near to the last line as she comes up behind him, sits down on the seat and slips off her shoes.

'All the birds are quiet in the woods,

Soon you will rest too.'

Olivia puts her cigarette into the corner of her mouth, closes one eye and claps like crazy. Annette places her hand on her breast and sighs. He could stand there, she thinks, and recite 'Humpty Dumpty' and they would think his words were made of twenty-four-carat gold.

Mrs Kaplan turns to her, smiling. 'We said we wouldn't allow him to leave the house unless he did some little thing.'

'Well, that was it,' he says, 'and I think that's as good a way as any to say goodnight.'

He looks at his wife.

'Oh, you should have done it in German,' she says.

'But then nobody would be able to understand it,' Olivia says, 'except maybe Michael!'

Mrs Kaplan and Annette turn to look at her.

'What did I say now?' she asks with a little laugh.

Her husband takes a step towards the door. 'I believe most things probably do sound better in the language that brought them about,' he says, 'and now I really must find my hat.'

Mrs Kaplan says, 'Well, it's beautiful no matter what language, in my opinion. It's the sentiment that counts.'

'Oh, but I wish he had done "La Lune Blanche", that's his other party piece. He does a wonderful job on that, too. And always in French.'

'Well, couldn't you do it now?' Mrs Kaplan asks him.

'Oh, I think that's enough from me for one evening,' he says, looking around. 'Now where did I put my hat?'

She thinks, If they ask me I'll do it. I'll stand up right there and I'll show those three little witches what it means to speak French.

She begins running through the lines in her head. *La lune blanche, Luit dans les bois. De chaque… De chaque…? Branche* – that's it. *Part une voix. Sous… sous… la? Sous la ramée* – yes, of course.

Olivia gets up and finds his hat under a chair and brings it back to him. Then she sits on the arm of the couch. Her hair under the light rich and dark. That hair again – *Ô bien-aimée* – and damn that Madam Cheruy!

'But what does it mean, Mr Aitch?' Michael says. '*La lune*, whatever you said.'

'Oh, you know, it means different things to different people. It's just about the moon, really, how it makes us feel, what it makes us see.'

She decides to step in. 'I have a soft spot for "La Lune Blanche", you know. When we started our romance—'

'It's getting a little late,' he says.

'Let her tell,' Annette cries. 'I wanna hear it!'

'Well, we were at the same art college. And our paths had crossed, of course, but then during one summer in Gloucester – on a retreat for artists, you know – we went sketching together and he began to quote "La Lune Blanche" and he couldn't believe it when I finished it for him. His face! He just couldn't believe it. Isn't that so?'

'Yes,' he says, 'yes, that's quite true.'

Annette gives a delighted laugh. 'But of course, you knew all along,' she says, 'how clever.'

'I don't understand – knew what?'

'Well, that he read French poetry. Don't tell me – you saw the book sticking out of his pocket and made it your business to learn it off and regurgitate it at just the right moment. You sly old thing. I was never much use at these female tricks myself – no wonder I don't have a husband!'

Annette laughs and Olivia laughs and she glances at her husband, now putting his hat on his head and seemingly unaware of the needles being jabbed into his wife.

'My grandmother happened to be French,' she says coldly. 'I take an interest in the language, always have done.'

She gathers up her purse, slips back into her shoes.

'Oh, come on,' Annette says, 'I was just kidding…'

She lifts her purse from under the seat where she'd earlier left it. 'Well, thank you for everything, Mrs Kaplan,' she says.

'Why don't I walk you out?'

'There's really no need.'

'But just the same, I would like to. Michael – fetch the flashlight, please, would you?'

Mrs Kaplan and Michael lead them down the pathway. Mrs Kaplan holds the flashlight while Michael chatters on: 'And Richie, he said he wanted to help me fix the kite up but he had something really, really important to do first, but he didn't come down and then when I went upstairs to look for him he was already sleeping.'

'He's tired,' Mrs Kaplan says. 'I'm sure he'll help you tomorrow. We are all a little tired, wouldn't you say?'

'I'm not!' Michael says.

As they get to the end of the path she hears Michael behind her ask if he can come by tomorrow. She doesn't seem to be able to answer him; she doesn't seem to be able to find a word.

'Why not leave it till the following day, Michael?' Mrs Kaplan says. 'I think we all need a little rest tomorrow.'

'I don't!' Michael says and Mrs Kaplan says, 'That's enough now, Michael. Say goodnight, there's a good boy.'

Michael and Mrs Kaplan stand watch at the end of the lane until they are safely centred on the road home, their voices calling out goodnight from behind the light. They turn, wave blindly into the beam and begin walking home, the world so still and silent, even the sea barely utters a sound.

On the way home, they say little or nothing. She looks at the moon, a chipped piece of marble stuck to the sky, and wonders again why he didn't give them 'La Lune Blanche'. He could have said, as she has so often heard him say before: Well, seeing as we have a moon tonight… And then begun. It was almost as if he was afraid to do it. As if something might show through his voice.

He says, 'I hope you're not too tired. It's been a long party.'

'I'm tired all right; don't know when I've stayed that long at a party – I'm surprised at you, I must say.'

'I'm a little surprised at myself.'

She says, 'Richie and Michael appeared to be getting along just fine. I saw you come back from the beach.'

'Yes,' he said, 'they were fighting earlier, but then down on the beach…'

'What?'

'It all seemed to change.'

They come near to the turn that leads to their house.

'Did you know Katherine Kaplan is not just seriously ill,' she says, 'that she's not expected to live past winter? That opera-singer woman told me.'

'Yes, I heard something too.'

She stops and looks up at him. 'Do you pity her?'

'Well, yes, I suppose I do,' he says. 'Don't you?'

'Of course I do! Poor girl.'

They walk on and he takes hold of her elbow as the road darkens around them.

When they get home they stand at the north window and watch the last of the fireworks break like electric dahlias over the hook of Provincetown.

'Go ahead, say it – I disgraced myself again,' she says.

'Did you? I wasn't aware.'

'I wasn't aware either. Until I overheard— those women. They said…'

'What? What did they say?'

'That I talk about our paintings – your paintings – as if they were our children. That I am… jealous and self-obsessed and, and—'

She begins to feel herself get weepy. 'Oh, never mind,' she says, 'the party was not a great success for me, if you must know.'

'You shouldn't,' he said, 'you shouldn't mind what people say.'

He takes her arm and draws her outside, where they stand on the back porch and continue to watch the display.

'And I did try, you know.'

'I'm sure you did.'

'I tried to be friendly but no matter what I said… And that Annette – did you hear what she said to me? As if I couldn't possibly speak French.'

'I wasn't really listening,' he says.

A new batch shoots up, this time in long spindles of colour. There is the shrill, painful sound of something about to explode. She wonders if people who were there at the air raids listen to it and are reminded of all the horror.

She puts her arm through his. 'Do you think I am a terrible person?' she asks.

'Why do you think I married you?' he says.

'You once said it was because I was an orphan and because I spoke French. Oh, and that I had curly hair.'

'Yes, that too. Come on, time for bed.'

'I'm not going near those women again,' she says.

'You don't have to.'

'You mix with them if you want, but as for me, well, you're just going to have to count me out.'

'If that's what you want.'

'I won't even get jealous. That's how strongly I feel about it.'

'Absolutely,' he says and pats her shoulder.

THEY LIE IN BED and talk of the dead. He remembers five departed men; she remembers eight departed women. She lies facing away from him, he curved right behind her, with his arms wrapped around her, the soles of her feet on the top of his. As if we are one big crustacean, she thinks, he the outer shell while I am the body.

They remember parents and relatives, the wife of a friend, and she begins counting up all who have died since they were married. He mumbles sleepily along as she goes through the list. Her tally comes to over fifty and he perks up briefly to tell her that is impossible.

'I'm counting the animals,' she says and he laughs, then almost at once falls silent. And now he has turned around and is facing the other way.

She lays her hand on his big, broad back, notes with a little sadness that it is not as straight as it used to be, the space between the blades a little wider, the shoulder blades a little further away from his back. She remembers how strong he used to be – those evenings when he could walk ten miles after a day's work; the days when he went sailing from dawn to dusk. How he enjoyed those long days while she strained not to feel abandoned.

He would come back sun-kissed, slightly smug and utterly attractive. She used to feel like flinging herself on him. But of course she never did. Instead, she usually greeted him with a little light sarcasm and a chilly shoulder. Once, on the advice of Mrs Sultz, she decided to change tack. She baked a blueberry pie, had a roast chicken dinner waiting in the oven. She watched him come up the slope from the garage, dusk all around him apart from that one slab of clear, ghostly light that catches at evening in the hollow. She had felt so completely in love with him. So content with her lot. Her strong, handsome husband coming up the hill to her, the aroma of her roasting chicken and sweet pastry waiting to greet him.

And the way his face had lit up with pleasure when he came in the door. A little boy, she had thought, whose mama has baked him a pie, and then at the tail-end of that thought, a bitter little kink occurred – that's all they want, really, a mama; a mama they're allowed to have sex with.

He even kissed her when he came in, pulled on her ponytail. Then laying his jacket on the table, he had pinched her through her corduroy slacks and said, 'You certainly are some baby.'

And she knew she should just stay quiet. Enjoy his pleasure and even the pleasure she had been feeling herself not a few seconds beforehand – where had all that disappeared to? But she could not do it. She could not let it lie.

'This is a once-off,' she snapped. 'Don't get too used to it.'

Nor could she just leave it at that.

'I can't divide myself the way you can. Can't spend all my time hitched to the stove. I can't do that and work too, you know.'

When she turned she saw the smile had gone from his eyes. Even then, she could not seem to stop herself.

'I do my bit,' he said. 'You don't think I do my bit?'

'Huh! Men always say that just because they make a few little gestures, go to the store or chop a few sticks of firewood. Well, I can't do it. Divide myself up like you do. Go off sailing for the day, come back and eat a feast that someone else has prepared for you, then go in and do a few hours' work.'

'I wasn't going to work,' he said, 'but I will now. And I don't want any dinner.'

She writes with her finger on his back.

'What's that?' he asks sleepily.

'Nothing.'

She hears him lightly snore and begins to write again: We are bone of each other's bone. Flesh of each other's flesh.

Die Trümmerfrauen

1

HE CAN SEE THE women. They are standing in a dark outline on a hill and the hill is made of rubble and the sky all around them is a pale grey colour.

On one side there is a tall building with the front torn away. On the other side, a building with no roof on it like someone has sliced through it, the way you would slice the top off a boiled egg. He is at the bottom of the hill, looking up at the women. They are pulling bricks apart with their hands, searching. Here and there little puffs of powdery dust rise up as if they were doing magic tricks. There is a sound of birds too, a horrible, wild screeching. One of the women finds a stick of wood; another one, a rod of steel. And then a woman at the far end of the line pulls out of the rubble an old clock. She dusts it off, shakes it and puts it to her ear. '*Es funktioniert! Tik-tak tik-tak!*' He can hear the women laughing. Down at the bottom of the hill he laughs too, without really knowing why.

His mother is up there – he knows that for sure, even if he can't say which one she is. From this distance, they all look alike, standing in their crooked line on the rubble hill, one foot up, one foot down. When they started to climb the hill he had been able to pick her out, but as they got near to the top and the pale grey sky, the women seemed to knot together before spreading out in a line and now he can no longer tell them apart. They are dressed alike, in coats that belong to men, and you can't even tell by their hair because they all wear it rolled up into dirty scarves knotted at the front. He wants her to turn around, to give him a special wave so that he will know her. He begs her in his mind. Even if he knows already that not one woman will lift her head – the dark is coming and there is so much work to be done.

Which one? Which one told him to stand there, to wait and be a good boy? *Sei ein guter Junge*. Which one gave him a little kiss and made him promise not to move? But something has changed since he made his promise. There is danger now that wasn't there before. It came with a big white bird that flew down a few moments ago and landed on a pile of nearby bricks. The bird staring at him now with his cold eye. He can see the bird's throat pushing in and out against its soft, smooth skin, and he can see too that long yellow beak with the dot of blood already on the tip of it.

He knows the bird is waiting for the dark and then it will attack. It will get to him before his mother has a chance to come skidding down the hill. He cannot just stand here and wait for the bird to fly at him, knock him down with its claws then break into his chest to get at his heart, peck, peck, peck. He has seen the big white birds pecking at a dead dog and so he knows how they work.

He wants to call out *Mutti! Mutti!* But if he does that then maybe the bird will decide to take its last chance and pounce. So he will not cry out but he will not run either. He will try to trick the bird instead. He takes a step sideways. The bird doesn't move. He takes another step and then another again. The bird makes a small, tight movement with its head but at least it does not try to follow him.

He can't remember if he already knew the gap was there before he started taking his side steps. Or if it just suddenly appeared. It is not like the other gaps, those narrow alleyways with walls made out of sandbags that are wide enough for people to walk up and down. The gap he chooses is so small you have to squeeze in sideways with first your elbow and then your knee and your shoulder: push, pushhhh, pushhhh until it lets you in.

And the feeling of being safe when at last he is in! The thought coming into his head: 'Here I will stay until the woman who is my mother comes to fetch me, here I will stay squeezed between the sandbags with their strange damp smell and their rough skin against my face. I will stay, where the bird can't get at me.'

He knows, even before he opens his eyes, that he is no longer a three-year-old boy in Berlin. He is a big boy now, an American boy. Mrs Kaplan said so yesterday. She said it in front of all those people and so that's how he knows it for sure. When she said it, he got so scared for a second. To see all those faces turning and looking at him. But then he thought he would burst with joy. A big American boy. An American boy in South Truro, on Cape Cod, in the county of Barnstable, in the state of Massachusetts, on the continent of God Bless America. And now here he is waking up in his usual bed and, even if he feels colder than he usually does, he is safe, safe, safe. So why does his heart hurt like there is somebody pinching it hard and fast?

He hears a seabird screaming outside the window and fingernails scratching the pane and an impatient drumming of fingers and a slow, steady *clack, clack* like the warning strike of a billy club against a table. And worse than all that – worse by a mile – he hears the voice of an angry woman.

He opens his eyes. Outside the rain is bashing down. A tree branch brushes off the glass of the window. The half-opened shutter hits against itself in the breeze. He pulls himself up on his elbows and listens. The woman's voice is muffled and yelling like crazy but it is nowhere nearby: it is downstairs in another room.

Across the way, Richie's bed is neatly made up, his pyjamas folded on top of his pillow. The light in the room is grey, a little like the light before dawn. But dawn is well past – he knows this because he was still awake at dawn. By now it is probably way past breakfast time, it could even be past lunch for all he knows.

He looks down and sees that he is fully dressed and lying on top of the coverlet. And he remembers, now, that he is dressed because he never got undressed in the first place and the bed is still made up because he never got inside it. He had been way too excited to sleep, had sat on the floor putting his kite together while Richie snored and groaned in his sleep. He had listened to the party downstairs wear itself out while he thought of all the things he could do when he went from being a big American boy to a big American man. People singing and shouting and then the sounds getting thinner, till there were just a few voices left and then, suddenly, none. And it had seemed then as if he was the only one awake in the whole of America.

When the kite was finished he put it on the bed and looked at it. He thought it was the most beautiful thing he had ever seen. He sat on the side of the bed and took it gently into his arms and longed for breakfast time to come round so that he could show it to Mrs Kaplan. He felt so happy just thinking about that, what she would say and how proud he would feel, that for a while he felt as if he could fly higher than any kite, all by himself – and that feeling is the last thing he remembers before falling asleep.

Downstairs a door slams. And now yelling again, this time clear and loud enough for him to recognize the voice of Richie's mom and Richie on the other end of it.

'But mom, I swear—'

'I'm warning you, Richie! I want the truth and I want it right now. Do you understand me?'

And he feels sorry for Richie, for whatever trouble he's gotten himself in – but at the same time, he feels pretty glad that he's not the one down there getting it.

He slips off the bed and goes to the window. Then he pulls back the shutter and looks out at the rainy day. Two men in sou'westers are carrying a table across the puddled lawn. Another two, in black cop-style capes, are hauling stacks of garden chairs round to the front of the house. He knows Frank is taking the piano back to Boston today and that the rest of the hired furniture is probably getting loaded up right now onto trucks and driven away. He would like to go down and watch all that; he would like to say goodbye to Frank too. And he would really like something to eat. But he doesn't want to have to pass Richie and his mom on the way or find himself stuck behind her yelling voice, trying to weasel his way round it.

He turns back into the room and sees his kite, blue and red with its tail curled around it, lying on its side on the floor. He picks it up and holds it out. He is admiring his craftsmanship, even down to the perfect alignment of the little bows along the tail, when the voice of Richie's mom suddenly appears again, this time coming up the stairs and now blasting into the hallway, and there's Richie's little squeal right behind it, 'Please, Mom, oh please don't, Mom, Mom, *pleeeease*.'

'I'm getting to the bottom of this, Richie Kaplan. Whatever is going on, I'm going to find out and you better hope, you just better hope—'

The door snaps open. And now she's right inside the room, dragging Richie by the sleeve of his sweater. She pulls him towards her, then pushes him back. Richie staggers then almost, but not quite, falls.

He tries not to look at Richie, nor at his mom still in her bathrobe with her hair all undone and her lips pale and her eyes gone crazy. He looks down at his kite, touches the bows, runs his finger along all the edges and wonders what – just *what* in hell Richie could have done?

Richie's mom picks up Richie's folded pyjamas. She shakes them out and throws them down on the floor. Then she begins tearing Richie's neatly made bed apart. She takes the pillowslip off and puts her arm inside it; she looks under the bed and behind the headboard. Then she gets started on his bedside locker. Richie's comic books come flying out of the locker, then she takes out his box, opens it up, turns it upside down, dropping baseball cards and candy wrappers and candy bars down on the bed. She picks up a candy bar and throws it at him. The candy bar bounces off Richie's raised shoulder. Then she steps over to him and slaps him right across the face. She turns away, sits down on the side of the bed and holds her head in her hands.

He wonders if Richie is crying and decides to take a quick peek. Richie looks scared: his face is white apart from the red flash from the slap and his eyes are nearly popping out of their sockets. But there are no tears in them. He tries to get Richie to look at him then, see if maybe he will give him a clue about what's going on. But Richie's wide eyes won't look near him; they just keep staring at his mom with her head in her hands.

After a minute, she takes one hand away, reaches into the pocket of her bathrobe and pulls out a pod of pills. Her fingers are shaking so much, the pod won't stay still in her hands. She stretches her arm out sideways to Richie and he takes the pod, opens it and gives it back to her. She drops two pills on the palm of her hand, then pops them into her mouth. Her throat gives one long, dry swallow. Then she gets up again.

'I'm going to search your bed now, Michael,' she says and he nods and takes a few steps back.

She drags the coverlet from his bed and shakes it out. She pulls the sheets off and shakes them out, then she gets down on her knees and looks under the bed. She gets back up and pokes around in his pillow, then she looks at the shelf over his bed and one by one begins picking up the books Mrs Kaplan loaned him. As she flicks through them, a letter falls out; a letter he had left there a couple of weeks ago and had forgotten all about. It was written to one of his non-existent friends. She opens the envelope and now he starts to sweat – what if she reads it? What if it's one of the letters where he wrote mean things about her and Richie? Or worse, what if it's one of the letters with all that lovey-dovey stuff in it about Katherine?

He can't believe it when he hears Richie say, 'It's a little rude to read other people's private letters – don't you think?'

She opens her mouth and widens her eyes as if she can't believe it either. Then she comes at Richie, pointing her finger. Richie gives a little jump.

'How dare you question me?' she says. 'How dare you? Not another word – do you understand? Not. Another. Word.'

She shakes the page of the letter out, looks inside the empty envelope then, without reading it, drops both down on the bed.

She starts on the closets next. First she goes to Richie's closet, pulling out all his clothes. His pants, long and short, his jeans and his T-shirts, his sweaters and his shirts, his shoes and his sneakers, his – who knows how many – pairs of pyjamas; his supply of socks balled into pairs and all of his folded snowy white underwear. And now there is a big pile of Richie's clothes on the floor. She steps over them and crosses the room to his closet.

His face burns and his legs begin to shake for the few seconds it takes her to get through his things. His two pairs of short pants, his couple of T-shirts, his one sweater, his one pair of sandals, his one spare pyjamas with the pocket torn off, his two pairs of socks and three single ones and his two stone-grey pairs of underwear. She opens a bag with his dirty laundry inside and one by one takes out a dirty sweater, two pairs of stained underwear and two more non-matching dirt-stiff socks. When she's done with all that, she steps over his little pile and begins walking to the door.

'You two stay right here,' she says. 'You don't leave this room till I come get you. Do you understand? And tidy up that mess.'

She stops at the door and glares back at Richie. 'On second thoughts,' she says, 'you come with me. Michael, don't you even dream about leaving this room.'

'Is it all right if I go to the bathroom?' he hears himself say.

She turns, then she comes back across the room and stops right in front of him. She stands there tightening her neck until it begins to look like the trunk of a tree. She pushes her lips together, then she sort of pops them open: 'Why, of course it's all right for you to go the bathroom, Michael, and I'll be sure to send something up for you to eat – after all, we don't have concentration camps here in America, do we? No, we certainly do not.'

She twirls away from him, grabs Richie, pushes him out and slams the door behind her.

When he gets back from the bathroom, he puts his clothes in the closet and carefully makes his bed again. He puts Richie's clothes back in the other closet and makes Richie's bed too. He puts all of Richie's things back in his box and puts the box back in the bedside locker, even the empty candy wrappers. Then he sits on the floor and begins tearing up the letter. He doesn't bother to read it himself, he just tears and tears it smaller and smaller, till all the sentences are words and all the words are just tiny specks of alphabet letters. Then he begins tearing the envelope until all that remains is a little hill of confetti on the floor. When he's done with that, he picks his kite up, wraps a towel around it and slips it into the space between his closet and the wall. He sits down on the side of the bed and every time he feels like crying, he pinches a piece of flesh on the top of his arm and gives it a tight, hard twist.

It seems like such a long time before Rosetta comes in with a glass of milk and a Swiss cheese sandwich and an apple and a small stack of cookies on a tray. She sits beside him on the bed and tells him to eat. He takes a small bite of the sandwich but can't seem to chew the bread. He pushes it into the pouch of his cheek and says, 'Rosetta, do you think Katherine might come see me?'

'Oh, Michael, Katherine is no help for you now.'

'Why not, what do you mean?'

'Oh, Michael,' she says, 'what you do it for?'

'Me? Do what? I swear it wasn't me that did whatever it was. I don't even know what she was looking for – I mean, I thought it was Richie was in trouble, that's what I thought.'

'Oh, Michael, you esteal on these people who was so good to you.'

'What are you talking about, Rosetta? What's that mean – esteal?'

'Oh, Michael.'

'Please stop saying "Oh, Michael, oh, Michael" and just tell me what did I do? Rosetta – what, *what*?'

Rosetta gets up and goes to the door. 'Esteal,' she says, 'you *esteal* like a thief.'

He walks up and down and he sits on the bed and he gets up again and sits on the chair and takes a gulp from the milk and every now and then he starts to cry. He bangs his head off the wall and goes to the window and eats a cookie and cries again. He pinches both arms and then he pinches the tops of his legs. He goes back to the window and looks out. It has stopped raining by now. The sun is trying to get out from the clouds. He wonders if he might get out too. He could easily do it: get out the window, hop over the verandah, down the wooden pole to the porch downstairs, jump off it onto the grass, sneak round by the edge of the trees, slip through the bushes then up the hill, over the field of long grass, then down the steps to the beach and on to his hidey-hole. He could throw all the things he has hidden in there in the sea: Richie's scouting knife and the US army medals and the cut-outs from magazines and the tin box with all the bits of cookies inside and the old watch and all the pencils and the little rubber ball. Then he could go back to the hidey-hole and kick over his traces, or even go to Mrs Aitch's house before anyone notices that he's missing. Except he is too ashamed now to face Mrs Aitch. He opens the window and steps out. Downstairs, the voices of men. He can hear Frank yelling, 'No, no, no, Jesus Christ. NO! You gotta move it from the back end. The bass end needs to be down, down. Down on the skid board. On it. On it, I said! You got it? You sure now? Okay, now remember what I told you – think of it as a racehorse, one wrong move and everything falls apart, easy, easy does it. Easy, that's it, okay, now we're talking.'

There are footsteps all over the wooden floor, voices all over the downstairs of the house. He would never get away without being seen. He will just have to wait for the dark to come in.

He is watching the grey skin peel off the sky and the sunlight starting to gush through and, now the small steamy patches that are beginning to creep along the grass, when he hears a new batch of sounds below. Footsteps. But different this time, lighter and not so slow and more than one set of them. The footsteps come across the back porch. There are no voices, just the sound of all these footsteps and then that stops. And now he sees, silently moving across the grass, Katherine wearing a raincoat with the belt drawn tight and Mrs Kaplan beside her with an umbrella in her hand and there's Richie's mom with a raincoat over her shoulders and Annette right behind them wearing no coat at all. And it comes to him then that Annette is the only one he didn't steal from and he realises that was because he has always known she would be the only one who would notice right away if the smallest thing went missing. Richie is there in the middle of the women, his mom dragging and pushing him along. They go through the bushes and, for a moment, they disappear, and now he sees them again, climbing one behind the other up the hill towards the long grass and the steps that lead to the beach.

Richie knows, he thinks, he knows about the hidey-hole. How could he know? And then after a moment – of course he knows; how could he not?

2

THE MORNING AFTER THE party they wake late and lie on in bed listening to the rain. She says, 'I hope it pours down all day. I hope it never stops raining. I hope it falls so densely that there's a wall of rain out there.'

'A wall of rain?' he says.

'Yes, that's what I really wish for – a wall of rain between us and the rest of the world so that, even for one day, we can stay hidden behind it – we don't need to go out. Do we?'

'Not if there's enough to eat.'

'I think so. I mean, we can manage. We got plenty of cans, there's bread, there's milk. And peaches.'

'All right then, we don't need to go out.'

She flicks her toes against the top sheet and, lifting her hands over her head, makes a few small cheerleading waves with her fists.

He smiles with his eyes and says, 'Breakfast?'

'Tea and buttered toast?'

'If you want.'

'In bed?'

'You bet,' he says and she laughs again, this time with a little whoop added on.

As soon as he gets out of bed an anxious sort of sadness begins to come over her. 'Oh, but that means you have to get up and leave me and you probably won't ever come back,' she says, putting on her little girl pout as if, really, she is only joking.

He doesn't answer and she notices that look of pain on his face.

'What's the matter – does it hurt?'

'A little.'

'And I thought you were doing so well. What brought it on?'

'Over-indulgence.'

'Did you?'

'A little wine, another piece of pie, that Mexican spice that was all over supper. A little wine again. And I probably spent too long on my feet.'

'Where does it hurt, exactly?'

'Behind here somewhere.'

'If it was a map of Manhattan? If your chest was Central Park?'

'If my chest was— well, it would be the Lower East Side. No, maybe a little
more over this way – Chinatown.'

'China—? Oh now, that is too bad. Would you like me to rub it for you?'

'It's better if I move around a little, eat something, maybe drink a cool glass
of water.'

'But will you come back?'

'There are some sketches I'd like to look over,' he says and then turning
around he takes hold of her hand and she feels…

Oh well, it doesn't matter what I feel, she thinks, that side of our life is over
now. The most I can hope for are a few small moments of companionship; the
occasional show of affection; that he might look at me sometimes when I speak
to him; that he might lie down beside me on mornings such as this and listen to
the rain.

She smiles at him and says, 'You are a dear. You are my dear.'

He pats her hand and then, turning his back to her, begins putting on
his pants.

Along with her tea and toast, he brings her a three-day-old copy of the *New
York Times*. She glances over the front page. Oh, but she doesn't want to read
about that now: army recruitment and communist outrage and death in Korea
– all that and the H-bomb too! She begins to skim through the smaller items
on the inner pages but that just makes her feel lonely for New York. Faces and
names she has never met and yet seem so personal to her; fashions and fads

that she's missing out on; and the small everyday city dramas that are still going on behind her back while she is stuck out here, miles from civilization, no one to talk to, no one to listen to either.

She slides the tray away from her, edges over to his side of the bed, turns on her belly and lets her hands fall down on the floor. The blood pushing into her head, she pats her hand blindly around until it comes across a book. She lifts it, reverses herself back to the distaff side and now she's upright again. Sliding the tray back to her, she pours another cup of tea, takes his pillow, props it into her back and opens the poems of Robert Frost with a small gasp of surprise as she lands on the line 'Something there is that doesn't love a wall.'

Later, on her way into the kitchen, she sees him, back bent over his worktable, leafing through sketches. He doesn't appear to notice her pass behind him, and when she puts the tray down on the worktop, he doesn't seem to hear the small clatter it makes. He is completely engrossed. She wants to tell him she's been reading *North of Boston*, to mention the coincidence of 'Mending Wall' and her earlier wish for a wall of rain to keep her at home, to reminisce with him about the other poems there – to say, 'Do you remember the first winter we were married, reading "The Oven Bird" on the train on our way to visit your mother?'

But she sees that he is deeply lost in thought and will not be easily found. He is looking at the ledger – why now, she wonders, is he looking at the ledger?

She stays in the doorway of the kitchen watching him. He opens a page of the ledger and holds it out at arm's length. Then he pulls a sketch from a spread on the table and places it on the lip of his easel. She sees now that it is a sketch of a painting he did a few years back – was it the summer of '43? The one with the buxom girl leaning against the porch; young man beside her, irrelevant. A night-time scene – although in those clothes, the girl doesn't seem to know it. Her legs, strong and straight, stretched out at an angle; stomach drum-taut beneath her bikini top.

And now he goes back to the ledger and flicks through it again. He stops, takes another sketch from the table and lays it on the easel. That one from three years ago. A New York painting. What is *she* doing here – surely he didn't take her with him all the way from New York? Another buxom one anyhow, flimsy dress curling round her big legs. She turned out to be a redhead under that hat. As did the girl in the next one he pulls – also from New York. But what could he be thinking or planning – and why bring all those old sketches from New York in the first place? She takes a few light steps forward and then stops as it occurs to her: the paper seems a little fresh, the sketches themselves a little too vivid. Could it be that he didn't bring any sketches from New York. But of course not – as if she wouldn't have noticed! These are new sketches.

So that's what he has been doing in here for the past few days, making new versions of old pictures. But why? Why would he want to keep them alive when he is usually happy to disown them as soon as the painting is done?

The women, strong legged and tall of stature. They could be sisters. They could be the same woman over and over, like an actress wearing different costumes and different coloured hair. They could be, of course, who else but Madame Cheruy. They are all reincarnations of his old French flame.

They begin to step in and out of her head: the woman sitting at the restaurant counter takes off her clothes and climbs up on a stage and now she is a burlesque dancer. The dancer has her hair darkened and bends over a bed in a foreign room. And now, in the same foreign room, she dons a short chemise and sits down on the floor, showing a frank lower half of herself. And suddenly there she is again, wearing a long red dress, standing by a piano, bringing her arms up and elegantly out before she begins to sing – 'You Do Something to Me'.

She can feel herself begin to rile up. Her heart jerks; a heat rockets up from her chest to her neck to her face. Her whole body swells, ready to explode. She almost lets fly at him. But then, at the very last second, she turns away and silently slips back into the bedroom.

She closes the door and, standing with her back to it, remembers the conversation she overheard last night; the cruel things that were said about her. (How does he put up with her? Does she *ever* stop talking about herself? I hear she has these terrible jealous rages.) She remembers other comments too that she has chosen to ignore over the years, from friends and enemies alike. Her possessive personality, her need to control her poor husband's life.

She presses her hands to her chest and draws in deep breaths. She will not prove all those women right. Those hateful women. She will not let anger be her master. Nor jealousy crack a whip. This time, she will stay in control. She will not allow herself to start a fight. It's not as if she hasn't always known that Madame Cheruy was his first love and for a man, they say, the first love cuts deepest. Nor is it the first time she has noticed the similarity between Madame Cheruy and the women in some of his paintings. To have another fight now would be pointless and utterly foolhardy. For how could it end, but with her usual tears and pain, the sound of a slamming door as he walks out, the sight of the Buick pulling away and, after that, the silent house.

She feels a sharp, hard pain in her hands. Her chest aches from a tightness inside it. She opens her fists and releases her fingers, feels her hands tingle with relief. Then she draws a few breaths and, after that, she gets up.

She goes to the drawer in her bureau, feels her way under her clothes. She takes out a book. Now she dries her eyes in the mirror, smooths back her hair and straightens her skirt. She puts her bare feet into shoes and comes into the studio.

'How are you feeling now?' she asks him.

'Hmmm?' he says.

'Any better – the pain, I mean?'

He glances back. 'Oh yes, much.'

She waits a moment. 'Oh, I forgot to say, I found this in the basement lying on the floor. It looks a little worse for wear, I'm afraid.'

He turns round to see.

'It's the Verlaine,' she says. 'The conversation about "La Lune Blanche" last night reminded me.' She holds the book up until she's sure he's seen it. Then she puts it down on the edge of the table.

'Oh, look,' she says turning to the window. 'It's stopped raining.'

~

HE WAITS TILL THE day after Labor Day before he ventures out again. Apart from the occasional ten-minute sit-down outside on his bench and a stroll in the evenings, he had been happy to stay home. There was the rain, and the shy light that came afterwards through the studio windows. In the background, the soothing sound of his wife sweeping the floors, the porch and the basement steps. And even on the second day, there had been a certain contentment in the house as he made a few drawings and she went about her general business, listening to and frequently contradicting a voice on the radio. He had been reluctant to leave the unexpected peace of all that.

On the first evening stroll he stayed close to home, circling a few adjacent pathways and wandering up a cart-road or two. He pushed through a meadow, stood on a hill and looked over the familiar terrain of grassland and scrub pine. There was a half-built house sitting on a saddle between two hills and he could hear the patter of the square-dance caller coming up from town on the warm evening breeze. At fall of dusk, he began to make his way back, careful to avoid the blacktop roads or any road wide enough for an automobile to pass through. He inhaled deeply of the ocean breeze and cautiously of the marsh pond with its latrine-scented air. And always he kept his back turned to the direction of the Kaplan house and his mind firmly closed against Katherine.

When he got back they ate supper and sat for a while. There was none of the usual post-party post-mortem, which had surprised him a little. Instead she handed him a copy of *North of Boston* and asked him to read to her. After that she suggested they speak French for half an hour, just to keep their hand in.

'French? You mean now?'

'Oh, *je t'en prie*,' she said with a gentle clasp of the hands.

The second evening he had gone a little further. He walked as the crow flies, cross country. That is, if it was a very slow crow. For a short time, he lost his sense of direction and it pleased him to know that after all these years he could still get lost out here. He ended back at Ryder Beach anyhow, standing on an overlook watching a brassy sunset and a row of gilded yachts strutting homeward through it. The sight revitalised him, although he didn't quite strut home himself and had to stop on the Quanset Road to rest awhile on the stump of an old stone wall.

From his stump he could see yet another house under construction – like so many built since the end of the war, trying to pass itself off as a traditional

Cape Codder. Only bigger and with more windows and probably a porch or two added on for good measure, and of course facing the wrong way. The house was half-done in white shingles; the shutters, already in place, were black. He thought the house seemed trapped somehow – and not just because it was half-caged in scaffolding. It looked all wrong, like a ship in dry dock. A similar sort of house began to build itself in his head; same clapboard shingles, same shutters but with a higher elevation and a window – a large bay window – jutting out from the front like a prow. The house rose and faded away before he was up and walking again. On the last evening he passed the walking girl out on one of her night-time treks. He hadn't seen her in a couple of weeks and was beginning to be a little concerned for her. He was glad to see her now and raised his hat to say goodnight as they passed each other along the cart-road. The girl looked straight ahead and kept walking as if she couldn't see him.

By the time he got back it was almost dark and she was waiting with a supper contrived solely from cans. And again, just like the first night, when he got home he stayed home and didn't think about Katherine; didn't think about her at all. Not even when he stepped outside for a few moments and the dark pressed down on him and the sea mournfully heaved.

All this living out of cans is beginning to have an effect on his gut; he feels a gnawing, creeping sensation as if there's an iron caterpillar in there, eating its way through his lower intestine. He goes into the kitchen, opens the pantry door, finds to his dismay quite a stack of cans remaining and decides to call time on their self-imposed siege.

He finds her sitting on the stoop in the afternoon sun, sorting through a box she has hauled up from the basement.

'Do you remember this?' she says, holding out a small rucksack. 'I packed it during the war in case we were raided. How you teased me! And look what I found inside. A can of condensed milk, soap, toothpaste, a cheque-book – as if the Germans wouldn't insist on cash!' She laughs.

He waits for her to finish examining her survival pack and then tells her they have run out of bicarbonate of soda. Bread too, milk, butter, just about anything that doesn't fit in a can.

'Would you like to go out for a drive? We could pick up whatever groceries we need on the way back?'

She shakes her head no.

He says, 'How about Orleans or Hyannis, maybe? That Portuguese woman who sells vegetables from her garden – remember her? You thought the potatoes were particularly good?'

Again the dismissive shake of the head.

'I have to pick up some poppy seed oil in Provincetown anyhow. We could have dinner there, if you'd like that?'

He runs through another few suggestions. As he does this the house with the black shutters rises up in his head again. It has taken the shape of a New York house with grey stone steps at one side; the big bay window has shifted a little.

'We could catch the afternoon show if we hurry,' he says, 'maybe have dinner later? Shop for groceries in between?'

'Oh no, I don't feel like the movies today. No, no.'

He feels he knows that window from somewhere – in fact, now that he thinks of it, the window has been lurking in his head for some time, just waiting for a house to latch itself onto. The day they took the boys to Provincetown – had he not gone looking for it then?

'We could stop by the Kaplans' if you want, bring the boys along?'

'I don't. No, really. I *don't*.'

'Well, how about I pick them up, I'll go grocery shopping and bring them back to see you?'

'No, no, no. I'm much too busy for company today.'

'Busy – how?'

'Well, I want to finish sorting that basement out and I'm going to complete that damned rug just to free myself up, maybe then I can start painting again – you may not have noticed but I've hardly picked up a brush this summer. And you – by the way. You owe me an hour. You better not even think about reneging. Remember? You promised to pose for me?'

'Well, yes, and I will, but this afternoon I thought we might—'

'Oh, but who would want to go driving around today? The day after Labor

313

Day Weekend – with all that traffic? Only someone crazy would even consider doing such a thing.'

He says, 'Well, all right, but you can't stay hidden here forever, you know.'

'Well, maybe not. But I can try.'

'Oh, come on now – it wasn't that bad.'

'I don't—!' she yells, and seems to startle herself more than she startles him.

She swallows hard and then starts over. 'I don't want to see any of those women. I don't want to see, not one of them.'

'Not even—?'

'No. Not even her.'

'I'll go get the bicarbonate and pick up some groceries.'

He is halfway down the steps to the garage when he hears her call out behind him. He turns and looks back up at her.

'The mail?' she shouts. 'The. Mail! Don't forget to collect it!'

He nods, waves, then turns back around to the steps, and he's glad that she can't see his face.

How could he have forgotten it – the expected letter from New York? As if it was never going to raise its ugly head again. He thinks of it, balled up and rotting somewhere on the side of a hill off Town Road and wonders if the rain had managed to turn it to pulp. And then he wonders what he's supposed to do about it now because one thing is certain: today is definitely not the day to tell her. Even if he had sworn to himself that, after the party, he would break it to her. She has been so quiet since then – a little too quiet, maybe, which is always a dangerous sign.

He backs out of the garage. When he glances up over the steering wheel, there she is, still standing at the top of the steps. He sounds the horn, she waves and he feels a sharp twinge in his belly.

The whine of heavy traffic comes up from the highway, and each time the road rises, he catches another glimpse of a long, sluggish line headed south towards the turnpikes. A few luggage-laden automobiles wobble ahead of him along Castle Road, leaving dust clouds and gas shimmers behind. But just before

314

town centre the traffic bottleneck sucks them in and he tags on behind and resigns himself to a long, slow progress of a few inches at a time. The opposite side of the road coming into town from the south is clear, apart from a couple of pick-up trucks and one or two local automobiles. He can see parking spaces outside the post office, although the gas station is crammed and he can barely make out the hats of the old boys' club sitting in their usual spot outside.

A few people are standing at the place where the bus stops, waiting on the Boston connection to come in from Hyannis. Otherwise, the only humans he can see are encased in automobiles that are trying to get out of town. He waits till he gains a couple more feet then breaks out of the line and points the nose of the Buick towards the grocery store.

He is about to turn in to a space when he sees the Kaplans' sedan parked a few spaces up. He scans the mirrors, above and each side of him, but it's not till he's out of the automobile that he sees Katherine, standing a few feet apart from the rest of the group at the bus stop. He is considering getting back in and driving off or maybe slipping through the door of the post office. But in any event, she has already seen him and is waving at him in an urgent kind of way and now walking in his direction. He returns her wave and waits for a moment before moving to meet her halfway.

She is wearing her hair tied back from her face and her face is clean of make-up. Her shoes are flat and she is dressed in slacks and a safari-style shirt.

She looks like a kid, he thinks, and then a few seconds later he changes his mind and thinks she looks like a sick woman heading for middle age.

She puts her hand on his arm before she even begins to speak. She leaves it there while she chews her lip and takes a few furtive glances around. Her fingernails are chipped orange, he notices, the fingers attached to them bone thin.

'Michael,' she says, 'is in the most *dreadful* trouble.'

She lowers her voice even though there is nobody around to hear what she's saying. 'I'm here to meet the Novaks. He's being sent home, you know. Olivia – she is insisting. Dreadful – I can't begin to tell you.'

Now she bends forward a little and begins to idly rub her side with her spare hand; the other hand remains on his arm.

'You see, he's been stealing,' she says. 'I mean – *stealing*.'

315

She lifts her hand from his arm, takes a packet of cigarettes out of her breast pocket, then brings a cigarette to her mouth, although she doesn't quite let it in. Her hand edges back and forward as if the cigarette weighs a ton. She pats all her pockets and finally indicates her need for a light with a lift of one eyebrow.

He gives an apologetic shrug.

'Do you have a lighter in the automobile?' she asks, already moving towards the Buick. 'The lighter from mine has disappeared.'

They sit inside while she lights the cigarette and begins to smoke it. She has one knee raised sideways and she is turned towards him. She keeps touching his arm and his shoulder and he thinks, Is she trying to kill me?

But she is telling him about Michael.

'I mean, I sort of knew he was taking stuff, you know, small things – silly things, like pretzels or pie. And there was a photograph taken from my picture album which I thought was sort of sweet. I figured, what harm – a poor boy like that and after what he must have been through. I mean, you don't have to be Freud to figure it out – do you?'

She takes a couple more blasts from the cigarette, and he watches the smoke slither over the top of the window where his wife usually sits.

'He has this secret place, you see – down your end of the beach. I've seen him scuttle out of it a couple of times. We went there yesterday and found his loot – you wouldn't believe. Oh boy, is Olivia livid.'

She stops suddenly, swings around and says, 'God damn it. There's the bus already.'

She stubs the cigarette out in the ashtray and turns to get out.

'I should tell you before I go that he's taken money. Quite a bit of it too.'

She shakes her head slowly and rolls her eyes. 'The money from the Orphan Fund. Maybe fifty dollars or so. He won't hand it over, either. We searched everywhere, including his secret nook. Olivia tore that apart.'

'I don't understand...' he begins.

'The book. People donate and write their name and details in the book so we can tell them later how much was raised. Anyhow, two envelopes were not accounted for and Mother telephoned the donors to check. Oh God, I better go, I have to deal with the Novaks now on top of everything else.'

She pushes the door open and over her shoulder says, 'If you or your wife would like to see him before he goes back to New York, I imagine they'll be staying tonight but leaving first thing. I mean, they'll hardly expect her to travel back tonight, not in her condition. Although Olivia is so livid, I wouldn't be surprised.'

She gets out, and he gets out. They walk side by side for a few steps then she turns left for the bus stop and he turns right for the grocery store.

He stands waiting to pay at the cash desk. The woman packing his groceries lifts her tired face and asks, 'Wife not with you today?'

He finds he has to resist the temptation to explain who Katherine is and why she was sitting in his automobile – even though the woman probably hasn't even noticed.

'I'll be glad to see the back of 'em. The visitors, I mean,' she says then with a sly little grin.

'I'm sure you could do with a rest,' he says.

'You can sing that. Every year seems they get more demanding.'

The till pings and he reaches for his pocketbook.

'You know what one of them asked yesterday? I mean, yesterday of all days?'

He hands over his money and waits to be told.

'She asked if the apple pie was home-made. Huh! Can you imagine?'

'Oh, I see,' he says.

'As if there's somethin' wrong with boughten cake,' she says, placing his change into his hand and closing his fingers over it.

Outside the grocery store he pretends to be busy settling the two brown bags in his arms while he watches Katherine and the Novaks cross over to the space where the Pontiac is waiting. The man short and swarthy, a little bandy at the knees; the woman heavily pregnant with her back arched and her feet pigeon-toed. And Katherine behind them, slower than she usually is, heavier in her step and just slightly stooped, walking as if she has a stitch in her side.

He puts the groceries in the trunk and gets into the driver's seat, is about

317

to back out and drive off when he remembers the cigarette in the ashtray. He releases it. Then he notices that she's left her packet of Chesterfields on the dashboard. He holds them in his hand for a moment; almost full. Then he gets out, walks to the trash can and drops the dead cigarette and the pack in after it. The last thing he needs now is to have a ready excuse to go looking for Katherine.

When he gets back to the house, his wife comes out of the bedroom to meet him, her feet bare and her face a little stiff as if she has banged her elbow or in some small way injured herself. She seems irked, angry even, and for a moment he thinks she may already have heard the news about Michael.

'Have you heard?' he asks.

'Heard what?'

'About Michael?'

'What about him?'

'Michael is in the most *dreadful* trouble,' he says just as Katherine had said.

'What sort of trouble?'

'I just ran into Katherine Kaplan – she was waiting to pick his parents up from the bus. He's been stealing – are you all right, you look a little—?'

'Stealing? What does that mean, stealing?'

'Money, it seems. Other things too – he's managed to accumulate quite a pile, it seems. He has a hiding place, just beneath our part of the beach.'

'You knew about it?'

'I saw him there once but didn't think there was any harm in it.'

'How much money?'

'Fifty dollars or thereabouts.'

'Fifty dollars!' she says. 'But why would Michael do such a stupid thing? And where is he supposed to have taken it from?'

'Orphan Fund money. There's this book, it seems, and when you put money in the envelope, you write your name and the amount in it. At the end of the day, it didn't add up, I guess, and so… Katherine says Olivia is livid. Wants to send him home.'

'He didn't take it.'

'Well, I'd like to think so too,' he says.

'No, I mean he didn't take it. I *know* he didn't take it. Olivia the Livid will just have to look elsewhere.'

She sits down and for a few seconds says nothing. Then she gets back up again.

'Richie took it,' she says.

'Richie?'

'Yes, Richie – he must have taken it.'

'Oh now…' he says.

'Don't you oh-now me. I saw him! With these two eyes, I saw him.'

'You better be pretty sure about this.'

'The envelopes, they were army Victory envelopes – right? The ones they used during the war?'

'I don't know.'

'Well, I do know. And I saw Richie with a couple of them hidden away in a room at the top of the house. I thought he was reading old letters from his father but, now that I think of it, there were dollars on the floor.'

'What time was this?'

'Just before the speech, I went to look for him. I knew there was something shifty about him, I *knew* it.'

'We better go up there and tell them,' he says.

'But I don't want to go!'

He goes into the kitchen and begins putting the groceries away.

'You have to, for Michael's sake.'

'You can go. Tell them I'm sick.'

'It has to come from you,' he says.

'I'll write a note to Mrs Kaplan.'

He comes to the door of the kitchen and looks out at her. 'It needs to come from you – you know that.'

'I don't want to see those women. I don't want to see them. And as for *you*!'

'Me?'

'The very thought of having to sit next to you on the way. Oh, this is all I need today, this is all in hell that I need!' she yells and then goes into the bedroom and slams the door behind her.

He can hear the sounds of her getting ready coming from the bedroom: the clip of the closet door and the swishing of clothes hangers along the rail.

He calls out to her: 'I'm going to have to eat something before we go. Would you like something? I'm going to have to go for oatmeal, see if I can settle this pain down – but I can fix you something else, if you want.'

There is no response for a moment and then the bedroom door opens and the sound of her bare feet slapping off the floor and now here she is, standing in the doorway of the kitchen, half-naked, glaring at him, her small face vicious and flushed.

She looks so deranged that he almost laughs.

'I want nothing from you,' she snarls, 'nothing!' And then she is gone as quickly as she arrived.

He fixes his oatmeal, eats it and goes into the studio where he sits on his rush chair and waits.

On the way down to the garage, she snaps at him again when he takes her elbow as they turn for the steps.

'Get off me!' she shouts. 'You put your hand anywhere in my direction and, I swear, I'll slice it off first chance I get.'

'I don't know why you're yelling at me – after all, I'm only asking that you help the boy out.'

'You think that's what's bothering me? You think *that*?'

'Well, what *is* bothering you then?' he asks but she is already bustling away from him.

3

AT THE TOP OF the front porch steps, the woman pauses and the man holding her elbow waits. She gives his arm a tight squeeze, letting him know this is the last place she wants to be; he gives her elbow a light squeeze letting her know that everything is going to be okay. Then, firmly, he pulls her on.

The girl who drove them here is walking ahead and she watches as her husband lets go of her elbow and falls into step beside the girl, leaving her to waddle behind. The girl, whose name she can't recall now – maybe Caroline or something – is talking about the sea and the weather and the traffic, and there's Harry responding with his smiley face: oh yeah, it's much cooler here than New York, and oh yeah, it looked pretty bad out there on the far side of the highway on the way in from Hyannis, and oh yeah, you can really smell it, the sea, you can feel it do you good.

As if this is a normal visit and Michael isn't up to his neck in trouble.

They come to a big door that is standing wide open. The girl goes in and Harry steps back, takes her elbow again and draws her forward.

In the lobby she can see through a half-opened door a room of people sitting around, including a man in uniform, and she thinks, oh my God what now, they've put him under military arrest?

Mrs Kaplan comes out to meet them and gives her a hug that she doesn't really want and then turns to Harry, smiles broad and bright at him and, in a voice that is both glad and sad, says, 'Harry!'

That's all, just the one word of his name. She lifts his hand and shakes it like she's trying to pull it off his wrist. Then she takes the overnight bag out of his other hand and puts it down on the stairs, three from the bottom.

The girl who drove them here reaches down, picks up the bag and begins to carry it up the stairs.

'Please leave that,' she says to her. 'I'm not sure we'll be staying.'

Harry throws her a look and she feels obliged to explain. 'I prefer to sleep in my own bed right now, near my own hospital – you know how it is.'

'Why, of course I do,' Mrs Kaplan says.

She knows that should be the end of the matter but she can't seem to help going on: 'I don't want to be, you know – impolite or anything, and we brought it like you said, just in case. But the journey wasn't all that bad and I slept on the train practically all the way from New York to Boston and then napped a little on the bus.'

'I understand,' Mrs Kaplan says.

'Only two weeks to go,' she says, 'that's not so long.'

'Indeed, it is not,' Mrs Kaplan says.

'Some people go early.'

'Yes, they do.'

The girl on the stairs looks at Mrs Kaplan like she's asking permission and Mrs Kaplan nods at the girl who then puts the bag back down, this time on the bottom step.

'Anyhow, if you don't mind, I'd just as soon…' she says and decides she'd better leave it at that.

What she really would have liked to say was that she would just as soon go home and empty the bag out for the second time in twenty-four hours and return to it all the brand new things that she had packed inside it weeks ago for the maternity ward. It had all been in there ready to go: her new lawn cotton nighties and the matinée coat that the girls in work bought her along with the wash bag, the beautiful blue bedside slippers and the baby layette, going-home diapers and everything else, including that little brushed cotton baby gown that made her nearly faint with love every time she looked at it. All of these precious things now stacked on the kitchen table with no bag to protect them. It had given her a bad feeling seeing it all sitting there as she walked out the door; it had seemed like a bad omen or something, even though she had no choice in the matter, because who has more than one overnight bag – except for maybe people like these?

The girl is standing next to Mrs Kaplan now. The daughter, of course – she hadn't thought of that until this moment. You could see it in their features when you put them side by side. Mother and daughter. Soon people would be able to say the same thing about her. Mother and daughter. It could, of course, be mother and son. But a daughter might be easier this time round. She could look her in the face, at least, without always having to think about poor little Jake.

'Where's Michael?' she asks the daughter, the mother, both. 'I'd like to see him now.'

'He's in his room,' Mrs Kaplan says, 'but I think we ought to have a little talk ourselves first, before you see him, don't you agree?'

And Harry, he says, 'Oh yeah, absolutely, Mrs Kaplan.'

She stands like a dope in the lobby, looking up the stairs in case Michael's face should suddenly appear. Mrs Kaplan walks ahead into the other room and her daughter follows. What must that be like to have a daughter follow you into a room? An adult daughter that once you carried around in the world who now walks the way you do, maybe talks the way you do too – what would that be like?

She straightens her shoulders. But she can't seem to make herself move, to go in there and sit around discussing Michael in front of strangers, army personnel included. Harry jerks his head at her as if to say, 'Come *on*.'

Then he takes a couple of steps back and says, 'Honey?' before putting his hand on her back and pushing her through the door.

The people in the other room get to their feet when they walk in, as if they are guests of honour instead of guests of shame. And before she knows it, she has been pushed into a chair by Mrs Kaplan, who tells her that it's the most comfortable chair in the house – 'My favourite easy chair by far,' she says, although it sounds like she's saying 'by faw'.

Then Mrs Kaplan sticks her head out the door and calls out the name Rosetta.

In a couple of seconds, a Mexican girl appears. Mrs Kaplan sends the girl off to make tea because 'There's nothing so refreshing after a long journey – now, is there?' And she nods in agreement even though it would be more honest to say, 'How the hell do I know? This is the first real journey I ever took.'

Mrs Kaplan then calls after the Mexican girl, 'Oh, and Rosetta? I think you could bring the sandwiches in now.'

The way she says it, with two little wary nods of her head and a worried look on her face, it's like the sandwiches have been waiting outside the door all morning and now they're going to come charging in and attack everyone.

'But maybe you would prefer a beer, Harry?' Mrs Kaplan says, as if Harry, being a working man, wouldn't understand such niceties as tea in a cup.

She can feel Harry look at her; she doesn't so much as glance his way, yet she sends the message across to him: 'Don't you dare, Harry Novak, don't you even think about it.'

'Oh no, Mrs Kaplan, thanks and all, but tea is fine with me,' Harry says even though he never touches the stuff, and she has to bite her lip to keep from grinning.

The army man has disappeared from the room, unless he is hiding behind one of the couches. But she sees now that this is a room with more than one way out of it. As well as the door they came in, there's steps going down to another room with windows all around and a big glass door so you can see right outside to another porch and then green trees and yellow grass and – is that? Yes, it is. The sea. Just over that hill, the sea!

So this is the house where Michael has been living, and out there is the hill he has been running up every morning, and on the other side would be the beach and the sea that he had told them about in his letter.

'The sea is everywhere,' was what he had said, 'even when you don't see it, you hear it.'

She feels the tears coming up in her eyes, just thinking about Michael jumping in the sea, happy and free, splashing around and now this... What would it be like? To go down there, free herself from the grip of her support stockings, walk over the sand and into the water, feel it creep up her legs, wet her underwear, her maternity smock, then lap against her big, hard belly like it was a rock. Mrs Kaplan is looking at her. She is looking at her like she's reading her mind. 'Would you like to go out and get some fresh air, Mrs Novak?' she says.

'The hill is a little steep for you to climb but if you would like to see the beach, I can take you a different way, along the road?'

The way she says it, like she owns that too.

'Oh no, thank you, Mrs Kaplan,' she says. 'I'm fine where I am.'

Harry may think the world of Mrs Kaplan. And no one can deny that she is a good person, like he always says, and a real lady too, like he always adds. But she can come across a little conceited too, sitting there with her hands in her lap, saying all those things about Michael, while the other women move around in the background like nuns in a convent.

Of course, they don't look like nuns, they just move like them, silent and superior, while Mrs Kaplan, the boss nun, runs through the list of the poor boy's sins. The women are so tall, and they are all, including Mrs Kaplan, good-looking. Maybe not so much the woman they introduced as 'a family friend', although she presents herself well, even if she acts like she's taken a course in 'how to smoke like a movie star' at night school.

'The sad truth is,' Mrs Kaplan is saying, 'he never really settled in. Not the way we would have hoped.'

'Well, we sure are sorry to hear that, Mrs Kaplan. I mean, we had no idea, did we, honey?' Harry says and she looks away and then, just to be polite, gives a belated half-nod.

'I mean, he didn't write much, maybe about two letters – was it, honey?'

'Mmm,' she says, 'about that.'

In one of his letters he said he had learned how to swim and she'd been so happy to know that. But then in the next letter, he said he'd rescued the dog from drowning and that he had to swim out a couple of miles to get the dog and bring it back in and then she wasn't so sure any more about the whole swimming story. That was the third and last letter he sent, the one she didn't show Harry. Although she did ask him: 'Dogs can swim – right?'

And he said, 'Sure, they do it by instinct.'

She would love to know if Michael can really swim, if he got that much at least out of his summer here. And, yes, she would love to know if he really did rescue the dog too because, who knows, anything is possible. And maybe it's a nervy dog or maybe it fell out of a boat or something. But she is not going to ask because probably it isn't true and the last thing she wants to do right now is to feed these people any more scraps about Michael.

A chiming sound comes from the direction of the lobby like a sound you might hear in the hospital. She puts her hand on her stomach and rubs it around a couple of times. She thinks: That thing I said earlier about hoping you're a girl, well, I don't mind what you are, so please, don't be offended in there.

And now the door opens and Mrs Kaplan holds it back while one of those hostess trolley contraptions comes jerkily through with the Mexican girl on the other end of it.

Mrs Kaplan starts filling up cups and passing them to her daughter to pass round to everyone else. The girl comes close to her and looks her straight in the face. They hold the look for a couple of seconds, no more. And she feels like she's just stepped into a refrigerator, her blood turns that cold. She remembers then, Harry telling her that the daughter was sick as hell. And she can see it now in her eyes that the light has already been switched off.

She can feel the cup and saucer rattle slightly in her hand. She wants to push the girl with her dead eyes away from the vicinity of the baby. The girl asks her something then gives her a little smile and, just like that, the light comes back on.

'One spoon or cube or whatever,' she says, even though she's not sure if she's even answering the right question.

Everything is starting to aggravate her. The silent women in the background, the stink of their cigarette smoke, the bitter edge of the tea when it hits her stomach, the smell of expensive perfume. Even the sound of the cups and plates is grating in on her teeth. But the thing that irritates the most, the thing that makes her want to yell through her teeth, is that Mrs Kaplan is not even mad at Michael. There's no calling him names, no saying he should get belted, nothing mean or spiteful, just a load of sugar-coated understanding when anyone can see all that's wanted here, all that's wanted from any of them, is that Michael should get out of their clean, shiny hair quick as he possibly can.

Harry says, 'I can't tell you how sorry we are, Mrs Kaplan.'

'Oh, please,' Mrs Kaplan says, 'there's no need to be sorry.'

And Harry looks so grateful, she could slap him too.

Mrs Kaplan says, 'Michael needs help.'

And Harry goes, 'Ah-ha, I see, well, yeah, sure, but in what way do you mean?'

'I'd like to talk to him now, please, Mrs Kaplan,' she says.

'But that's the thing, Mrs Novak, he won't come down,' Mrs Kaplan says. 'He's refusing, absolutely.'

'Well, I can go up to him then,' she says.

Then the girl, the daughter, says, 'Mother, let me go talk to him.'

And this aggravates her too now, because who says Mrs Kaplan has to be in charge of who gets to talk to Michael?

'Oh yes, do go up, dear. Do go and have a word with him. Let him know that Mr and Mrs Novak are here.'

Mrs Kaplan says, 'Katherine, you see, has a special friendship with Michael, if he's going to talk to anyone...' and the girl is gone out the door.

She hears a big, impatient sigh break out at the other side of the room and a voice say, 'Well, I don't know about anyone else but I could do with a drink.'

The voice belongs to the redhead whose name she thinks could also be Mrs Kaplan. Of course, the daughter-in-law, Mrs Kaplan Junior. She gets up, goes to the buffet at the side and begins unscrewing bottles with a swift, professional hand. Then she picks up a soda syphon and in two sharp shots fills two glasses and hands one of them to the friend.

The friend says, 'Oh, thank you, Olivia. This is all so upsetting, so... I don't know, I just don't know.'

And she feels like saying, 'And you are who now? And how come this is any of your business?'

But then it occurs to her that maybe Michael stole from her too and so she keeps her mouth shut and turns her head the opposite way.

A beautiful rosewood dining table stands a couple of feet away, pushed in against the wall. And in the middle of it, all laid out, is an odd assortment of things: a peculiar mess in an otherwise immaculate room. She lets her eye wander over it. She sees a pocket knife and a square tin box, a couple of old candy bar wrappers, a packet of cookies and packs of bubblegum. There's a few pencils and a long stick thing with a sort of wooden ball on the top of it. There's a photograph of two blondes and a man laughing outside a house and what looks like an electric cigarette lighter out of an automobile along with a silver cigarette case.

It makes no sense to her why all these things should be laid out on the table until she sees the scraps of paper and realizes then that these are all the things that Michael has stolen. The scraps are just like the ones he used to play with in their old apartment, cut out from magazine pages and knitting patterns, figures and little scenes that he carried around with him in his suitcase. And what harm in that? And what harm in the other useless bits of garbage either? What's the difference, she would love to ask Mrs Kaplan, between playing with these and, say, a box of tin soldiers?

But she knows the little pieces of curled-up paper are not the real issue, nor anything else on the table for that matter, including that nail file, the inch ruler, the pack of playing cards. It's the fifty-four dollars that changes everything. Fifty-four dollars of orphan money. That's almost as much as Harry takes home in a week, without overtime.

She looks back into the room. Mrs Kaplan Junior or Olivia or whatever she's called is leaning forward now, resting her elbow on her crossed leg, which she swings elegantly from side to side. She is wearing a beautiful blue and white skirt that's so fresh and full looking that when it sways off her knee it makes it seem like a sail on a boat.

'We are not judging Michael in any way – please understand that,' she is saying. 'But just the same…'

She can't see the blue and white sail now because the original Mrs Kaplan is standing in front of her, pushing a plate of sandwiches into her chest.

'We thought you might have eaten lunch in the dining-caw,' she says (caw!), 'and so we didn't hold lunch – I hope we did right?'

'Oh yes, thank you,' she says, even though they already had a mountain of sandwiches that she made herself to eat on the train because who has the kind of money to throw away on dining-car lunches except maybe the Kaplans and their kind?

She sits forward, slides the nearest sandwich to her, puts it on the small plate that is resting on the arm of her chair. She tries to sit back again but has difficulty getting comfortable. There is nothing easy about Mrs Kaplan's easy chair; in fact it feels like she's trapped in it. Otherwise she might jump up on her feet and yell out at the top of her voice, 'Oh, for crying out loud, what's fifty-four bucks to you people?'

She can feel herself bristling all over; her skin feels hot and too tight on her body. The baby can feel it too and starts acting up. She gets a heel in one side, then a head butt on the other side, then a punch right out front. It's like the baby is mad with her for not standing up for Michael and is trying to beat her up from the inside. She places her hand on her stomach and silently says, Fifty-four dollars, if it wasn't for that...

She turns in her easy chair, tries one side for a few seconds, then the other side, but it's just no use. There is no comfort to be found in this chair, in this room, in this house.

'Are you sure I can't offer you a bottle of beer, Harry?' Mrs Kaplan is saying to Harry and she feels like saying, He told you no and who says you can call him Harry, anyhow? It's Mr Novak to you – I don't hear you dishing out your first name!

If she could just take her shoes off. If she could take them off and put them up on that foot stool that's just sitting there unoccupied. She is thinking about how good that would feel when Mrs Kaplan Junior says, 'The thing is, he doesn't appear to know right from wrong. He just doesn't *get* it.'

'Oh, excuse me, but I disagree,' she hears herself say. 'He's a very sensitive boy as it happens.'

Mrs Kaplan Junior leans forward again; the sail of her skirt sways. 'I think it's important to say, Mrs Novak,' she begins and then stops. There's a sound of tinkling coming from the vicinity of her hand and for a moment she thinks she must be wearing a charm bracelet, but when she takes a closer look she sees the tinkling is coming from the ice in her now empty glass.

'What I am trying to say is that we want you to know that we don't in any way blame you for all this.'

'Oh, you don't?' she says.

'Oh no, Mrs Novak, not at all.'

'And excuse me, but why should you blame us? He wasn't under our care when he took the fifty-four bucks, was he? I mean, we didn't leave that kind of money lying around.'

Harry is looking at her with a look of panic on his face. She can feel her temper coming up from her toes and pulls herself back.

'Excuse me, Mrs Kaplan,' she says, 'but I need to use the bathroom.'

She tries to lift herself out of the chair and Harry comes over and hoists her to her feet.

Mrs Kaplan gets up. 'Let me show you.'

'Oh no, please. *Please!* I mean, I'd rather go alone. I mean, how hard can it be to find?'

Mrs Kaplan nods and says of course. Then she gives her directions that go straight in one ear and right out the other.

As she comes out of the room she hears the sound of a door bell. She looks through the dim lobby. The door is already open, the sunlight bouncing around in the doorway in small, rough shapes. After a few seconds, the light begins to settle and now she can make out the shape of two people standing there with their backs to the open door. A very tall man and a much smaller woman. She hears a sound behind her and when she turns the girl called Rosetta appears from the side of the stairs. Rosetta stops, points back down the hallway and says, 'Go down there, you will find a window seat – just front of it, there is the bathroom.'

She is about to move off when Rosetta puts her hand on her arm. Rosetta lowers her voice. Her face seems to nuzzle the air as she speaks. 'Michael, he is a good boy,' she says. 'I don't know, maybe he take the money, but he is a good boy, that's what I want to say to you.'

Rosetta turns away from her then and goes to answer the already opened door.

She barely makes it into the bathroom before she breaks down and cries.

When she comes back into the living-room, there's the tall man standing at the back with his hat in his hands, and the small woman is standing in the centre facing Mrs Kaplan, and there is Rosetta criss-crossing the room as she loads up the hostess trolley.

'You're not listening to me, Mrs Kaplan,' the small woman is saying. 'I'm telling you that I will not say a word about the matter until I've spoken to Richie.'

The small woman's chin is stuck up in the air, her fists are clenched by her sides; there's a sort of blaze in her eyes.

The minute she sets eyes on her, she thinks: Oh, now, this is more like it, this is what we need around here – someone who knows how to speak their mind.

Mrs Kaplan junior stands up suddenly and, straightening down the sail of her blue and white skirt, says, 'And we *told* you, *that* is not possible right now.'

The small woman ignores her and continues to look only at the original Mrs Kaplan.

'I need to speak to Richie – that's all I'm prepared to say for now.'

'He's gone to pick up his dog,' Mrs Kaplan says. 'Mrs Dutra's daughter, I believe, she works in the pet shop anyhow – well, she has been taking care of Buster.'

'Well, I'll just have to wait then.'

'I think I have a right to know why you wish to speak to my son,' Mrs Kaplan Junior says, her voice all choppy and alarmed now. Again, the small woman completely ignores her.

And she thinks, as Harry helps her to get back into the easy chair: Oh, I like her. I certainly do.

'He's on his way to Provincetown, he may be some time,' Mrs Kaplan says. 'He's catching the bus at the end of the road and then Mrs Dutra's daughter is going to take him home when she closes up.'

'What time did he leave?'

'About ten minutes ago.'

The little woman looks at her wrist-watch.

The tall man says, 'I'll drive you to the bus stop.'

'No, thank you,' she says. 'I don't mind walking and better I speak to Richie alone.'

'You won't make it if you walk – the bus will be gone. Look, let me drive you and I'll wait for you while you have a talk with him and then drive you both back.'

The little woman nods and makes for the door; the man begins to follow. He stops when he comes to her chair and says, 'You must be Michael's folks?'

The little woman sticks her little head back round the door and yaps at her husband. 'Well, come if you're coming – we can do all that later.'

The man begins to move away. At the door Mrs Kaplan stops him. 'Is this really necessary, do you think?' she asks.

The man nods his head a few times and says, 'I believe so, Mrs Kaplan. Yes.'

There is a long silence when the couple leave the room, which she decides not to worry about. She lays her head back and turns her eyes towards the sea. The light has changed and now everything out there seems to have mellowed somehow; the hill and the grass seem softer, the gentle sway of the trees and the sea. Her eyes grow heavy and her head begins to nod.

She can hear, over by the window, the boy Richie's mother and her friend squawking like something you'd hear in a barnyard.

'Of course she's half-crazy – anybody can tell!'

'What do you mean *half*?'

'Just who she thinks—'

'Oh, pay no attention, dear.'

'I've a good mind to drive down to the bus stop myself and get Richie – if I hurry I should pass them out, the way they crawl along…'

'Oh, don't bother.'

'He is *my* son… and, Mother, I have to say, I don't know why you let them walk all over you like that.'

Mrs Kaplan says, 'But what could I do? They spend so much time with Michael and Richie likes them, he may open up and—'

'Oh, they probably won't even make it,' Annette says. 'The bus will be gone by the time they get down there. Here, let me fix you a drink. Mrs Kaplan is right, she's probably just going to question Richie, try to find out what really happened. Oh, but she is so pushy! And her manners! That poor man…'

332

The next voice she hears belongs to Harry.

'She hardly slept all night with the worry.'

She opens her eyes.

Mrs Kaplan says, 'Are you feeling all right, Mrs Novak? You're looking a little pale.'

'What? Oh no, no, I'm fine. I'm—'

'She is looking a little pale,' Mrs Kaplan says to Harry.

'She's tired out, is all,' Harry says.

Mrs Kaplan gets up and comes over to her. 'Come with me,' she says, 'I'll show you where you can lie down.'

'Oh no, thank you, I'm okay now, really I am,' she says, while at the same time she allows Mrs Kaplan to help her to her feet and draw her towards the door.

Harry steps forward but Mrs Kaplan says, 'That's all right, Harry, you stay where you are, I'll take care of her now.'

Mrs Kaplan sits her down on a big bed, takes off her shoes and says, 'Why don't we take those support stockings off, make things a little more comfortable for you?'

And at first she is mortified and can only hope her feet are not stinking and then she thinks what the heck, as Mrs Kaplan rolls them off her sweaty legs and lays them on the end of the bed. Now Mrs Kaplan is lifting her iron-heavy legs and putting them up on the bed and drawing over her a satin quilt that feels soft against her skin, soft and cool, like water.

Mrs Kaplan closes over the shutters. 'There's a bathroom right over there,' she says. 'Now you try to get some rest and I'll call you in an hour or so.'

'It's so quiet here,' she hears herself say, 'there's so much silence.'

'Can't you hear the sea?' Mrs Kaplan says. 'Shh, listen. That's it. Keep listening and before you know it you will have fallen asleep.'

When Mrs Kaplan closes the door and her steps sound down the hallway, she thinks: I will give her five minutes to get downstairs and out of range then I'm getting up and I'm looking for Michael.

~

HE DROPS HIS WIFE at the corner and drives a little further on to make a turn in the road. Then he comes back and pulls over and now the Buick is pointed towards home. He can see, through the mirror, Richie sitting on the grass spur by the bus stop and his wife bustling towards him. Richie's head goes up and now he is standing and staring at her. His wife appears to be doing most of the talking while Richie stands, his arms stiff by his side, his head down on his chest.

After a few moments, she sits down on the grass and pulls Richie's arm to sit down beside her. He peers into the side mirror at the distorted picture they make – like two kids from this distance, brother and sister maybe. And that's when he remembers that he has forgotten to send the cheque to his sister.

He leans over to the glove compartment and pushes the lid open. He puts his hand in and begins rummaging through the bits of paper in there but there are no letters inside. As he tries to recall where he could have left the mail, he notices a flutter of shadows through the side mirror and now he sees Richie and his wife crossing the road and heading his way.

She puts the boy in the back seat and closes the door behind him. Like the arresting officer, he thinks. She sits up front then, twists herself around and says, 'Richie, all you have to do is tell the truth.'

'They won't believe me,' Richie says, his words catching in the back of his throat, 'and I'm scared.'

'Did you mean to pin the blame on Michael?' she says. 'Just tell me that much, Richie.'

'No, I mean, I don't know. At first, I did. But then—'

He pulls out onto the road and starts driving.

Richie calls out from the back seat, 'Oh, please, sir. Please don't take me back there and make me face them all. Please, sir, I'll tell you everything, but please don't make me stand there in front of everyone. I have the money here, sir, I'll give it back.'

Richie sits forward and shoves a tight roll of dollars over the back of the seat, no bigger than a bullet cigar.

'I had it in my pocket, just hoping for a chance to give it back but— Please, I'm sorry, I really am. Please, sir, don't make me…'

He looks at the boy through the mirror, the terror in his eyes, the way his whole mouth is shaking. He can see his chest moving up and down, his breath getting shorter.

'Do you have your rescue inhaler, Richie?' he asks.

'No, sir, but I'm all right. I just feel so awful, that's all.'

'Supposing you tell us what happened, Richie, then when we get back to the house, maybe we could ask your grandmother if you could talk to her in private?' he says.

Richie gnaws on his bottom lip.

'Why don't you just tell us why you did it, son?'

'I… I was mad at him and wanted him to get in trouble. I was planning to put the envelopes in his hiding place that he thinks I'm so dumb I don't know about but then— Then when we got back from the beach and we had such a good time with you and Aunt Katherine and I was sorry then and meant to put them back. And I tried to, sir. But they were counting the money already, you see, in the kitchen and checking the book and I couldn't get anywhere near it. I knew my mom, she'd go crazy, and I was just too scared to admit it… So I told her about Michael's hiding place on the beach and—'

'But why were you so mad at him?' he asks.

'Well, because. Because he was so mean to me, I guess, and wouldn't be my friend and then he went off with the Westin boys. And—'

'Yes, but to pin the blame on somebody else, Richie. Do you understand what a terrible thing it is to do something like that?' she says.

'Yes, ma'am, I do.'

'A dishonourable thing to do, Richie, and I know you are not a dishonourable boy.'

And now the tears start to come. 'It was supposed to be—' Richie says. 'It was supposed— It was—'

'Slow down, son,' he says. 'Slow down, take a deep breath, that's it. Now tell me, what are you trying to say?'

'A day for my father. It was supposed to be *his* day. So why did Michael have to be the one in the centre of everything, the one to get the speech made about him and the kite and everything. Why not me? That's what I thought, if you want to know the truth, sir. He never even knew his father. But I knew mine. I *remember* and it just made me feel… well, why not me?'

And now Richie puts his hands on his face and starts to sob.

He pulls into the parking space.

'You two wait here,' he says. 'I'm going up to the house to fetch your grandmother.'

~

WHEN SHE WAKES UP, she can see by the clock on the bedside table that she's been out for an hour and a half. So much for Mrs Kaplan saying she was going to call her! Almost five in the afternoon – how were they ever going to get back to New York at this rate?

She has to use a series of little bounces to get herself off the bed and barely makes it into the bathroom where she feels she could pee for the rest of her life. Mid-stream, she hears a knock on the bedroom door and she hadn't even thought to close the door of the bathroom. The knock sounds a second time; she clears her throat and over the downpour calls out, 'Just a minute.'

The door opens anyway and she nearly pops the baby out right into the toilet until she realizes it's only Harry.

'Don't you come in here,' she says. 'You know I can't go if there's anybody watching.'

'Sounds like you're doing just fine,' Harry says.

When she comes out, Harry is putting a tray down on the end of the bed. He says, 'With Mrs Kaplan's compliments – keeps the blood pressure level, she says.'

She takes a peek at the tray: a cup of coffee and a sandwich.

'Another sandwich!' she says. 'Why doesn't somebody just slice me up and slather me all over with butter?'

Harry laughs. 'Just wait till you hear this,' he begins.

'Has Michael surfaced?'

'It was the other kid,' Harry says, all excited and looking around like he's afraid someone is listening to him.

'What other kid – what are you talking about?'

Harry lowers his voice. 'I'm telling you, the other kid, he took the money.'

'You mean—? Not the grandson! How do you know this? What happened, Harry, tell me, before I burst, what happened?'

'The other kid did it, I'm telling you.'

'Where's Michael? Does he know?'

'He's packing. We're going home. That is, if you feel up to it. There's a Captain Hartman down there – he's giving us a ride to the terminal in Boston so we don't have to worry about missing any train. You happy to go?'

'I couldn't be happier.'

'It'll be all hours before we get home?'

'I don't care, Harry. Let's go.'

A few minutes later, she's back in the easy chair and Mrs Kaplan Junior is no longer in the room but the friend has stayed and is over in the corner, keeping her head down. Mrs Kaplan is apologizing, trying to explain her grandson's behaviour away.

'He was angry at Michael and only wanted to teach him a lesson. He never meant it to go this far, you know. I can't tell you how sorry he is. How sorry we all are, Harry, Mrs Novak.'

'Where is he anyhow?' she asks. 'Don't you think he could show his face, maybe apologize on his own behalf?'

'He's too upset. Katherine is putting him to bed now. But he has apologized to Michael. They've settled their little differences, I'm very glad to say.'

'That's all right, Mrs Kaplan,' Harry says. 'We understand.'

'Maybe you understand, Harry,' she says, 'but not me. And what I'd like to know is this, when did he intend coming clean – before Michael was sent off to reform school or after?'

'Oh now, Mrs Novak, it would never have come to that,' Mrs Kaplan says.

'Easy for you to say that, Mrs Kaplan, but the world's a little different when it comes to people like us.'

The little woman who saved Michael is standing by the rosewood table looking at all the things Michael has stolen and she thinks, Please let there be nothing belonging to her, not after she saved him and all.

'This is all that Michael took?' she asks.

'Yes,' Mrs Kaplan says, 'I'm sure it doesn't seem like very much now.'

'No. And this, who is this in the photograph?' She lifts up a picture and Mrs Kaplan goes over to it.

'Oh, that's Katherine and two friends. A house they used to rent during the summer.'

'I wouldn't have known her, not at first.'

'That was before she got sick – her hair, well, it was a different colour then.'

'I see,' the little woman says and puts the photograph back down on the table, and then she comes over and stands right next to her. 'Mrs Novak, I know how you feel, I sympathize, I really do, but Richie has his own troubles,' she says, 'and he *is* sorry, I'm convinced. He did try to put the money back, you know, but it didn't work out and then he just panicked. I think we should just leave it at that. Anyhow, it's getting late and I'm sure you want to get going now. And you know, you must not forget that Michael did steal quite a few things. He is not above blame.'

She looks up at the little woman, who is so direct in the way she speaks, in the way she looks too, that there doesn't seem to be anything left to say. And so she says nothing and just nods.

The tall man and his little wife begin to leave now. The man stops at Mrs Kaplan's chair and says, 'We can pick up the dog, if you like.'

'Oh, Buster! I'd forgotten all about Buster. Maybe I should telephone the pet shop and ask if they could keep him for another day.'

'It might be good for Richie to have him here,' he says. 'We don't mind doing it. I need to pick up something in Provincetown anyway. We can take care of it on the way home.'

And then the man and the woman leave, quietly and without any fuss.

Through the window she sees the army captain walking around the side of the house and a few seconds later he is lifting his head and calling out to someone unseen, and now she sees the side of the tall man, his shoulder, his elbow, the tilt of his hat.

338

The baby gives her a kick. She leans forward to take it, then she sits back and feels a sigh move through her whole body.

The next time the door opens, Michael walks in.

And now he is standing there in front of her, the brown suitcase that Harry bought him in his hand. He's a little tired-looking but he's filled out and sun-kissed all over. She wants to tell him he looks beautiful, but of course she can't say that to a boy.

'Michael, you look so different!' she says. 'I swear I wouldn't know you.'

'You look different too.'

She laughs and taps her stomach. 'Been at the cookie jar again – you know how it is.'

Michael smiles.

'But you!' she says. 'I don't know, you look like…'

'I look like what?'

She wants to say you look like the son of a gentleman but she sees Harry beaming from ear to ear over there and she just smiles and says, 'You look ter-rific, Michael.'

Mrs Kaplan says, 'I'm so glad you think so. Despite everything, I think the vacation did him the world of— But, Michael, what about your kite?'

'I don't need it,' he says without looking at her.

'But after all the trouble you took over it?'

'I don't want it now,' he says and keeps staring at the floor.

Mrs Kaplan nods. 'I understand,' she says quietly.

Michael's head comes up suddenly and begins turning side to side. 'Where's Mrs Aitch?' he asks.

'Oh, they have just left, Michael,' Mrs Kaplan says.

He drops the suitcase and he's out of the room before she knows it.

~

SHE IS QUIET ON the way to Provincetown and he puts this down to the effect of Michael's farewell. He's a little upset himself. They are neither of them used to all that emotion in one day and he can't seem to get the little scene out of his head. They had just taken leave of Captain Hartman and were almost back at the parking space when they heard the boy calling out her 'Mrs Aitch' name. And there he was suddenly, half-running, half-skidding through the dusk and down the lane and just about managing to come to a halt before throwing himself right at her.

The boy so tall that all he had been able to see of his wife was the top of her head trapped in his awkward embrace and her left hand placing a few feeble pats on his back.

'Oh now, oh now.' She had repeated this little chant a few times before pulling herself free. 'Well, that's a fine thing – trying to smother me. And I thought we were supposed to be friends!'

'I don't want to leave you,' the boy said and then broke down in tears.

A look of shock came over his wife's face and then, as if she had been looking around for something to say, her eyes began to flicker, her lips to twitch, although she managed to collect herself well enough.

'I'm afraid you're going to have to, Michael,' she said, 'but just think now about all that is waiting for you when you get back to civilization – new house, new school, new *baby*. A little brother or sister. Someone who will arrive into the world and find you there, already waiting. Remember that now – it will be your home first. You will be the one showing him or her what's what. And that's quite a responsibility, you know. You can't go stealing things, you know – all that has got to stop.'

The boy had nodded, pulled the cuff of his sweater down over the heel of his hand and swiped it over his eyes. 'Where is this New Jersey anyway – is it far?'

'Oh, a train ride away from New York. It's nothing.'

'Can I come see you?'

She doesn't answer for a moment and the look on the boy's face – at once fearful and puzzled and so he intervenes and says.

'Of course you can come see us, Michael.'

'So long as you don't go sneaking off without permission. You hear me now? I won't allow that,' she says.

'But how will I find you?'

340

'Oh, just find Washington Square,' she says a little vaguely, 'and you'll find us all right.'

He shook the boy's hand and for a moment it had seemed like they might embrace, but the boy turned away suddenly. He turned away and went running back up the lane to the house that was standing gloomy now in the half-light, except for a single rectangle of pale yellow that had broken out in an upstairs window.

As they come to the turn for the highway to Provincetown, he sees the walking girl up ahead making for Castle Road. He wonders whether to point her out to his wife, who usually has something to say on the subject.

'There she goes,' he says and points ahead to the figure bobbing up the hill. His wife looks up and regards the girl for a second then, without comment, puts her head down again.

In fact, she doesn't open her mouth until they get into town and then it's only to instruct him on where to find a parking spot.

'What's wrong with right here?' he asks.

'Oh, nothing, once you don't mind being towed away. Ten dollars it costs to get a car out now. But if you don't mind, then why should I?'

He moves on.

'How about here then?' he asks, pulling into a space opposite the library and she gives an indifferent shrug.

He says, 'I'll pick up the order and be right back. We can go get the dog then.'

She raises one hand and vaguely swats him away.

When he comes back ten minutes later, her seat is empty.

He puts the package in the trunk and goes looking for her.

He walks around for maybe twenty minutes before he sees her at a distance, sitting on a quayside boulder in the West End of town, the dog sitting squarely beside her. He makes his way down to her, past the cramped crooked houses and the clumsy signage of back street enterprises: *Live Bait. Auto Repares. Clams Anyway You Like.*

When he comes up behind her, the dog turns and flaps a tongue at him. Then, tongue first, it turns back to her. She places a hand on the flat of the dog's head while they both ignore him and stay staring into the black water.

From open windows comes the sound of frying. The scent of clams, helped along by garlic, tomatoes. It reaches down into his stomach and pokes him in the gut. He needs to eat and he needs to do it soon.

But there is a stillness all around that he is loath to disrupt. The soft clanging sounds of the harbour, the slap of water. Nothing moves apart from the fidget of a moored boat or the ruffle of the dog's coat when it lifts its nose to the breeze. He can hear far-off dance music coming from the centre of town and, close by, the low voices of fishermen, gathered around a lamp, speaking Portuguese. And a smell that takes him right back to boyhood, of wood-shaving and tar and boiled fish oil rubbed into wood.

The dog turns to look back at him a couple of times. It looks like it has eyebrows, quizzical eyebrows as if it expects him to say or do something. In the end, he just asks her if she would like to eat something.

'No, I would not,' she says.

'What about the dog – you think maybe he's a little hungry?'

'Oh, I'm sure Mrs Dutra's daughter fed him well enough.'

He waits for a moment and tries again. 'I'm pretty hungry myself.'

And, when there's no response to that: 'We could probably get a table somewhere, if we hurry. I'm sure Buster won't mind waiting in the car.'

'Oh, don't waste your money on me,' she says, 'you go if you want, I'm not stopping you.'

'I'm not going to leave you here alone,' he says. 'And I need to eat, you know that, otherwise I'm in for another night of pain.'

He expects a bite back, a sarcastic remark at least. But all she does is lean over and let out an exasperated and childlike sigh. Then she stands and pulls the dog to its feet.

He has soup and a lobster roll. She has coffee and prods a piece of pie with a fork.

'He can always come visit,' he says, 'Michael, I mean. If that's what is upsetting you?'

'I know who you mean,' she says, 'and I'm not upset about that.'

'Well, do you want to tell me what's on your mind?'

'You mean what's on my mind generally or right now?'

'Well, now.'

'I was just thinking,' she says.

'About?'

'Your old friend Mac – I was wondering how he's doing without a wife.'

'What brought that into your head?'

'You never went to her funeral.'

'No. We decided not—'

'*You* decided not.'

'It was in California and how long ago was that anyhow?'

'He is supposed to be one of your great friends. But can male artists really have friends, I wonder? Or is it just too much ego for one relationship?'

He looks around for the waitress, signals for the cheque.

'I wrote him a letter,' he says, reaching back to pull out his wallet.

She wraps the pie in a napkin, stands up and walks out. He pays the cheque and follows.

They walk back down Commercial Street, pouches of light and music along the way. A voice pushes out of a bar, a piano accompanies it, 'That lucky old sun…'

There are few people out: after-dinner strollers, a couple of servicemen, one or two lone wolves.

He says, 'It's much quieter now the season's done.'

She says nothing.

When they get back to the automobile, she opens the door and looks at him across the roof.

'A cold fish of a letter it was too.'

'What was?'

She gets into the passenger seat, kneels up on it and holds out the pie to the dog sitting up on the back seat who sniffs, takes a couple of licks but doesn't partake.

'What was?' he asks again.

'Your so-called letter of condolence,' she says and he decides to let it go.

*

343

The air is solid and unwieldy. He rolls the window down full but still has some difficulty breathing. His gut is burning, his head is beginning to ache and the dog's frantic panting in the back seat is not helping any.

A short way out of Provincetown, he sees a roadside stand selling beach-plum jelly and decides to pull over.

He looks down on the dark stretch of the bay below – the sea appears life-less, draped and dark like a bolt of black satin cloth. But the cool night air at least, on the crest of this hill, pours down on his head and over his face.

'Had a good evening?' the woman behind the stand asks, her voice a little worn.

He says, 'All right. How about you?'

'No, not so good. Probably pack up tomorrow or next day anyhow. Not the best season we've ever had, truth be told.'

He feels moved to ask for a second jar and the woman pulls it from the crate behind her. Then she holds her palm under the lamplight and pushes her finger around counting his change. It brings him an odd sense of peace, watching this woman push a few cents around her dirt-stained, worn-down palm. He wishes he could just stay here for a while, watching her, but he says, 'Oh, that's all right; you keep the change,' and turns away.

As he comes back to the automobile, the dog regards him intently through the side window while, up front, his wife, leaning her elbow through the open window, covers her face with the span of her hand.

She kicks off the second he sits back in. She starts off a little cryptically, which draws him in before he has time to think about it.

'How big a house can become,' she sighs, 'how small a double bed.'

'Do you want to explain?' he says, pulling out from the lay-by and onto the road.

'I'm talking about what is ahead of me now, when we get back to the house.'

He drives on for a few minutes and then says, 'I thought you'd be happy about Michael. I don't mean about his leaving, I mean—'

'Because I got him off the hook?'

'I don't see that you need to put it that way – the boy was innocent.'

'Not all that innocent. He still stole plenty, whatever way you dress it up. It doesn't matter, anyhow – the Kaplans are done with him now. You can bet on that.'

'I'm not sure that is altogether fair.'

'They are cold people.'

'What are you talking about?'

'That's why you get on so well with them.'

'Have it your own way,' he says.

She stays with her head turned away from him as they come along Depot Road. They take the hill and as the road twists by the pond she whips around and yells, 'You *disgust* me!'

Behind him he feels the dog flinch.

On Fisher Road, he drives past the turn for their house and continues down to the end where he pulls over at the Kaplans' parking space. He gets out and opens the back door. The dog turns its head away.

'Come on, boy,' he says, 'you're home now.'

The dog, just like the last time, pretends not to hear him.

'Come on, out. Out *now*.'

He reaches in and the dog recoils. He goes round to the other side, leans in and begins to push; the dog might as well be made out of concrete.

He sits right in, next to the dog, and, pushing his hip against it, gradually bumps it to move along the seat until one final push forces it out. The dog jumps on the ground and he pulls the door shut behind it. He gets out and gets back in the front.

'We better wait,' he says, 'in case he follows us. Last time I took him back, Katherine had to whistle for him before he'd go home.'

'Sure now it was the dog she was whistling for?' she asks.

He watches the dog slope up the hill, glancing back once or twice over its shoulder. Then just before the top, it stops, turns its body into a slight curve, the white blaze of its chest showing up in the dark.

Her face is turned right in to the window. He wonders if she may be crying.

He softens his voice. 'What's the matter?' he says. 'Is it Michael? Richie then?'

345

She shakes her head, but does not look at him.

'Well, if not the boys then what?' he says. 'I mean, you were fine when I left this morning.'

'Yes, I was, wasn't I? But that was before I realized the sort of man I am married to.'

He turns the car and is about to drive off when she opens her purse and takes something out. A handful of letters. She pulls one out.

'What is that?' he asks.

'Oh now, isn't that a good question!'

He switches on the overhead light and sees that it is the letter he had written to New York and he remembers then where he had left the mail – in the pocket of his other jacket.

'I was going to tell you,' he says.

'Well, forgive me if I don't quite believe that.'

'Of course I was going to tell you. You would have found out anyhow as soon as we got back to New York.'

They sit in silence staring out at the dark. The lights of an oncoming automobile pass on the other side of the road, the outline of a young couple inside, heading for the beach, her head on his shoulder. It makes him feel a general pity for everyone he knows, not least of all himself.

He begins to drive. Further along, coming out of a side road, the walking girl appears again. She is headed eastward in the direction of the Old County Road, walking away from them into a dark silence. Her walk, caught in his headlights, is measured and mechanical. No longer a girl, of course, she gets thinner each year, her stride a little more twisted. Her knees look like two knobs on a pair of bedposts, yet there is something about the sight of her that he can't help but envy.

'I mean, bad enough that you keep it secret from me,' she says, 'but to laugh at me behind my back that way.'

'I didn't laugh at you.'

'Oh yes, you did. Turning it all into a joke.'

'I was just trying to lighten things up a little. He did his best – I didn't want him to feel bad about it. Look, I would have told you but you were upset after the party and then all this with Michael and Richie.'

'To betray your own wife.'

'I'm sorry I disappoint you,' he says.

'I'm sure you couldn't care less what I think or how much you disappoint me. Of course, Katherine now. That would be different.'

'Katherine? Oh, so it's Katherine now – what happened to Olivia?'

'At least I know now what the attraction was in Eastham. What, nothing to say about that? She looks different now, not so husky and no longer blonde. I saw the photograph. It was on the table, there in the Kaplans' little display of stolen goods. She's the girl in last year's painting. Michael spotted it straight away when I showed him the sketches but I didn't believe him. Or maybe I just didn't want to. In any case, I saw the way you looked at her at Mrs Kaplan's party, and when I looked at that photograph today, it all began to make sense. You never told me she went stargazing with you.'

'She invited herself along – so what?'

'You never told me.'

'I've done nothing to be ashamed of.'

'I don't even care that she is young and pretty – God knows, the poor girl doesn't have all that much time left.'

He opens his mouth to say something but she is ahead of him.

'I don't care about her, I said. What I care about is my wasted life. *My* life. I had something once, I had spark and potential and creativity, it was there in me. It was always in *me*. But with the coming of you—'

'Couldn't this wait at least until we get home?'

He makes the turn and begins driving up the road that leads to their house, the trees closing in on him like a fist.

'That's what it's all about – isn't it?' she says. 'You being in control.'

'Oh, *please*,' he says.

'Not allowing me to paint. Not allowing me to *drive*. I see kids around here, sixteen years of age, driving around. Kids who hardly know they've been born. Oh, but not me. I'm not allowed. Because I married a man who likes to keep me on a tight leash.'

347

'If you must know, I don't like you to drive because you are a danger on the road – to yourself and to others.'

'Oh, that's a lie but not the worst lie you told in recent times.'

'I had no idea who she was last year – she was just a girl in a doorway.'

'I'm not talking about Katherine, I don't care about that. It's this! This that breaks my heart.' She waves the envelope again. 'You and your give-nothing-take-all friends.'

'He tried everywhere, everyone he knew but—' he says.

'I'm not buying that. It's the same old story, the female artist is pushed out of the way by the male, by the big-egoed—'

She slaps the envelope on the side of his face, the corner catching in his eye.

The car jolts and abruptly stops. But she keeps coming at him, slapping him with the envelope and now pounding his arm with the side of her fist.

'You killed everything in me,' she screams, 'every artistic bone in my—'

'That's not true,' he says from under the cover of his arm.

'Stomped it all out of me, bit by bit, you just wouldn't allow it.'

'That's not true,' he says again, quietly, as if to himself.

'After everything I gave up for you. After the way I made your career, pushing you forward while I stayed in the background. Because I thought. My. Turn. Would. Come. That you would help *me*. Oh, the stupidity of women. I thought. I thought.'

She stops hitting him now and begins sobbing. He brings his arms back down, puts his hand on the driving wheel and turns the key. As the engine slowly moves them on, he looks straight ahead at the slope of the cart-road leading up to the garage and the flight of steps and the house at the top of the hill. He turns off the engine and gets out.

He walks round by the rear of the car and then straight on past it, back the way he has just driven.

He hears her call out through the window, 'What are you doing?'

Then he hears the door open as she gets out and shouts again, 'What are you *doing*?'

He stops but he keeps his back to her.

'What the hell are you—?' she says. 'Get back in the car.'

He turns and takes a few steps back to her.

'I didn't kill anything in you. Because there was nothing to kill,' he says, 'nothing to stomp out.'

'What are you talking about? Get back in the car.'

'I'm not getting back in. I'm not going back in the house, I'm done. I'm done with all this.'

'Oh, now you're just being childish.'

'I'm done.'

'Oh, now, you really are.'

'I've had it,' he says. 'Those things you said, about me killing your talent, I can't allow you to say those things any more.'

She puts her hands over her ears and squeezes her eyes shut. 'I'm much too upset to listen to all this nonsense, I will not listen to it.'

She opens her eyes again. 'Now get in the car.'

'You could have done other things, you know. You could have been a writer, maybe.'

'But I don't want to be a writer. Why are you even saying this? I'm an artist. A painter.'

'No you're not.'

'What?'

He comes back to her and looks straight at her. 'You ever consider the possibility that the reason you've had no luck as a painter is because you don't have any talent?'

'Oh, you're just trying to hurt me now, that's what you're doing. I see it now. Go ahead, do your worst.'

'I'm sorry I took so long to tell you this.'

She gives a short, uncertain laugh. 'Oh yes, kick me when I'm down,' she begins but he is already walking away.

He can hear her screaming behind him. 'Kick me when I'm down, why don't you! Coward, coward, you disgusting coward!'

He continues to walk.

'And don't come back! Do you hear me? Don't you dare come back, I mean that. Oh yes, I mean it!'

He walks to the end of the cart-road, then turns for the lane that leads out to the blacktop road where he can no longer hear her.

4

IN THE MIDDLE OF the night, she walks around the house talking to herself just to hear the sound of a voice. She says, 'He is just trying to scare me now. But what do I care – he'll be the one to catch cold. He could catch pneumonia out there this time of the year when the nights start to chill, and who is going to nurse him then – the Kaplans? Oh, I think not!'

Or maybe – she thinks as she goes into the kitchen to boil water for tea – maybe I could be the one to get pneumonia? See how he'd feel then! I could take this sweater off, go outside wearing only my nightie, go down to the beach, walk in the sea up to my neck and then come out, stand in the sea breeze and let the cold, wet cloth dry into my skin, right through to my bones and—

The water for the tea begins to bubble up, distracting her. 'Oh, what childish nonsense you're talking now,' she says. 'He's the one walking around in the cold night air, not you. Stooping to his level, that's what you're doing, you know, oh yes. And you are *so* much better than that.'

While she waits for the tea to draw she pulls a few Pilot crackers out of a bag, then searches for something to spread on them. But all she can find is a small blob of butter in the corner of the dish. She remembers now the beach-plum jelly in the trunk of the Buick. Then she remembers the Buick itself with the key still in it. What if he has already come back? What if he has been and has driven off again? Oh, why had she not thought to take the key with her? He could be halfway to New York by now. After that, he could go anywhere he liked. All he would need to do is promise one painting in the foreseeable future and they would be throwing dollars at him from the sidelines, enough for him to drown in. He could go anywhere he had a mind to go. Abroad even – France! He could be gone by tomorrow. To *France*.

She rushes out of the kitchen and across the studio. But through the window, she can't see a thing beyond darkness. She opens the window into the silence.

She pulls the rush-back chair over, kneels up on it, screens her hands around her eyes and peers out again. And now she can just about make it out, still crouched like a great big turtle at the bottom of the hill, caught between the two gateposts. She gives a small scornful laugh. 'France – as if!' and then, climbing down off the chair, 'Back to his sister would be about the size of it and see how long he would last then, living with that mean old shrew!'

For a moment, she considers going down there and retrieving the jelly but she is too weak now after all the upheaval to go blundering around in the dark and she feels the need, too, for some sort of nourishment before facing into or even thinking about anything else. Crackers and butter will do just fine; she was never all that keen on beach-plum jelly anyhow. It was just another item on a long list of items endured for the sake of harmony. 'Well, no more!' she says raising a determined fist. '*No* more,' and then she begins to cry again.

Back in the kitchen, she blows her nose, takes the tea and a whole heap of crackers rubbed over with butter to the table. She sits and looks up at the clock on the shelf above the kitchen sink. Almost two-thirty in the morning. She will not sleep now. She had tried that earlier, telling herself this is what adults do instead of prowling through the wilderness in the middle of the night: they get undressed, put on their nightclothes, climb into bed, read for a while and then, as their eyes grow heavy, they put the book down and go to sleep.

But no sentence ever written had the power to get by the hellfire blazing in her head, and each word read had flamed up on contact and disintegrated. Inside her, it felt like there were demons twisting and turning, clawing at her stomach. She worked herself up so she could hardly think and, before she knew it, she was sitting bolt upright, screeching and growling through barred teeth. She had bashed her head off the bed head, had tried ripping the coverlet apart with her hands. She had even bit into the pillow before starting out on her hair, tugging and plucking and, oh, but if anyone had seen her, they would have wrapped her up in a straitjacket and rolled her off to Bellevue.

And why get so upset over nothing? When all he had been doing was trying to hurt her. Playing dirty, that's what he had been at. Drawing the blade across the sharpening stone before sticking the knife in. To say she had no talent, that she wasn't an artist! As if a man like him could spend all those years with someone who wasn't an artist.

In the end, she had run out of steam.

And now here she is, wide awake and sitting in the kitchen in the middle of the night, stuffing dry crackers down her neck, her throat feeling as if it is clogged with sand.

Standing up from the table, she goes to the sink, pours a long glass of water and comes back out to the studio.

She pulls the Dutch door fully open, stands by the storm door and presses her head into the screen and listens to the sea. The sound irritates her – she feels she has been listening to it for far too long. And always going over the same old thing unless the wind dictates otherwise, and even then it soon reverts to the same old thing – breath sucking in and breath sucking out through gritted teeth. And she thinks, I will go crazy if I stay here much longer, in this place where nothing ever changes: the sea, the four-note cry of the damned whip-poorwill; the people even, with their mundane conversations about weather and fishing and village-pump politics.

How she longs for New York! To be back where there is more to hear in the evening than the birds and the sea. Human voices. Where she can run into a neighbour on the stairs and have some sort of interaction. Or go walking down Carmine Street and listen to the women cackling on stoops in all their strange tongues. Where even in stillness there is purpose: the men playing chess in the park, the street girls sitting on a certain bench waiting to be picked up. And the sense that everything around is constantly evolving; turning and moving; walking and wheeling. Changing, and for ever – not just until the tide takes a turn. But above all, the voices. Instead of the same moronic four-note song of a bird that never shows its face or the come-day-go-day in-and-out sound of the sea.

✳

She continues to move around the house, pausing without really stopping to look out a window. Window by window. Her legs ache, she longs to sit down and rest but each time she lingers, she feels a sort of piercing of the heart and a small, cold rush coming out of it, like oil out of the ground, and so she keeps moving.

The next time she finds herself in the kitchen, the clock shows three-fifteen. She stares up wondering what it feels like to watch time pass by. Long – that's how it feels – who could know one minute would take so long? She eyes the shelf surrounding the clock and begins to wonder if she could make a picture out of it. The shapes of the items on each side: the circles of dishes, the stubby handle on the saucepan and the lines of light on the coffee pot. Beneath the shelf, the deep sink, with its lead-white highlights, the copper on the piping and the sink's undercarriage that he had once said looked like the udder of a porcelain cow.

She would need to add something to it: flowers in a vase or maybe a plant or…? Or something. The clock moves to the next minute and she decides to forget about the picture, to clean the whole area instead: the shelf and everything on it, the sink, even the small patch of floor beneath it. By the time she has finished all that, he will have returned. And if not – well, then she could begin to worry again.

She heats up the water, climbs up on a chair and takes everything down bar the clock. She polishes the coffeepot, washes and replaces the other items, then starts on the sink, down to every little bar on the dial of the plug-hole. She cleans everything in the vicinity, from a washer on the pipe to the small neat candle holder at the side of the cabinet that he fixed there years ago. She works on, calmed by the sound of her own light grunting, the splash and squeeze of the wash rag in water, the no-nonsense smell of Old Dutch cleaner. As she nears the end of the task she begins to worry that he will come back before she is quite done. She does not want him finding her here, dishevelled and on her knees, scrubbing with all her might the small patch of linoleum beneath their kitchen sink.

When she stands and looks again at the clock fewer than twenty minutes have gone past. Twenty minutes! After all that work. 'Everything is against me,' she says, 'everything – including time.'

She feels her blood begin to heat up again, her stomach tighten and a rile-up of anger and despair begins to return. She slaps the heel of her hand against her forehead, shakes her head from side to side and says, 'Stop! Stop now, you hear me? Get out of the kitchen, do something else, anything else. Just *stop*.'

She goes outside to the chaise longue and lies on her side. After a while, a sort of half-dream, half-memory begins to come into her head. A conversation from a long time ago that had, in fact, happened, although she can't recall when or where. She had been a listener rather than a participator in the conversation and he had been there, surrounded as usual by admirers – all men. And for some reason, she had been trying to be good, to not interrupt, to let the men speak – although why on earth she had been doing that she cannot recall. And he was wearing his good tweed suit, so it must have been in New York. They were talking about trains. They were talking about what one sees from a train. What *he* sees. 'Everything looks so much better from a moving train,' he had said. 'Everything has a life that is glimpsed only for a few seconds.'

And she could remember thinking at the time, Oh, he likes that of course, looking down from his lofty heights at the world diminished: small people, small houses, the miniature lives that these tiny people are leading.

It had been the first time such doubts about him had come into her mind and maybe that is why she remembers it now.

His admirers continued to coo around him, and she had imagined him then standing on the edge of the world like a lighthouse on the headland. Looking down from a height. She had thought of all the poor small birds that had flown towards the lighthouse, attracted by the light, and crashed and died, battered and fallen. But they had been talking about trains, not lighthouses, and she had been trying to be good, to not interrupt or at least to not say anything too wayward. And so she had said simply, 'At his height, he is used to the bird's eye view. And how he loves to ride in trains.'

But even as she had said that, the image had risen again, the birds flying and crashing and falling.

And now as she lies on her side on the chaise longue, she can see it again: the lamp on the lighthouse, turning slowly and with great certainty, while the birds, without the least hesitation, continue to hurl themselves against it.

She stands up from the chaise longue. His lighthouse paintings, she decides, have all been self-portraits.

Now in the bedroom, she pulls her journal out from the bottom of the closet, sits on the end of the bed and begins to flick back over the years.

She reads words of love and words of venom; sentences that jump up and scratch her in the eye; others that seem to reach out and caress her. She finds whole passages that stand twisted and black like the gates of a madhouse and passages that read like a bed of roses. Sometimes she finds herself laughing as a memory is awakened; other times her heart stops with shame for something she has written.

This journal that she has always referred to as her *liber veritas*. But the only real truth she sees in it now is the harsh truth of herself – the truth she has heard so many times from others over the years, but has almost always refused to believe. Yet here it is, everything they say about her: resentment, jealousy, selfishness. And here too, in her own handwriting, countless references to his paintings as if they were children. (*I christened this one; I was at the conception of that one.*)

And again, although in a darker way, when it comes to her own pictures. (*My stillborn bastards are left ignored in the studio. I should have smothered that one at birth.*)

Her hand shakes as she turns the pages, year after year, all that pain and hate. How could she have endured it? How could he have put up with the demands of her possessive nature? Possessive to the point of madness.

She slams the book shut, then closes her eyes. 'Yes, I am possessive. And so what if I am?'

Because she wants all of him. She wants him and all the other versions of him that existed even before she knew him. She wants the little boy at the window reaching out from his mother's arms to touch the lights on the Hudson River. She wants the young man, gauche and clear-eyed, walking the streets of Paris. She wants to stand behind him when he wrote his funny letters home to Nyack; to stand before him when he entered Madam Cheruy's boudoir. She wants to shadow the salesman as, disconsolate, he walked the streets of New York – to know what he may not even have known then, that it was all coming in: the sidewalks, the buildings, the room through a window, the black shadows and of course the light. She wants to own his body, to be his soul. That is all she has ever wanted.

She knew it the first time she stood yelling at him on the street all those years ago when they had their first fight. And she knew it yesterday when Michael came running down the lane to throw his arms around her. She had found herself having to fight the urge to push the poor boy away, to swallow the words, 'But I don't want you to visit me. I have enough. *We* are enough already: my husband and I, the flesh of my flesh, the bone of my bone.'

When she looks up again, darkness has started to wear away and daylight is taking over. She gets up, throws on an old coat and a pair of shoes, then takes a pillow from the bed and goes outside and begins down the steps through the low-slung ropes of early fall mist. When she gets to the Buick, she doubles the pillow over and places it on the driver's seat and then bends over and pulls at the lever until the seat jumps and moves forward. She sits in, puts her hands on the wheel and says, 'Don't think about it now; don't make a thing of it – just do it, just…'

She turns on the gas and the car gives a little jerk. Beneath her she feels the bumps on the cart-road, trying to shrug her off the seat. Her hands tighten on the rim of the wheel and she keeps her foot steady on the gas until bit by bit, bump by bump, she comes up to the garage.

'Now,' she says, 'now, ease off the gas. Nice and… that's it.'

She gets out and opens the garage, takes a few deep breaths and gets back in.

'It's an automobile, not an aeroplane,' she says. 'What's the worst that can happen?'

As she comes to the open garage door she feels the front wheels waver and, closing her eyes, she decides to push on blindly. She feels the movement beneath her, a few seconds of gliding and then slowly she brings the Buick to a halt. She puts her head on the wheel and laughs.

*

Back in the house she decides to carry on as if nothing has happened.

She goes to the bathroom, washes her face and generally freshens up. She is about to get dressed when she remembers the pink dress she found while cleaning the basement the other day. A dress she had bought in Orleans a few summers ago and had forgotten about. She removes it from the closet and lays it on the bed. Then she fixes her hair, puts on a little perfume and smudges two dots of lipstick on her wheat-pale face.

The sun rises. It flushes through the house, a light so strong that her tired eyes can hardly bear to look at it. She stands at the entrance to the studio and watches it fly at her, from every window and door, every pane of glass, crossing and re-crossing her path and flaunting itself all over. And she tries not to think, I am dressed and standing here, a witness to the rising of the sun and soon that will be done – and then what?

An unruly stack of old newspapers and magazines catches her eye. She will go to them now in a moment, pull them out from under his worktable and begin to sort through them. She will throw out most, keep a few and cut out pieces from others. If he hasn't appeared by the time that is done – well then, she'd better start thinking about the future.

She is about to make her way over there when she senses something outside.

She goes to the window, kneels up on the rush-back chair and looks out, her heart clipping in her chest. The light has toned down a little over the back hills. She leans forward a little more, holding on to the window ledge to keep herself steady. But there is no one. Not on the lane at the bottom of the hill, not out on the cart-road. There is not so much as a shadow near the garage, nor coming up the steps. No one!

'Oh now,' she says aloud, 'oh now, who would have thought it? He has left me. He is gone.'

She is about to get down off the chair when a shadow moves somewhere to her right. And there he is suddenly coming from the rough meadow that lies south of the house, coming across it and getting nearer with every long step.

She turns back to the front, pretends not to see him. She squints her eyes at the sun as if nothing has brought her to the window but a mild curiosity about

the weather. She can see from the tail of her eye that he has stopped and is looking at her kneeling up on the chair, leaning into the window. Her heart strains
to hold on to the sudden rush of joy. The last line from 'La Lune Blanche' comes
into her head, 'C'est l'heure exquise'. The exquisite hour. Even if it is at the
wrong end of the day.

She waits another second or two and then, moving away from the window,
goes out to the kitchen and puts on the coffee pot.

Cape Cod Morning

HE KEEPS IT WITH him for another couple of weeks, the vision of a woman, just after sunrise, leaning into a window, looking out, and he no longer thinks he has lost his hold on the world.

It takes a little while before he finds the window he has been looking for, but it turns out to belong to a house in Orleans. It had been there all along, at the end of the street where he'd parked on the day Michael found his box of Conté Crayons lying on the grass.

The shape and mood of the house he retains from the half-built construction he found on a stroll during that period of unusual peace that followed Mrs Kaplan's party. He thinks about the light on the grass for a long time. He thinks about what to use in order to show that light up. The sky comes and goes in his mind; the stone steps at the side are tried again and abandoned again, until he decides that only a dark forest belongs there, fronted by a few innocent-looking trees that don't seem to know what is lurking behind them.

The windows and the shutters are just as he first envisaged. The house is twisted to face west instead of east; the fall of shadow altered to suit the rising, rather than the setting, of the sun. The lines of the shingles are already etched in his mind.

But whatever else may happen before or after he takes it to the canvas, the picture is about the woman. The woman with her anxious arms pressed down on the ledge as she leans out from her post, her face resigned and ready for the worst, but at the same time hopeful.

When the painting is about finished, she asks him, 'What should I write in the ledger?'

'Oh, whatever you think,' he says.

'Yes, but I don't want to say anything – you know – it's such a nice picture.'

'Say whatever you feel is right.'

It would not be the first time she has doctored the notes to enhance her involvement. And what does he care – he is done with the picture by then anyhow.

Although in the future, whenever he is asked, as he often is, 'Which is your favourite?' it will be this picture that invariably comes to mind.

They have one more encounter with the Kaplans before they leave for New York. Or Olivia and her friend Annette Staines, at any rate. They are in Hyannis celebrating the fact that he has finished the picture and he is about to call for the cheque when he sees Olivia veering across the floor with Annette trotting close behind.

They sit down at their own invitation, Olivia raising her hand for the waiter before he has time to ask if they would care for a drink. His wife unusually quiet, although he can see her back has gone up and that her ponytail is practically bristling. He just about manages to ask after Richie and Mrs Kaplan. He cannot seem to bring himself to ask about Katherine or Michael.

'We just left Richie to his new school yesterday,' Annette says. 'Oh and a fine little place it is too.'

'Is that so? And how is he?'

'Still upset about everything,' Olivia says, 'if you must know, very much so. Of course he got most of the blame. But anyhow, Mrs Kaplan and Katherine returned to Boston last week, and we had a job holding him back with us so that we could take him to see the specialist before he started school.'

'And how did that go?' he asks.

'Fine, he'll grow out it. I just hope he settles in, that's all. To school, I mean.'

'Oh, of course he will,' Annette declares. 'I mean, such a fine school.'

Olivia takes a long drink from the cocktail and then suddenly leans in and blurts out: 'There was something about that boy, you know. All the upset he brought to us, the Novaks and you of course. Well, I don't care what anybody says, there was something odd about him. Though why that should surprise anyone… You know – he never got bitten, the whole summer, not even when the mosquitoes were so big they could practically talk to you. Not so much as a wood tick. He left here with not a mark on him. Completely unscathed. Never even said thank you when he left. Well, I guess some people are just made that way—'

His wife stands up and her head wags a little. She says, 'I'm going to the restroom now and when I get back I hope to find you both gone.'

He stands out to let her by and as she passes he squeezes her arm and resists the temptation to kiss her. He stays on his feet. Olivia looks up at him, at first surprised, and then she gathers herself and rises. Annette hurriedly finishes her drink and stands.

Olivia says, 'That cigarette case he stole was a gift to me, you know, a gift from my late husband on our wedding day. Not that anyone seemed to care a damn about that.'

When they get home, he draws his small sketch of the painting in the ledger and as he does so she asks him a few questions: what was the first thought that came into his head when he saw her in the window that morning? Where and how did he come up with the window, the idea of a prow? Then she asks him a few technical questions – the answers to which she probably already knows. When he's finished his thumbnail sketch, he passes her the ledger and she writes her own description beneath it along with the name, which she has chosen.

And that will be the last conversation they have about the painting or about that Cape Cod morning.

~

SHE WOULD NOT MENTION that night to him; she would not ask him where or how he had spent all those hours. He would finish his painting and they would pack up and go back to New York and the rest of the fall would pass and the winter would come and spring again, and by the time they got back to the Cape the following summer, there would be new people renting the Kaplan house.

In New York they would sit one day in an afternoon theatre, watching a British movie, and she would begin to sense something coming from him that she had never noticed before. She would look at the screen and she would look at him and then at the screen again where a blond-haired boy was running through the streets of London with his legs like a colt and his funny way of talking.

And she would know that he missed the boys, or Michael anyway, a boy who had looked enough like him to be mistaken for his son.

And one summer years later, while waiting in line at the post office in Truro, she would pick up a copy of the *Boston Globe* that someone had left lying on a shelf. And she would happen to glance at the name of a soldier lost in Vietnam and think for a second that she had read the name R. Kaplan. But she would not look twice, she would put the newspaper down and wait her turn in the line, and she would send off her mail and collect her mail and say nothing about it when she got back, not even to herself.

And as for Michael. One day, she would think she had seen him: a tall, thin tramp with long fairish hair that was embedded with dirt, lying drunk on the grass in Washington Park. Another time, she would think she had seen him: a tall, handsome businessman, getting out of a cab on Fifth Avenue.

But she could not be sure about any of this.

The only thing she would know for certain was that she would look over the banister in the house in Washington Square and watch her husband trudge upwards, stopping now and then for a little rest as he climbed all the way up the seventy-four steps to their apartment. And that the rests would become more frequent, and that the journey would take longer and longer, and that soon enough there would be as many stairs to climb as years already lived and then if they were lucky – or maybe not so lucky – the years would outnumber the stairs, until there would only be one of them left to make the climb, and then the stairs would be insurmountable.

THE END

Acknowledgements

The author would like to thank, and acknowledge, the following for their assistance:

The staff of Truro Library, North Truro, Cape Cod
Dr Naemi Stilman, Fisher Beach, Cape Cod
Helen Addison, Addison Art Gallery, Cape Cod
Lisbeth Wiley Chapman, Hopper Tours, Cape Cod
Alec and Anne Marshall, Cape Cod

The author would like to acknowledge the following publications:

Provincetown Advocate
The New York Times
The Wildflowers of Cape Cod by W.A. Hinds and H.R. Hathaway
Berlin by Antony Beevor
The Past is Myself by Christabel Bielenberg
Holst: The Planets by Richard Greene
My Pamet: Cape Cod Chronicle by Tom Kane
New England StarWatch: The Essential Guide to Our Night Sky by Mike Lynch
The Long Road Home: The Aftermath of the Second World War by Ben Shephard
Cape Cod by Henry David Thoreau

The author would also like to acknowledge the following contributors to books, films, articles and interviews used as references throughout this work:

Jean-Pierre De Villers
Karin Ek
Lloyd Goodrich
Gail Levin
Deborah Lyons
Michel de Montaigne

John Morse
Brian O'Doherty
Didier Ottinger
Elena Pontiggia
Wim Wenders

The author would like to thank and acknowledge the following art galleries and museums:

The Metropolitan Museum of Art, New York
Smithsonian American Art Museum, Washington D.C.
Renwick Gallery, Washington D.C.
Whitney Museum of American Art, New York
Yale University Art Gallery, Connecticut
Edward Hopper House Museum & Study Center, New York

Thanks also to:

The Orchestre Symphonique de Montréal for their live performance of
    The Planets by Gustav Holst.

Finally, special thanks go to Professor Thomas Lynch, St James's Hospital, Dublin.

Note on the author

CHRISTINE DWYER HICKEY IS an award-winning novelist and short-story writer. Twice winner of the Listowel Writers' Week short story competition, she was also a prize-winner in the prestigious Observer/Penguin short story competition. Her bestselling novel *Tatty* was chosen as one of the 50 Irish Books of the Decade and has been selected as the 2020 Dublin One City One Book choice. It was also longlisted for the Orange Prize and shortlisted for the Hughes & Hughes Irish Novel of the Year Award, for which her novel *The Dancer* was also shortlisted. *Last Train from Liguria* was nominated for the Prix L'Européen de Littérature and *The Cold Eye of Heaven* won Irish Novel of the Year 2012 and was nominated for the IMPAC 2013 award. *The Narrow Land* has been shortlisted for the 2019 Irish Book Awards. She lives in Dublin.